T0286360

Books by Jean Stone

A Vineyard Season
A Vineyard Wedding
A Vineyard Crossing
A Vineyard Morning
A Vineyard Summer
A Vineyard Christmas
Vineyard Magic
Beach Roses
Trust Fund Babies
Off Season
The Summer House
Tides of the Heart
Places By the Sea
Birthday Girls
Ivy Secrets
First Loves
Sins of Innocence
Four Steps to the Altar
Three Times a Charm
Twice Upon a Wedding
Once Upon a Bride

Books by Jean Stone writing as Abby Drake

The Secrets Sisters Keep
Perfect Little Ladies
Good Little Wives

UP-ISLAND
HARBOR

JEAN STONE

KENSINGTON
PUBLISHING CORP.

www.kensingtonbooks.com

ISBN: 978-1-4967-4301-5 (ebook)

ISBN: 978-1-4967-4300-8

First Kensington Trade Paperback Printing: April 2024

10 9 8 7 6 5 4 3 2

Printed in the United States of America

In memory of my sister, Joan Adams,
who taught me the magic of reading

Chapter 1

An ice cream shack sat at the foot of the hill at Menemsha Harbor. It had the same kind of silver-colored shingles that Grandma Nancy's cottage had, the same white trim. It also had a white wood window that Mr. Fuller pulled down into a shelf every morning at eleven o'clock, a quiet announcement that he was open for business.

"You know the rules," Grandma whispered. "A double-dip vanilla and strawberry cone if you help me shuck corn for dinner." It was a small cone, not as big as "double-dip" made it sound, but Maddie always remembered the tasty treat from the last summer she'd been there, racing down the hill as fast as her five-year-old, skinny little legs could go.

As memories went, that was the most vivid one she had of Martha's Vineyard, of the tiny fishing village called Menemsha that Grandma once told her meant "still water," where old wooden boats were moored in the harbor every afternoon, having chugged out to the Atlantic Ocean before dawn, way earlier than Maddie roused from the small cot in the house where her mother grew up. Her mother's name was Hannah. Until Maddie had opened the letter that arrived last week, she'd forgotten that her grandmother's name was Nancy. Nancy Clieg. Unlike Hannah, Grandma Nancy had been alive until two and a half weeks ago, four decades after the summer when Maddie had her last double-dip.

Standing at the top of the slope in front of the cottage whose shingles had visibly tarnished, Maddie pulled an envelope from her purse and read the letter for the umpteenth time since it showed up in her office mailbox at the college in Green Hills, Massachusetts. Green Hills was in Berkshire County (often just called the Berkshires); it was as far northwest as one could go in the whole state. Martha's Vineyard, however, was as far southeast as one could go, not counting Nantucket. In between, Massachusetts had a lot of people, something like seven million. One of them was named Brandon J. Morgan, Esq., an attorney with an office on Marlborough Street, Boston. According to the return address, he also had a place on North Road in Chilmark. Chilmark was on the Vineyard. The village of Menemsha and its harbor were part of Chilmark. And so there she was.

The letter had stunned her.

> *Dear Ms. Clarke,*
>
> *Perhaps by now you have learned that your grandmother, Nancy Clieg, age 89, unfortunately passed away on June 30th. She liked telling people that she'd lived a good, long, satisfying life, having stayed in the "same damn place" where she'd been "birthed." Nancy was one of our island's beloved characters, and she will be missed. She hadn't wanted a fullblown funeral, but she did ask to have her ashes scattered off the beach at Menemsha Bight, the curve of blue water where the harbor meets the ocean. She often said that, framed as it was by the small mounds of sand dunes, the tall beach grass, and the*

long-standing rock jetty—all of which are watched over by the
cottages up on the hill and by the reassuring presence of our
Coast Guard station—the bight is, without a sailor's doubt,
the most beautiful place on earth.

Flicking her gaze from the letter down to the harbor now, where the sun's rays of mid-July danced on the water, Maddie could not disagree. Nor could she tell if the place had changed since she'd been five, though the pleasure boats seemed larger and more streamlined. The commercial fishing boats, however, appeared unaltered, with riggings of tall poles supported by taut cables that reached upward, creating a crisscross pattern against the cloudless sky like a game of pick-up sticks splayed on a blue canvas. But even from this distance, as Maddie studied the boats, she could tell that their wooden hulls and decks seemed weather worn and in need of paint. Like her, they were noticeably older.

She laughed. Thankfully, no one would recognize her today based on how she'd looked back then, when she often dressed in her favorite white T-shirt that Grandma had embroidered with a big sequined star. She usually wore it with bright pink shorts that had a drawstring at the waist, which she often fidgeted with as she shifted from one bare foot to the other, waiting her turn at Mr. Fuller's ice cream shack. Her eyes were blue (like the sky and like her father's), and her hair was thick and straight, which it still was, though it now looked more charcoal than the shiny onyx of her youth. These days, she kept it trimmed just above her shoulders because an assistant professor needed to look, well, professorial, especially since she was on tenure track, competing with two others for the coveted position. Another big change was that each summer that little Maddie had come to the island, she rarely wore shoes. Which also would not be appropriate for a middle-aged, New England divorcée despite the non-dress code of the twenty-first century.

Glancing down at her short-sleeved, ivory knit top, her mid-calf, faded black skirt, and her everyday tan canvas sandals, it was obvious that, haircut aside, sometime between ages five and forty-five, she'd become disinterested in how she looked. It was obvious that, yes, Maddie, too, was weather-worn. And a bit less vibrant.

"Just a little," she said aloud, then went back to her reading.

> *Included with this letter please find a copy of your grand-mother's Last Will and Testament. As you will note, she has left her entire estate—her worldly belongings, her small crafts business, the cottage and two outbuildings, and her prop-erty—to you, the only child of her only child. All she asks is for you to scatter her ashes off the beach at Menemsha at sunset. And to remember that she always loved you. Very much.*

The last part hit Maddie's heart with a thwack. How could she have remembered that her grandmother had loved her when all of this felt so . . . perplexing? Perhaps the attorney did not know the rest of the story.

She read on.

> *I'll be traveling between my offices in Boston and Chil-mark this summer. Please let me know when you can come to the island so I can be there in person to meet you and explain what this entails and to answer any questions you might have. I am also enclosing the key to the cottage so you will be able to make yourself at home, the place Nancy loved so much and now belongs to you.*

Most of all, please accept my condolences on your loss.
Sincerely,
Brandon J. Morgan, Esq.
P.S. I'm sorry for the delay in getting this letter to you.
It initially went to an address on Broadside Road in Green
Hills but it came back marked "Return to Sender." But then
I located you at the college, so I'm sending it there. Please let
me know you've received it. Thank you.
—BJM

As she folded the letter, her nostalgic mood started to dissipate. How could she have lost something—someone—she hadn't known she still had?

Stuffing the letter back into the envelope, she paused for a moment, then plucked out a brass key that hung from a metal chain and was accompanied by a fluorescent tag imprinted: "Shirley's Hardware, Vineyard Haven." The key was shiny and looked almost new, as if it had never been used, as if Grandma never locked her house. Maddie was glad she'd called the attorney's phone number in Chilmark right away; his assistant scheduled a meeting for ten o'clock Monday. Tomorrow. There was no sense dragging this out when Maddie had her career to tend to, including one more article to write and try to get published before the tenure committee made its decision. She'd done the research; the outline, then the writing, should be easy. If she were a die-hard optimist.

Gingerly navigating three flat granite rocks that served as steps to the front entrance, she opened the screen door and inserted the key into the lock on the heavy inside door, which, like the fishing boats, could do with a new coat of paint. It took a few tries for the tumblers to come to attention; then, using her shoulder, she delivered a determined shove that sprung the rusty hinges open.

She was greeted by strong scents of must and dust; she blinked to adjust her vision to the near darkness. Then she tiptoed into the room. It was hot and humid—"muggy" she thought Grandma Nancy would have called it—and eased into the past, which, childhood memories aside, Maddie refused to allow to divert her future. She'd worked too hard toward achieving her goal in Green Hills; there was no room left in her life for a rundown cottage on an island she barely remembered.

She made it into the living room. Suddenly, the shadow of a small critter streaked across the wide plank floor. Maddie squealed, as if she were five again. Glad no one was there to hear her overreact, she prayed it was only a tiny mouse, though it had seemed bigger. Maybe it was merely a dust ball that blew in on the ocean breeze. *Sure*, she thought with a snicker.

Fumbling through her purse, she quickly flicked on the flashlight app of her phone. By then, however, the invader was apparently gone.

She sighed.

Assuming that the electricity had been turned off, she swung the light beam around the room; it landed on a pair of old gingham curtains that sagged from an ancient rod. She walked over, pulled the curtains apart, and unlatched the pair of windows they'd been covering. Then she raised the slightly rotting wood sashes and invited the sunshine and salt air inside.

That done, she wove her way through a maze of furnishings, boxes, and stacks of what looked like magazines, and went toward the opposite end of the room—a galley-like kitchen—where she pushed matching gingham curtains apart. Then she opened two small windows over the chipped enamel sink, a single window on the back door, and one on the side-wall behind an unpolished square wooden table, where a single chair sat, as if waiting for Grandma.

Maddie moved back to the center of the room that stretched from one end to the other, kitchen to living room, living room to kitchen, with no walls between. The sparse furnishings looked vaguely familiar, though the place seemed smaller than she remembered.

In the center of the living room, a threadbare plaid sofa faced a stone fireplace; a matching chair was tucked into a corner and offered views of both inside the cottage and out to the front yard. What looked like a handwoven lap blanket was draped over the back of the chair. Had her grandmother often sat there, watching the world of Martha's Vineyard float by?

The fireplace stood on the outside wall near the chair; atop the mantel sat an odd-looking, purple-and-white half of a quahog shell that was scuffed and had a large crack; it hardly seemed like a memento that someone would have wanted to save. Next to the shell was a small, lopsided pottery bowl decorated with a childlike painting of a single daisy. But a larger item dominated the space: an acrylic-on-canvas depiction of Menemsha Beach at sunset.

Maddie recognized the painting. She knew if she stepped closer, she'd see the artist's signature: *Hannah Clieg*. Her mother. For years, a similar canvas had stood on the mantel over the fireplace on Broadside Road in Green Hills, the home where Maddie was raised. One day, like her mother, the painting was gone. Her father must have stored it in the attic, as if that part of his life was long over. The image she studied now, however, was slightly different: her mother had added two silhouettes—a woman and a child—walking along the shoreline, holding hands. She'd probably captured that sweet sentiment after witnessing it one summer. Perhaps the figures had been tourists; Hannah had often painted them, always careful to disguise their faces.

Maybe, when her mother had been a young girl with an untrained eye, she'd also painted the daisy on the pottery bowl.

Rubbing her arms, Maddie was surprised that a chill had snuck into the room. There was so little she remembered about her mother—her beautiful mother who'd been killed in a car accident. Hit-and-run. It happened so long ago that Maddie rarely thought about her anymore. And yet . . .

She quickly tamped down her emotions, pushing them into a dark recess in her mind where she'd learned to push those kinds of things so she could keep moving, so scary feelings would not bog her down. After all, years ago she figured out that crying didn't do any good; it wouldn't bring her mother back. So she stiffened her upper lip now before foolish tears formed, and she continued to scan the cottage.

There wasn't much to see: the place was hardly bigger than the entry hall of her ex-husband's house that he shared with his silly society wife. Luckily, Maddie had had the good sense to get out of her brief marriage when their son, Rafe, was only three. By the time she and Owen had tied the traditional knot, her mother had been dead many years; her father, however, had continued to wear his sorrow like a nineteenth-century mourning shawl. Maddie had hoped that her marriage into a wealthy, well-known family in the Berkshires who would protect her (a laughable expectation) and provide her with security (the ultimate punch line) might help assuage her father's grief.

She'd been wrong.

"Yoo-hoo!" A singsongy female voice that seemed more cheerful than necessary jerked Maddie back to the present.

A short, stocky woman stood outside the screen door. Her arms were cupped at her waist; she held a woven basket. She was smiling broadly.

"Are you Maddie?" Ms. Cheery asked.

"I am."

The visitor looked thirtysomething. She had long light brown hair contained by a red bandanna; she was dressed in an outdated denim jumper and a butter yellow T-shirt. Her round face was absent of makeup; her cheeks were rosy, likely from the sun.

"I'm Lisa Jenkins. Your neighbor. My house is down the hill on the left." She twitched her chin in that direction. "I saw your car in our lot, so I figured it was you."

The "lot" was a small area halfway up the hill from the road where the driveway ended. It was barely big enough to park three cars. From there, a narrow sandy path led to Grandma Nancy's cottage, which was just up the hill from where Maddie's visitor named Lisa apparently lived.

"I ran into Evelyn—your attorney's mother—at the post office yesterday. She said you were coming. I'm so sorry about Nancy, um, your grandmother." She held out the basket; in it, an embroidered tea towel was wrapped around something shaped like a football. "This is one of her baskets. She made them out back in the big shed. They always sold out at the artisan fairs." The young woman hastily jibber-jabbered, the way Maddie's students often did. "Anyway, I didn't know if any of her baskets are left. Just in case, I brought you this because you should have one. It's yours to keep. She gave it to me for my birthday." She took a short breath, then peeled back a corner of the cloth, revealing a loaf of bread nestled inside. "This is for you, too. I made it this morning."

Maddie kind of remembered that Grandma Nancy was always busy with a project; one of them might have been making baskets. She opened the screen door.

"Please," she said, "won't you come in?"

Lisa shook her head. "No, thanks. I have errands to run

while the tourists are still on the beach. It's the only time there's a hare's chance of getting to up-island Cronig's on a Sunday in summer." Her face scrunched into a frown that revealed a few lines; her arms and hands looked very tan, the kind of tan one gets from working in a garden or mowing the yard, not from lazing on a beach towel. "I also wanted to tell you to please let me know if you hear too much noise from our place. My husband's a lobsterman, so he works long hours, but we have a seven-year-old boy who likes to pretend he's an action figure and a four-year-old girl who shrieks at nothing."

Maddie laughed. "It sounds like a lively household."

"That's one way of putting it. Plus, our place is about the same size as this one, so it's kind of crowded."

Lisa seemed nice enough, but Maddie knew there was no point in making friends where she wouldn't be living. She examined the gift. "Well, thanks for the bread. Are you sure you don't want the basket back?"

Lisa shook her head again. "No. Please. Keep it. And the towel. It was one of Nancy's, too." She gestured to Maddie's phone. "You can turn off the flashlight. I reminded Evelyn to make sure the power was on for you."

"Oh. Well. Thanks." Maddie felt idiotic for not having tried to flip on a switch. She turned off the flashlight and slipped the phone into her pocket.

"No problem," Lisa replied. Then, as she turned to descend the granite steps, she dropped her gaze to her footing. Suddenly, she stopped. "I found her, you know."

Maddie blinked. "What?"

"I found Nancy after she fell. They figured that by then she'd been dead five or six hours." She spoke robotically, as if her words had been choreographed.

A shiver wriggled up Maddie's spine. "My grandmother *fell?*"

Lisa nodded.

"Is that how she died?" Then Maddie realized that the attorney hadn't specified Nancy's cause of death, only that she had "unfortunately passed away."

The young woman nodded again. "Sorry. I thought you knew."

Maddie drilled her gaze back to the granite steps. "This is where she fell? And lay dead for five or six hours?" She backed into the house.

"It was so sad," Lisa continued. "I might have heard her if she'd yelled for help, but I guess it happened while I was at work. I'm an administrative assistant at the town hall." She lowered her voice, then pointed to a sharp corner of the top granite slab. "She was right there. The police said it looked like she caught her foot on the edge. Lost her balance. Hit her head. At least, that's what I heard at work."

In spite of the background noise—boats in the harbor, traffic on the street, and people (and dogs) yipping everywhere, Maddie's ears plugged up. Totally blocked. As if she'd gone deaf.

"Right here?" she asked again, as if she had misunderstood. Her gaze remained riveted on the steps. She tried, but failed, to picture her grandmother. She tightened her grip on the basket.

"I'm afraid so," Lisa said.

Maddie wondered why on earth she'd assumed her grandmother had simply died in her sleep. Or in a nursing home, where she'd lingered for a while with a terminal disease. It never had occurred to her that Grandma Nancy had been lying on the ground at her own front door. Alone. For hours.

A small ache rose inside her. She lifted her eyes and considered the bread-baking neighbor. "It must have been awful for her. And for you, too. To have found her that way. I'm so sorry, Lisa." It wasn't the right time to admit that she hadn't seen her grandmother in years and could hardly remember what she looked like. After Maddie's mother died when Maddie was still five, her father said it was time to sever "those island ties," because her grandmother lived too far away to maintain a connection. Which was easy to understand back in the age before cell phones, the internet, and godawful social media. When Maddie turned ten, she asked her father if she could visit Grandma. But he said the woman had been old and feeble and that she had died. Maddie hadn't questioned him. Why would she have? She'd been too young to realize that, realistically, the woman would still have been too young to typically become feeble and die.

With a slow shrug, Lisa said, "I keep thinking she might have had a stroke or something before she fell. If you hear anything, will you let me know?"

"Of course."

"I don't want to pry, but what with you being her only family, and, well . . . she was my friend." She paused again, as if searching for words. "I know it probably was a freak accident. But if anyone knew her own turf it was Nancy. She might have been old, but she was as sure-footed as I am."

"I'll let you know if I learn anything," Maddie said, half wondering if Lisa was trying to suggest that something sinister had occurred.

Lisa nodded and mumbled a few words about her husband coming home soon. Then she lifted an arm in a short wave and headed toward the path.

And Maddie remained standing in the doorway, gripping the woven basket by its wide handle, watching Lisa disappear through the tangled overgrowth of tall grass and beach roses that crept down to the harbor. And all Maddie could think of was that nothing could bring back the past. It could not bring back her mother; it could not bring back her grandmother, no matter how she had died. Or when. And the sooner Maddie got the cottage cleaned out and sold, the better.

Chapter 2

Maddie left the front door open, intending to sweep out the dust and the sand and whatever else Nancy left behind at the time of her unexpected departure. With any luck, the fresh air would help cool off the place. Setting the basket on the counter, she removed the bread, wrapped the tea towel more tightly around it, and put it in the oven in case the streaking critter showed up again. She wondered if she should have asked Lisa for advice on rodent removal; it wasn't something Maddie had ever dealt with in Green Hills, in the sunlit, second floor of a lovely Victorian home nestled among tall pine trees. The house was a former faculty residence on the campus of the college where her father, Professor Stephen Clarke, taught political science. If any mice dared to take up tenancy in the house, her father no doubt would have alerted the property manager without telling her. After all, he wasn't given to making a fuss about much of anything.

When Maddie and Owen separated, her father suggested that she and Rafe move in with him. (Though technically retired now, the professor still taught a course or two and had been allowed to remain in the Victorian—seniority was paramount in the academic world.) It hadn't taken long for Maddie to decide: her father was a good influence on his grandson, and she liked how he showed Rafe that, contrary to Owen's belief, having a rich life didn't have to mean having hefty financial investments. In any event, other than an occasional raccoon that Maddie heard rooting through the trash cans in the driveway when she was up late grading papers, her experience with critters was nil. Which was how she liked it.

Returning to her task at hand, she found a broom that must have seen better days, but, as the old saying went, "none of them were recent," and surveyed the rest of the cottage. Two modest bedrooms. One bathroom, which she expected would be ancient but had been noticeably renovated. A sleek, walk-in shower now stood where an old claw-foot porcelain tub used to be. The old one hadn't had a shower . . . the shower was outside, loosely enclosed by a makeshift stall of wood slats that were wide enough so people could peek between them. By mistake, Maddie once saw Grandma Nancy's wrinkly backside through them; she'd quickly scampered away.

And then she remembered something else: the outdoor shower was tucked into an alcove of the house that was created when another room, tinier than the others, had been added behind her mother's childhood room; like a fairy-tale portal, the room was accessed through a miniature door at the back of her mother's bedroom closet. The secret place fit an old army cot, a nightstand, and a seaman's chest that once belonged to Maddie's great-grandfather and was where Grandma stored Maddie's dolls, books, and a few toys. The room had a single, round window that opened like a porthole; Grandma said Maddie could fit through it in an emergency.

Closing her eyes, she could almost hear her mother's sweet laughter and her gentle voice. "It's your special place, honey. Grandma had it built just for you."

By a man with long black hair in a ponytail, Maddie suddenly remembered. He'd banged his hammer day after day because he hadn't been able to finish before Maddie and her mother arrived that summer. He was a nice man, though. Tall and skinny. And she'd never seen a ponytail on a man before, let alone one that reached halfway down his back. But she didn't remember his name, if anyone had told her.

She laughed now, surprised that though she had few memories of those early years, she could picture the man with the ponytail who'd built her a room. It might have been the year before their last visit there, which meant Maddie would have been four. Grandma said they should call it Maddie's Hobbit House.

"Hobbits are happy little people," Grandma had explained. "Sometimes they live underground because they love to hide." Maddie wasn't sure what she had to hide from, but she loved the special space that Grandma—and the man with the ponytail—had built just for her.

Happy to have unleashed another memory, Maddie started down the hall now, toward the closet where the small door led to the room. Then her phone rang.

She stopped. As badly as she wanted to ignore the call, she realized it could be the attorney, trying to confirm their meeting for tomorrow.

But the caller was not Brandon J. Morgan; it was her son.

She decided not to answer. It was bad enough she'd lied to her father, saying she was going to visit friends in Boston. But Maddie never lied to her son. She was not, however, ready to tell Rafe what she was really doing. Or that his grandfather—the esteemed Stephen Clarke, PhD—had either lied to her decades ago, or someone had given him misinformation about her grandmother's supposed death. Which was hard to believe, because what would have been the motive for either to have happened? But the timing had been rather convenient:

he'd never told her Grandma was dead until Maddie said she wanted to see her again. Yes, she thought, she shouldn't talk to Rafe yet. So, with her emotions now too raw for her liking, she set the phone on a table in the hallway and decided to change her clothes and go for a run. Like Rafe, Maddie's Hobbit House would wait.

In the early days of her marriage, physical exertion became Maddie's go-to way to put off doing boring, housewifely stuff she simply did not want to do. Owen's shirts needed ironing? She looked for volunteer positions around town instead. Clean clothes should be folded? Browsing through the Clark Art Institute in nearby Williamstown seemed far more important. Kitchen floor needed scrubbing? Maybe after she'd run a mile or two—no sense staying inside and wasting a beautiful afternoon. Soon, running became her favorite way to put off inevitable domestic tasks. Not marathon running or anything as honorable, just a mile or two whenever she felt a need to procrastinate.

She'd stepped up her running a year after she and Owen were divorced, after he'd found a younger (of course), perkier, more doting young woman who, with her blonde locks and professionally-applied makeup, looked more suitable on his pompous arm than Maddie had. Had he been pompous when she'd married him? Had she thought the pros of the marriage would outweigh the cons?

A therapist encouraged Maddie to put her thoughts down on paper, which seemed like a good idea until she reread what she'd written. It was depressing, self-indulgent, and whining, not at all like the woman who had returned to college with aspirations to teach . . . something. She'd finally landed on journalism, hoping to show young people how important it was to write captivating, concise, factual news stories, with the emphasis on factual. Eyeing that goal seemed a more productive way to work through her husbandless situation—and more pleasant than keeping a diary.

But now, with the afternoon sun making it too hot for a run, she was sitting in her idling car with the air conditioner cranked up, drumming her fingers on the steering wheel, as if the digital exercise could make the long line of vehicles ahead of her move faster. Or rather, could make them move at all.

Lisa had been right; according to GPS, the quickest route to West Tisbury and up-island Cronig's Market was clogged with an unending queue of traffic. She doubted that State Road instead of North Road would have made a difference, though GPS did show a Chilmark General Store at a nearby place called Beetlebung Corner. She had no idea what a beetlebung was or what the store near it might offer. But she'd need enough groceries to last a few days, and Lisa had mentioned Cronig's, so she should probably tough it out and go there. Maddie had never liked food shopping, but if she hadn't spent so much time digging through one of her grandmother's outbuildings—which, though not much bigger than a shed, had been crammed with rakes and hoes and shovels and gardening tools, gloves, boots, and empty egg crates and sacks of mulch and several unidentifiable objects—she wouldn't be sitting where she was now, stuck behind an oversized pickup truck, her car creeping forward about half a foot every few minutes. While she waited, the light of day started to dwindle, and shade from the trees that edged the road became dense. She deduced that slow-moving beachgoers were heading back to their summer homes. Or their rentals.

She wanted to scream.

Instead, she decided to think about what kind of rubble she'd find the next day in the other outbuilding-slash-shed. Maybe she shouldn't bother with it. Maybe she could sell the entire property and structures "as is," including the furnishings—the threadbare, faded curtains, the stacks of useless periodicals and who knew what else, as well as the critter that hadn't showed its four-legged self again.

If Rafe were there, he'd be annoyed that his mother didn't want to find and make friends with whatever it was. Unlike Maddie, her son found nature fascinating.

She laughed, crept two or three more feet toward her destination, and thought about how lucky she was to have him. From the day he'd been born, Rafe's existence proved that she'd done at least one thing right in her life. Of course, he wasn't perfect, but he came darn close. With a crop of thick black hair and the coppery-burnished skin of Maddie's Iberian heritage (thanks to her mother's Portuguese fisherman ancestor who, Maddie had been told, had made his way to the Vineyard in the nineteenth century), and the blue eyes of Owen's Irish roots combined with her father's Scottish/ British ones, Rafe was handsome. He was also tall: by age twelve, he'd sprouted past Maddie's five feet six inches; now, at nearly twenty-two, he was well over six feet tall with a rugged physique, thanks to the past few years he'd spent on the rowing team at Amherst College, where he also was on the dean's list. In itself, that was a miracle, because his major was business, a topic he was only moderately interested in. But his father had insisted, because he fully expected that after grad school Rafe would join him in his investment firm. Maddie at least encouraged Rafe to minor in environmental studies; it was, after all, what he really wanted.

Yes, she thought now, her son was close to perfect, if she did say so herself. He was even a caring half brother to the nine-year-old twin daughters whom Owen and what's-her-name had proudly produced; the girls seemed sweet enough, but neither one could hold the smallest tea candle to Rafe when it came to brains.

Maddie wondered how—and if—the inheritance from

Grandma Nancy's bequest, no matter the number of dollar signs that went with it, might give Rafe a more secure future so he wouldn't need to kowtow to his father's wishes. How she wished her son had known he had a great-grandmother who'd been alive and well and living on Martha's Vineyard all these years and who would have adored him.

Even worse, he'd never had the chance to feel one of Grandma's hugs.

Sitting, waiting, the engine still idling, Maddie's sorrow surfaced again. But she knew that though Rafe was sensitive, he was emotionally stronger than she was. And he was sensible—a gene that must have come from her father. Or possibly her mother. So Maddie set her jaw firmly, fished out her phone, and told the software to text Rafe and say: "I'll be back by the end of the week." She'd tell him everything then. Hopefully, he wouldn't be angry for not having known his great-grandma. Or for thinking that Maddie's father had kept it from them for whatever reason.

Her mood now subdued, she considered parking the car and walking to Cronig's, wherever it was. Then her phone pinged.

Gramps said you're in Boston, the text read. *I didn't know you have friends there.*

Maddie waited a few seconds while her mind scrambled, searching for a cohesive reply. She typed it herself so Siri wouldn't screw it up.

Ha ha! I've finally been able to keep a secret from you.

And it was true. For now, like her hobbit house, this would remain a secret. One that, so far, only she and Brandon J. Morgan, Esq. knew. And apparently Evelyn, his mother. And Lisa Jenkins. There might be others, but Maddie hadn't yet met them, so they didn't count. Until then, it was a secret she felt compelled to get to the bottom of without the input or influence of her son, her father, or, God forbid, her ex-husband.

So she turned off the GPS and dropped her phone back into her purse. Then she made a sloppy U-turn and headed back to the harbor. Hopefully the food truck she'd spotted there earlier was still open; she'd worry about everything else tomorrow. After she went for a run. And after she met with the attorney.

The burrito threatened to keep her awake even though she was exhausted. She had, after all, left Green Hills at six o'clock that morning, spent four hours driving, another hour waiting to board the ferry, followed by almost another hour on the boat between the crossing and the waiting to disembark, and then over half an hour on State Road. The getting to Grandma's had not been half the fun. Nor had plowing through the cache of gardening things or sitting in the blistering sun in her aborted attempt to buy groceries.

Welcome to Martha's Vineyard in summer, she thought now as the burrito bebopped in her esophagus. Though it had tasted delicious, Maddie often forgot (or wanted to forget) that along with middle age she sometimes developed indigestion after consuming spicy food. And she never seemed to have an antacid when she needed one. The only alternative now was to gnaw on her neighbor's homemade bread, which actually helped. Maybe as a thank-you she should give Lisa first dibs on anything in the house or on the property. After all, Maddie lived in a house that was not even hers, and that one was well furnished, mostly with books. She needed nothing.

But after making sure both the front and back doors were locked (she wondered if Vineyarders would have been insulted by that), she went into the front bedroom (her grandmother's, she remembered), pulled back the curtains (sheers that were equally as ancient as the gingham ones), opened the windows, and stretched out on the lumpy mattress of the double bed. She shifted her focus from her heartburn to wondering what treasures might be in the cottage, buried in closets or bureaus or under the beds. Were there photos? Scrapbooks? Family memories that Maddie had not known existed? Would she be able to learn some things about her mother's and grandmother's lives? And how much would that matter at this point in hers?

She decided she was too tired to think about all that now. What she wanted was to sleep. But, though the aftermath of the burrito finally was in check, it soon became apparent that under the lumpy mattress, squeaky metal springs threatened to keep her awake. So she pulled herself up and relocated across the hall, to what had been her mother's room. She pulled back the old sheers and opened the window in there, too, hoping that light breeze would reach that side of the house. Thankfully, the twin bed was lump- and squeak-free. The room also held a small rolltop desk and a vintage maple bureau that Maddie was too tired to investigate, but added to her mental list of things to attempt tomorrow, after her run and her meeting and maybe her shopping.

She closed her eyes and slept without trying.

In the morning, she gathered her senses and ruled out the run; there was too much else she needed to do. So she showered (the inside shower, not the out), dressed in the navy-blue sundress she'd brought, and brushed back her hair, which overnight had become uncontrollable, thanks to damp air that, this close to the sea, had permeated the night. Securing her unruly tresses with a headband, she dabbed a quick layer of mascara on her lashes and slipped into her sandals—the only shoes she'd brought besides her trainers.

Car keys and purse in hand, she opened the front door before nine o'clock and inhaled the clear, sunny morning that wasn't yet hot. With a sliver of uncertainty, she stepped onto the first granite slab. But as she moved down to the next, she felt unsteady. Not because she feared tripping or falling or smacking her head . . . but because of a sudden feeling that she was being watched.

She paused. She took a deep, eyes-closed kind of breath, and tried to shake off the feeling.

Then, stoically, she continued down the hill.

So that was Madelyn Clarke. Maddie, she was called. She was pretty, though she seemed unaware of it.

From a vantage point in the woods, up the hill from the cottage, it would be easy to check on her over the next few days or however long she was there. It was comfortable enough, sitting there, watching. The thermos of iced coffee was nearly depleted, as was half a family-size bag of Cheetos, for which friends would be appalled if they found out it was serving as breakfast.

It had been an interesting yet unsettling outing, to feel like a bird of prey, an osprey, perhaps, one of those who had come back to the island, a wide-winged bird who hovered aloft, patiently studying the ocean below, waiting, waiting, for the perfect time to plunge.

But the vantage point here was over land, not open water. And, for now, it was time to go. Before the morning rush of beach crowds arrived to spread out their blankets, unfold their chairs, unscrew their water bottles, and probably be fried. They would stay all day.

So, yes, it was time to go until tomorrow. Maddie Clarke, after all, would be too busy to realize that someone was spying on her, hoping she'd reveal how things were going to play out.

Spying—or today's word, "stalking"—was not very nice, but sometimes you did things you did not always like when you'd made a promise . . . no matter how long ago.

Chapter 3

Intuition was not new to Maddie. Sometimes it came at her like an electrical current, a startling, frightening zap, an *Oh my God* sensation. Other times it was as if a fun message was delivered by an impish spirit, letting her know something great was going to happen: she'd be given an award; she'd meet an interesting man; she'd have something published somewhere that it mattered. Other times, it was creepy, more like a foreboding, a dark cloud slithering across her grave: the sensation she'd just had felt like that.

Not looking over her shoulder, not wanting to know why she'd felt what she'd felt, and why on earth anyone would be wasting time watching her, she kept her eyes on the ground and walked briskly down the path, passing Lisa's house and the mini lot where Maddie had parked her car, until she reached Basin Road.

She craved a cup of coffee.

A burger-and-hot-dog stand stood in the place where Mr. Fuller's ice cream shack once stood—a sign said it would open at ten. The food truck was still closed, too, as was the Homeport—a restaurant across the street. Then she spotted the fish market, where she and her mother had often bought

fresh shellfish for dinner—scallops, quahogs, lobsters, whatever the day boats provided. But even if the market sold coffee, it wouldn't be open until ten thirty. With a rush of
exasperation, she walked at a fast clip back to her car, set her
GPS, and headed toward the Chilmark General Store. If they
didn't have coffee, maybe she could get a bottle of orange
juice. And a doughnut. Once she'd had caffeine and sugar,
surely she'd be able to forget her demons and concentrate on
meeting the attorney. At this hour, traffic should be heading
to the beach—this time in the opposite direction.

The parking lot at the general store was packed, as was the
inside. Easily spotting the take-out line, Maddie fixed her gaze
on several chalkboards. The menu offered breakfast and lunch
selections, from wild blueberry scones to rosemary-roasted
chicken. When it was her turn, she decided she wasn't hungry
after all, so she ordered only a large coffee with milk and
sugar. Thankfully, no one asked who she was or why she was
there—most likely because at this time of year, out-of-towners
must be in the majority. Even better, the sense that she'd been
being watched had almost evaporated.

Weaving her way out the front door, she dodged the cluster of rocking-chair porch-sitters who nodded *Good morning*
greetings, but didn't try to engage her in conversation. Once
safely inside her car, doors locked, windows rolled up, air
conditioner humming, she gulped her coffee and allowed herself another deep breath. Then she began the short trip to
Brandon J. Morgan Esq.'s in-season address.

"Madelyn," the not-quite-middle-aged man said with a
smile. He wore pale blue pressed chino shorts and a white
short-sleeved collared shirt. His attire was similar to that of
Maddie's ex-husband, though Owen stuck to long pants, even
when the temperature soared. The attorney's unkempt wisp
of reddish-blond hair drooped over his forehead; that, and a

warm smile, made him look wholesome. Down-to-earth, not drop-dead desirable. Much more relaxing for Maddie to be around than her stuffed-shirt ex.

"It's nice to meet you," he added. "Is it okay if I call you Madelyn?"

She stood on the front porch, which was drenched with pots of so many summer flowers Van Gogh would have drooled. The house was a large country farmhouse (on a prosperous farm); it was well cared for and cordial.

"Actually," she replied, "most people call me Maddie."

He nodded twice, then attempted to brush back the droop of his hair so it would stay on top of his head. His effort was futile.

"Then Maddie it is. And I'm Brandon." He stepped aside, making room for her to enter. "Welcome to the Vineyard. And welcome to this rambling old house that's been in my family for generations—five at last count. Or maybe it's six."

"Six generations, dear," came a feminine voice as Maddie stepped into the foyer. "Though it's had some work done from time to time." The woman stood in a rectangle of sunlight in what looked like a parlor; its decor was a palette of fresh pastels that added a sunny glow to her white hair.

"Hello, Maddie," she said. She wore a pale yellow cardigan and short-cropped white pants that looked brand-new that season and spoke of tidy breeding. "You probably don't remember me. I'm Evelyn Morgan. I was in school with your mother. And I knew you when you were a little girl." She did not look as old as Maddie's mother would have been—was that approaching seventy already?

And then the weight of what the woman said sunk in. Evelyn Morgan had known her mother, and she remembered . . . her. Maddie. *When she'd been a little girl.* Her throat tightened; she didn't know if she could speak.

"Brandon?" Evelyn said with a slight Radcliffe or Wellesley accent leftover from the days of all-female Ivy League colleges. "Why don't you bring Maddie into your office while I fix iced tea. Or maybe you'd prefer iced coffee?"

To say Maddie was stunned minimized her gut-constricting reaction. Which she knew was ridiculous. For God's sake, her mother had grown up on the Vineyard. Of course people would have known her, maybe even had been friends with her. Maddie tried to smile.

"Iced tea would be nice," she managed to eke out.

Like her son, Evelyn nodded twice. "I make it from herbs that grow wild on the island." She smiled warmly and then disappeared in one direction, while Brandon guided Maddie into another high-ceilinged room.

She sat in one of two comfortable chairs facing a large mahogany desk that whispered classic antique, though a trio of oversized computer monitors stationed across it transformed the look into a workstation at NASA's mission control. The room was substantial: one wall had bowed windows with a pastoral view of stone walls and rolling meadows thick with wildflowers; the opposite wall featured built-in, floor-to-ceiling bookcases that spanned the entire width and were filled with rows of books, many of which were only accessible by a library ladder that trolleyed from one end to the other. Maddie calculated two thousand books, maybe more, some with plain, law-book-looking spines, others with colorful jackets, perhaps those were nonfiction books or novels. In a way, she felt transported to a classic nineteenth-century office on Beacon Hill, the kind frequented by high-society clients. But, of course, the view outside was not a narrow cobblestone road lined with gas streetlamps.

It was the Vineyard. In its storied glory.

"You look as if my mother took you by surprise," Brandon said as he sat behind the desk and observed her through a gap in the monitor lineup.

She forced another smile. "It hadn't occurred to me that anyone would remember my mother. Let alone, me, when I was a kid."

"My mom grew up here. My dad didn't, but he was here every summer from the time he was born, which I guess counts." His light green eyes swept the room. "How his ancestors managed to amass six generations of stuff—some of which is still here—amazes me."

"It's lovely," Maddie said. "Did you spend summers here, too?"

"I did. The rest of the time we were in Boston until my dad retired ten years ago. That's when he was diagnosed with lung cancer, and my parents came back here for good. The following year, my dad died, but as you can see, my mother stayed. I'm on- and off-island a lot in the summer, less off-season. I had a wife, but she . . . let's just say she preferred to stay put. No kids, which made things easier." He laughed. "Sorry. That was way too much information."

Maddie tried to look empathetic but wasn't sure if she succeeded.

"Anyway . . . ," Brandon began again, as he picked up a small stack of papers neatly layered on the desk, "as I said in my letter, your grandmother was quite a lady."

"I don't remember her very well. I was five when my mother . . . died—after that, I didn't come back to the Vineyard. Until now." She swallowed her embarrassment. "I . . . I was told that my grandmother died years ago."

Brandon nodded again, as if he already knew that. Or perhaps he was just being kind. Still, Maddie supposed that the island was a small community, especially off-season; maybe Grandma Nancy had fabricated a story the way Maddie's father had—if that was what he'd done.

"I'm so sorry, Maddie. My letter must have been a shock."

She said it was.

"Well," he continued, sidestepping a question of had-she-been-lied-to-and-if-so-why, "thanks for coming all the way out here. I figured you might want to see the cottage before we met. No matter what you decide to do with it."

She hesitated.

"Also," he continued, "now that you're here, if you have any questions, we can meet again. Unfortunately, I'm back and forth to Boston a lot right now, but I'll help however I can. Once we receive the death certificate, Nancy can be cremated. Then you can go forward with scattering her ashes, and we can settle the estate."

"Thank you," she said. She raised her chin—a trick she'd once taught herself to help shore up confidence. "Actually, I'd like to sell the place as soon as possible. It's a busy time of year for me; the fall semester at Green Hills will be starting soon, and I'll need to go back to work." She hoped he didn't think she was being impatient, greedy, or, worst of all, disrespectful of her grandmother.

"Well, you can't put the cottage on the market until the certificate arrives, but you'll be pleased to know it should sell quickly. It goes without saying that the location is highly desirable. And I don't think I mentioned that Nancy put her estate into a trust for you, so there shouldn't be any entanglements or lag time if you decide to sell."

She'd just told him that she planned to sell. Hadn't he been listening? She fidgeted with the small pearl bracelet on her wrist.

"Not knowing what your plans would be," he continued, "I haven't had the cottage appraised yet. My best guess is it will go for over a million. One-four. Or one-five."

Maddie must have heard him wrong. Did he mean a million *dollars*? A million *and a half*? For that tiny old house? She wondered if he'd seen it lately.

"And, of course, there are the other properties," he added.

"Other properties?" Maddie asked, her words popping out in a squeak.

"Your grandmother also owned two parcels in Aquinnah. They aren't on tribal land, so you're free to sell it. One is about two acres; the other is close to three. They're near the water, so together their market value is around three to four million. Give or take. Add that to the cottage and . . ."

Maddie no longer wanted to listen. She knew how to do math. But had her grandmother known the value of her un-tapped wealth?

Three to four million dollars?

Plus the cottage?

Her heart started to palpitate. To date, Maddie's 401(k) was just shy of one hundred thousand dollars, which she thought was pretty good, considering she'd only started work-ing full-time eight years ago. Prior to that, she'd been an ad-junct for a few years and hadn't saved a dime. Before that, she was an adult student, trying to make up for having married a man who hadn't wanted his wife to work but to serve on charitable boards and play golf. Not that there was anything wrong with those things, but they hadn't done a damn thing to build financial independence for her. She hadn't even scored in the divorce settlement, foregoing alimony for more child support and for Owen to pay all of Rafe's education.

She stood up abruptly. "Thank you for the information, Mr. Morgan. I need a day or two to think about this." The truth was, her stomach was now in three-to-four-million-plus-the-cottage knots. Give or take.

He stood, too. He was taller than she was, nearly as tall as Rafe. He had a kind face. A gentle face. She hoped she hadn't insulted him. But she couldn't listen any longer.

"Wait," he said. "Let me give you something. . . ." He shuffled through the papers and extracted a few. "These are copies of the assessors' parcel maps for the land in Aquinnah. It will give you an idea of the scope of the lots. And where they're located. As you can see, one is on the opposite side of the basin, not far from the cottage and close to the bike ferry dock; the other is off Clay Pit Road, near Lobsterville Beach."

She glanced at the maps, but the lines and squiggles, the numbers and landmarks meant nothing to her. She turned without taking them and simply said, "I'll be in touch." Then she darted from the room too fast; she nearly bumped into his mother, who was approaching, balancing a tray that was rattling. It held a small plate of what looked like homemade biscuits and glasses filled with ice.

"Good day," Maddie said, as if she, too, were from a proper, old Boston family like the Morgans. Wealthy New England aristocrats, which, come to think of it, Maddie also might now be considered. Minus the aristocrat part.

Turning the knob on the front door, her fingers fidgeting worse than before, she walked briskly onto the porch, down the steps, and out to her car. Then she flicked on the ignition, fastened her seat belt, revved the engine, and sped off the premises, leaving a cloud of dust and shards of clamshells in her wake.

Halfway back to the cottage, she realized she hadn't asked if the medical examiner had determined Grandma Nancy's official cause of death.

She forgot to get food.

After arriving at the cottage she supposed she now could call home, Maddie sat at the kitchen table, gnawing on another piece of Lisa's bread that had a soothing, savory touch of rosemary. She hadn't yet figured out if she should return to the food truck for a veggie wrap or go straight to the fish market for a lobster roll, which might be a more fitting way to celebrate. But celebrating felt wrong. It wasn't as if Maddie had won the lottery or the Pulitzer Prize for teaching good journalism, not that there was a prize for that. Instead, her windfall had come from an unhappy event—her grandmother was dead. Which in itself felt like a dream.

She wondered again if her father knew that Nancy had been alive and presumably well, and on the island this whole time, that she'd been making baskets and embroidering tea towels and gifting them to neighbors on their birthdays. Then Maddie vaguely remembered that her grandmother had come to her mother's funeral, and that she hadn't been alone. She'd arrived with a few people in an old camping trailer that she wanted to park in the driveway. But Maddie's what-will-the-neighbors-think? father had said no.

She hadn't thought about that in years.

As she sipped water that tasted straight from a freshwater well, Maddie thought she recalled her father's brusque "no" not because he'd raised his voice (he rarely did), but because he'd described the camper as a "house on wheels," and told Maddie he could not allow it to be parked on college property without a permit, which he didn't have. She wanted to ask if he could ask the college if Grandma could at least stay in the house. But the night before, Maddie had heard him crying in the bedroom that he'd shared with her mother, and she didn't want him to cry anymore. So she said nothing.

Had the funeral really been the last time Maddie had seen her grandmother? And, if so, why? Maybe she'd find an answer in the voluminous boxes or stacks of papers in the cottage or tucked between the pages of tattered magazines—maybe a letter to Grandma Nancy from Stephen Clarke would appear, reading something like: "Don't contact us again. Ever."

Would her reserved, well-respected father have done that? She had no idea.

Closing her eyes, she tried to grasp the full meaning of her inheritance. Millions of dollars' worth of property. It seemed so bizarre that it had landed in the lap of an ordinary assistant journalism professor from an ordinary town, a woman who now knew so little about so much.

One thing she did know was that she needed to tell Rafe.

And that she had to stop trying to think straight on an empty stomach.

Though she might have preferred to sit there, brooding, Maddie opened her eyes and went into motion in order to jog down the hill to find some food. She collected some cash, her phone, and the key to the cottage (unlike Grandma Nancy, Maddie locked doors). Then she realized she needed to change into her Nikes if she was going to run. But as she slipped out of her sandals, a now familiar "Yoo-hoo!" rang through the screen door.

Chapter 4

"Yoo-hoo, yourself," Maddie said as she set down her things and went to the door. "No work at the town hall today?"

Lisa shook her head. "I took the afternoon off. Charlie—that's my son—had a dental appointment. It looks like he's going to need braces pretty soon." She sighed and adjusted her silver headband that looked nicer than the red bandanna had. "We'll probably have to get a third mortgage to pay for that."

Perhaps Lisa had come calling in search of a loan. As an islander, she no doubt was tuned in to the property values. Maddie folded her arms.

"I know the feeling. My son needed them, too. It wasn't much fun on an adjunct teacher's salary." She didn't want to add that Owen had covered the cost.

Looking off toward Vineyard Sound, Lisa sighed and said, "With any luck, Loren, my daughter, won't need them. But she's only four, so who knows. Anyway, I just stopped to see if you're settling in okay."

Settling in? Did Lisa think Maddie planned to live there? She leaned against the doorjamb.

"Thanks, I'm fine. Right now I'm digging through my grandmother's paperwork—I have a lot to do."

"Of course. I'll let you get back to it." Lisa half turned away and then pivoted back. "Oh, I almost forgot. I wanted to warn you about CiCi."

Maddie winced. "And CiCi is . . . ?"

"Her real name is Cleo. Cleo Cochran. But she goes by her initials. C.C. Get it?"

Yes, Maddie got it.

"Anyway, she came into the town hall today and asked if I know what your plans are. Like if you're going to sell this place."

"Why? Does she want to buy it?"

"No. CiCi's a real estate agent."

Good grief, Maddie thought. Word seemed to travel around the Vineyard faster than it did around the campus at Green Hills. She would not have thought that possible.

"She's a good person," Lisa continued. "Though I've heard she can come across a little . . . strong."

"Thanks for the warning. I'll be sure to find a hiding place."

"There's a great little place off the back bedroom," Lisa said, "but only if you know how to get there. Nancy used to let my daughter go in and play with anything she wanted. Loren loves it there."

Maddie checked a knee-jerk move to say, "No! No one's allowed in there but me!" Which she quickly realized sounded rather pitiful.

Then Lisa waved. "Gotta go check on Charlie. Good luck with your paperwork." Then she trundled down the path, leaving Maddie still startled by her reaction.

The line at the gray-shingled shack with the bright blue trim was long. As Maddie inched closer to the fish-shaped wooden sign that hung near the entrance, she tuned out the happy lilt of summer voices and let her thoughts drift back to her "hobbit house," her one-room special place, where she'd loved talking to the yarn dolls Grandma Nancy made for her. She told her dolls everything, like how much fun she had at Grandma's and how she wished Daddy was there, too. But he had to teach summer school in July and August, and her mother said it was fun to sneak away—just the girls—and jump into the ocean waves with Grandma. She was right.

When they got back to Green Hills, Maddie and Mommy always spent Labor Day weekend with Daddy at a lake in the Berkshires, where the water was ice-cold and there were bugs that bit her, leaving little pink lumps that itched at night. She tried not to cry, because Mommy said it was Daddy's only chance to have a vacation and she wouldn't want to spoil it for him. One thing Maddie hadn't minded was going in the row-boat with Daddy to fish. She wouldn't have liked to put the worm on the hook, but he did that for her. The best fun was surprising Mommy after they'd docked the boat and walked up the rocky slope to the rental cottage and Daddy called out: "Toss the coals on the grill, Hannah! We caught dinner!"

After her mother died, Maddie tried to reinvent the hobbit house in her bedroom closet in Green Hills. She moved her shoes and the storage bins where her winter clothes were kept in summer, and where her summer things went in winter. But even doing that didn't leave much room. So she put the toys, most of her dolls, and all the books except for one under her bed, which left enough space in the closet for two dolls, the book, and her. When Daddy saw it, however, he said if she went inside and closed the door she might suffocate. It was no fun leaving the door open, so Maddie abandoned it.

"Next!" A man's voice pierced her ears and reinstated her attention.

She stepped forward. "One lobster roll. And a bowl of chowder. Both to go."

"The roll comes with chips."

"That's fine."

Once back at the cottage, her dinner in the refrigerator, her lunch on the table, Maddie sat down and reflected on all the memories she'd recollected in the past twenty-four hours. If anyone had asked—and more than once, they probably had—what her childhood had been like, chances were she'd had little to tell. Rather than dwelling on what, if anything, that might imply, she picked up the lobster roll and took a bite. Like so many flashbacks she'd been having, the taste was happily familiar.

When she finished eating, she went directly to the closet in her mother's bedroom.

In the back, she found the door—"The perfect size for the Seven Dwarfs," her grandmother had said. Maddie opened it, crouched, and wriggled in.

The room was much the same, though the cot was now covered with a puffy pink blanket. Several of Maddie's favorite yarn dolls, however, were nestled in a basket that sat atop the seaman's chest. She remembered every one of them.

Setting the basket on the floor, she lifted the lid of the chest; her heart quivered, her eyes teared up. Inside were her childhood clothes, including the pink shorts with the drawstring waist and the white T-shirt with the big sequined star. She held the T-shirt up and wondered how she'd ever been that small. Below the clothes were a few dozen children's books: Golden Books, Sesame Street, Dr. Seuss's *The Cat in the Hat* and *Horton Hears a Who!* Grandma Nancy had read Maddie a whole book every night when they were there. When she reached "The End," Grandma kissed three of her fingertips and touched them to Maddie's forehead while whispering a word Maddie didn't know but sounded like it was about a cow. Whatever it had meant, whenever she heard it, Maddie fell sound asleep.

Picking up a doll with orange yarn hair, she stretched out

on the cot. Unlike in earlier years, it wasn't long enough now to fit her legs past her knees. So she curled up, hugged the doll close to her chest, and shut her eyes.

Which was when it occurred to her that her mother's closet—the secret passageway leading to her hobbit house— had been empty. Gone were her mother's clothes. Gone were boxes of her mother's shoes and purses and memories like the high school yearbook that Maddie liked to look through because many of its pages included drawings that her mother had made of popular venues on the island: the Flying Horses Carousel, the Capawock movie theater, the lighthouse at the cliffs. Maddie hadn't seen any of those things in Green Hills; they must not have crossed over to the mainland the way her mother had.

And now they were gone from the Vineyard, too. Maybe it had made Grandma sad to see them there. So she'd packed them away. Or thrown them out.

Chapter 5

The next thing Maddie knew, an onrush of muted shouting filled the room. It was nearly dark; she knew right away that outside it was sunset. And that she'd slept.

Rubbing the remnants of sleep from her eyes, she untangled her body, shook a few kinks from her limbs, and ran her fingers through her hair. Picking up the two yarn dolls, she crawled back through the tiny door and into the hollow closet.

Once again in the living room, she set the dolls on the sofa as if to make it look like she had company. Then she opened the front door, where she was greeted by a full, day's end panorama—a glow of pink, yellow, and tangerine blazed across the evening sky, accompanied by a symphony of cheering from an audience that stood on the shore, many of whom were on the water's edge, as if that would bring them closer to the enchantment, help them see better, help them see more.

It was the same shoreline from which Maddie's grandmother wanted her ashes scattered into Menemsha Bight. At sunset.

According to Maddie's hazy memory, no one knew when or how the tradition of clapping for the sunset had begun; someone might have started it spontaneously, without intention. But people had so much fun with it that island chatter had spread the word about its spectacle, long before social media could have sent it spiraling, viraling as the most striking sunset in the universe. The sight was downright magnificent, climaxing when the orange ball dropped into the sea like a flaming rock.

Maddie might have forgotten this if it hadn't been for her mother's penchant for painting the scene. And yet, no matter how many Hannah Clieg canvases existed of the last arc of the sun as it dipped and bowed into the water, to Maddie, each one had looked different. In fact, a Menemsha sunset still hung over her bed in Green Hills. Unlike her father, she had not dismissed her mother from her life. Or her love of the times they'd spent on the island, a love that had resurfaced—and seemed to be growing—with each hour she was there.

She stood another moment, just watching, enjoying. Then, as the afterglow of sunset began to disappear, she turned to go back inside. Which was when she noticed that something (a shadow?) or someone (a man?) was slowly moving up the hill, walking toward . . . her. Trespassing on her land.

Her senses went on alert. Her shoulders squared; her jaw tightened. Could it be the same someone she'd thought had been watching her? Then, as her fight-or-flight instinct began to kick in, the man (yes, it was a man) drew close enough for her to see: it was Brandon J. Morgan, Esq. And he was holding what looked like a briefcase.

"Hey, Maddie," he said jovially. "You're just the person I was looking for. I thought I might see you on the beach."

"Is it something urgent?" Her voice sounded professor-stern, which hadn't been her intention. She was still a bit shaken.

"Not at all. Sometimes I come here with my mother to watch the sunset. She's still down there with the rest of the holders-on. As if they can't come back tomorrow and watch it happen all over again."

Maddie finally relaxed. She laughed.

"Anyway," he continued, "you left this morning before I could give you these." He unzipped his briefcase and pulled out several papers. "The parcel maps of Nancy's Aquinnah properties. They're yours now. Well, almost. They will be once we've wrapped up the legalities."

Staring at a neat pile of paper as if assessing whether touching them would sting, Maddie hesitated. Then, because she felt she did not have a choice, she took them from him.

"Thank you." It took effort for her to sound pleased. "It was nice of you to bring them. I'm sorry I ran off earlier—I guess it was all too much for me. . . ." She tucked the maps under her arm. "I'd invite you in for a glass of wine or something, but I'm afraid all I have is a bowl of chowder that I picked up earlier." She didn't know why she thought offering her attorney a drink would be expected. Or appropriate.

"Thanks for the offer," he replied with a friendly smile, "but I'll have to take a rain check." He glanced back toward the beach. "My mother likes to get home in time to settle in and watch *Amanpour and Company*. It's not on until midnight; I keep telling her I can record it so she can see it in the morning, but she gives me one of those annoyed-mother looks—you might know the type—and tells me to go to bed and let her watch it in peace. So I do." Then, as if realizing what he'd just said, he grimaced. "Oh, Maddie. I'm sorry. When I said 'those annoyed-mother looks' I forgot that . . ."

She brushed it off. "It's fine, Brandon. I'm sure my mother looked at me that way once or twice. I know my father has. And still does."

"My father did, too. It must have been in a parents' manual in the 1980s, though you might think they'd have tossed it out once we came of age." He rezipped the briefcase. "Speaking of parents, I'd better brave the crowd and find my remaining one. I'll give you a buzz when we're ready to proceed with the paperwork. And you can decide when you want to scatter the ashes. If you want to, that is."

The ashes. Right.

"I was thinking I might want to have a small service on the beach. Though my grandmother didn't want, as you called it, a full-blown funeral, I wondered if a few people might like to attend?" She hadn't thought about that until right now. After all, Lisa might like to be there. Maybe Brandon's mother, too. And others, who Maddie didn't know. If, as Brandon had said in his letter, Nancy had been one of the island's beloved characters, it only seemed fair to invite her neighbors and friends. As long as it could happen soon.

"It makes sense, yes. But I'll double-check with my mother and let you know about that, too." He waved and headed back toward the beach.

And Maddie was left feeling as if the magical embers of the sunset were smoldering in her stomach the way the remnants of the burrito had done last night. She wondered if her intuition for something unpleasant—or at least, unknown—was rearing its head again.

As badly as she wanted to dismiss it, Maddie genuinely felt that something was wrong. If not wrong, maybe off-kilter. Though her intuition—her "gift," her father called it—sometimes had been real, other times it hadn't. After her divorce, when she'd gone back to college, she hadn't known what to major in. One day, while scrolling through the college catalog, she read a three-sentence course description on archaeology—and had one of those electrical-current zaps. The description said that the class explored cultures of ancient civilizations through excavated pottery and petroglyphs that depicted horses, birds, and godlike creatures in the netherworld, and were found on the walls of caves. It sounded fascinating. Almost as if it was calling to her.

Her father had said archaeology was interesting, as long as she stuck to the facts and didn't get caught up in romanticizing it. She knew he often thought her intuitions were solely a product of her imagination; sometimes, he'd been right. Now, however, she remembered that when he'd told her Grandma Nancy died, a strange foreboding had enveloped her. But she'd never questioned the validity of what he said. Because her father would not lie to her.

"Pick a subject you can live with," he'd recommended about her choice of study. "Because you'll be teaching it for a long time."

Maddie then considered art history—she loved exploring art museums, partly because original paintings reminded her of her mother. But thinking about her mother every day into the future felt like an invitation for depression.

So Maddie chose the history, processes, and effects of journalism, all of which were important in learning how to craft in-depth, honest (not opinionated) stories. She felt strongly that responsible journalism was past due for a resurgence as a viable career—one for which she could help her students prepare. Most likely, her choice had been influenced by her father's penchant for political science.

Sitting on the lumpy, faded sofa, staring out the window at the starry night sky, she wondered why she was thinking about all that now. She supposed she should disregard a hunch that Brandon was omitting, or perhaps sidestepping, the truth. Why wouldn't a woman who'd been nearly ninety want to have her friends gather to say goodbye? Why would he have to ask his mother? Maybe Grandma Nancy hadn't had as many friends as he'd suggested in the letter and he'd been trying to spare Maddie's feelings.

She might never know the answer because she didn't really know him. And he was an attorney. She'd seen enough late-night comedy to know what that could mean.

But because it was illogical for her to give her intuition credence when her job was teaching the importance of sticking to facts, Maddie dismissed her wariness as unfounded. Then she got up, went into the kitchen, and heated the chowder. After that, maybe she'd sit outside and count fireflies, the way she, her mother, and Grandma Nancy liked to do.

Hmmm . . . , she thought. Another lovely memory had reappeared. She decided to allow that one to quiet her mind.

Having discovered that the cot in her hobbit house wouldn't afford her adult body a good night's sleep, Maddie spent the night on her mother's old bed again. She awoke early the next morning, ready for a run. Outside the front window, a fuzzy gray mist draped its dreamlike haze across the dunes. The beach would be quiet: sunbathers weren't likely to show up until the fog had lifted, so she headed down to the water. Maybe it was low tide and the sand would be wet but slightly firm, perfect for running.

Changing into shorts, a T-shirt, and her Nikes, she left the cottage, locking the door behind her.

Once outside, she followed a path that circumvented the road; along the way, she was astounded by a tall bronze sculpture rising high above the beach grass and shimmering with dew. The piece depicted a man who stood poised, his harpoon aimed at a large swordfish that curved upward toward the sky. She didn't remember it; maybe it was installed at some point in the past forty years. She laughed at the notion that so much time had passed since she had been there.

Jogging past the harpooner through the gray air toward the water, listening to the soothing cries of the morning gulls and the restful putt-putt of a fishing boat as it chugged out of the harbor, she tried to clear her mind. But a single thought kept barging in:

Three to four.

Million.

Plus the cottage.

For a total of somewhere north or south of five.

She put her hands on her hips and exhaled a loud groan. Then she resumed her running position and continued her trek.

Not surprisingly, with the inheritance on its way, getting tenure no longer seemed as important. Which made her kind of sad. She'd worked hard to get to this point. She'd worked hard and sacrificed a lot. With a father who'd kept pushing her to do her best, to be her best, everything had been in her favor. Tuition was fully paid because her father had been grandfathered into that perk for the offspring of a tenured professor. As soon as she'd moved back into the historic house where she'd grown up, she recognized that her son felt safe and loved there, too. Plus it hadn't been long before he was busy inspecting the many nooks and crannies within the hundred-year-old walls.

But even with everything in Maddie's favor, it took many grueling years for her to get her PhD. In the process, she'd had too few stolen hours with Rafe, too little time seeing friends, and, God help her, less time for dating. After several futile attempts at the latter, she gave up: one man was too old; another, too young. But then came Harry Miller, who was "single, never married, no kids, a veterinarian." Perfect. Well, not quite. After dating for six or so months, one evening he picked her up; they were going to an outdoor concert on the lawn at Tanglewood. Maddie had packed a picnic supper for them. But when she set it on the back seat of his car, she picked up a piece of paper that she thought was trash. Instead, it was a sixth-grade report card for a child named Harry

Miller Jr. She asked; Harry (apparently Harry Sr.) replied. Yes, he had a wife and three kids stashed in Great Barrington— he'd "forgotten" to tell her about them.

Maddie immediately retrieved her picnic basket, told him to get lost, and resurrected the "Onward!" spirit she'd developed after her divorce. She buried her hurt and herself in her dissertation and finally reached her goal a month before her thirty-seventh birthday. And now it looked like she was a shoo-in for tenure.

Even with her hard work and her father's connections, she'd never thought she'd be so lucky.

"Now you're an official nepo baby," Rafe had said when she first learned she was on tenure track.

She had no idea what "nepo" meant.

"Think nepotism," he responded. "Nepo is what kids of celebrities are called when they get famous, too. Get it?" At the time he was fourteen, sometimes too smart for his age.

"Well, this nepo has earned it," she said.

He agreed. Though on Wednesday nights and every other custodial weekend, Rafe was still exposed to his father's money-driven life, unlike Owen, Rafe had a heart. She was glad he'd witnessed how much hard work it could take to reach a goal.

And now, as she made it down to the beach, only to see it was high tide—not helpful for running—she peeled off her sneakers and socks and let the cool sand cushion her bare feet. Then she walked, while still thinking, still wondering.

Could she be a worthwhile professor if she wasn't mentally hungry? If she didn't need to struggle to build a financial future?

Maybe she should keep her old Volvo so she'd stay humble.

Letting the gentle waves tickle her toes, she knew that, in spite of her good fortune, it wasn't right that she hadn't been able (or allowed?) to reconnect with Grandma Nancy. Maddie would have liked that. A whole lot.

"Madelyn!" It sounded like a woman's voice, muffled through the cloak of fog.

Maddie kept walking.

"Madelyn Clarke? Is that you?"

She stopped. Was it Lisa? Or Evelyn? Or had someone else found out she was there? Her heart started to beat faster, while the *thump-thump* of footsteps grew louder, trotting through the sand, heading toward her.

"I guess they call you Maddie." The voice was closer, less muted now. "We haven't met, but I think you'll be glad we finally did!"

Just as Maddie decided she should pick up her pace, an ethereal figure moved through the remaining mist and stopped next to her.

"Cleo Cochran," she said, extending a hand. "But call me CiCi. For my initials."

Of course, Maddie thought. CiCi. The real estate agent Lisa had warned her about.

"Hello," Maddie said, giving up, giving in, and shaking her hand.

The woman was younger than Brandon's mother, but not by much. Even in the haze, her cerulean, three-quarter-sleeve top and matching capris stood out, as did the gaudy pink-and-blue earrings that dangled from the short crop of her bleached-blonde hair.

"I went to your grandmother's cottage first. You weren't there, but you left the light on, so I figured you came down here. Most people new to the island can't get enough of walking on the beach."

Maddie wasn't sure if that was a compliment.

"Anyway," CiCi continued as one eyebrow lifted higher

than the other, "from what I've heard, I can make you a rich woman." She winked as if she were a used-car salesman.

Apparently, no one had told her that Maddie wasn't ready to talk business.

"My grandmother just died," she said. "I'm not ready to discuss her real estate. And certainly not at this hour."

The woman's multi-lined forehead crinkled. "Fine. I'll come back another time." She turned to leave.

"Wait," Maddie said. "Do you have a card? I'll contact you when I have something to say."

CiCi pulled a card from her pocket as if it had been waiting for the invitation.

Maddie took the card, forced a smile, then turned and resumed walking, that time at a faster clip.

And, again, she would have sworn that someone—not CiCi—was watching her.

So CiCi was on the hunt. Was Maddie going to sell? It was too soon to know. College professors were good at mulling things over, weren't they? Would she research her topic to death, not daring to make a hasty decision?

Things would be easier if that weren't the case now. Maybe CiCi would get on her game and pressure Maddie. And help put an end to this insanity.

Chapter 6

After Maddie shook off her paranoia (*Who the heck would want to watch me, anyway?*), she showered (inside again) and dressed (jeans, T-shirt, her boring tan sandals), and decided to check the second outbuilding to see how much more junk she'd have to get rid of. Then she could move on to what was guaranteed to be the biggest job of all: sorting through every closet and drawer inside the cottage. As much as she'd love to hire someone to do it, she didn't want to. There might be important papers that needed tending to or family mementos she could save for Rafe—not that he'd want them, but at least he'd have the option.

She found an empty trash barrel next to the outdoor shower and dragged it up the backyard hill. When she reached the shed, however, she noticed a rusty door latch with a silver padlock hooked through it. And it was locked.

"Seriously?" she said aloud. It was hard to believe that Grandma Nancy didn't lock the front door to the house but had secured this bedraggled hut.

Dropping the barrel, Maddie jiggled the padlock; it didn't budge. Even worse, a small window next to the door had been covered from the inside with what looked like a cardboard remnant—so she couldn't even peer in. This must be where Lisa said Grandma Nancy wove her baskets. Maybe a sizable inventory remained inside; maybe Grandma had wanted to protect her business more than everything else. Maybe once Maddie got around to tackling the heaps in the cottage, she'd find the key. She could always call a locksmith. Lisa might know one. But right then, Lisa would be at work.

Maddie sighed. She decided she at least could go to Cronig's. Then she'd be able to cross food shopping off her to-do list.

Though the fog had lifted, the morning was overcast and the temperature was cool, which might not do much to cut down on traffic. Without a beach-worthy day, more people might be driving around the streets, browsing through festivals, spending money in the town shops, or hiking in Menemsha Hills. There must be an abundance of things to do; it felt odd that Maddie knew so little about the place that was about to hand her a few million dollars.

After pulling a long-sleeved shirt over her T-shirt and grabbing her purse, she was on her way to up-island Cronig's in a blink. But as she wheeled toward the main road, preparing to turn left, she realized she'd be driving right past Brandon's. Why not stop there first and ask if he knew CiCi? Maybe he'd recommend someone else, someone trustworthy who would set a fair price and could arrange a solid deal that would not have repercussions. Or wouldn't take too much time. She assumed she'd need someone who was well connected to the island. Someone aware of values, trends, and, hopefully, potential buyers.

While there, she could also ask Brandon if a key to the padlock was tucked in Nancy's file.

Brilliant, she thought as she smiled to no one but herself.

It wasn't long before she reached the Morgans. Evelyn

was out on the *veranda*—a word that Maddie's father said was passed down by his Scottish ancestors that described a porch with a view of a beautiful lawn. Not that she knew if it was true.

Evelyn was tending to the myriad of flowers in large pots that hung and stood and sat strategically around and displayed a full palette of summer colors. She waved when she saw the Volvo. Maddie wondered if islanders were as friendly to people who weren't millionaires. By the condition of her car, it must be evident that she had not been one of those. Until now. Presumably.

She parked, got out, and walked toward the house.

"Good morning," she called.

"You caught me tending my captive crops," Evelyn responded, pressing one hand against her lower back as Maddie walked toward her. "I let the wildflowers and the blueberry bushes in the meadow take care of themselves, and I've become too old and creaky to bend down and dig in the dirt around the house. So I settle for mothering these beauties."

"Old" and "creaky" were hardly words Maddie would use for Evelyn. In fact, it wouldn't be surprising if, in spite of being older, the woman was in better physical shape than Maddie, who, in spite of her penchant for running, spent most of her time either standing in front of a classroom or sitting at a desk grading reams of students' papers.

"Your flowers are beautiful," she said.

Evelyn took off her green gloves and wiped her brow. "Thank you. The colors are extra vivid on a cloudy day."

Maddie hadn't considered that.

"I hate to drop in," she said, "but I was on my way to Cronig's and wondered if Brandon might have a minute. I have a couple of quick questions."

Setting the gloves on a small gardening cart, Evelyn abandoned her pots and went down the steps toward Maddie. That day her capris were light gray, her polo shirt, pale aqua. Once again, her white hair was tidily in place. "I'm sorry, dear, but Brandon isn't home. Is there something I can help you with?"

Maddie smiled. "Maybe. I can't find a key to the padlock on my grandmother's large outbuilding. I'm starting to sort through her things, and I'd like to see what's in there." She was mildly proud of herself for saying "things" instead of "junk." And for not admitting that she was trying to decide what to save, what to sell, and, mostly, what to dump.

The woman folded her arms and looked at her pleasantly. "My son should be back any minute. Would you like to join me in the front garden and have tea while we wait?" She gestured toward a shady spot in the side yard where a white wrought-iron table and two chairs stood amid more pots of blossoms.

Maddie said that would be nice, and she followed Evelyn, sat down and looked around. "You've created a lovely little Eden here."

Evelyn laughed. "Thank you. Around back there's another outdoor space that seats six or eight. But I think this one is cozier when a friend drops by to say hello. Now, if you'll excuse me, I'll go get the tea. Hot or iced?"

"Iced is fine."

Though the sky remained overcast, Maddie supposed that any moment the sun would "burn off" the clouds—another of Grandma Nancy's sayings that Maddie recollected as she sat, relishing the floral scents, the stillness of the day, and mostly the ocean air—all of which evoked more memories, both surprising and wonderful.

"Your mother was a terrific artist," Evelyn said when she returned, carrying the same tray she'd carried the day before.

"She was," Maddie said, as if she'd ever known the depth of her mother's talent. She'd seen only a few canvases—the pair of Menemsha sunsets that had graced their home in Green Hills, and the one on the mantel in her grandmother's cottage.

"So you were in school with her?"

"Every year, right through high school. Our class was smaller than classes are today, and we all knew each other. Your grandmother usually picked us up in her old pickup; she had to go past the house where I grew up. My mom didn't drive, and my dad usually didn't get home until late. He was a fisherman like your grandfather."

Maddie took a big gulp of tea. She hadn't known her grandfather was a fisherman. She didn't, in fact, know anything about him. At least, not that she recalled.

"He died when we were in elementary school," Evelyn said quietly. "It was hard on your grandmother. And your mother."

"I didn't know that. Thanks for telling me." She wondered if she meant that. Or if the less she knew about her family, the better.

"But your mom!" Evelyn perked up. "Hannah was so much fun. So creative. And always curious."

She handed Maddie a plate that had the same kind of biscuits she'd planned to offer her the day before. This time, Maddie took one. It was a scone . . . with cranberries and a light icing on top. She wondered if the berries were from the island, if there was a bog there.

Before she could ask, Evelyn continued.

"Your mom was always busy doing one thing or another. After high school we rarely saw each other; I went off island to college, got married, and came back. She got married and left, but you know that. We occasionally saw each other when she was here with you. Every one of those summers, I tried to get her to teach the kids' painting class at the old school. But she was doing her own work, which she was so good at." She laughed again, as if recalling happy memories. Then she stopped. "Wait. You were in the program one season. I taught the kids how to paint a flower on a piece of small pottery. Do you remember?"

Maddie bit into the scone so she wouldn't have to answer. She chewed. Then she murmured something she hoped sounded as if she were thinking.

"Winnie Lathrop—oh, Winnie is a wonderful potter," Evelyn went on. "She's still at it. She makes jewelry, too. Gorgeous wampum earrings and bracelets. Anyway, every year, Winnie donated bowls—mostly they were seconds that I thought were lovely but had a tiny flaw or two, so because she's a perfectionist, she refused to sell them. The kids, of course, loved them. They got to decorate them and take them home. It was great fun for all of us."

A small bowl with a tiny flaw—like listing a little? And painted with a flower? Swallowing at last, Maddie asked, "Could I have painted a daisy on one?" The bowl on her grandmother's mantel took on new importance. Maybe her mother hadn't painted it. Maybe *she* had. Little Maddie. The girl with a hobbit house.

"A daisy!" Evelyn cried. "You *do* remember! Yes, daisies were easy to teach. Lord knows I don't have an ounce of the talent your mother had."

Just then, a vehicle pulled into the long driveway. A Volvo like Maddie's. Well, not really like hers. It was a new one; an upgraded model. With a gleaming finish and no visible rust.

"Oh, good," Evelyn said as she stood up. "Brandon's home. Maybe he can find your padlock key."

Maddie and Brandon went into his office while Evelyn carried the refreshments back to her kitchen, allowing her son privacy with his client. He wore what looked like the same shorts he'd had on the day before, but a T-shirt instead of a button-down. He was no longer an Owen clone.

She sat in the same chair she'd sat in yesterday, now with one more reason to be dumbfounded. The bowl. The daisy. It had been easier when she'd first arrived and felt little connection to . . . everything.

"Nice to see you again," Brandon said with a smile.

"Thanks." Maddie didn't want to say she thought it was nice to see him, too. At least, not *that* way. She'd become man-shy after Harry, and it suited her. "I promise I won't keep you," she said. "I can't find a key to a padlock on one of my grandmother's outbuildings. I thought you might have it in her file. There's probably not much of value in the shed, but I'll need to clean it out. . . ."

Before she continued, Brandon was shaking his head. "A padlock? Nope, sorry. I haven't seen a key. Did you look everywhere in the cottage? Did you go through all the drawers?"

She was embarrassed to admit she hadn't yet started searching the house. Or that she'd figured because he'd had the key to the front door, he'd have that one, too.

"Maybe I haven't looked hard enough." She tried to look pensive and not embarrassed. "But I do have another question. What do you know about CiCi Cochran?"

He chuckled. "CiCi? Has she hunted you down already?"

Maddie hissed. "You could say that. I'm learning that news travels fast here."

"Yup. That's how it works. Sometimes the grapevine is helpful. Other times . . ." His words trailed off. He grinned again.

It must have been the grin that made Maddie at last feel comfortable enough, so she pressed her hands to her face and confessed, "I have no idea what I'm doing! I'm just an assistant college professor praying for tenure. I'm a single mom who lives with her father and her son. The only thing of value I ever sold was my last Volvo because it had over two hundred thousand miles on it." She dropped her hands to her lap. "Even then, all I did was get another one just like it. Only newer, of course. Though that one's now old, too."

Brandon was laughing, but in a friendly way. "CiCi will be fine. She can come across a little . . . pushy. And maybe she is. But she's a good agent. And she's been here forever, so she knows the island. Knows how to sell it. And she'll get you the best money possible."

For some reason, his endorsement surprised her. "So I don't need to interview others?"

He shrugged. "It's up to you. She comes across as eccentric, but you won't do much better. Especially up-island." He paused, then put his elbows on the desk and leaned toward her. "So, you're sure about selling?"

She sat back. "Well. Yes." She wondered if he was disappointed. "My life is back in Green Hills. I'm hoping I make tenure this year. And . . ." She realized she'd already told him that. And everything else he needed to know about her.

He waved her off. "I wasn't prying. I just want you to be sure. One thing about the Vineyard is that when property goes up for sale, it sells fast. Lightning fast. And once it's gone. Well, it's gone." His grin returned. "I'm sure you know what you're doing, though. You must be pretty smart. To be a college professor."

It was her turn to laugh. Then she stood up. "Well, thanks." She fidgeted a few seconds, then said, "Oh, there's something else. Your mother said your grandfather—her father—was a fisherman. Same as mine."

Brandon stood, too. "Yup. Gramps was a pretty good one, too."

"So your whole family knew mine."

"I guess so. Yes."

She stared at her hands. "Do you know if my grandfather was cremated? Like my grandmother wants to be? Or if he's buried somewhere on the island where I might see his grave?" She had no idea why she decided she'd like to see a grave, a headstone engraved with the name of a man she'd never known.

Brandon walked around the desk and leaned against it, facing her. "So you don't know what happened," he said softly. "Would you like me to tell you?"

She frowned. "Yes. Of course."

"Okay. But it was a long time ago, Maddie. Before either you or I was born. When I was a kid, I remember my grandfather—my mother's father—talking about yours. Butchie, he called him. They were good friends. Then one day, Butchie Clieg's boat capsized in a storm off Georges Bank. They used to fish there for cod. Haddock. 'It must be the best fish, 'cuz everybody likes it,' Gramps used to say." He lowered his voice. "Anyway, Butchie died at sea in that storm. I'm so sorry, Maddie."

It didn't seem right for Maddie to say it didn't matter, that, until that moment, she'd never actually wondered about him. So she simply said, "Honestly, Brandon, it's okay. I never knew him. When your mother mentioned him, I realized I didn't know anything about him. At least, not that I remember. Anyway, I'm glad I do now. Thank you." She turned to go.

"Your mother was still young when it happened," Brandon added. "My mom probably knows more."

Maddie adjusted her purse on her shoulder. "It's okay, Brandon. I really appreciate what you've told me." She willed her positive spirit to return. "Now I'm off to Cronig's for food. Then I'll turn the cottage upside down until I find that darn key to the padlock!"

"Let me know if you want a locksmith. That might be easier. Besides, if you turn the cottage upside down, you might decrease its value."

"For which CiCi would never forgive me."

"No, she wouldn't. But mark my word, she'd still be able to find you a buyer."

Chapter 7

Coffee, a few premade meals to stick in the microwave, a couple of salads, a small frozen pizza, and the splurge of a pint of Cape Cod Creamery's ice cream (Vineyard Vanilla flavor): as Maddie unpacked the basic staples that she thought should last the rest of the week—which would surely be long enough for her to have to stay there—she mused about how interesting it was that some families from similar backgrounds wound up having money when others did not.

Evelyn—the daughter of a fisherman, as Hannah had been—wound up living in a lovely house on a gorgeous piece of land, while Hannah's mother had still lived in a small cottage with a small yard accessible by a sandy path that rippled up the hill through tall grass and wild beach roses and closely abutted the neighbors' properties. In Evelyn's case, she'd married money. In Hannah's, she'd married a college professor.

Maddie consoled herself by knowing that her ancestors had a better view of a sunset and the sea than the inhabitants of North Road did. Still, it would be nice to learn something about her background other than her mother's Iberian genetics that her father once said was why Maddie had such thick, beautiful hair. "To-die-for hair" a high school friend once called it. Maybe Maddie would learn more when she tackled the boxes and stacks of papers in the cottage. And she'd at least be able to tell Rafe some interesting stories.

Besides, if she were about to become a millionaire, it would be nice to know where the money had come from in the first place. Especially when it came to the land, since, somehow, someone in her past had been able to buy the nearly five acres.

She decided it was time for a field trip, a scouting mission to view her inheritance.

Folding the paper shopping bags, saving them for a recycle bin, she found a canning jar in a kitchen cupboard, washed it out, filled it with fresh tap water, and screwed the top on tightly. Then she grabbed her phone, purse, and the maps Brandon had given her. But before going to the car, she went up to the shed she'd plowed through the day before and retrieved Grandma Nancy's gardening boots. There was no point getting her sandals mucky or wet—which might be a strong possibility when someone lived on an island.

She set her GPS for West Basin Road, Aquinnah, which she decided must be close by, considering that the address of the cottage was Basin Road, Menemsha, without the "West." Unfortunately, she hadn't discerned that between here and Aquinnah was lots of water: Menemsha Basin, Menemsha Inlet, Menemsha Creek. And, of course, Menemsha Harbor. There was the bike ferry that Brandon mentioned—apparently it was only for people who were traveling from here to there on foot or with bicycles. Looking at the GPS map, it appeared that the ferry would be faster and easier than to drive clear out to State Road and circle back.

With the maps, her phone, and the jar of water in hand, she put the keys and a few dollars in the pocket of her jeans, got out of her car, and locked her purse and Grandma's boots inside, keeping everything safe.

Safe, she thought, rhymed with Rafe. She wished he were

there now, sharing her adventure. He would have loved it. And he most likely would have found a way to rent kayaks or a canoe to cross to the other side to add to the fun.

As she walked down the road toward the water, she was amazed at the number of people meandering around on such a cloudy day, drifting in and out of the few small shops, sitting on big rocks, talking in low voices while watching the water or waiting in line for sandwiches or ice cream, hopefully the kind that Mr. Fuller used to sell. Maddie smiled and kept walking until she reached a blue-and-white sign shaped like a surfboard. It read: BIKE FERRY. AQUINNAH VIA MENEMSHA. $5 ONE WAY. $8 ROUND TRIP. It seemed simple enough. But nothing was in sight that looked like a ferry.

"Excuse me," she asked a young woman who stood near the sign, holding the handlebars of a red bicycle. "Is this where we get the bike ferry to Aquinnah?"

The girl squinted. She seemed around the same age as Maddie's students. Rafe's age. She pointed across the channel. "It's over there," she said. "I already rang the bell. It'll be back in a minute."

"Thank you," Maddie said. "It's been a long time since I've been here." She supposed that the girl didn't care about that or about the rest of Maddie's story. Maybe she'd be more interested if Rafe was there. The boy—the young man, she corrected herself—turned even more heads than his father once had.

Then the girl announced, "Here it comes."

Holding her hand to her forehead to shield the gray glare off the water, Maddie said, "All I see is what looks like a pontoon boat with an awning over part of it."

"That's it," came the answer. "No need for anything bigger. My grandfather said it started off as just a raft with a railing to hold on to and a tiny motor. Or something like that."

Maddie fumbled in her pocket and withdrew a five-dollar bill and three ones. She was about to ask if she should tip the captain (if that's what he was called), but the girl was removing her helmet, strapping it around the handle of her bike, and grasping the handlebars more tightly, making ready to be piped aboard.

After a successful "crossing" to the other side, and with her maps unfolded, Maddie began her expedition by following the road. All around her was beach sand, dunes, and sea grass—there were no landmarks for Grandma Nancy's properties. Not that she expected a sign that read, THIS WAY TO GRANDMA'S, but a hint would have been nice. She continued to walk along the narrow road: a long curve of the beach was on her right—the ocean side—and a few sections of tall, wood-slat fencing stood here and there, dividing the pavement and the sand, perhaps an effort to minimize the amount of sand that wind gusts blew onto the asphalt. That close to the water, there were no tress, no shade to help protect much of anything.

Opposite the beach side of the road, wild plants sprawled in abundance, all of which displayed healthy blossoms, some pink, some white against lush green leaves—*Beach roses*, Maddie thought. Hadn't her grandmother once made jam and tea from them?

Other than the beach roses and bits of wild vegetation, the land was mostly barren, shaped by soft-looking dunes and a smattering of small ponds. Maddie would love to investigate them but wasn't sure she should: the ground around them might be trickier to navigate than it appeared, and she'd left Grandma's boots back in Menemsha. Besides, it might be tribal land that Brandon spoke about. Or private land that belonged to the owners of the few houses in the distance that stood on higher ground. No matter the case, she wouldn't want to trespass.

She walked farther than she'd thought she'd have to, but, according to the map, when West Basin stopped, she turned at Lobsterville Road. After a while, her calves started to ache, a sign that she should have worn sneakers, not sandals.

Finally, she found Clay Pit Road.

"Aha!" she said aloud though no one but seagulls must have heard, as no people were in sight.

She headed up the street, hoping to find the property that supposedly was "off it," whatever that meant. If someone stopped her, she'd show them her parcel maps and ask if they had any idea where the boundaries were. Surely, someone would know.

Her enthusiasm propelled her, aching calves and all, toward a large dune, hoping she'd be better able to get her bearings once she was on the other side. Which was when Maddie's usual common sense deserted her.

It was two thirty when, out of necessity, Maddie called Brandon.

"Thanks for not letting this go to voice mail," she said when he answered. "My choice was to call either you or the EMTs."

"The *EMTs?*"

"Yes. I've had a little mishap." By then she was sitting on the sand, having landed on her butt, after her body had hurtled down the large dune from the top to the bottom. She supposed her jeans were embedded with countless granules of sand, much like her hands, the flesh of her palms stinging as if they'd been burned. She'd managed to take off her sandals, but by the way her right foot was swelling, it did not appear that standing up would be happening anytime soon.

"Are you bleeding?" Brandon asked. "Did you hit your head? Where are you?" His questions burst forth in a rush, each one faster than the last, as if he were a contestant on one of the game shows that, oddly, her father enjoyed watching since he'd retired.

"I'm okay, but I fell," she said. "I tumbled down a dune, and I think I sprained my ankle. I don't think I can stand on it."

"Are you near your cottage?"

The fact that he'd called it her cottage didn't escape her. At least he hadn't asked if she'd tripped over the granite slab that had caused Grandma Nancy's "unfortunate" passing.

"Not exactly." Maddie was mortified to tell him that, as competent as she was at some things, going on an adventure alone—not counting running—had never been one of her strong suits. So she tried to sound lighthearted when she said she'd taken the bike ferry across the harbor while armed with the parcel maps. She would have preferred, at that moment, to cry.

"So . . . ," she continued, "I'm near Clay Pit Road. On the wrong side of the dune, which means I can't see anyone and no one can see me. Not that anyone's around. So how's that for an afternoon jaunt?"

"And you sprained your ankle."

"Well, the dune was higher than I thought. When I fell, my right foot went in the wrong direction. And now it hurts. A lot."

"Oh, Maddie," he said, "I'm really sorry, but I can't be much of a lifesaver. You need the Tri-Town ambulance. Call nine-one-one. Right now. The responders can find you through your phone ping. I'd run over and join them, but I'm on the boat."

The boat? "Oh, Brandon, I'm the one who's sorry. Sorry to bother you. I didn't know you have a boat. How nice that must be."

"It would be, I suppose. But I don't have a boat. I'm on the *big* one. The ferry. Islanders just call it 'the boat.' I'm heading back to Boston for a few days."

Maddie was reminded that he was her attorney, not her son, not even her friend. But other than his mother and Lisa (and CiCi, which would be a stretch), Maddie knew no one else there. Not a soul. Which reinforced her decision to get things sorted and the real estate put on the market, so she, too, could get on the big *boat* and leave.

"Let me know how everything turns out," he added.

She thanked him, disconnected, and dialed 9-1-1. A calm voice on the other end told her to keep her line open until the ambulance located her. While she waited, Maddie sat back on the sand, sipped water from the canning jar, and tried very hard to employ mindful meditation to ease the increasing pain in her foot. But she'd gone to only one free meditation class, which no doubt was why she wasn't getting any worthwhile results.

Her foot wasn't sprained. It was broken. In two places.

"Is there someone we can call?" a nurse asked some three hours later, after the EMTs had located Maddie, assessed the state of her foot, and driven her down-island to the hospital, where she was welcomed, scanned, and plaster-casted. She was surprised that they still used plaster in these days of technology and innovation. At least they'd cut the right leg off her jeans above her knee so she wouldn't be naked below her panty line. And thank goodness no surgery had been required.

After rejecting the idea to phone Rafe or her father, and

before she could say, "No, there's no one you can call," a woman's voice came from outside the private room in the ER, where Maddie was sitting on the bed, staring at the plaster that seemed too enormous when she'd broken only her foot, not her whole leg.

"She'll be going with me," the woman in the hallway said.

It was Evelyn. Who would probably be a better savior than Lisa Jenkins. Or CiCi Cochran. And, unlike Rafe or her father, Evelyn wasn't hours away, so Maddie would avoid a lengthy explanation about why she was there in the first place. Brandon must have called his mother, which was how she already knew.

"Evelyn?" Maddie asked.

The woman stepped into the room. "Brandon feels terrible that he wasn't here to help."

"But he did help," Maddie said. "I didn't know if nine-one-one would reach the EMTs. Especially out there, where it seems isolated."

"Believe it or not, the island has made it into the twenty-first century. And now it's my turn, not my son's, to take over. You are my old friend's daughter, and you have no one here." She said it matter-of-factly. "You'll need to sign your life away before we can spring you from this place. It's a lovely hospital—all of us on the island are proud of it—but there's no place like home, correct? And for the next few days, your home will be mine."

"But . . ."

Evelyn wagged a finger. "No buts. You've seen our house. It's huge. When Brandon's not around, I often think I must be crazy to insist on staying there alone. And he'll be bringing his friend back with him this weekend, so we'll have a grand time. Maybe I'll feel like the lucky summer resident I once was, a woman who spent time arranging clambakes on the beach, playing croquet on the lawn, and scheduling tennis lessons for my guests. Suffice it to say, you won't be playing croquet or tennis, but you will stay with us for the foreseeable days. I will not take no for an answer. Your mother, God bless her, would have expected no less of me."

Of course, there was no way Maddie could or would decline Evelyn's offer after that monologue.

"Before you go," a gray-haired woman in a pink smock said as she entered the room carrying a tablet, "we need to schedule your return appointment. The doctor wants to see you one week from today. I recommend the one o'clock slot, so you can get here early and take advantage of lunch at our café. Chowder, sandwiches, hot meals, you name it. It's all great. And cheap."

"Then one o'clock it is," Maddie said. There was no point in saying she'd planned to be on the ferry by the weekend, since it appeared that she was stuck on the Vineyard. For now.

She started to climb down from the table just as the orthopedic doctor strode into the room and held out a pair of metal crutches.

"There will be no ambulation until you learn how to operate these," he said. "They'll be your constant companions for the next three to six weeks, depending on how long it takes the fractures to heal."

Maddie's new companions were gunmetal silver with wide cuffs above the elbows, which she knew would help stabilize her. Rafe had used the same type when he'd sprained his ankle playing hockey on the frog pond near their home. He, however, also had a mild concussion, which she expected wasn't likely from falling down a pillow of a dune.

"And for the next two or three days," the doctor was saying, "keep your foot elevated above your heart as often as possible."

Good grief, she thought. *What have I done to myself?* When she'd asked the doctor how it had been possible that she'd broken a bone by falling where she had, he'd said, "We have no idea." Which hadn't been terribly helpful, but at least he'd been honest.

Honesty was always the best route to take, no matter the situation. It was an unpleasant reminder of what Maddie had to do next.

"I need to call my son," she said abruptly. "And my father."

And there it was. Sooner or later, she was going to have to tell them the truth about where she was and what had happened. She was going to have to admit that she'd inherited Grandma Nancy's estate, though she wouldn't yet tell them everything—every dollar—it entailed. She doubted they'd be able to absorb the details if she spewed it all out at once. Especially her father, who was now going to have to come up with a good reason why he'd lied to her about Grandma dying when Maddie was ten. If he had lied back then.

Then Evelyn asked, "Would you like to call them now? I can step outside; I'm sure these nice people will give you privacy." She spoke as if she had any authority over the nurse or the doctor who still stood there, holding the crutches.

"You'll excuse me, then," the doctor said. "I'll see you next week." He handed the crutches to the nurse and exited.

Maddie told Evelyn the phone calls could wait until they got to her house. "But I have one request," she said. "Could we detour to the cottage so I can pick up a few things?"

Evelyn seemed pleased that her houseguest was going to go with her willingly. "Only if you tell me where to find what you need and wait in the car until I collect everything. And by the way, did you ever find the key to that padlock?"

Maddie laughed, because she no longer cared about what

might or might not be stashed in the mysterious outbuilding. While sitting in the sand before the ambulance arrived, she'd made the decision to sort through the papers, but that was all. A salvage company could come and haul away the rest.

Then the nurse showed her the proper way to use the crutches, and soon after that an orderly arrived with a wheelchair for her departure. Evelyn took charge of the crutches, and they went on their way.

Chapter 8

Maddie and Evelyn shared one of the premade meals and the salad she'd picked up at Cronig's. With the exception of the ice cream and a few unexciting things in the freezer, Evelyn had collected the perishables as well as a couple of changes of clothes for Maddie, who'd also requested her laptop in case she was inspired to work on the outline for her article.

After dinner, she called Rafe and told him where she was.

"Mom . . . ," he said after a short pause, "I thought you were in Boston. Why the heck are you on Martha's Vineyard? Are you alone or is that a secret, too?"

He must have thought she was with a man. A boyfriend, if that word still applied when someone was over forty. She took a cautious breath. "I'm not alone, Rafe. I have friends here." She did not, however, specify that she had friends there *now*, people she hadn't met until the past couple of days. She looked around the guest room in the Morgans' Chilmark home, at the tall windows that nearly touched a cream-colored hand-carved cornice. She admired the view from the bed where she lay, her legs out straight, her right one elevated above her heart, as the doctor had instructed. She gazed past the ivory floor-length draperies, out to the bountiful meadow, then decided that she hadn't outright lied to Rafe because it appeared that, yes, indeed, she now had three friends on the island. Not counting CiCi.

"I came here for the funeral of a relative I hadn't seen in years."

"You went to Martha's Vineyard for a funeral? I didn't think you had any relatives left there. Were they on vacation? Did they live in Boston? Did you go there first?"

Maddie realized that even stretching the truth could be confusing to both the bearer and the listener. "It's too complicated to get into on the phone. I promise I'll tell you all about it when I see you. Can you possibly get here? We could have a few days together before you go back to school."

"Does Grandpa know where you are?"

She paused. "Not yet. And I want to wait until I get home to tell him. So please don't tell him, okay?"

"Sure. But how long will you be there?" Her son pressed for answers.

So she said there was a minor glitch in her schedule. She confessed about her broken foot. She didn't mention that she'd done it while exploring the dunes across from Menemsha Harbor. He might ask too many questions she didn't want to answer. Yet.

"Geez, Mom. I can't believe you broke it."

"It's fine, honey. I didn't need surgery. But they did give me a clumsy cast and a couple of crutches like the kind you had when you sprained your ankle playing hockey. Remember when you did that?"

"I was nine, Mom. And I was down the street from our house, not on an island where I hardly knew anybody."

"Well, my situation really isn't much different. It's just a small twist in my otherwise boring life. At least it's summer, and this is a great place to be. Which is why I'd love it if you could get here. And right now, I'm not able to drive home because, unfortunately, it's my right foot. The one that works the gas pedal." She hoped he'd see some humor in that and make up a joke about it. But he didn't.

"Do you have to stay there until the cast comes off?"

"I hope not. Right now, the plan is for me to see the doctor again next week." Maybe she should at least give the ortho man a chance. Especially if Rafe could come and she could tell him about her grandmother when they were together right there on the island, where Maddie's memories of Grandma Nancy had been formed. He'd like that. "By then, the doctor should be able to tell how my foot's healing. So I'll be here until then."

Lifting her head, she glanced over at the tray Evelyn had brought her. A small teapot was on it, along with two "bedtime chocolates," as she'd called them: once a caregiving mother, always one. And it was evident that Evelyn cared deeply for her son.

Rafe paused, which Maddie knew meant he was thinking, not because he was angry with her the way her father might be when he learned what was going on.

"But, Mom, I'm still working at the river," he finally said.

As he'd done every summer since starting high school, Rafe was a volunteer, cleaning up the banks of the Hoosic River in the Berkshires, learning ways to protect the earth and its wildlife. It wasn't exactly a job for a business major, especially since Owen had wanted him to spend the summer as an intern at his firm because he said it would look good on his grad school application. But because Rafe preferred to be outdoors, not in-, he'd begged Maddie to convince his father this would be his last summer to be "a kid," and that after college was over, he'd have plenty of years to do the things he didn't want to do.

So Maddie intervened and told her ex that a volunteer job helping the environment was trendy, and that key words like "environment" and "volunteering" tipped the scales toward a grad school applicant being accepted. Especially if, in his essay, Rafe tied it in with a goal of wanting to go into business to help the environment on a larger scale.

"If I can find someone to take my place, maybe I can get there next Tuesday or Wednesday," he added now. "Will that be too late?"

"It should be perfect. My appointment is Tuesday. Maybe the doctor will say I can leave anytime. We could stay a couple of days here, then go home together."

Rafe groaned. "I can't believe you can't drive. What about your car?"

She said she wasn't going to worry about that yet. Then she realized she could sell it right there on the island—or donate it to someone in need. She'd be able to afford to do that, wouldn't she? Either way, she'd never have to return. Which would be more than fine with her.

"I could take the bus so we'd only have one car over there," Rafe continued. "Then I could drive us home in yours, and you wouldn't have to worry about how or when to get it."

Maddie pondered that. "The bus might take too long. You might need to go through Boston."

"Don't worry. I'll figure something out. But when I get there, how will I find you? And where is Martha's Vineyard, anyway? I know it's an island, and it's off Cape Cod, right? So, is there a bridge?"

"My son knows nothing about my grandmother," Maddie told Evelyn the next morning. "He doesn't know anything about the Vineyard, either. He asked me if there was a bridge."

Evelyn smiled. "My father told me that in the olden days

when he was a boy, he went with his father to bring their catch to the fish market in New Bedford. They crossed Vineyard Sound in their canoe. They used the canoe to fish, and they used it for transportation. Later, when he had an honest-to-goodness fishing boat, he used it to get to New Bedford, too. He said it took less time than driving down-island in his pickup and taking the ferry to the mainland. When your mother and I were girls, we went with him a few times."

Maddie set down her coffee mug. They were sitting in the breakfast room, an octagon-shaped, glassed-in space that overlooked the meadow. The sun was out; it warmed the many colors of the tall wildflowers that waved in the breeze.

"It's bizarre, isn't it?" she asked. "That I'm upset because my son knows nothing about his great-grandmother, when I know practically nothing about my mother, let alone my grandmother. You've told me more about them—and my grandfather—than I ever knew."

"Your mom and I were raised the same way. But as I said, our paths went in different directions. Brandon's dad went to law school to be a lawyer like his dad and his dad's dad, and I didn't want him to be in Boston without me. It was hard enough when we'd been separated during our undergrad years—he went to Harvard; I was lucky enough to get a scholarship to Smith."

"What a coincidence," Maddie said. "My son is going to Amherst, just across the Connecticut River from Smith." She wondered if the Ivy League women's college was where Evelyn had learned proper manners—or if she'd learned them by marrying a proper summer boy. "But you came back to the island. . . ."

Evelyn nodded. "The Vineyard was and is and always will be home. This house had been in my husband's family for such a long time—it started as a seasonal place, but he always said that it felt like home, too. I was the island kid whose parents had little money, much like your mother's family. After I got married, we stayed in Boston off-season, where my husband had his law practice, and where we raised Brandon. But we cherished our summers here. But right after my husband turned sixty, we learned he had lung cancer; he said this was where he wanted to be if he was going to live. Or if he was going to die."

"Oh, Evelyn, I'm so sorry."

The woman offered a slight smile. "Brandon took over his dad's practice, which keeps both of us, and frankly, this place afloat. But my husband and I had a wonderful life together. Not many people can say that, so I have no right to complain." She leaned across the table and patted Maddie's hand. "But enough about me. You're the one who deserves to complain this morning. How do you feel? Any pain?"

Maddie shook her head. "I took a pain pill last night, but only half of one today." She'd thought she'd need the extra help before hobbling down the hall when Evelyn called her to breakfast. Thankfully, the "hospital room," as her benefactor cheerfully described the guest room, was on the main floor and not upstairs with the rest of the bedrooms. Maddie didn't want to ask if Evelyn's husband had died there.

"That sounds like progress to me," Evelyn said.

"Let's hope." Then Maddie tried to reposition her weight onto her left side as if that might help an ache that was resuming in her foot. "It would be nice if I could take a shower."

"Your discharge papers say not today but maybe tomorrow if your pain stays under control, and if you're not teeter-tottering from the medication. I'll help you wrap a plastic bag around it and secure it so water can't get in."

"Thank you. I don't know what I would have done without you."

"If my son hadn't been halfway to Boston, I'm sure he would have come back to help."

"Speaking of sons," Maddie said with hesitance, "would you be able to drive me to the cottage again today? I hate to keep imposing, but before Rafe comes next week, I'd like to spend some time going through my grandmother's papers. Maybe I can find things of hers—or my mother's—that will interest him." She didn't add that it would give Maddie something to do other than stare at the walls of her attorney's house, lovely as they were.

"Hmm," Evelyn said. "You remind me of your mother. Never wanting to give up, give in, or just relax. Don't worry. That's a marvelous way to be. But I think you should wait a couple of days before you start wandering around the cottage on your own. Give the healing process a chance to begin, you know? Besides, you need to elevate that foot, remember? Also, I'd like to go with you to be sure you don't overdo it and lose your balance. I do, however, have a few commitments in the next couple of days. They're not critical, but they must be done."

Though Maddie was listening, it was hard to get past Evelyn's comment that Maddie was like her mother—never wanting to give up, give in, or just relax. She hadn't known that about her. There was so much she hadn't known.

"But if you stay put and behave," Evelyn continued, "I'll bring you to the cottage on Saturday. And I'll drive you to your appointment next Tuesday. And to pick up your son, if he's able to get here, and if he needs a ride. Unless Brandon's back by then, in which case, perhaps he'd like to do that." Evelyn was a well-organized woman. Maddie had a sense that she'd still want to help even if a hefty attorney's fee for settling the estate wasn't involved.

"You win," she said. "As long as you promise to wrap the

plastic bag extra tight tomorrow so I can have a very long, very hot shower."

"Deal." Evelyn stood up and began to clear the dishes. "And, for the record, it's nice to have someone need me again." She checked her watch. "But I'll leave you alone for now; I'm chairing a meeting at the library this morning, then I have a luncheon engagement. Before I leave, I'll bring my husband's walker in here; I recommend that you relocate to the sunroom, and you'll be able to get around the house more easily than with the crutches. It has a seat, which will be good for carrying your phone or a book or whatever, and you can hang your purse from one of the handles. And help yourself to lunch—I've left some things in the refrigerator. Read or listen to music, but don't spend too much time on your computer. It wouldn't be restful. And remember to keep your foot elevated as much as possible. And behave yourself, okay?"

Maddie agreed and sipped her coffee again. She liked that this woman had been her mother's friend. Which made Maddie wonder if this unpredictable diversion had been meant to be.

The sunroom was peaceful beyond words. A soothing buzz of honeybees wafted through the screen door on a quiet breeze, their sounds merging with the scents of the wildflowers. Maddie was reclined on the thick cushion of a lounge chair; her foot was propped above her heart, because sometimes she actually followed directions. With her laptop by her side (against her caregiver's orders), she tried to gather the momentum to fine-tune the outline for the article she planned to write—a nonfiction piece about a woman who'd won a large settlement in a malpractice suit. Maddie had based her research on how the national story had been recounted much differently in the Northeast, Midwest, Deep South, and the

West—which combined to provide a prime example of how regional media coverage often fed their audiences varied slants of the same story, based on their political and/or cultural leanings. Once the article was published she'd introduce it to her classroom.

But, before opening her laptop, and with the bees providing their sweet symphony, Maddie began to doze. And then, for the first time in many years, she saw her grandmother.

They were together in a classroom, the only classroom in a child-size, one-room schoolhouse that she somehow knew was up-island in Aquinnah. In the dream, Maddie was young; she sat at a small wooden desk with a top that flipped up, revealing a compartment where she'd stored her possessions: a pad of paper, some colored pencils, a drawing of a daisy. Best of all, her grandmother stood at the front of the room, holding a piece of chalk, then turning to the slate board on the wall and printing a single word: *"wuneekeesuq."* She said it was from the ancient Wôpanâak language and was a traditional word that meant "Good day." She then explained that because they lived on what once was Wampanoag land, it would be nice for the children to greet tribal members this way.

For some reason, Grandma Nancy was not home making baskets. She looked the same way as she had looked so long ago: she wore her long black hair in a braid, her arms and legs were long and spindly. Her cotton skirt was pretty; it had colorful beads and some embroidery. Maddie assumed Grandma had made the skirt.

Then, as she stirred from sleep, Maddie wondered if Grandma had picked that Wampanoag word to teach her because, in spite of the drama the day before, she would have a good day today.

Wuneekeesuq.

Then she woke up.

★   ★   ★

It wasn't such a bad thing that Maddie broke her foot. It should, after all, mean she won't be able to escape from the island easily. At least, not without help.

And she'd have plenty of time to think.

So, in a few days—or less—no matter what her condition, she might make a decision about everything.

And I can go home.

Chapter 9

Evelyn hadn't returned by one thirty, and Maddie was hungry. After her strange dream, she'd managed to accomplish a little on her outline, which nonetheless felt good. Almost as if things would return to normal soon.

She tried not to laugh at that naive notion.

After a few practice tries, the struggle to stand up became easier; she even wheeled the walker to the bathroom without losing her balance. Buoyed by that success, she proceeded to the kitchen, where a large Post-it adorned the refrigerator door. In perfect penmanship, it read:

> *Chicken salad sandwich in here is for you. I put iced tea in the pink thermal water bottle. Make sure to try one of my special peanut butter cookies in the jar next to the sink!*
>
> *~E*
>
> *P.S. Joe, my property caretaker, might stop by this afternoon. He'll no doubt want iced tea and a cookie, too. He can get them himself.*

Evelyn was likely sending the caretaker to check up on Maddie. Having a nursemaid felt odd; though Maddie's dad was great at running to Whole Foods for chicken soup if she had a cold, he wasn't a warm-fuzzy kind of man.

But now she was being, well, mothered, she supposed. Not smothered (thankfully) but taken care of.

It was nice.

After collecting her lunch, she took the long way back to the sunroom, scouting each room on the first floor, all of which were spacious and meticulously furnished and designed, a blend of old and new. The living room had a thick-cushioned, contemporary sofa that sported eight or ten toss pillows in a mix of colors and designs that complemented a number of what looked like real antiques—a pair of wingback chairs, two delicately painted porcelain vases, and, atop the mantel of a wide fireplace, a gleaming wood-and-brass clock that stood, patiently ticking, tocking. It sounded like the old ship's clock in the board of directors' room at the college, where Maddie had been invited to tea on a few occasions.

Next to the living room, a dining room displayed a sleek glass-topped table that synced well with ornately carved mahogany chairs that had padded, silk-covered seats. A few contemporary paintings graced the red-and-cream, French toile-patterned walls: the combination was appealing. Maddie wondered whether Evelyn or Brandon had been the curator.

As she kept snooping, Maddie saw that even the music room aspired to museum-quality dignity and comfort, from its baby grand piano to interesting pieces of sculpture that stood on pedestals on either side of the windows. Two cozy sitting areas were on each end of a wall of bookshelves that held not only books but also mementos that had clearly come from other countries, other lands—Southeast Asia, Africa, India.

Together, the decor invoked *House Beautiful* on Martha's Vineyard.

At that point, Maddie's foot began to ache again—a dull warning that it was time to elevate. Besides, sneaking around someone's house unchaperoned would be considered impolite.

Rolling the walker back to the sunroom, she sat upright on the lounge chair while eating her lunch. Once finished, she raised her foot again and tipped back into a nearly prone position. She wondered if, even with the deluge of money, she'd be able to create such a warm, welcoming home for friends and strangers alike to visit. If that was what she wanted. And how long it would take for her to know.

The man who took care of Evelyn's property arrived just before three o'clock.

"I'm in the sunroom," she replied, after he'd called out her name. "And I hope you're Joe, because I'm not expecting anyone else."

Footsteps padded across the wood floors, the sounds muffled when they crossed the Oriental rugs.

"I hope I'm Joe, too," the voice replied. "Because I'm too darned old now to be anyone else."

He stepped into the sunroom and circled around to face Maddie, who remained prone, her foot propped in a way that would please Evelyn when she came home, whenever that would be.

Joe was tall and lanky, with dark eyes and a deeply tanned, leathery complexion that spoke to having spent years in the sun. Threads of gray ran through his black hair; as he turned to pull a chair closer to the patient, she noticed that his hair wasn't only long but also was in a ponytail, tied back with what looked like a thin cord of straw.

It occurred to her that he might be a full-blooded member of the Wampanoag tribe. Should she greet him by saying, "*Wuneekeesuq*"? But she'd learned the word in what had only been a dream; she'd feel foolish if it wasn't real, if it wasn't a word her deep memory had recalled.

So she simply said, "Hello. I'm Maddie." Then she thought about the man with the ponytail who'd built her hobbit house. Had he been Wampanoag, too? In elementary school in Green Hills, she'd been taught that the tribe had purportedly dined with the Pilgrims at the first Thanksgiving, which was now well recognized as a myth. She knew little else about them.

Her visitor pressed his lips into a broad smile and nodded. "I kind of figured you were her. I'm Joe Thurston."

"And I kind of figured you're Joe." She mirrored his smile. "But I didn't know your last name until now."

He laughed. "Not everybody does. Folks mostly just call me Joe." He gestured toward her foot. "How's it doing?" His voice was soft, almost whispery, as though it had some gravel in it. Or tiny grains of beach sand. It also sounded oddly familiar, which might be because other islanders sounded the same, having breathed the same, salty, often sandy air that circled the perimeter, keeping pace with the tides.

"I'm not in much pain today, thanks, so that's good. But I never would have thought that a tumble down a small dune could break a bone."

"Sometimes our earth has a mind of her own," he said. Then he asked where it happened; she admitted she was looking for a piece of property that belonged to her grandmother.

"Nancy," he said.

Maddie was startled. Then she wondered why she was surprised that he knew who her grandmother was. She had no idea how many people lived on the Vineyard year-round, especially up-island, but she imagined that the number wasn't large. Which also meant that Joe must know why Maddie was there.

"The place off Clay Pit?" he asked.

"Yes." So, yes, he not only knew about her grandmother, but he also must know why Maddie was there.

"Darn pretty area. When I was a kid, Nancy showed me where to forage for berries out there."

Maddie had no idea how old he was. The same age as Evelyn? "You knew my grandmother well, then."

He nodded again. "You could say that. And I know she'd be sorry to hear that you broke your foot on her property."

Maddie grinned and decided not to correct him by saying that the "place off Clay Pit" actually belonged to her now. Or, rather, it almost did.

Then she had another of her intuitions—one of the pleasant kind. "By any chance, did you build a room on the back of my grandmother's cottage years ago?" Was that why his voice was so familiar?

His dark eyes studied hers. "You have a good memory."

"Hardly!" She laughed, glad that her "gift" had worked in such a nice way, if that's what had happened. "I might have been four? I loved that room. If I stared at you then, I apologize. Back then I'd never seen a man in a ponytail."

"I hope it didn't traumatize you."

"Not at all. I found it . . . curious."

"Good for you. Lots of men have ponytails today, so I'm no longer a curiosity. And by the way, you were only three when I built that room. You were a happy little girl." He cocked a half smile and stood up. "Evelyn mentioned there might be some iced tea in the fridge?"

"Help yourself. It's very good."

"I'd put money on it that your grandmother taught Evelyn how to make it. I have no idea who'll be able to take Nancy's place teaching kids the important parts of island life." He snorted, not in a cynical way, but in the sad way that grief sometimes triggers.

Joe returned with tea and cookies (yes, he clearly knew where they were stashed) and sat back down. Just as he took a bite, Evelyn arrived. She was carrying two large bags.

"Oh, good, you have a visitor," she said as if she'd had no idea Joe would be there. She settled onto one of the chairs facing Maddie and handed her the bags. "I had time between my engagements to pick up a few things for you. I wasn't sure if Nancy had a washer and dryer in the cottage, and I expect you'll be staying on the island a bit longer than you'd planned."

Maddie opened the bags: one held two cotton nightgowns and three short-sleeve tops, each in a different pastel; the other had a lightweight denim jacket and two elastic-waist, A-line skirts, one white, one denim. Both skirts had pockets. "For carrying things when you're on crutches," Evelyn said.

Maddie was stunned.

"Did I guess the sizes correctly?" her new patron asked.

"I'm sure they'll be fine. And thank you so much. I'll re-imburse you . . ."

"No, you won't. Consider them get-well gifts to my old friend's daughter. I thought the skirts would be better than shorts—they'll be easier for you to get in and out of without worrying about the cast. There are some new underthings in there, too."

"Thank you, Evelyn. It's so thoughtful."

The woman smiled. "Believe me, it's my pleasure. Now," she said matter-of-factly, "did you have lunch?"

"Yes. It was delicious."

Evelyn turned to Joe. "And I see you found the cookies."

"Right where they always are," Joe said. "You want one? Or some tea?"

"Thanks, but no. I only had salad for lunch, but my meeting at the library included coffee and carrot cake with wonderful cream cheese frosting."

Judging by her slim physique, Evelyn didn't often indulge in cake.

"So," she asked Joe, "have you been entertaining my houseguest with tales of the good old days?"

"Only a little. I didn't want to bore her."

"And did you tell her everything . . . important?"

He paused. He blinked. "Depends on what you mean." He turned to Maddie and gave her a half smile again, which made her wonder what Evelyn was talking about.

"You know full well what I mean. Did you tell Maddie about your parents? Specifically, your father?" She eyed him with a narrow look that hinted, *Don't make me pry it out of you.*

When Joe didn't reply, Maddie braced herself in case whatever was coming next was going to make her uncomfortable. She could have been having another intuitive moment, or was just being insecure.

Evelyn folded her hands in her lap. "Joe's been a friend of my family's—and my late husband's—for as long as any of us can remember."

Again, the caretaker made no comment. Instead, he stared into his glass of tea as if he was reading leaves that were on the bottom.

"Isn't that right, Joe?" Evelyn demanded. "And, by the way, that was your cue to tell Maddie what you were going to tell her."

Yes, Maddie's intuition had been trying to tell her something. That time, it felt like a warning.

He lifted his chin, then looked straight at her. "Okay.

Here goes." He drew in a long breath. "Your grandmother and I . . . well, we had the same father."

His last two words hung in the air like spray from a Vineyard skunk, as Grandma Nancy liked to say when fish went bad. The black-and-white creatures were all over the island; when she'd been a kid, Maddie remembered they were rampant up-island. Grandma once said she knew a man who hadn't known any better so he twirled skunks by the tail and tossed them into the woods behind the cottage. He was never sprayed, not once. God, Maddie wondered now, where were these crazy memories coming from?

Finally, she spoke. "I don't understand."

Joe's eyes moved to Evelyn, then back to Maddie. "Our father was Isaac Thurston. Your grandmother was my half sister. I'm Joe Thurston, Isaac's son. Nancy was Nancy Thurston before she married Butchie Clieg."

Maddie was confused. "My grandmother was your sister? But . . . but she was almost ninety. Old enough to be your mother."

"True. I'm sixty-seven," he said. "Nancy's mother died when she was young—and, by the way, I'm sorry you lost yours. Hannah was a sweetheart. Anyway, after a bunch of years, Isaac wanted another wife. It had been hard for him, raising your grandma alone, 'cuz he was a fisherman like your grandfather Butchie became, and he was out to sea seven days a week, so Nancy mostly was raised by the women of the tribe. Isaac tried his best, and he did okay, but he finally asked the tribal elders to pick another wife for him. They'd chosen Nancy's mother for him, too. The story goes that the elders knew the ideal woman: she was a lot younger than Isaac, but I guess my father charmed her. It seemed like a good fit, so the elders arranged his wedding to the woman who became my mother. Her name was Violet. Like the plant. A few years after that, Isaac's daughter, Nancy, who

by then wasn't yet twenty, married Butchie Clieg, and everybody was happy."

Maddie thought about her father, who hadn't married
again but had not been a fisherman who worked seven days a
week. Nor did he have tribal elders to help him find another
wife.

"So," Maddie said, "you were my mother's uncle. . . ."
Her words trailed off, and Joe nodded. Then Maddie realized
this was pretty cool. Like her mother, Stephen Clarke was an
only child, so Maddie had never had aunts, uncles, cousins.
And now she knew something about . . . what was Joe to her?
A great-half-uncle once removed? She had no idea how genealogy worked—until now, she'd had little interest in it. But
whatever Joe was to her, yes, it was pretty neat. Rafe would
think so, too. Especially since it meant they had a relative who
was a Wampanoag, a Native American.

And that's when Maddie's brain came to a freaking-
screeching halt. Because she'd realized something else: if Joe
Thurston was a Wampanoag, Grandma Nancy had been, too.
And because the tribal elders had picked Nancy's mother—his
first wife—for Isaac Thurston . . . she, too, must have been a
Wampanoag.

Her throat closed up a little, the way it often did when
anxiety rushed in—or when she wanted to cry. She stared
at Joe.

"So . . . Nancy's mother was Wampanoag? And her husband was, too?"

Joe nodded. "Yes. Both of them. Full-blooded."

Which meant that Maddie's mother had been a Wampanoag, too. An Indigenous person.

And, therefore, so was Maddie.

She was not half exotic Iberian, not 50 percent descended
from a Portuguese fisherman, as her father had told her. Maddie Clarke was a Wampanoag Native American on her

mother's side. She'd always known that her father was part Scottish, part British, that he'd once traced his British ancestors back to the *Mayflower*, to the same people who'd survived their first winter in America, thanks to the kindness of the Wampanoags.

She looked at Evelyn, then back to Joe. She hoped that one of them would say more. But they stayed silent.

She tried to sift through what she'd been told. Was it true? Or had her mother really thought she had Iberian heritage? But that would have been ridiculous. Hannah, after all, had grown up on the Vineyard. She'd grown up among her people. Of course she'd known the truth.

Maddie had questions, lots of questions. But right then she was numb, and her foot was throbbing. It was hard to think straight.

"Why didn't anyone tell me?" was the first question she uttered. She couldn't tell if she sounded angry or upset. Or plain stupefied, which, frankly, she was. "My father said my mother's family was Iberian. Why would he have lied?" Then her whole body became agitated, every nerve crackling, combusting, going on alert.

Evelyn reached over and patted the armrest of the lounge chair as if it were Maddie's arm. But Maddie didn't want to be comforted. More than anything, she wanted—needed—to get back to the cottage and scour the place room by room, corner by corner. Closet by closet. She wanted answers. . . .

But she was trapped in a house that wasn't hers, with a woman who claimed to have been her mother's friend, and a man who claimed to be Grandma Nancy's half brother, and who, for all Maddie knew, wasn't Wampanoag at all but another descendant of the same fisherman, who at some point could have believed it would be more acceptable to claim to be a Native American than a Portuguese immigrant, at least on Martha's Vineyard.

Was it as simple as that? If so, why didn't Evelyn and Joe seem to know it?

Of course, as badly as Maddie wanted to escape, she didn't have her car. And with what felt like a fifty-pound sack of potatoes strapped from the toes of her right foot nearly up to her knee, she was hardly able to get off the damn lounge chair, let alone walk out to North Road and hitchhike her way back to Menemsha Harbor.

"Maddie, dear," Evelyn said in her motherly tone, which Maddie now found irritating. "Why don't we wait until Brandon gets home? I'm sure he can help straighten this out."

She wanted to ask why she thought Brandon Morgan, Esq., who, like Evelyn, clearly was Whiter-than-White, could manage to do that. He hadn't even been able to get a letter to her on the first try. Shifting her gaze out the window, she noticed a pond in the distance that she hadn't seen before. She wondered how many more surprises would be in store, and if any of them—including her inheritance—would turn out not to be as it had seemed.

"If you'll both excuse me," she said, "I'd like to take a shower now." She looked at Brandon's mother. "And thank you, Evelyn, but I'll manage to put the plastic around the cast by myself."

Chapter 10

Maddie didn't care if she had to call an Uber or a taxi or had to take whatever public transportation was available: early tomorrow morning, she was going back to the cottage. If she made it down the driveway on her crutches, surely she would be able to flag down a vehicle and find out where a bus stop was, if there were bus stops on the island. Maybe whoever she asked would offer her a lift. Hitching a ride most likely would be safe: she doubted that many kidnappers were on Martha's Vineyard. Or that anyone would try to harm a middle-aged woman whose leg was in a cast and who was brandishing two metal sticks.

She could have called Lisa, but she didn't want to. She certainly wouldn't call CiCi. So either the bus or the hitch-hiking would have to do.

No matter what it took, she would get out of there. She'd gladly exchange the cushy bedroom for Grandma's bed with the squeaky springs. After all, the cottage was more of a home to Maddie than this exquisitely decorated, professionally land-scaped, perfectly gardened, impressive island retreat. Maddie's roots were in a ramshackle cottage that overlooked Menemsha

Harbor. They were not in Chilmark with her mother's old school chum.

She had no idea why she was angry with Evelyn. Or angry with Joe, her great-or-whatever-half-uncle. That night, she could not get to sleep. She knew she needed to talk to her father. But the initial shock at the news had simmered into anger at him, too, and she hated being angry until she knew if it was justified.

Whoever had or had not lied to her, there must be answers in the clutter in the cottage—old letters, documents, newspaper clippings that were scattered, stacked up, or burrowed in those rickety walls—there must be documentation that would reveal the truth. God knew, Maddie didn't have the patience to wait for a DNA test.

She closed her eyes; she tried to keep her breathing steady, meditative. Again, the exercise wasn't working, but what little she was doing might keep her from losing her mind.

The strangest part was if she were half-Wampanoag, and if her father had known all these years, why had he concealed it? Had he hesitated to accept a Native American into his *Mayflower* genealogy? Evelyn's family—and her late husband—were White. Yet Evelyn had grown up among the Wampanoags. Some islanders might be of mixed blood—perhaps descended from the first, uninvited immigrants who'd traded a few beaver pelts and a meager amount of wampum for the land. The land that had belonged to Maddie's ancestors.

Then another thought emerged: Had Hannah Clieg turned her back on her heritage in order to gain the husband whom she wanted? Had Maddie's father also been duped? Hannah Clieg and Stephen Clarke were married in the early 1970s. It was hard to believe that sort of racism was still going on. And yet . . . Maddie was educated; Maddie knew differently. She knew that things weren't always as they seemed. Or as they should have been.

If she could have tossed and turned, she might have worn herself out enough to sleep. But tossing and turning was hardly doable encumbered as she was by the cast.

Lying awake, mulling over what might be the big lie of her life, Maddie heard the ship's clock in the drawing room chime eight bells. At one of the college teas she'd attended, she learned that the ship's clock did not chime the hour but signaled the four-hour shift changes of a sailor's watch: eight bells in the morning at four o'clock, eight, and noon; in the afternoon the eight repeated at four o'clock, eight, and midnight.

The eight bells now must mean it was midnight.

At twelve thirty, the chimes rang once; at one o'clock, twice; at one thirty there were three chimes; at two o'clock there were four; at two thirty, five; and on and on every hour and on the half hour in a repetitive configuration until it returned to the eight bells for the next watch. To Maddie, it was positively confusing. In his study in Green Hills, her father had a long-case clock that he'd inherited from his father, who'd inherited it from his father, none of whom were Native Americans. Maddie had never liked that he'd turned off the chimes.

"The trouble with clocks that gong," he'd explained, "is that when you wake up during the night and hear the chime, you have absolutely no idea what time it is. So you wait for the next half hour, thinking you'll be able to figure it out. By then, however, you're awake for the rest of the night. At least I am."

Now, when she heard the clock strike again, it chimed four bells. She calculated that it was either two o'clock, six o'clock, or ten. The pale light that leaked around the edges of the drapes and snuck into the room suggested that the sun had recently dawned. Six o'clock, then. In the morning.

Time to get up and activate her plan.

She started by popping a pain pill.

The house was quiet. Evelyn must still be asleep.

Maddie quietly packed her cross-body carry-on bag. Rafe had given it to her the previous spring, hoping she'd fly to Philadelphia to watch him row in the Dad Vail Regatta. "You have to come, Mom!" he'd exclaimed as she'd unwrapped the gift. "It's the biggest—and the coolest—college regatta in the country; it's a nearly seventy-five-year-old tradition." Maddie had hardly traveled—she'd been too wrapped up in school, either as a student or as a teacher. She'd gone to England once with a group from the college; another time she went on a cruise up the Mississippi River with some old high school friends. And when her father retired, he took Rafe and her to Scotland to learn about their ancestors. They spent two weeks in the Highlands, visiting castles, ancient ruins, and quaint hamlets; they trekked through lavender-covered hills and silent, ancient battlefields, and enjoyed boat tours on peaceful glacial lochs. It was a wonderful bonding trip, and her father discovered things that he hadn't known, including that the Clarkes had descended from Clan Cameron.

He'd never mentioned that on her mother's side there was another, even older clan.

As for the regatta, Rafe had been so excited that she wouldn't, couldn't, say no. It had been fun; she was glad she'd gone. And now she was really glad he'd given her the carry-on, which, like the pockets in the skirts Evelyn had bought, would enable her to keep her hands free for the crutches.

Zipping the last of her things into the bag now, she wondered if, after her inheritance came through, she would travel more. Maybe she could find one of those interesting groups that combined learning with sightseeing. She'd like that, especially since she'd recently read that many trips catered to singles. After all, her friends would still be working. The thought of which made her sad.

Enough of that, she thought, expelling a tired sigh.

Thankfully, notations about the regatta events remained in a side pocket of the bag. Maddie turned it over to the blank side and scribbled a note to Evelyn.

I'm getting a ride back to the cottage, she wrote. *I'll be in touch later. Thanks for your help and your kindness.* She signed it a simple "M." Then she stuck the note in the pocket of the new denim skirt she'd put on, and cross-bodied the carry-on.

Walking tenuously so as not to trip on an edge of one of the Oriental rugs or, worse, make too much noise while traversing the polished wood floors, she slipped out of the guest room and maneuvered her way down the hall, one unsure step at a time. She made it to the front door at last, relieved.

But the door was locked.

Of course it was, she thought. Grandma Nancy must have been the lone islander left who thought that tourists were the only ones who locked their doors.

Examining the lock more closely, Maddie saw it was a dead bolt, the kind that needed a key to open, even from the inside. She thought those had been banned in case of fire or God knew what else, so no one would be trapped inside the way she was right now.

She tried not to panic. For all she knew, Evelyn was an early riser, someone who liked to stroll through her gardens first thing in the morning before the dew was off her much-beloved blossoms.

Letting out a whimper, Maddie wondered why she felt she needed to escape before the woman caught her. After all, Evelyn—like everyone else there—had been nothing but nice to her. But, unlike what Maddie had told Rafe, none of these people really were her friends. *None* of them. She supposed she needed to be less trusting of strangers, less stupidly naive. But at the moment, she apparently had no choice but to stay put: she was definitely locked in. A prisoner in Chilmark.

Resigning herself to wait for Evelyn to rise and allow her to leave (perhaps offer to drive her? *Dream on*, she mused), Maddie decided she might as well make coffee. But as she began to hobble toward the kitchen, she spotted something shiny on a side table in the foyer: a key. It rested in plain sight at the base of a lovely floral arrangement that stood in an exquisite crystal vase.

Her eyes darted around, as if she were a thief. Plucking the key up from its spot, she spun, well, sort of spun, around, stuck it into the lock, and twisted it. She steeled herself, grasped the knob, and turned. The door opened.

Moving back to the table, she fished the note out of her pocket, dropped it next to the vase of flowers, and set the key on top of it. Then she went out the front door, glanced around the porch to be sure Evelyn hadn't come out there earlier, and made her way down the front stairs.

But as Maddie limped toward the driveway, something in her peripheral vision diverted her attention. She jerked her head back to the house; in an upstairs window, she thought she saw the ghostly wisp of a curtain quivering.

She paused. She waited. But when the curtain didn't quiver again, Maddie decided it had either been her imagination or her guilt; it hadn't given her the same creepy feeling as when she'd thought she was being watched.

Please God, she mused. *Not that again.*

Taking a deep breath, she gripped the crutches with determination and proceeded to totter down the driveway toward the street.

★ ★ ★

As if to prove that miracles could happen on the Vineyard, in less than twenty minutes, Maddie was at the cottage. She'd been offered a ride by an old farmer in a pickup who was toting three sheep in the bed of the truck. He said she looked like she needed a lift; he was headed to Aquinnah but said he didn't mind veering off to Menemsha for a lady in distress.

She decided that an old man in a pickup with three sheep in the back so early in the morning most likely wasn't dangerous. And she'd walked far enough to know that going the rest of the way under her waning steam was not a doable option. So she started to hop into the cab as best as she could, then allowed him to get out, walk around to the passenger side, and give her a hoist.

When they reached Basin Road, he drove up the driveway to the pull-off where he helped her out, tipped his baseball cap, and told her to have a lovely day.

Even if he'd been planted by Evelyn to keep an eye out for her runaway guest, he'd been pleasant. Cordial. And not once had he asked what she was doing out at that hour with a cast on her foot and leg and crutches to boot. He hadn't even asked her name. She felt guilty for not having asked his.

Though Lisa's bread was now four days old, Maddie decided it was still edible. Barely. She sliced off a piece and dropped it into the toaster, then put the kettle on to boil water for the instant coffee she'd bought. While she waited for the electrical elements to do their thing, she scrounged through a couple of cupboards until she landed on a jar of preserves that wasn't yet opened.

"A veritable feast," she said to no one.

Because the container of cream had also made its way to Evelyn's, Maddie sinfully added a heaping tablespoon of Vineyard Vanilla ice cream to the mug of coffee and spread the jam on toast.

After she was infused with food and drink, she got to work.

She started in her grandmother's bedroom, which seemed the most likely place for someone to sequester details about the past.

The closet was narrow, and not very deep. Around a stash of a few plastic bins, the dusty floor was in need of a good cleaning. Shoes sat on top of the bins: a pair of old sneakers, an equally old pair of black flats, and a pair of lace-up boots made for rugged terrain, as if there was any of that there. A wooden pole ran the width of the closet and held several shirts—a few flannel, the others cotton and seersucker. A few lightweight summer dresses also hung there, as did two long corduroy skirts—one dark brown, one navy blue—and a beige cotton skirt with colorful beads woven into a diamond-shaped pattern above the hemline.

She blinked.

It resembled the skirt Grandma had worn in Maddie's dream.

Trying not to read too much into that coincidence, she surveyed the contents of the bins: threadbare sweaters, hats, and mittens. And yet, compared with the rest of the place, the closet could be called tidy—except for several cardboard boxes, all of which seemed overstuffed and old. However, placed on a shelf that rested above the clothes pole, the boxes did look interesting, as if they might hold secrets. But in order to reach them, Maddie would have to climb up on a chair. Which would be risky, what with the cast and all.

"Damn. Damn, damn." She groaned.

Cursing, however, did not change the situation. So she raised one crutch and poked at one of the boxes on top. She managed to get it to move . . . then it came crashing to the floor, its lid bursting off, its contents careening all over the place.

"Damn!" she said again, that time shouting it.

Which did no good, either, though it did evoke a shiver of low laughter from the living room.

Maddie froze. Had she imagined it, or was someone out there? Her eyes flashed around the room, searching for something to arm herself with against an intruder. But just as she remembered she could wield a crutch, Joe Thurston walked into the room.

"Sorry to interrupt," he said in that gentle voice of his. "But it looks like you could use a little help."

Her first instinct was to tell him to go away. Then she remembered that, related or not, he had built her hobbit house. If Grandma Nancy had trusted him, maybe she should, too.

"I'd ask how you knew I'd be here, but I suppose there's no need to."

"Evelyn didn't want to bother you. She knows that a boatload of emotional stuff has been dumped on you, so she suggested I stop by. And don't worry—you don't have to call me Uncle Joe if you don't want to."

Staring back into the closet, wishing her foot would *please* stop throbbing, Maddie laughed. But then, she did something she was neither prepared nor known to do: she started to cry.

He let her cry for several seconds, then helped her to the faded pink-flowered boudoir chair in the corner and got her to sit.

While she tried to compose herself, she saw his gaze travel to the closet and the mess all over the floor. "Okay, let's get some air in here so we can breathe," he said. He went to the windows and opened both of them. Then he looked over at Maddie. "If you want to see what's in those boxes, I can take them off the shelf. Not that you should get your hopes up, 'cuz my sister was a wicked packrat."

Brushing back her tears, Maddie smiled. She told him to go ahead, then watched him gather the papers and files that were strewn in all directions. Next, he removed the boxes, one at a time, and lined them up on the bed so she'd be able to reach them without much effort. Then he stepped into the closet and vanished behind the clothes. After a few seconds, his feet emerged first: they kicked out one metal container, then another. And one more. They were the height and width of a standard file box, and seven or eight inches deep. Either Joe had just seen them, or he'd known that they were there.

"Done. Be careful of these, though," he said, touching the containers. "They're fireproof, which translates to heavy. You might want to wait until your son gets here."

Unsure if she'd told him Rafe was coming, she decided to stop wondering how anyone on the island found out so much so fast.

She looked at the cartons and the steel containers and quietly asked, "Is it true, Joe? Am I really Native American?"

He reached behind his neck and appeared to tighten the straw cord that held his ponytail in place. "I could say yes, but it's better for you to find out for yourself." He nodded toward the boxes. "If you can't find what you're looking for in here, let me know. I'll help you go through the junk in the living room. Sooner or later, you'll run into the truth. After that, you can decide what—if anything—you want to do about it. When it comes to this stuff, there aren't any rules."

She thanked him, and he said he'd be on his way for now but that she should call whenever she wanted—whether for a particular reason or for none at all. He peeled a flap of cardboard off one of the boxes and wrote his number on it.

Rising from the chair, she thanked him again, grabbed the crutches, and followed him to the front door.

"It will be fine," he said. "You'll see. Worse things happen in life."

Like being married to Owen, she thought, though it seemed like an odd time to have that pop into her brain.

Then Joe waved, turned around, and jogged down the path.

Maddie watched him go, feeling that, in spite of his congeniality, it was too soon to let down her guard. But on her way through the living room, back toward the bedroom and the boxes, she caught sight of her mother's canvas on the mantel, and the odd-looking quahog shell. And the pottery bowl that listed just a little and had a painting of a daisy on the front. *Her* painting, according to Evelyn. Evidence that Maddie had been there before. A reminder that she'd been happy. And she had belonged.

Chapter 11

After spending a couple of hours sitting on the bed, perusing her grandmother's treasures in the cardboard boxes, Maddie had found directions for basket weaving; recipes for Indian pudding, succotash, dried herring; a yellowed set of blueprints for a building labeled "Gay Head Processing Plant," dated 1961, and which, she'd supposed, was intended to process fish. She could ask Brandon—or Evelyn—if it was ever built. If she felt she needed to know.

Not having unearthed anything pertinent to her search, she abandoned the boxes and opened one of the steel containers . . . which was where, while digging through files of seemingly unrelated items—paid invoices and bank statements with dwindling balances, random handwritten notes including one about someone having gone clamming at a place called Red Beach planning to make chowder, and lists of basket sales at fairs over many years—she found a Bible.

It wasn't much longer or wider than her hand, fingers included. Its black leather cover was faded, unraveling at the edges. The type inside was hard to read because it was so small. But halfway through the tissue-thin pages, an insert was attached: a foldout record of family lineage. Someone—her grandmother?—had printed a title: "Praying Indians of the Wampanoag People of Gay Head. Thurston."

What followed was a list of what apparently were Indigenous names that went as far back as the 1600s, but Maddie neither recognized them nor felt a connection to. Until she landed on the significance: *Isaac Thurston, Walks with Thunder, 1897–1989.* She presumed he was her great-grandfather, Joe's father and Nancy's; Walks with Thunder must have been his Wampanoag name.

He wasn't exactly a nineteenth-century Portuguese fisherman.

She stared at the page.

Then she went back to reading: *Wife—Sarah Nightingale, Earth Talker. Daughter—Nancy. Wed to Bernard "Butchie" Clieg, June 7, 1953. Children—Hannah, Born May 13, 1954.* No other names were listed. There was no reference to her grandfather's death or to Hannah's marriage to Stephen Clarke. And there was no mention of Madelyn, Hannah's only child. It was as if Grandma Clieg stopped recording the lineage prematurely. As if the world had stopped revolving when Hannah married and left the island, leaving her roots behind.

Then she realized there weren't any Wampanoag names noted for Nancy, Butchie, or Hannah. Perhaps the trend had stopped with her great-grandparents' generation. Or as "Praying Indians," they'd stopped using them. She knew that she had much to learn about their culture.

But Maddie also recognized that the entries seemed to prove that Evelyn and Joe were right: Maddie was half Wampanoag. Half Native American. Half Indigenous person. As she sat on the bed that had once been her grandmother's, her feelings started to ride a wave that rolled from numbness to bewilderment. She wondered if this was how adopted children felt when they learned the truth about their birth.

Returning to the box, she spotted a large envelope tucked

in the back; she pulled it out. Its clasp was half broken, as if it had been opened and closed too often. Inside was an 8 x 10 black-and-white grainy photo: a young woman and a young man, standing straight and close together, facing the camera. The man was dressed in simple pants and a fringed tunic that looked made of some type of hide; the woman wore a similar tunic as well as an ankle-length skirt with a design around the hemline; three long necklaces of what looked like wampum floated down her chest. Draped across her right shoulder was a woven blanket. Both the man and woman had long, dark hair; both wore tall moccasins. The demeanor of the figures dated it perhaps many decades but not centuries ago, because they were smiling.

Turning the photo over, hoping for identification, she saw a newspaper clipping taped to it. The photo was reproduced; the headline read: "Nancy Thurston Weds Bernard Clieg at Gay Head."

Maddie stared at the clipping. She remembered reading somewhere, perhaps in the 1990s, that the name of the town called Gay Head had been reverted back to Aquinnah—its original name.

Slowly, she read the article about the wedding. It said that the couple—both members of the Gay Head Wampanoag Tribe—had chosen a traditional ceremony, complete with fire circle, songs and drumming, and Wampanoag clothing. It added that Nancy wore a blanket woven by her grandmother Gladys Nightingale, Spotted Fawn, and noted that the bride chose to take her husband's surname, Clieg.

It hadn't occurred to Maddie that her grandmother would have done otherwise. She had, however, once used a newspaper story in one of her classes that explained that Indigenous people of North America once were a matrilineal society, where women controlled their property and belongings. She'd used it as an example of how journalism could document cultural trends even in small ways. Perhaps in some tribes, married women retained their maiden names, too.

The important thing was that Maddie now knew that she, too, had Indigenous roots.

She looked at the photo again. In addition to her grandparents' smiling faces, she saw that, yes, in spite of the shades of black and white, the couple's skin hinted of coppery tones. The article made it clear that both of them were members of Wampanoag Nation. And, yes, the bride resembled a younger version of Grandma Nancy.

With her eyes still riveted on the image, Maddie pressed a palm to her cheek, to the coppery tone of her flesh. It was a shade lighter than the skin of the couple now smiling up at her, but coppery, nonetheless.

Ignoring the fact that her foot was throbbing again, she pushed aside the boxes and stretched out on the mattress. She closed her eyes, wishing she could call up a clear vision of her grandmother the way she'd seen her in her dream at the old schoolhouse and more memories of her time with her. Had they walked on the beach together, collecting pieces of wampum like the ones on the necklace in the wedding picture? Had Grandma sung songs to Maddie at bedtime like the ones that were sung on her wedding day?

As hard as Maddie wanted to conjure a few details, she kept returning to the definitive truth: she was 50 percent Wampanoag, had been since the day she was born. Would be until the day she died. She had deserved to know that. And to know who had kept it from her. Maybe she should confront her father before she told her son, because Rafe, too, was entitled to know why it had been hidden from him.

A breeze quivered through the screen at the open window, as if trying to tell Maddie what to do. But its message was too veiled for her to hear.

* * *

"You-hoo!" The singsongy voice chirped from the front door, jolting Maddie out of sleep. "Maddie? Are you here?"

She pulled her thoughts together. "One minute, Lisa." She sat up, dragged her casted leg off the side of the bed and finagled her body upright. Grabbing the crutches, she maneuvered into the living room.

"Your door was open," Lisa said. "I heard you fell. . . ." Her eyes dropped to Maddie's cast. "Oh. Look at your leg."

"It's not as bad as it looks. And it's only my foot."

"Well, your foot's still important, isn't it?"

Maddie had no response for that. Instead, she asked, "How did you find out?"

"Jeff Fuller came into the town hall this afternoon. He's also a neighbor, but you can't see his place from here. Anyway, he said he saw Bucky Williams bring you home and that you were on crutches. He stopped Bucky on North Road and asked what was going on."

So Bucky Williams was the man in the pickup with the three sheep in the back. But Jeff Fuller? She almost asked if he was related to Mr. Fuller who once owned the ice cream shack, but she was too tired for another history lesson. Chances were, he was a son or a grandson. People on the island seemed to live near one another, travel in the same small circles, or were related. Sometimes all three.

"Do you need help?" Lisa asked. "Do you have food? What can I do?" Chirp. Chirp. Chirp.

"I'm fine, Lisa, but thanks. My son will be here in a few days, and I have plenty of food until then." The "plenty of food" was comprised of only the pizza, ice cream, jam, and coffee, but the less said to Lisa, the shorter the visit. She hoped.

"Do you have books to read? I can go to the library. Nancy didn't want to pay for cable TV, but I think there's an old radio in the kitchen. She liked to listen to small craft advisories on Vineyard Sound."

Maddie didn't ask why her grandmother had done that. If she'd still owned a boat, surely Brandon would have included that in his laundry list of Maddie's inheritance.

"I spoke to CiCi today," Lisa continued. "She said the two of you had a nice chat."

Maddie leaned against a chair, needing to take her weight off her foot but not wanting to sit, for fear Lisa would think it was an invitation to do the same. "CiCi knows I haven't made a decision about this place yet. But I have her card."

"If she doesn't drive you crazy, she could use the business. She assumed you inherited everything, and I wasn't sure, but I figured she was right."

If her neighbor was expecting an answer, Maddie did not comply.

Then Lisa looked over her shoulder back down the hill. "If you're sure I can't help, I guess I'll be off. I've got to pick up the kids from day camp, and I don't have a clue what to make for dinner."

Maddie stood up straight again. "Well, thanks for stopping, Lisa. I'll let you know if I need anything."

"Great. Just holler down the hill. One of us will hear you!"

Then, blessedly, she departed.

Maddie wriggled over to the chair by the gingham-framed windows and sat. She wondered if Lisa knew that Maddie was Wampanoag . . . or that she'd only just found out.

Not that it mattered.

To anyone but Maddie.

And Rafe, as soon as she told him.

Glancing over at the table, she noticed she'd left her phone there. It must be nearly five o'clock—two bells. Time to stop procrastinating and call her father.

"Where are you? When are you coming home?"

Maddie's father was not a gruff man. Except when he was

worried about his family. She had no idea if he'd been like that before her mother died, but Maddie did know that she and Rafe were all Stephen Clarke had. His students—who had filled his days with activity and his nights by grading their papers—had disappeared into his bottomless pit called retirement. From time to time he saw one of his former fellow professors, but most of them still worked, and many of those who had retired, had moved back to the towns they were originally from. Back to where they had brothers, sisters, cousins, and the rest, maybe even a parent or two. And while her father did have a couple of cousins in the Midwest, their only connection was an annual Christmas letter about the good things in their lives.

With a quiet sigh, she knew that, first, she needed to let him get his worry out of his system. Then it would be her turn.

"Dad," she said, "I'm fine. I hurt my foot, that's all. I'm going to stay a few more days, but I'll be home next week."

"Rafe said you broke it."

"It's not a bad break. I didn't need surgery."

He paused; he must have closed his eyes and was taking a moment to regain his usual calm demeanor. "At least there are good doctors in Boston."

She bit her lip, glad he couldn't see her. "Yes, there are." It wasn't a lie, even though she didn't happen to be there.

"How did you do it?" He'd begun to sound normal again.

It was a good time to tell him the rest, to say that she was on the Vineyard, to tell him about Grandma Nancy. Maybe not to outright accuse him of lying, but to suggest that someone had lied to him years ago. But the words did not want to come out.

"I lost my balance walking down a hill. It was a silly misstep."

He didn't say she should be more careful. He didn't ask if

she'd been alone when it happened. If he thought she'd been with a man, he would not invade her privacy. He was a good dad. The thought of which made her feel guilty for what she was about to say.

Then she reassessed: *Wait. I'm the one who's feeling guilty? Seriously?*

"There's a letter here for you from Don Jarvis," her father said, changing the subject, which he was adept at.

Don Jarvis was the head of the English department at the college. He was also the chair of the tenure committee.

"Oh," she said.

Her father laughed. "Oh? That's all you can say?"

"Well. I don't know. It's unexpected." Had the committee already made a decision? Would they do that in the middle of summer? She still hadn't written the article about the media coverage of the malpractice case. Which meant it wouldn't count toward her list of publications, which might have affected their selection.

She was sitting at the kitchen table, her right leg propped on the chair opposite her. From there she could see out the front window—not all the way to the water, but as far as the dunes and the few houses below. She wondered how she'd feel if the college rejected her, especially if she no longer needed a guaranteed job. Which brought her back to the question of if she didn't teach, what in God's name would she do all day? Would she wind up watching game shows with her father, their lunches set on the old TV trays?

"Would you like me to open it for you?"

"Oh, Dad . . ."

"Sorry. I don't mean to pry. But if they've made a decision I thought you'd want to know. You could celebrate with your friends."

It took a moment to remember she wasn't with her friends. "It might be a rejection," she said. "It might be to tell me they selected Elliott or Manchino." They were her competition: Elliott was younger but she thought better qualified; Manchino was a wizard at getting published. And though Maddie knew her credentials were more than adequate, her lack of confidence often trounced that assumption.

"Okay," her father said, "The letter will be here when you get home."

"No," she said, resigned. "Open it. Read it to me." If they rejected her, she might as well know now. It might help her decide how to realign her future.

He laughed. She knew he liked it when she was spontaneous; he often said her mother had been. Hannah Clieg. Artist. Spontaneous woman. Wampanoag. Too bad he'd left out that last detail.

She put her elbows on the table and covered her eyes with her hands, as she listened to the sound of paper being torn. Leave it to the college to put their declaration on official letterhead and not send it in an email.

"'Dear Madelyn,'" her father began. "'I hope you are enjoying your summer. Classes will be back in session before we know it, so take advantage of every quiet day!'"

It was an odd opening for what should be a formal letter. She told her stomach not to lurch and her heart not to sink; after all, it wasn't as if she would still need Green Hills College.

But she had worked so hard . . .

"'I'm writing to let you know that Dr. Elliott has accepted . . .'"

Her stomach lurched, her heart sank in spite of her instructions.

"A position at Remilard University in Chicago."

Her father paused.

Maddie paused.

Then she cried, *What?*

He repeated the sentence. And he kept reading. "'You and Dr. Manchino are now the only remaining candidates for tenure here at Green Hills. The committee decided to let both of you know about this unexpected change. See you in a few weeks. Sincerely, Don Jarvis.'"

Maddie listened as her father refolded the paper. It was like him to return it to the envelope. Neat. Efficient.

"You have one less competitor, Madelyn. That's great news."

"I guess. But Mark Manchino has a lot of publications. . . ."

"And you are a brilliant woman who knows the rules and plays by them. Manchino, however, is headstrong."

"If you say so. Let's talk about this when I get home, okay? I need to go out and get dinner."

"Okay. I hope your foot feels better. And have a nice time."

A nice time? Oh. Right. He assumed she'd be dining at a lovely Boston restaurant with her lovely Boston friends. Whoever they might be.

"Thanks, Dad. I'll see you soon." She disconnected the call and sat perfectly still. She hadn't breathed a word about Grandma Nancy. She hadn't told him about the inheritance. She hadn't told him anything. Maybe because her future was proving as difficult to unpack as the history boxed up in the cottage. Would it have been easier if she'd been rejected for tenure, so her future wouldn't be fraught with so much doubt?

Besides, she'd already decided to sell everything and leave the island.

Hadn't she?

Right then, however, Maddie was sick of thinking. And she was hungry again. Maybe she could make the pizza last for a couple of meals, then find out which restaurants would deliver.

But as Maddie struggled to stand, the silhouette of a male appeared at the screen door, shaded by the late-day rays of the sun.

"I've come with gifts," Brandon, the silhouette, said. He was holding what looked like a casserole dish in one hand and a canvas bag in the other. Wildflowers were poking out of the top.

From watching through the window and seeing her reaction when she'd scanned the Bible, Maddie obviously finally knew the truth about her heritage. It was strange she hadn't known before; maybe her father hadn't wanted her to feel any ties to the island. For whatever reason.

Then again, Maddie seemed to have a mind of her own; maybe she'd finally be able to choose whichever road she wanted. Her son was an adult now; maybe she'd let him make his own choice, too.

Spying was good for some things, but not if one was supposed to be able to read the target's mind.

In any case, it definitely was time to move closer. All this waiting and wondering has been risky. Not to mention tiresome.

Chapter 12

"Seafood strudel," Brandon said, as he raised the casserole dish and stepped into the cottage. "Salad in the bag, and a bottle of wine. Does that work for you?"

Maddie smiled. "You're back from the big city."

"All true. And I shall dine with you, if that's okay. I feel terrible for abandoning you in your hour of need."

"You did not abandon me. You told me how to get the EMTs. And you told your mother I was en route to the hospital."

He rolled his eyes. "I hope she wasn't too . . . controlling. My mother thrives on being in charge. Speaking of whom, I have two more bags in my car for you. She bought you clothes?"

Maddie hung her head. "She was a lifesaver. I'm embarrassed that I snuck out of the house after all she did for me. But I was afraid she'd try to stop me." She raised her head and began again to try to stand.

"Stay where you are. I can find my way around a kitchen. But please, let's not talk about Evelyn anymore. She's a tough nut for me to live up to. With the emphasis on 'nut.'"

She hoped Brandon didn't think she wanted a relationship. As with most men since married-with-children Harry, Maddie felt little chemistry, even with the caring ones.

"Thanks for bringing dinner," she said. "People are being so nice. Lisa, my neighbor down the hill, has offered to help. So has Joe. But I hate to bother anyone. Unless I can't find a restaurant to deliver."

He uncorked the wine. "A lot of places still do since those scary first days of Covid. But never fear. You're on Evelyn Morgan's radar now. Don't forget, she was a friend of your mother's. Which gives you added points, despite that, technically, you're a wash-ashore."

Maddie half listened to his last sentence. Instead, she smoothed the top of the table, her mind drifting.

"Brandon? Did you know I never knew that my grandmother was Wampanoag? That my mother was, too?"

He poured the wine into a couple of canning jars and set one in front of her. "I love this island," he said. "I've always been happy that my mom kept the house here. Unlike in the city, where people tend to make friends only with those of like minds and backgrounds, the Vineyard is a tapestry of all kinds of folks—from artists to attorneys, from fishermen to presidents. And everyone in between. Some are happy, some are grumpy, some are outgoing, some keep to themselves. It doesn't matter. If you happen to be quirky, that's not a problem, either. Your grandmother was delightful. And, yes, she was a little quirky, but quirky is accepted here. I have no idea why you weren't told about your heritage, but I have a hard time believing it was her choice. If you'd had the chance to know her longer, I think you'd agree." He sat down and sipped from the jar. "Sorry if that sounded like a closing argument. I'm not even a trial lawyer."

Maddie smiled again. "You might have made a good one. And as I told you, my memories of my grandmother—and the island—are pretty vague. It's funny, though. The longer I'm here the more I remember."

"In my experience, the past can be a pain in the neck. My mother's still irked about my divorce. Mostly because she has no grandkids to hover over. But you have a son. And a husband, too?"

"My son's a good kid. I'm very lucky. As for the husband, I'm lucky there, too. Because now another woman has to put up with his egomania."

"Ahh . . . ," Brandon said, raising his glass, "here's to divorce."

They clinked.

"I'm not against marriage, though," Brandon continued. "In fact, I'm about to jump into it again. If you're around on Labor Day, you're welcome to come to the wedding out on the beach at Lambert's Cove."

Once again, Maddie felt relieved. She wondered if she would become a content spinster. Perhaps she already was.

"Well, congratulations. Is the lucky lady an islander or from Boston?"

"Actually, the lucky lady is a man. My mother wasn't crazy about that, either. Not at first. But she adores Jeremy. Which helps."

"You're gay? I can't believe that's still a big deal."

"My mother doesn't mind the 'gay' part. She's just disappointed—again—that I won't carry on the Morgan line of descent."

"There are surrogates."

He laughed. "Jeremy and I have talked about that. We might even do it. But I'm not going to tell Mom yet. She'll start shopping for baby clothes and convert one of the bedrooms into a nursery. So please, mum's the word. No pun intended."

Maddie smiled. "Well, it's terrific news, Brandon. Have you and Jeremy been together long?"

"Let's say we're a few years past due at the altar. That's why I went to Boston on Tuesday. Jeremy's condo sold; I handled the closing. My place up there is big enough for both of us. But though I love my clients in the city, I hope my husband and I can spend more time down here."

He stood up and went back to the kitchen, setting the casserole dish in the microwave. And Maddie felt a small wave of envy for the fact that his life seemed neatly wrapped up with a well-suited partner, a successful career, and even a mother he clearly loved. He was the kind of person she'd like to have as a friend.

Then again, she remembered she didn't really know him.

Maddie slept surprisingly well for having to navigate her now weighty lower extremity and the fact that she hadn't taken a pain pill. Lying on her back in her mother's childhood bed, staring at the ceiling, which, like the rest of the place, was overdue for a fresh coat of paint, she assumed she might need to repair and redecorate before putting it on the market. Now that she'd started to go through Grandma's things, she sensed it might not be as quick a task as she had hoped. She'd barely started with the boxes she'd already opened, and she needed to assess the linen closet, the kitchen cabinets, and the piles of magazines and papers that waited in the corners of the living room. Not to mention the junk in the locked outbuilding. She forgot to ask Brandon for the name of a locksmith; she'd consult Google instead. Surely there was one on the island.

But first, she needed to tend to herself.

Once out of bed, she found a box of plastic trash bags she'd brought from Green Hills, intending to use them to pack Grandma's belongings. She never would have dreamed she'd be wrapping one around her right appendage if she wanted to shower.

After tying it tightly, she managed to get clean without getting soaked in the wrong places. When she was finished, she brushed her teeth and her hair and dressed in the skirt and top that she'd arrived in on Sunday. Then she went into the bedroom and, exhausted, she collapsed on the bed.

A few minutes later, she heard a knock on her door, followed by "Hello?"

It was a woman's voice that Maddie didn't recognize.

She considered not getting up; hopefully, Evelyn, Brandon, Lisa, or Joe hadn't sent the island militia to check up on her. But after another round of "Hello," Maddie hauled herself off the bed—again—and limped—again—to the living room. She reached the door in time to see a large man, a small woman, and a little girl moving back down the path.

Out of curiosity, she called, "Hello? I'm here."

The visitors turned around.

"Hi!" the woman replied. She was young, much younger than the man, who looked old enough to be her father. She had a full head of pixie-cut dark hair, a stark contrast to the big man's bald head. On one hip, she carried another, younger child. "Is Nancy around?" She headed back toward the cottage, the others following.

Maddie leaned on the doorjamb and waited until they nearly reached the granite steps.

"I'm Maddie Clarke, Nancy's granddaughter," she said through the screen. "I'm sorry to tell you, but my grandmother died a couple of weeks ago."

They stopped at the steps. Maddie decided not to mention the connection with Grandma Nancy's demise.

"Oh no. I'm so sorry," the young woman said.

"That's too bad," the big man added, nodding.

"I'm Francine Flanagan, and these two little imps are Bella"—a lovely little girl with dark hair and round black eyes—"and Reggie"—the younger one, who looked almost ready to be a toddler. He was dressed in blue as if he were a sailor. Francine brushed back a lock of the boy's flyaway hair and adjusted him on her hip.

The man extended his hand. "And I'm Rex Winsted. Friend of Francine and her husband. And these two little ones."

Maddie opened the screen and shook his hand. "Did you know my grandmother?"

"Not really," Francine replied. "I learned about her a few years ago when Bella was an infant. I was given one of Nancy's baskets, which I carted Bella around in until she got too big. Reggie's outgrown it now, too. I live on Chappaquiddick, but we came up-island today so Rex could check on his cabin. It's across the channel from you. I have a friend who's pregnant, and I wanted to buy her a basket. One of Nancy's."

"You live on Chappaquiddick?" Maddie asked. "Isn't that a different island?"

"Actually, it's part of Edgartown," Francine said. "I manage the Vineyard Inn over there; my husband, Jonas, and I live on the property. Rex helps out when we need an extra hand. His sister is married to one of the owners."

The connection was probably less complicated than it sounded, but Maddie saw no need to question it. "I'm really sorry," she said, "but I haven't seen any of my grandmother's baskets, except one that a neighbor gave me, but it's not big enough for a baby."

"Thanks, anyway. It was worth a try." Francine looked at Maddie's leg. "I hope that didn't happen here."

"Sadly, yes. Walking on a sand dune, if you can believe it."

"I can," Rex said. "They can be tricky if you're not used to them."

"I'm not. I'm from Green Hills, which is so far west it borders New York. I came to the island to clean out my grandmother's place. Unfortunately," she added with a laugh, "I came alone."

"Oh, gosh. Well, if you need anything, please call the Inn," Francine said. "There's always someone there who'd be glad to come up and help."

"And I'm in these parts a lot," Rex added. "Thanks to my cabin over there." He gestured toward the harbor.

"Thank you," Maddie said. "That's so nice. And it was nice to meet you both."

They began to walk away, and Maddie started to shut the door when she thought of the outbuilding.

"Wait!" she cried, calling after them.

The little group turned around. "There might be baskets out back in the shed. But I need a locksmith to open the padlock. I'll let you know what I find once I can get inside."

The big man—Rex—chuckled. "If you can wait while I go to my truck, I might have a solution."

Maddie and Francine sat on aged Adirondack chairs—one might have once been painted green, the other white or yellow—in the backyard. The kids were parked on an old beach towel that Maddie dug out of the linen closet; Reggie was watching his big sister playing with Maddie's yarn dolls that she'd brought outside.

"Just like Grandma Claire's!" Bella had exclaimed when she saw them. Francine explained that Bella's grandma had presented a few to Bella a while ago.

"They're her favorites," she added.

With a tiny twinge, Maddie wondered if Nancy had taught Bella's grandma how to make them.

Rex had returned with a toolkit and was kneeling at the door to the shed.

"He knows how to do everything," Francine said. "He owns the Lord James restaurant in Edgartown. He always says, 'When you own a restaurant, you have to be a jack of every trade known to man. And then some.'" She tried unsuccessfully to mimic Rex's deep voice and then laughed. "I didn't know that included breaking into padlocks."

Maddie was enjoying the company. "It won't be the end of the world if he can't, but I'll be selling the property—"

"Really? You're going to sell?" Francine looked bewildered.

Taken aback, Maddie did not know what to say. "Well, I . . . I mean, well, Green Hills is a long trip. . . . I teach at the college there—"

"I'm so sorry," Francine interrupted. She sheepishly lowered her dark eyes—the color of which mirrored her little girl's. "It's none of my business. Sometimes we islanders get too cozy."

Maddie smiled. "It's fine. I don't mind. The truth is, I haven't been on the Vineyard in decades, and I thought my grandmother died years ago."

"Really?"

Maddie nodded. "I hadn't seen her since I was five. My memory of her—and of this place—is vague."

"I understand. But I'm sorry. It's just that I was surprised when you said you're going to sell. Sometimes people who inherit property here are overjoyed. Even if they can come only for vacations."

"I also have a son who lives in Green Hills. And a father who's getting older."

Then the sound of metal splitting startled them both.

"Got it!" Rex exclaimed.

If it weren't for her cast, Maddie might have jumped up and hugged him.

"Wonderful!" she cried. Even with Francine's help, it took a couple of minutes for her to get up off the Adirondack. Then, bolstered by the crutches, she walked up to him.

He was eyeing the shed. "I don't know why Nancy bothered with a padlock when one good swing of a ball-peen hammer would bring this place down." He unhooked the remnants of the lock. "Want me to open it?"

"Sure. Please."

Francine stayed by the chairs, monitoring her kids.

After a couple of tugs, the rusty latch ended up in Rex's hand, and the door flopped open. In spite of the sunshine outside, the inside was dark. The cardboard over the only window didn't help.

Grabbing a flashlight—again, from his toolkit—Rex directed the beam from one corner to the other, from top to bottom. Nothing was there. Not a carton, not a barrel, not even a mouse.

"How strange," Maddie said. "Why would she have locked an empty shed?"

"Good question," Rex replied. The two of them remained standing, peering inside, as if any second something would appear.

"Something wrong?" Francine called over to them.

"Something wrong?" little Bella echoed, as she set down Maddie's dolls.

"Not really," Maddie said. "Except I'm afraid there aren't any baskets in here, after all."

Francine put the dolls and the beach towel inside the back door of the cottage, then the adults said their goodbyes, and Maddie thanked Rex again for his help. Francine invited

Maddie to come to "Chappy" to see the Inn whenever she had the chance. She added that one of them would love to give her an unofficial golf cart tour of their island. Both Francine and Rex were so nice, Maddie didn't want to tell them she'd be there only a few more days. Or that she couldn't drive with the cast still on her foot. She didn't want them to think she didn't like the Vineyard. Or worse, didn't like them.

It was odd, however, that the outbuilding was empty. Especially since the cottage was filled with so many bits and pieces. And yet, there were no signs of the baskets that Grandma had apparently loved making.

But, buoyed by the company, Maddie set the dolls back on the sofa and opened all the windows and the doors.

Then she thought of someone who might know how—and why—the baskets were no longer there.

Chapter 13

Joe answered his phone on the first ring.

"Afraid I can't help," he said after Maddie asked if he knew why the shed had been locked but was empty. "Except to say that my sister didn't always do what one might expect."

"I guess it doesn't matter," Maddie replied. "It seemed curious, that's all." She was at the kitchen table again, seated where she'd decided it was easiest to get up and down when she wanted. She again rested her leg on the opposite chair—she figured that was elevated enough, as nearly seventy-two hours had passed.

"Right. Well, I'm glad you got to meet Rex," Joe said. "He's a character. Had his share of troubles when he was younger but turned out a decent man. Dependable, too."

She was beginning to think that most of the island people could be called "characters." The "tapestry" of the island, as Brandon had said.

"But I'm glad you called," Joe continued. "I was going to check in later. How's the foot?"

"Fine. It hardly hurts right now."

"Good. 'Cuz I wanted to ask if you'd feel up to a ride tomorrow."

"A ride? Where?"

"I was going to suggest a kayak, but that might be tough on your leg. So how about a canoe?"

"You want me to go somewhere in a canoe? It sounds great, but is it a good idea with this cast? What if it gets wet? What if we capsize?" As soon as she said that, she was embarrassed.

"I usually take people in separate kayaks. But it will be safer if you're in the canoe. With me. As for capsizing . . . first, you'll be wearing a life vest. Second, I haven't tipped a canoe in all of my sixty-seven years. Not counting the times I did it on purpose."

She laughed. "You tipped a canoe intentionally?"

"Sure. Lots of times. Kid stuff. But you'll be perfectly safe. I thought you'd like to experience a piece of your . . . heritage."

She paused, then asked, "What piece?"

"The flat waters. Calm waters. Not the ocean. We can start in Menemsha Pond and go to Nashaquitsa, then Stonewall. They're some of the waters our ancestors cared for, where our tribe runs a hatchery and a natural herring run, and where the shellfishing is great. The ponds are also known for their rich eelgrass beds, tons of birds, and all kinds of island wildlife." Then he added, "The waters give us so much, Maddie. And we give back to them by keeping our commitment to take care of them."

Listening to Joe, Maddie felt thousands of miles from Green Hills, from her small college office, from her father. From her world.

"If you don't believe me," Joe added, his voice sparkling now, "believe the carbon dating that proves that our Wampanoag link to the ponds goes back ten thousand years."

She was speechless. She ran a finger around the top of her cast and wondered how her ancestors would have treated a broken bone. Whatever their medicinal methods, she sensed they were often successful.

She inhaled, slowly exhaled. "I guess I'd be foolish not to take you up on it."

"It's up to you. But I expect that your grandmother would have wanted you to know a few things about our past."

If he was trying to guilt her into going, it was working. "No pressure, right?"

He laughed. "None at all."

She pictured his happy, leathery face. He was a kind, well-meaning man. And an honest-to-goodness blood relation. "What time?"

"Five thirty?"

She cringed. "In the morning?"

"You bet. Just about daybreak. The best time to feel the spirits of our tribe."

Maddie knew she liked knowing what was what and when. She liked being grounded by day-to-day routines. Unlike her son, she wasn't much for adventures. Crossing the channel on the bike ferry had been an exception. And look where that had landed her. But now, she thought about Rafe. He would love this. He would love knowing about their heritage. He was the adventurer in the family. So she would do this. For him.

"Shall I meet you at the bike ferry?"

"I'll come and get you. No sense wearing yourself out gimping down to the harbor on those crutches."

Before tackling the rest of the boxes, Maddie went into the bathroom. While washing her hands, she studied her face in the mirror. She'd always thought it was an ordinary face. Not beautiful, but not terribly ugly. And though she moisturized daily, her only makeup was eyeliner, mascara, and a touch of blush. Ever since high school, female friends her age had remarked on her skin: it was smooth and unblemished, clear yet creamy, its light coppery shade making her look as if she had a year-round, early-summer tan. More than one friend claimed to be envious. But to Maddie, it was just her face, where a couple of thin lines now appeared at the corners of her blue eyes. Blue eyes, not black like Joe's. And Joe's skin was a little darker, probably because both his parents, not just one, had been Wampanoag.

Oddly for Maddie, not once had she considered that her ancestors were different from those of her friends, especially since she'd thought her mother's side had emigrated from Europe. She had a feeling that her old pals would be even more envious if they learned that she was half Native American.

Turning off the water, she hobbled back to the bedroom. Then she sliced through the sealing tape on a carton marked "Baskets"; maybe it held samples of Grandma's work. Instead of baskets, she found handwritten notes. Instructions. And diagrams. Lots of diagrams.

Ash or Hickory, one sheet read. Following that were apparently locations. One read: *Menemsha Hills. Grove by the ancient pathway, halfway toward the water on left. Left at roadside ditches of fiddleheads. Walk in fifty feet. Harvest thick, wide splints, one and a half to two inches by a few feet long. (This will provide strength and room to make dots with a knife tip and create shapes of shells, rabbits, butterflies, etc.)*

Behind the papers, Maddie found black-and-white photos of different patterns and designs, as well as notebooks with records of the quantities and types of baskets she'd made, where she'd sold them, when, and for how much. The earliest entries were dated "Fall 1949." Nancy would have been fourteen years old.

As she kept sorting, Maddie also came across a number of recipes and instructions for other things like embroidery and beading—all of which Maddie suspected were from Wampanoag traditions.

Hours passed quickly. Finally, she finished examining the contents of two entire boxes. She stood up and stretched, then made her way into the living room and over to the fireplace, where she lifted the small pottery bowl. It was somewhat unsteady—one of Winnie Lathrop's "seconds"—but, to Maddie, it now was beautiful. She wished she remembered painting the daisy. She wished she remembered Evelyn teaching her, when her own mother was elsewhere on the island, being a real artist. Maddie decided she'd take the little bowl home to Green Hills, a keepsake of her time on the Vineyard then— and now.

Setting it back on the mantel, she moved to the front door. As she looked down the hill, through the tall beach grass, she saw Lisa hanging sheets on an outdoor clothesline. She wondered if her neighbor knew about Nancy's collection of basket notes and other things, and if she might be interested in having them. It seemed better than tossing them out. Besides, after meeting Francine and Rex, Maddie had decided that making friends wasn't so bad.

She cupped her hands and shouted: "Hey, neighbor!"

But Lisa kept working.

So Maddie yelled: "Lisa!"

The clothes hanging stopped. Lisa looked up toward the cottage and waved. And in less than a minute she stood next to the notorious granite steps.

"You need something? How's the foot?"

"The foot's fine, thanks. But I have two questions."

She asked if she'd like Nancy's old basket instructions.

"I'd love to see them!" Lisa chirped.

They went into the bedroom, where Maddie spread the instructions and photos on the bed.

"The diagrams don't look like the one you gave me," Maddie said. "Maybe she made more than one kind."

Lisa examined every page. "I've never seen this type, with the wide splints of wood. I think they're really old. I wonder . . . ," she continued, then stopped. "I bet someone at the Aquinnah Cultural Center will know. They might be the type the Wampanoags made before anyone could order parts through the mail or online. Back when they gathered the 'ingredients' for lots of things right here on the island and nearly everything was made by hand." She'd stopped chirping, her tone having grown serious. "Most likely, they're the first ones Nancy made. And thank you, Maddie, but I shouldn't take these. If you don't want them, they should go to the tribe."

To the tribe. Once again, Maddie wondered if everyone but her had known that Nancy Clieg had been Wampanoag, if everyone but her had known that 50 percent of her carried Indigenous genes.

"Of course they should have them," Maddie said quietly. "They should probably have these entire boxes. There are other crafts and photos. Lots of recipes, most of which use corn, squash, and beans."

Lisa nodded again. "Corn, squash, beans. They're called the Three Sisters. Staples for the tribe for as long as anyone remembers, and probably before then." She was a nice person, after all. Someone who seemed to care about people and traditions.

"Second question," Maddie said. "Would you mind giving me your cell number? It occurred to me if I'm going to be dragging my leg around here for the next few days, I should probably know who I can call if I need to. I have a couple of other numbers. And CiCi's, of course. But I'm not ready to tackle her yet."

"You're going to sell?" She had the same look of surprise that Francine had had.

So Maddie simply nodded because she didn't want to feel as if she had to make excuses for herself and her decision.

Before Lisa left, she invited Maddie for a cookout at six o'clock the following night. She said it would be only her husband, her, and the kids. Her in-laws had planned to come for the weekend but couldn't get a boat reservation until next week. Maddie stopped herself from saying that was another reason why she couldn't live on the Vineyard: How on earth did people exist there when too many tourists, mechanical boat failures, or bad weather that could ground ferries and planes—any day, any time—well, how did people exist if they couldn't get to the mainland? She supposed the tribal members would laugh if she asked them that question. Some Wampanoag she was turning out to be.

Once Lisa was gone, Maddie returned to the boxes and piles of her grandmother's things. She decided to sort through them again, separating the personal mementos from those that might be of historic tribal interest. She felt as if she was on a long journey.

By midafternoon, she was hungry again; she went to the back door and stood in the breeze that wafted through the screen. Realizing she was on the verge of becoming too sentimental, she heated the leftover strudel and wolfed it down.

Before resuming her tasks, she closed and locked the front door. The playful voices floating up from the beach, the symphony of busy seagulls in the sky, and the occasional horn blast of a boat, coming or going, in or out of the harbor, filtered through the window screens. Which was almost enchanting. If her leg wasn't confined by the darn cast, she would have left the cottage and gone for a run or strolled barefoot in the sand, her toes sinking into its warmth.

Amazing, she thought. Her first time on the island in forty years and now she couldn't even walk on the beach.

She forced herself to return to the bedroom and peruse the contents of another box, that one a plethora of sewing patterns in a range of sizes for simple yet practical clothing for both men and women. It appeared that her grandmother had designed them all.

Standing as she worked, comfortably leaning against the bureau, her back to the doorway, she read, sorted, and used the hard surface to help her stack the papers. She was so engrossed she didn't hear the back door close. She didn't hear footsteps crossing the living room; she didn't sense that someone had walked into the room.

"Maddie?"

In a gut reaction, she quickly—too quickly—spun around. She landed on the floor, her good leg twisted beneath the not-good foot.

She grimaced. She didn't know what was more upsetting: the fact that her left leg and her butt were rocked with pain or that her ex-husband stood next to the bed. She decided they were equally dreadful.

"Jesus, Maddie, what are you doing?"

She supposed she should give him credit for helping her up off the floor and onto the boudoir chair.

"How'd you break your foot?"

"I fell climbing a sand dune. It's not as big a deal as it looks." She couldn't believe that Rafe had told him where she was. How else would he have known? Even worse, had her son told her father, too?

Owen stared at the cast. "Are you here alone? The front door was locked, but the back door wasn't. I opened the flimsy screen door and marched right in. I could have been anyone."

She wanted to tell him she wished he *had* been anyone. Anyone but him. Instead, she said, "I have friends here."

"Seriously?"

She ignored the barb. "At least I'm where I'm supposed to be. Unlike you. How did you find me? And, more important, why?"

He smiled the smile she used to think made his blue eyes light up a room. Now those same eyes looked small and uninteresting. Even devious. His hair now sprouted major hints of gray, and he'd developed saggy jowls. His silly society wife no doubt would make sure he found a plastic surgeon. And soon.

"You're forgetting that I'm smart," he said smugly. "I overheard our son's side of his phone call with you; I heard him say you broke your foot. And that you were on the Vineyard for a funeral—something about a relative? I put two and two together and remembered that your mother was from here. I looked up her obituary. I forgot her maiden name, if I'd ever known it. But I found the obit on Google. *Hannah Clieg Clarke*, it read. Your grandmother's name was in the write-up, too. *Nancy Clieg, Martha's Vineyard.* Rocket scientist stuff, right?" He chuckled like the pompous ass he was.

"That's why you're here, right?" he kept blathering. "Because somebody died? Was it your grandmother? I couldn't find her obit."

Maddie decided to reply, if only to shut him up.

"If, in fact, my grandmother did die, did you come all this way to offer condolences?" It was weird being in the same room with him without Rafe there as insulation. Weird and uncomfortable. They'd always been civilized when an event involving their son called for them to be together. But as the years had passed and Owen's ego swelled to the size of the Gay Head Cliffs, Maddie made it a point to stay out of his presence.

He sat on the edge of the bed as if he belonged there and heaved an annoying sigh. "I sure didn't come all this way to fight with my former wife. I was concerned when I realized you broke your foot. I thought you might need help."

Out of politeness, she didn't laugh. This was the same man who'd been on the golf course with a client when Rafe was born, too busy to help her then. She doubted he'd turned over a new leaf. Unless there was something in it for him.

She looked away.

"I really did come to help, Maddie, and not just with your foot. Your mother's obit said she was an only child. I know that you were hers. I thought if your grandmother died, maybe, as her only heir, you could use financial guidance."

And there it was. The real reason he'd showed up was money—of course it was. She wished she could bolt upright, stomp over to him, and shove a finger an inch from his arrogant face. She would have ordered him to leave her alone. To get off the island (preferably, the planet) and mind his own business. But the pain in her foot pulsated fiercely now, and she didn't dare stand up, let alone bolt or stomp.

Closing her eyes, she said, "Go home, Owen. You're not needed here. Not to help me with my foot. And definitely not for my financial situation. I'm perfectly capable of handling things. Just as I've done since we divorced. Now go. Please."

When she sensed he hadn't moved, she opened her eyes. He was still there. "Didn't you hear me?"

"I didn't come all this way to leave, Maddie. Was it your grandmother who died or wasn't it?"

Her foot threatened to jump out of the cast; her brain threatened to jump out of her head. She had no idea how to get rid of the man she used to sleep with. "My grandmother has been dead since I was ten."

"Seriously?"

"Yes. My father told me that way back then."

He folded his arms. "Google would have had her obit in the archives, too."

"Not everyone wants their death publicized."

"Okay, so if it wasn't her, who was the 'relative'? And why was whoever it was living in this house—if you could call it that—at the same address I found when I googled 'Nancy Clieg'?"

On top of the other pains, he was giving her a headache. "As I said, Owen, this isn't your business. Not to mention that I'm tired and I need to go to bed. So please leave. I do not want you here."

His eyes narrowed. "You're keeping something from me."

"Get out," she said, sharply that time. "And if you breathe one word of this to Rafe, you'll never see him again."

He leaned down, his face too close to hers. "What the hell does that mean?"

"It means I have some influence over our son. And if I tell him you were being abusive to me, he will cut you out of his life."

He backed off and began to pace, a timeworn method he applied when trying to formulate a cutting remark.

Then Maddie remembered her phone in her pocket. She slipped it out, careful to keep it from his sight. Grateful she now had Lisa's number, she tapped the screen.

Lisa answered before Owen had stopped pacing and spotted the phone.

"I'm having a problem with a prowler here at the cottage," Maddie said. "Could you please send your husband over? And I believe you said he owns a shotgun?"

Owen retreated from the room. But she did not hang up until she heard the flimsy screen of the back door rattle closed.

"Never mind," she said to Lisa. "Problem solved. It was just an ex-husband who needed a reminder that he's neither wanted nor needed."

After disconnecting, Maddie went into the kitchen, closed and locked the back door, and shut and locked every window in the place.

Chapter 14

Five o'clock was no time for anyone on the Vineyard to rise and shine unless he or she needed to catch fish for a living. Especially if they'd been awake most of the night, worried that Owen had figured out she was going to inherit a small fortune and that he'd somehow try to grab some of it for himself.

She willed herself not to start overthinking again. Instead, she used all her mental energy—and it did take all of it—to be ready for canoeing when Joe knocked on the door.

He was prompt: five thirty. The sun was almost, though not quite, awake, too.

Before she knew it, she was seated in the front of the canoe, not caring that her position was somewhat awkward since she'd wrapped her cast in a plastic bag "just in case." Her right leg stuck out straight; her left one was buckled under the small seat and now throbbed more than her right foot. But she'd decided not to take a pill: she wanted to be able to absorb everything about this experience so she'd always remember it.

Joe showed her how to work the paddle, then took the seat behind her. Calmly, steadily, they moved into Menemsha Pond. The water was as quiet as they were; the only sound was each gentle stroke of their paddles. As the sun climbed higher in the cloudless sky, its warmth embraced her face, lifting her mood. She closed her eyes and wondered how to describe something so peaceful. "Just go with it, Mom," Rafe often said when she was obsessing about anything, from polishing her CV for the tenure committee to trying to create their weekly food shopping list. This, however, seemed far more important than those kinds of things. Best of all, she knew that Joe would keep her safe. She'd started to trust him. Her half uncle, once removed. Or at least that's what she decided he was.

Then a song flitted through the silence. "Mockingbird," Joe said.

Maddie opened her eyes.

"Piping plovers," he said, as he pointed to a group of black-and-white birds on the shoreline. "Great black-backed gull." He nodded to a different bird that bobbed sleepily on the water.

She took it all in, every bit. After a while, he announced they'd reached Nashaquitsa Pond. "We just call her 'Quitsa,'" he said. "Saves time." A minute or so later, he added, "To our right is an eelgrass bed, like the ones I told you about. Look below the surface and you'll see it."

Maddie stretched her neck, leaned close to the water, and saw tall, thin, green shafts performing a ballet in time with the gentle current. "It's so beautiful."

"A few years ago," Joe said, "we got a grant from the National Fish and Wildlife that helped us restore the beds here. Eelgrass gives off oxygen, so it plays a big role in our ecosystem. Wherever, however it grows, so grow the shellfish and other aquatic life. This spot's terrific for scallops and littlenecks."

All Maddie could think of was Rafe; he would love to be in the canoe right now, listening intensely to all that Joe was saying. He would also love Joe. And he would have loved

Nancy, from what Maddie had already seen. Joe and Nancy lived amid nature. The way Rafe loved. Then she told Joe about her son, about his passion for the outdoors.

Joe did not seem surprised. "Sure. It's part of his heritage." Maddie couldn't see his face, but she was sure he was smiling as he said it.

"Look," he added, gesturing toward a sudden swirl of water. "It's a sign that the juvenile shellfish are growing up, testing their capabilities. It causes the eelgrass to undulate. Like ribbons would. If ribbons could swim."

Maddie looked.

Maddie watched.

Maddie was mesmerized.

They went on paddling, one careful stroke after another, trying not to disturb the grasses below the surface. She wondered how many times her grandmother had been on these ponds, immersing herself in watching the gifts of the earth. She wished she and Grandma Nancy had spent more time together.

Then Maddie decided to ask the question that had been gnawing at her. "Joe?" she whispered, "I've been wondering something. Do you think that falling was what killed my grandmother? She apparently knew her way around her property well. Had she become . . . frail? Or off-balance?"

Joe was slow to respond. He looked into the water, as if searching for an answer. Then he said, "I know Nancy's death seems strange. But life—and death—often are, aren't they?"

It seemed like a bizarre answer to what Maddie thought had been a straightforward question. But clearly, Joe did not want to talk about Nancy's death. And Maddie wasn't going to argue with that.

What she'd really wanted was to outright ask if he thought someone killed her. Someone who might know the value of the properties and might not have known about Maddie.

Someone who thought Nancy had no legal heirs and somehow thought they could reap the rewards. But though Maddie had started to trust Joe, she wasn't yet ready to be so
direct. So she simply said, "That's true." And let it go at that.

They were gone all morning. After exploring the ponds
for more than two hours, they got into Joe's pickup and went
to the Chilmark General Store for coffee and breakfast sandwiches. Then he drove toward Aquinnah.

"You do know why they call this part of the Vineyard up-
island, don't you? Even though it's the southwest side of the
island?"

Maddie reluctantly said, "I don't have a clue."

"Lots of people don't. It goes back to the whaling days,
long before GPS, when sailors used latitude and longitude as
their only coordinates. Here in the western hemisphere, the
farther west you go, the higher the longitudinal number.
Nantucket is east of the Vineyard. The longitude there is
70.09, while in Aquinnah it's 70.80. When you're on the
Vineyard, to get to Aquinnah, you have to head west, so the
number goes up."

She wanted to say, "Good grief," but settled on saying, "It
makes sense. I guess."

He laughed. "If you're not a sailor, it must seem pretty
weird."

Then he took a right onto Lobsterville Road.

"I figured as long as we're up this way, you might as well
have a look at your properties. With that thing on your leg,
you'll have to stay in the truck, but at least you can see some
of it from the road."

It was no surprise that Joe knew about the properties.
Maybe he'd witnessed Nancy's will; maybe that was how he
knew Maddie would inherit it all. Or maybe Nancy told him.
Who knew how he would have felt about that.

Lobsterville Road was bumpy, narrow, and on both sides thick with trees. At the foot of every dirt side road, wood slats in the shape of arrows were nailed to many trees; they were stacked one above the other. Each was painted a different color and sported a name printed in block letters—Smith, Randall, Allsop, and so on.

"Most of those are names of the homeowners," Joe said, as he pointed to one group of signs. "It's how renters found where they were supposed to go long before GPS."

Then they turned onto an obscure, even more narrow, sandy road. Partway down, Joe stopped.

"Here's the first parcel."

There was no driveway, no colorful wood slats with the name of an owner nailed to a tree. There were just trees. And patches of undergrowth here and there.

"There's a small pine grove in the back, a nice little spot," he said. "There's also a pond and bushes of wild berries nearby. It's a nice piece of property. And within walking distance to Lobsterville Beach." He sounded like a real estate agent, though not as intense as CiCi.

"Nothing's ever been built on it?"

"Nope. It used to belong to the tribe—both of Nancy's parcels over here did. We were slowly 'dispossessed'—that's an interesting word—of our land, which I won't get into now. By the mid-nineteenth century, when we had about two and a half thousand acres, a small amount went to members of the tribe and the rest was for communal use. It wasn't until 1987 that the federal government recognized us as a viable Native American tribe. Of those two and a half thousand acres, they put less than five hundred into a trust for us. It's complicated. Nancy's lots aren't part of those five hundred acres, though."

"But if Wampanoags are now a federally recognized tribe, isn't there a reservation?"

Joe shook his head. "What we have is called a 'formal land-in-trust reservation.' Like I said, it's complicated."

She looked at him in disbelief. Even Maddie knew that Wampanoags were the first Native Americans to welcome the Pilgrims in 1620, and had taught them how to live off the land and survive.

"But, Joe . . . ," she began, then he raised a finger to his lips and shushed her.

"We live our lives. We try to be kind. And we are still here."

She sat back on the seat, understanding the message. It would take a while, she knew, to fully grasp this way of thinking.

They continued on Lobsterville Road toward the water, where he went right then left onto West Basin Road. The road west of Basin Road in Menemsha. Owen would have groused at her big deduction. Like the way he'd googled her grandmother, he'd say it hardly was rocket science. Then Joe told her that the second parcel was actually tucked between tribal acres.

"We have some rights of way to the water," he said. "And some acreage has been given back to us here and there. Donated by generous folks. They're not official tribal lands, but . . ." His words trailed off.

They reached the property off Clay Pit Road—most of it was obscured by the dunes. In the distance, a few houses stood atop a hill; they had walls of windows that faced the sea.

Maddie remembered the area well; the ambulance had carried her out of there on a stretcher.

"Thank you so much for this, Joe. But, thanks to the medication for my foot, I'm tired now. I need to go back to the cottage and rest. It sure has been an incredible morning, though."

"My pleasure. As I told you earlier, I'll do anything to

help my niece learn how much or how little she wants to know about our people."

She smiled; she had no idea how much or how little that would be.

But after he dropped her off and she loped up the path toward the cottage, Maddie suddenly wondered if Joe's real reason for taking her out—and for his history lesson—had been to try to convince her to give her grandmother's land back to the tribe. Three to four million dollars' worth, give or take.

Then she wondered if she'd misplaced her trust in Grandma Nancy's half brother.

After her good, yet confusing, morning, Maddie not only needed a nap but also a pain pill. She took the pill first, then, because her grandmother's squeaky-springed bed was covered with papers and boxes, she lay down in her mother's old room and slept until after five o'clock. Which gave her an hour to wrap her leg in plastic again, take a shower, and dress in one of the new tops and the white skirt Evelyn bought her. Then she'd be ready for the cookout at Lisa's.

Just before six, while she poked through the refrigerator looking for something to contribute to the supper but coming up empty, she heard a light tap on the front door. With her skills at using the crutches greatly improved, it took only seconds for her to get there. A young, towheaded boy was standing on the front steps. He had blue eyes and summer freckles, and he was dressed in shorts and a T-shirt with a dinosaur printed on the front.

"I'm Charlie. My mom said you broke your leg and I should help you down to our house."

Maddie smiled. "That's very nice of you, Charlie. Lucky for me, I only broke my foot, not my whole leg. But I do have a pretty cool cast. See?" She held out her leg for him to inspect.

"Yeah. Cool," he said. "I broke my arm once. I slipped on the jetty."

"Ouch. That must have hurt."

He nodded. "I wasn't supposed to be out there by myself."

"And I wasn't supposed to be doing what I was doing, either." She grabbed her phone and her keys and double-checked the lock on the front door in case Owen hadn't found his way off the island. "Okay, Charlie, lead the way! Knowing you're with me will be a huge help."

He smiled; Maddie could tell that his bottom teeth were crooked and overcrowded and, yes, they appeared to be in need of braces. Lisa had been truthful, which Maddie found nicely reassuring.

It turned out that having an escort wasn't her only surprise. When she and Charlie reached the backyard, Brandon greeted her. He quickly introduced Jeremy, who, with silver hair and pewter-colored eyes, was dressed in all white—shirt, long white pants, and sandals—and he wore a grin as broad as Brandon's. Maddie was charmed. It turned out that Lisa knew them through Nancy. Of course.

Then Lisa appeared with her daughter, who, like Charlie, examined Maddie's cast. Then Maddie met Mickey, Lisa's husband, who was tending to corn on the cob on the grill. He was tall, thin, and tanned, perhaps like many fishermen.

And then, from the house, came Evelyn, carrying a large platter of oysters that she set atop a wooden picnic table.

"Evelyn . . . ," Maddie said, making her way to the table. "I'm so glad to see you. I'm sorry for sneaking out—"

But Evelyn stopped her. "No apologies, dear. You were overwhelmed. You've had more than your share of surprises in the past days. Now make yourself comfortable. And have an oyster."

The evening was joyful—and the most fun Maddie had in a long time.

They ate and ate and drank lots of iced tea. And they laughed, mostly at Brandon's way of telling stories about the island when he'd been young. When Jeremy produced a fiddle, Evelyn taught them a few old sailing songs, and they sang and laughed a little more. It was fabulous.

Then, as sunset approached, Brandon drove Maddie and his mother to the beach while the rest of their party walked. When he dropped them off, he gave them each a folding chair. The women stayed on the pavement at the edge of the sand, away from young kids licking soft-serve cones from the Galley, and from teenagers, who still wore their skimpy swimwear, though the time for sunning was long past.

"Well," Maddie said when she and Evelyn were alone. "It's been such a nice evening. My new clothes fit perfectly. Thank you again."

"They look nice on you," Evelyn said. "I'm glad you like them. And I do hope you're feeling more comfortable here, Maddie. Not that it matters if you're planning to leave."

"Mmm," Maddie said as she looked at the crowd on the beach, out over the water, and up to the late-day sky. "I'm hoping to get tenure this year. I've worked hard to get it." It seemed as if she'd said that too many times. Maybe she was trying to remind herself not to get sidetracked from her goal.

"I'm sure you have. You're your mother's daughter. She worked hard, too. At her art."

"But how could she ever have left the island, Evelyn? And why didn't she tell me about our heritage?"

Evelyn sighed. "I know she was in love with your dad. And I know she was afraid if she stayed here she'd never paint anything more than Menemsha sunsets."

"But they're so beautiful."

"Yes, they are. But your father unintentionally opened a new world for her, and she saw the chance to step into it. But I know she loved it here—it was home, after all. And don't forget she brought you back every summer to see your grandmother. I think she would have kept coming if . . ."

Maddie closed her eyes for a few seconds. Then she said, "I know. But I don't understand why she pretended to be Iberian."

"Oh, honey," Evelyn said, patting Maddie's hand, "there are some things about people that we'll never figure out. But I don't think she was trying to hide her heritage; I think she simply wanted to wait until you were a little older. Old enough to understand. As one of—at the time—only a couple of hundred tribal members, maybe she was afraid you'd feel stigmatized on the mainland." She paused. "I do know that Hannah was never malicious. And that, above all, she was proud of being Wampanoag."

They sat for a moment, watching the sky glow red and yellow, a perfect replica of her mother's paintings. Then the rest of their party arrived, and the orange ball dropped into the sea. The applause burst out; cheers filled the air.

And Maddie smiled.

Chapter 15

One week.

When Maddie woke up late Sunday morning, she couldn't believe she'd been on the island only a week. With all that had happened, it seemed more like a month. Or a year. But as nice as last night had been, she knew she had to be careful not to get drawn in by her new friends; the island, after all, was their home, not hers. If they were on a mission to keep her from selling the cottage to wealthy summer people who'd tear it down and build a concrete-and-glass monstrosity, Maddie had no control over that. Maybe Brandon could lobby for a town ordinance that dictated housing parameters. If there wasn't already one.

And if anyone planned to encourage her to give the parcels in Aquinnah back to the tribe, she would have to deal with that. After all, the land had been theirs in the first place. And yet . . .

She wished she knew what her grandmother would want her to do.

After foregoing the rigmarole of taking a shower, she washed and dressed in the new denim skirt and one of her old tops. Then she went into the kitchen, hunting for breakfast.

She'd long since finished Lisa's bread, and everything else was lunch or dinner food. Including the pizza still in the freezer. So she settled on coffee.

Once it started to brew, she sat at the table and checked her phone: a message from Brandon had arrived an hour earlier.

Fun time last night. Jeremy likes you. Check your front door.

Curious, she got up and unlocked the door. A small bag hung from the knob; inside were three plump blueberry muffins and a note.

Freshly made this morning. Enjoy. Below that was the shape of a heart and a signature: ~E.

Maddie sighed. She wasn't used to this much attention. If she were back in Green Hills with her cast and crutches, her father would have gladly gone to the bakery and picked up muffins for their breakfast. They would not, however, have been warmed by the morning sun, and they would not have the aroma of fresh-picked wild berries.

She limited herself to half a delicious muffin, wrapped the rest for later, and put one in the freezer to save for Rafe. If he could get there.

Then she knew she had to get back to business. Surprisingly, she'd organized the contents of all the boxes in her grandmother's bedroom. Today she'd tackle the mess of magazines and papers in the corners of the living room. Again, she'd set aside anything of interest to the tribe.

She blew through the first pile in mere minutes—all, indeed, were women's magazines (some from years ago) that she tossed into a bag for recycling. But another steel box had been buried at the bottom of the stack. It had a lock, but it was open.

Instead of being crammed with things, this container had well-organized manila file folders—each had a tab marked with a name. They were in alphabetical order: Aitkens, Ashbury, Barton, and so on. She grabbed at a handful and pulled out the A's, the B's, the C's.

The files were filled with photos: some black-and-white, some color; some old, some more recent. Most were close-up, portrait-style images of people. Maddie now recognized the Wampanoag facial features—high cheekbones, eyes set widely apart, smooth skin—she knew she had the same ones. On the back of each photo, someone—Grandma Nancy?—had penned a name and date. Most were from the 1950s and 1960s, some as late as the 1990s.

Then she came to a thick file labeled "Cranberry." First there was a series of color photos of all ages of people who were gathering what looked like cranberries and placing them in cloth bags. Behind those were more photos—also in color. These showed Wampanoags in Native American dress, dancing and drumming. Maddie turned one over: *Cranberry Day, 1989. The tradition resumes.*

Then she remembered the tradition: on Cranberry Day, in the fall, Wampanoag children didn't have to go to school; they spent hours picking cranberries with the adults—some used wooden cranberry scoops handed down for generations. After the picking, everyone gathered for a wonderful feast and celebration.

She looked back at the photos. How on earth had she re-membered that? Had she seen these pictures long ago? Had Grandma Nancy told her the story? Then a small chill rippled up Maddie's spine. *I have been there,* her memory told her. *I have picked the berries with Grandma.*

She was certain that her intuitive brain had triggered the connection.

"I have a feeling that you'll be very appreciated by the tribe," she told the photos, as she carefully replaced them in the files and the files in the container. Which was when she heard a *ting-ting* of metal fall to the bottom.

She stared at the box, wondering if she should investigate or . . . not. After a few seconds, her inquiring mind prevailed: she pulled out all the files to see if something else was there.

Something was.

Another damn key.

A piece of paper was folded like an origami and threaded through a hole on top of the silver thing. Maddie unbound the paper. On it a note read:

> *Whoever finds this (I hope it's my granddaughter), this is not the key to the padlock of the big shed. That one I threw out by mistake. But it doesn't matter. I locked it by habit after I emptied everything that was in there and moved it to my storage unit at the airport with other things.*

Maddie laughed.

> *This one fits a large fireproof cabinet in my storage unit, which is #373. My security passcode into the unit is 5-1-3-5-4. Inside the cabinet are my most valued posses-sions (not counting the painting, the bowl, and the quahog shell on the mantel). Also in the unit, you'll find some of my baskets—I sold the rest to pay my heating bill.*
> *—Nancy Clieg*
> *P.S. If this is not my granddaughter, please see that everything in the storage unit is shipped to her in Green Hills, Mass. I think her surname is still Clarke.*

Maddie reread the note. Then she put the files in the metal box again, closed the lid, reached for her phone, and called Brandon. She might not know if she could trust any of her new friends, but Brandon was her attorney. And attorneys weren't allowed to lie. Were they?

★ ★ ★

"Please thank your mother for the wonderful muffins," she said when he answered. "They were a nice surprise."

He started to say something, but Maddie interrupted. What she had to ask couldn't wait.

"Could you and Jeremy take me to the airport today?"

"Going somewhere?"

"Not exactly." Then she told him about the note. And the key. "There must be something there that my grandmother really wanted me to see. I'd like to go today because my son won't be here until Tuesday or Wednesday, and I don't want to wait—"

"Absolutely," Brandon interrupted. "Besides, this might save my life and Jeremy's, too, because he wants to try windsurfing today."

"Wow. I never dreamed I'd save two lives with a single phone call."

Brandon laughed. "Noon? Maybe after we can find a fun place for lunch."

Maddie agreed, and they hung up. She hauled herself from the sofa, grabbed her crutches, purse, keys, and then hooked the key to the mysterious cabinet onto the same ring. She read her grandmother's note again, dropped it, along with her keys, into her purse, and then made her way to the bedroom. Lunch on Martha's Vineyard was definitely worthy of changing into something nicer than denim and an old top.

It took longer to get to the airport than Maddie expected. She kept forgetting that the island wasn't small. The weekend traffic didn't help.

Brandon came alone because his mother railroaded Jeremy into staying with her and reviewing her plans for the Labor Day wedding ceremony. Maddie would not be attending;

she'd be back in Green Hills by then, back in the real world, her world. Clearing out the storage unit would put her a step closer.

They finally made it to the airport and Brandon found the storage center. After passing through the security gates, they easily located unit #373. Without hesitating, Maddie keyed in the security code. The door started to open.

"You remembered the number?" Brandon asked. "I'm impressed."

"It was easy. Five-one-three-five-four. It stands for May 13, 1954," she replied. "My mother's birthday."

He exhaled like Maddie would have exhaled if she weren't holding her breath, anxious about what they were going to find.

The first thing they saw was an old pickup, parked almost the whole length of the unit. For a moment, neither of them spoke.

Then Brandon said, "Well. It's a truck."

Maddie let out her breath. "I wonder what year it is."

"Last century, I believe."

"Or the one before."

They edged toward it, as if expecting to be greeted by a calamity, not the multitude of cardboard boxes that were piled in the truck bed and reached halfway to the ceiling. At least the cardboard wouldn't need a key.

Brandon tried the passenger door of the cab; it was open. An ignition key was on the seat, resting on another note. He read the contents to Maddie.

Here's the key to Orson. Butchie named him that after an old friend who some folks thought had been lost at sea, but he'd really snuck off island to get away from his bad-tempered wife. Butchie always kept Orson's secret, but that was back in 1963, and to my knowledge, none of the parties involved are still around.

On my 80th birthday I drove to the DMV and turned in my driver's license. I could still drive this old thing fine—it runs like an ornery top, but it still runs. My reflexes, however, weren't as good as they once were, so rather than run over a gang of wild turkeys or a bunch of tourists, I opted to give up the ghost.

So here's Orson. Whoever finds him—Maddie, I hope it's you—can have him. The title's in the glove box. My brother, Joe, made me have seat belts installed two decades ago. Enjoy.

Nancy

"The truck would have been yours anyway. Based on her will," Brandon said.

It seemed like a moot point.

Maddie couldn't see if anything was behind the truck, thanks to the barricade of boxes. Curious about the contents, she pulled one from the bottom; the tall pile on top of it somersaulted toward her. Not unlike the way the box had careened from the shelf in her grandmother's closet, only there were more of them.

"What the . . . ?" Brandon stopped futzing inside the cab and rushed over to her. "Are you okay?"

She laughed. Cartons surrounded her on the floor. "I'm fine. They barely grazed me."

Brandon picked one up. "Lightweight. Must not be packed with canning jars or other heavy stuff." He stood the boxes on the floor next to the truck's front wheel. "From now on, don't go poking through things without me. Okay? It could be dangerous."

She flashed a smile of thanks.

"Come on," she said. "Let's see if anything's behind here. Like maybe the storage cabinet. The boxes can wait until Rafe's here."

Once they reached the tailgate, they saw a metal cabinet— it was large, maybe six feet high, four feet wide, and a foot and a half deep. There was just enough space to try to unlock it once they squeezed behind the truck.

Maddie inserted the key into the lock and held her breath again. Then . . . *Click.* Her eyebrows shot up.

"Oh, boy," she said as she opened the double doors.

Inside, five horizontal shelves spanned the width of the cabinet. Each shelf was neatly covered by a canvas drape.

"At least it's not another truck," Brandon said.

"That's very funny. For an attorney."

Studying the shapes beneath the drape, she sensed what was there—a number of vertical slots . . . each of which likely held a painting standing neatly, separated by dividers, protected by the climate-controlled air in the storage unit, better for preservation than the cottage or its outbuildings. She almost caught a whiff of decades-old acrylics, almost envisioned more views of Menemsha sunsets. Of course she couldn't be sure that the artist was her mother. She wouldn't know until she uncovered them.

"And we're waiting for . . . what, exactly?" Brandon asked.

Maddie paused, then whispered, "I think they might be my mother's paintings."

"Oh," he said. "Wow."

"Yeah." Her lower lip started to quiver. She thought she might cry.

"Do you want me to look first?" he asked.

She almost said yes. Then she realized if her grandmother had saved them, had preserved them for her, Maddie should have the courage, and the gratitude, to do the honors.

"Thanks," she said, "but I've got this."

Stretching her arm to the top row, she nudged the tarp until it cascaded down the cabinet, exposing row after row of artist's canvases that, indeed, were standing between wooden dividers so they didn't touch one another. Starting on the right side of the top row, she gingerly removed the first one.

It wasn't a Menemsha sunset. Instead, it was a portrait of a girl with the beautiful complexion of a Wampanoag, the same jet-black hair and high, prominent cheekbones. Her clothing was pale beige, perhaps the color of deer hide—perhaps it even was deer hide; she wore a beaded headband around her forehead. She might have been eleven or twelve years old.

"White wampum," Brandon said as he pointed to the pieces woven into the headband. "It's amazing, isn't it? She might have collected the shells, separated the white from the purple, and crafted the beads herself."

Maddie nodded. She knew that wampum—some white, some purple, most a combination of both—came from the interior of quahog shells. She'd loved picking up the pieces of it on a beach with her grandmother while her mother sat at a nearby easel. And Maddie had seen a perfect example in the photo of Grandma Nancy's wedding costume.

After staring at the painting another moment, Maddie's eyes moved to the small signature on the bottom: *Hannah Clieg, 1971.* Her mother had painted the portrait when she was seventeen.

"She was a good artist, wasn't she?" Maddie asked Brandon.

"I'll say. Do you want to look at more now . . . or take them to the cottage and go through them there?"

"If you don't mind, let's look now. I don't want to take them until I decide what to do with them. At least I know they're safe here." The last thing she wanted was for Owen to return and break into the cottage when she wasn't there and make off with these wonderful paintings. No matter what they might be worth in dollars, they were more valuable to her.

So the process began. Hannah had painted the canvases in the top three rows before she'd married Maddie's father and left the island. Several others were portraits—some in various styles of Wampanoag traditional dress, some of individuals simply sitting. They were in a range of ages, and none were named. The oldest was a man who wasn't dressed in traditional Wampanoag clothing but in a denim shirt; he wore a rawhide necklace with a wampum pendant hanging from it that had been carved into the shape of an arrowhead. Other paintings were Vineyard landscapes and seascapes, some of which were sunny, others, cloaked in fog. And there were sunsets. Lots of sunsets. All were beautiful. And seemed very accomplished for someone so young.

The bottom row was different. They were later landscapes, most of which were dated after Maddie was born. They were not of the Vineyard, but of the Berkshire Hills: blanketed by snow, illuminated by shades of autumn leaves, vibrant with spring greens. There were a few portraits, too, though none looked as interesting as those of the Wampanoags. Yes, Maddie thought, the paintings on the bottom row were missing something. They were missing Hannah's heritage. Her heart. Her home.

Where the heck did Maddie go with Brandon? Did he take her to the boat? Was she going home? She couldn't drive her car—was someone meeting her on the other side? Her son? Her father?

And wasn't she supposed to be recuperating?

It might be a good time to snoop around inside the cottage, to see if there were any clues about what she planned to do. Unless she'd left the island . . . in which case, all of this would have been a total waste of time.

Chapter 16

Over an hour passed while Maddie and Brandon perused the paintings. It was exhilarating. And confounding. Because Maddie had no idea what to do with the collection.

"Why not choose a few that you like best and donate the rest to the cultural center?" Brandon suggested.

"Great idea. I'll do it when Rafe is here. I think he'd like to see all of them. And maybe he'll want a couple. For now, however, let's go to lunch. I'm famished."

They were driving to Edgartown, to the restaurant Brandon's mother wanted to cater Brandon and Jeremy's wedding. Maddie asked questions about the wedding plans, but his answers all were, "I have no idea. That's Jeremy's and my mother's problem." Then he chuckled. "All I want to know about is the food. I love good food, so it's the only thing I can relate to."

The trip into town passed quickly, and soon they reached a sign that read: HISTORIC VILLAGE. Maddie had heard of Edgartown but didn't expect both sides of the narrow streets to be lined with stately white colonial houses that nearly hugged the redbrick sidewalks. Many of the houses had wide, welcoming porches rimmed by perfect plantings of fat-blossomed hydrangea bushes. She guessed that most of the homes were built in the eighteenth or nineteenth century, when the whaling industry was booming and the town must have been bustling with needed services: blacksmiths, candle-makers, and dry-goods shops, instead of the present day restaurants, clothes boutiques, and surf gear retailers.

As they sat in traffic on the single lane of Main Street, the sun was bright and warm, the air conditioner inside the car hummed, and Maddie decided that the town was extraordinary. Picture-perfect, like Menemsha Harbor, but in a different-lifestyle way.

Then Brandon groaned.

"I should have taken my mother's handicapped tag," he said. "Actually, I wouldn't. It's illegal to do that."

Maddie was startled. "Your mother's handicapped?" Surely, it was a joke.

He flicked his eyes from the street to Maddie, then back again. "She didn't tell you? Well, she does like to deny it. She doesn't even use the tag when she's by herself—God forbid that anyone would think she was not 'tip-top.' But, yes, Mom has a heart condition. I thought you knew."

She flinched. "I had no idea."

"It's been about five years since her diagnosis. It's controlled by medication, but she has more bad days than she'll admit."

"Oh, Brandon, I'm sorry. Though I haven't seen anything slow her down in this past week."

He snickered. "She hides it well."

Maddie wondered if all the people here were as resilient as Evelyn, or as pragmatic as Grandma Nancy, who'd relinquished her driver's license when she'd turned eighty. Maddie suspected she could learn a lot from islanders. More than from the journalism topics she researched for her classes.

Just then a parking space opened up catty-corner from a bookstore. Brandon quickly slipped his vehicle in.

"It's an easy walk from here to the Lord James," he said. "My mother thinks it's the best restaurant on the island."

Maddie thought for a second. Then she smiled. "I've heard of it. And I think I've met the owner."

Brandon looked at her curiously. Then he got out, went around the front of the Volvo, and opened the door for her. She grabbed her crutches, shimmied out, and stepped onto the sidewalk with surprising agility. She might not be as resilient as Evelyn or as pragmatic as her grandmother, but Maddie knew a few things about how to cope with the unexpected.

After a short walk to a crosswalk, they went down a slight slope to the restaurant.

"Any chance of a table for two for lunch?" Brandon asked a young blonde hostess.

She studied a tablet while Maddie leaned on her crutches.

"It's about a forty-minute wait," the hostess said.

"Seriously?" Brandon asked.

"I'm sorry. On such a beautiful day, you'd think everyone would be at the beach. Or out on their boats."

Maddie looked into the dining room. An expanse of windows showcased the harbor where the sun shined off a crowd of gleaming white yachts that peacefully bobbed on the quiet water.

She turned to Brandon. "We can wait. Or, I can if you can."

"Sure," he said. "If you want."

Maddie wanted. And she wouldn't mind seeing the big man named Rex who'd rescued the padlock off the shed. If he was around.

"Name?" the hostess asked.

"Morgan. Brandon Morgan."

The hostess consulted her tablet again. "Oh, yes, Mr. Morgan. We have a table waiting for you."

"You do?"

She smiled. "A woman called earlier and said you'd be arriving with a guest. She didn't say when, but our owner had
just come in, so he spoke with her."

Brandon rolled his eyes.

Maddie laughed.

They both knew that the woman had been his mother.
Resilient Evelyn.

The table was by a large window that offered a close-up of
sunbathers on the decks of the gleaming yachts; others in their
company sported broad-brimmed hats and were lounging
with their feet resting on railings. A few powerboats glided
past at low speed; a couple of dinghies transported passengers
from their pleasure vessels to what looked like the town dock.
Edgartown Harbor had a much different look than the up-
island one.

Maddie and Brandon were seated less than a minute when
the big man named Rex came over and greeted them.

"Maddie," he said with a wide grin, "nice to see you
again. And, Brandon, always a pleasure."

"Did my mother tell you to say that?" Brandon snickered.

"Actually, she did. Right after she said I had to show you
a wedding menu that you won't be able to resist. By the way,
congratulations, man. It's about time. Jeremy's a lucky guy."

Brandon blushed.

"I didn't realize you're also a caterer," Maddie said.

"Technically, we're not. But Brandon's family and mine
go way back. My mother worked for her sometimes."

"Was she a chef, too?"

"My mother?" Rex asked. "Nope. She couldn't boil an
egg. She played the flute, though. But as far as I know, not for
Evelyn. She did secretarial work for her. Or rather, for the
charitable foundation that Evelyn was the chairperson of."

Brandon laughed. "What he's too shy to say is that Mrs. Winsted was an accomplished flautist. She played at the Metropolitan Opera in Manhattan. Until she met Rex's father and moved to the Vineyard. Where he was born and raised."

"I'm impressed," Maddie said.

"Don't be. Please. And I'll only cater the wedding if Brandon chooses the menu."

"And if my mother approves," Brandon said, a Cheshire grin forming.

"Some things are better left unspoken." Rex winked at Maddie, then pulled out a chair. "Mind if I join you for a minute? Unless you're in a hurry for food."

"I'm fine," Maddie said.

"I'm hungry," her lunch partner said. "So make it quick." His simpy grin implied that he was toying with Rex.

"I'd like to amend what I said earlier," Rex said. "You are definitely the lucky groom. Lucky that Jeremy can put up with you." He pulled a sheet of paper from his white chef's jacket and handed it to Brandon. "But seriously, here's what I have in mind. Look it over. Show Evelyn. Share it with Maddie, if you want. I have a feeling her taste is much more refined than yours."

Maddie lowered her gaze as warmth rose in her cheeks. She had no idea why Rex assumed that.

"Touché," Brandon said. "Now, please, get us each a glass of champagne. We're in Edgartown, so we need to look the part. Unlike the owner of the Lord James."

Rex stood up and swatted Brandon's arm with the wedding menu. "Shall I select something for your lunch?"

"Please," Brandon said. "Shellfish, Maddie?"

"Absolutely."

"You heard the woman. But try to make it something that hasn't been kicking around in the freezer for eight or ten months."

"I'll do my best." Rex bowed and disappeared through the swinging doors into the kitchen.

Maddie laughed. "Do you two always trade barbs?"

"Absolutely. Barbs are good among friends."

She had an urge to ask if Rex was married or involved with someone. It was something she hadn't wondered about anyone in a long time. But aside from being too timid to ask, she knew it would be pointless. Even if Rex were available, it hardly mattered. Maddie would be gone sooner than later.

Their champagne arrived along with an appetizer of six oysters accented with fresh lemon wedges. They each were served a delectable-looking pink sauce in a small dipping bowl. Brandon's sauce came with a note from Rex:

> *The sauce is a mignonette. That's French for "Eat it. You'll like it."*

"Oooh, oysters," came a woman's voice from behind Maddie. "Bet they don't have those where you come from. Not fresh ones, anyways."

Maddie turned her head and saw CiCi. That day, the real estate agent was dressed in a white A-line shift that seemed too short for a woman her age. She wore chunky beads in rainbow colors and matching earrings that dangled to her shoulders and evoked "thrift shop." She was smiling, though, which buffered her attire.

"Hello, CiCi," Maddie said, trying to be kind. "Do you know Brandon?"

"Attorney Morgan, of course I do." CiCi nodded; Brandon nodded in return. "So you two are a long way from up-island. What brings you to Edgartown?"

Brandon looked at his plate. "Lunch."

CiCi tee-heed, which she also was too old to do. Maddie

almost felt sorry for her. "Well, because you're in a restaurant, I guess lunch is an appropriate activity."

She was trying to be funny, Maddie thought, so she smiled. "What brings you here, CiCi?"

"Oh, a client," she said with an elongated sigh. "So many clients these days. Speaking of which, I have a couple of folks who are very interested in your property, Maddie. I think you'd be wise to list it before the season's over. Get your best price while the skies are sunny, you know?" She pursed her pink-painted lips.

"I still haven't decided, but I have your card."

CiCi nodded. "Well, okay, then. I promise I won't bug you. Enjoy your meal. Ta-ta!" She swished away as if she were a ballroom dancer.

Brandon looked at Maddie. "Were you putting her off or are you serious?"

"About what?" Maddie asked as she dipped her seafood fork in the sauce, poked it into an oyster, then slid it into her mouth.

"You told her you haven't decided. I thought it was a done deal that you're going to sell."

She chewed, shrugged, swallowed. "I'm going to wait for my son's input. After all, he's going to find out that he's part Wampanoag, too. His opinion deserves consideration."

"Good idea. I wish I could meet him, but Jeremy and I have to go back to Boston tomorrow. We both have work to do up there. But we'll be back in a few days."

Their lunch of scallops and fresh greens arrived. The presentation was dazzling.

"These look fabulous," Maddie said. "Let's check out your wedding menu and see if they're on it."

Brandon handed her the menu. At least he didn't ask if her indecision about selling the property had anything to do with

how she'd lowered her gaze and blushed when Rex had com-
plimented her. Maybe he hadn't noticed.

She didn't get home until after five o'clock. Her foot was
hurting. Big-time.

It was almost three hours since she'd had the champagne,
so she took a pain pill. After that, she wiggled out of her clothes
and into her new cotton nightie, grabbed two pillows and an
old, fuzzy blanket, and reclined on Grandma Nancy's old couch,
propping up her head on one of the pillows and her right foot
on the other one.

There, she thought and closed her eyes.

She wanted to think about Rex. But for some reason,
Owen drifted into her mind. Had he actually driven all the
way from Green Hills to the Vineyard because he thought she
was coming into money? He'd probably already researched
the island's real estate values. Did he honestly think she'd en-
trust her inheritance to him?

Closing her eyes, she really, really wanted a nap. She really
wanted the pain in her foot to go away instead of yelling at her
for having done too much walking that day. But it had been
worth it to see her mother's wonderful paintings. And she
liked Brandon's idea for her to keep a few and donate the rest
to the cultural center. Grandma Nancy might have liked that,
too. As for the ones her mother painted after she left the Vineyard . . . Maddie didn't know what to do with them. Even an
amateur as she was could tell they weren't Hannah Clieg's best
work. It was as if she'd been trying to be someone she wasn't.
And why were those on the island? Had she sold some of
them at one of the artisan fairs when she and Maddie were
there with Grandma?

Slowly, Maddie drifted into sleep, her questions unan-
swered.

Then her phone rang. She stirred; she considered not answering it. But . . . maybe it was Rafe.

Blindly reaching to the table for her phone, she picked it up.

"Mom?"

The sound of his voice always evoked a smile.

"Hi, honey."

"Are you okay? How's your foot?"

"Not too bad. As long as I behave."

He laughed. "I've never known you not to." He was right, of course. Rafe had only known his mother as someone who played by the rules.

"I'm sorry you wound up with such a predictable mother." She didn't add that the label might change now, if she dared to look beyond her conventional life in tiresome—*Yes, tiresome*—Green Hills.

"Being predictable isn't always a bad thing."

Of course Rafe was being kind.

"Thanks," she said. "But seriously. Will you be able to get here Tuesday?"

"I will."

Happiness filled her. She hauled herself to an upright position, the blanket tangling around her cast.

"I'm so glad," she said.

"What time's your appointment?"

"One o'clock."

"Okay. I'll drive to Falmouth—you were right, the bus would take forever. I'll park at the ferry lot in Falmouth; from there I can get a shuttle to the pier, wherever it is. I can make the ferry that arrives in Vineyard Haven at two o'clock. Can you pick me up if your appointment's near there?"

Evelyn had offered to take her to the doctor. She wouldn't be Maddie's first choice of someone to meet-and-greet Rafe, but so be it.

"Two o'clock might be tight, depending on my appointment. But wait for me outside the terminal. I'll text you if I'm not already there. Oh, and I have to have someone drive me," she added, "so I won't be alone. Okay?"

"Sure. Gotta run, work's calling. Love you."

"Drive carefully, honey," Maddie said, but by then, he'd hung up. Rafe, after all, was almost as predictable as she was. So she knew that—without a doubt—the news of his heritage was going to rock his world.

Chapter 17

She thought about calling Evelyn to ask if she'd still be able to take her to the hospital Tuesday, but she didn't want to interrupt Evelyn's time with Brandon and Jeremy. The men would be off to Boston tomorrow; Monday would be plenty of time to confirm her offer.

Then she remembered Evelyn's heart condition. She certainly was active and vivacious and didn't seem prone to self-pity. Hopefully she'd stay that way for a long while.

As for Maddie, she was thankful for good health; before last week's "incident," she'd been in a hospital only when Rafe was born. Even her dad—now seventy-two—had only occasional lower back pain that sent him to a chiropractor a few times a year. She wondered if, like her grandmother, her mother would have lived to almost ninety, if Hannah had inherited Nancy's long-life genetics. Maybe Maddie had.

Which reminded her it was time to get up and get back to clearing out her grandmother's things; the fact that she was slow-moving these days wasn't a good enough excuse to ignore what needed to be done.

Following Brandon's suggestion about distribution of the paintings, she decided to create three piles: one for things to keep; one for things to toss out; the third one for the cultural center, if they wanted them. With a concrete goal, she got to work.

Hours later, much of the living room clutter was under control. She'd skipped dinner but was thirsty for tea. So, a little achy and a lot tired, Maddie limped into the kitchen and put on the kettle. But as she waited for the water to boil, a small shadow on the floor by the back door caught her eye; she was sure nothing had been there before. Inching closer, she grasped the door handle and stooped. Which was when she realized it was a thermos.

A thermos?

Picking it up, she shook it gently; it seemed empty.

Slowly, she unscrewed the lid, took a tentative breath, and sniffed the interior. Coffee? Maybe. But none was left.

Maddie squinted. Where had it come from? Or, more specifically, who had put it there?

An icy sensation rippled through her. That intuition thing again.

So she did the only thing she knew that she could do: she checked the locks on the doors and closed the windows, then crept down the hall, looked in the closets, and had to take the chance no one was hiding elsewhere. Most likely, she wouldn't be able to crawl under the beds or into her hobbit house with her cast on. So she burrowed under the bed covers in her mother's bedroom and hoped she was safe.

She didn't sleep until dawn.

The next thing Maddie knew, someone was knocking on the door.

Not again, she thought. *Go away!*

She didn't want to get up. Her phone informed her it was seven forty-five; whatever the intrusion was, it must be important.

At least she'd survived the night without an uninvited guest. Maybe the thermos had been there all along. Maybe Brandon left it there the other day, and she simply hadn't noticed.

Hauling herself out of bed, she grabbed a cotton housecoat from her grandmother's closet and sneezed twice from the dust. Then she lumbered into the hallway, praying it wasn't Owen again. But as she rounded the corner, she saw that it wasn't. It was her father. And he was standing in the kitchen.

"Well. I finally found you."

"Dad?" she asked as if it could be Stephen Clarke's long-lost twin or a doppelgänger.

"Maddie?" he asked with a touch of sarcasm.

"What are you doing here?"

"I could ask you the same thing."

"But how . . . ?" Had Rafe told him where to find her? Why would he have done that when she'd asked him not to?

"Your former husband stopped by to see me yesterday."

She closed her eyes. "But how did you get in?"

"Your grandmother always kept a spare key under the flowerpot at the back door in case she got locked out. It was still there."

"Oh." For a moment she forgot she was angry with him. He looked older, he looked tired. His hair had thinned over the past years, it was now wispy gray-white. His neck was puckery; he still was thin, and his dimples remained in place on either side of his mouth. They'd always been visible even when he wasn't happy. Like now.

He set down his overnight bag; apparently, he intended to stay. Which didn't please her.

She asked if he wanted coffee.

"I'm sorry I lied to you, Dad," she said while her back was

to him as he sat at the table and she fussed in the kitchen, starting the coffee, getting out mugs, and setting one of the blueberry muffins on a plate for her dad.

"I guess the attorney found you after all," he said. "Sorry,
but I opened the letter before I returned it."

So at least she had one answer: her father hadn't wanted
her to know that her grandmother died a few weeks—not
decades—ago. There was so much she could say. So much to
ask. But Maddie's brain was still clogged with sleep, and now
her nerves crackled again. "How did you get here?"

"I drove to the Cape yesterday and stayed at a hotel in
Woods Hole. I left the car there this morning and walked to
the early boat. I took a taxi up here. At least I remembered
how to do all that." It had been a long time since he'd been to
the island, too; he'd never said much about his visits before he
and her mother had married. As far as Maddie knew, he hadn't
been back since then.

She put the half muffin that she hadn't yet eaten yesterday
on a plate for herself, as if this were an ordinary day, and that
next they'd be reading the *New York Times*—she on her laptop, he, the print version.

"Do you need help?" he asked as he stood up again. He
seemed to move more slowly than she was used to seeing him
move. When had that happened? Gradually, over time? Or
only since he'd seen Brandon's letter?

"Owen showed up unannounced, too," she began, ignoring his question. "I think he saw dollar signs in my future."

"Enough to take you back to court to try to get you to pay
the last of Rafe's education." His comment was not a question.

She snorted. "At least Rafe's a senior."

"There's always grad school."

"I'll manage." She stirred milk into her coffee, then asked
if he'd bring the plates and mugs to the table.

While he did as she asked, she sat down, and then so did he, and they fell silent again. She thought of the ship's clock at Evelyn's, almost hearing it tick-tock in the background.

"What about the . . . college?"

"Do you mean 'what about tenure'?"

He nodded.

She forced a short laugh. "I don't know yet if I have it, Dad."

"You'll get it. Manchino's too young."

There was no point reminding him that Manchino had published two books and more articles than Maddie had. He was a single guy without a son or a father to take care of and seemed to devote all his spare time to studying or writing. Besides, Maddie and her father had more important things to discuss.

"Dad?" she asked. "Why didn't I know? Why didn't anyone tell me that Mom was a Native American? That I'm one, too? And who made up that story about us being Iberian?" Now that she'd started, the questions tumbled out, the muscles in her face tightening with each one. "And what about Grandma? Why did you tell me years ago that she was dead? I had a right to know the truth. And now so does Rafe." Her hands shook; she folded them, hoping he wouldn't notice.

He stared at his muffin as if wondering whether or not it was safe to eat. "It's a long story, Maddie."

"I have time."

Breaking off a piece of the muffin, he put it in his mouth, then brushed a few crumbs from the front of his short-sleeved white shirt. In spite of it being summer and he was on the island, Dad wore a collared shirt, dress pants, a belt. And shoes. Slip-on, leather shoes. With socks. Back when he'd been teaching, he always added a tie and sports jacket to complete his conventional ensemble.

"When your mother and I started seeing each other, she

said she envied me. That she'd give anything to see what it was like to live on the mainland. With lots of places to go and lots of things to do. I thought she was joking. She was the happiest, most talented, prettiest young woman I'd ever met. And she loved her life here."

Nearly the same way Evelyn had described her.

Maddie lowered her eyes. Whenever she thought about her mother, yes, she did remember how happy she was. And how much she made Maddie feel loved. Her father's words, however, felt as if he'd rehearsed them all the way from Green Hills.

Her lip started to quiver; she swallowed her tears.

"Hannah intended to tell you everything before you started first grade. She thought you'd be able to understand it better then. She also wanted to share her culture with our community—but not until you knew first." He paused, took another bite, perhaps rehearsing again. "I never did figure out why she wanted to wait. But then she was gone . . . and I . . . well, I never told you because I didn't know how. I didn't want to confuse you. And then you were grown up and it was too late. I convinced myself there was no need because you'd never have to come back . . . here." He let out a big whoosh, as if to say, *Thank God, that's over.*

Squeezing her hands together, holding in her rising anger, Maddie said, "But Grandma Nancy came to Mommy's funeral." She was startled to hear the word "Mommy" come out. But it had been what she'd called her mother. She'd missed out on the growing-up years when a child often shifts from calling her mother Mommy to Mom and sometimes Mother.

Her father nodded, his eyes still focused on the damn muffin instead of on her. "Yes. Your grandmother was at the funeral."

"Which was the last time I saw her. When you wouldn't let her park the camper in the driveway."

He nodded again.

And for an instant, Maddie had a strange feeling that he was preparing to lie to her again, that he needed to hold back the truth.

"Your grandmother and I argued," he said at last. "But not about the camper. She wanted you to continue to come to the island every summer, even without your mother. I could not let that happen."

"Why not? She was my grandmother, Dad. She wouldn't have hurt me."

He pushed the plate away. He put his face in his hands. "It was complicated, Maddie." He stood up and started to pace. He paused at the fireplace and looked at the mantel, at her mother's sunset painting. Then he returned to his pacing. "Time passed." He huffed, and she sensed another fabrication forming. "I thought it was better to keep you home, not share you with a woman whose ways and whose culture I didn't know much about. So I said she was dead. For which I am sorry. But once I'd done it, there wasn't a good way to take it back. It never occurred to me that you'd find out otherwise."

Maddie let his monologue sink in. "You never spoke to her again?"

"No." It came out in a whisper. "I couldn't." He didn't elaborate.

So Maddie simply sat there, hands still clasped together, tears spilling down her cheeks. She remembered her grandmother reading to her, kissing her fingertips, then touching Maddie's forehead with them when the story was done and whispering the word about a cow.

Her father returned to the chair and sat. He made a soft noise, as if he'd been wounded by the emotions he'd buried in a deep recess in his mind, like the kind she'd carved out in hers. "Oh, Maddie," he said, extending his hand, reaching for hers.

She pulled away.

After a few minutes, anger dried her tears. Yes, she thought, she was angry. She'd never thought of her father as a stupid man. Yet now . . .

She tucked a lock of hair behind her ear. "Rafe's coming tomorrow," she said brusquely.

"I know."

"Does he know you're here?"

"No. He's at his father's this weekend. And working on the river. I can leave today if you want."

She wished she could get up and pace the way he had. Even better, go outside for a long run. She sighed. "Yes. It will be better if you're not here. I need time to tell Rafe what's going on. He'll have questions; I want to be the one to give him answers. And I need to do it alone."

Her father didn't respond. Maddie couldn't remember when—or if—they'd ever argued. It was painful for her; it must be for him, too. *You should have thought about that before you lied to me*, she wanted to blurt out.

Then he said, "I know you want to protect your son. The way I tried to protect you."

She wanted to remind him it was hardly the same thing, because she had every intention of telling Rafe everything. She bit her lip again. "Well, Rafe's not a child. And I want him to meet some people and experience a little of the island before I decide what to do."

"Before you decide what to do about what?"

"My grandmother left me her whole estate, Dad. It's worth a lot of money. Owen was right about that."

"Oh" was all he said, his voice weak.

And that's when, for some stupid reason, she started to feel sorry for him. Sorry he'd lost the only woman he'd ever loved. Sorry he'd made a hasty choice in telling Maddie that Grandma was dead, then didn't feel he could reverse it. And she was sorry that she had to dismiss him now, especially after all he'd done for her and her son. Her father had made a mistake. Over the years, Maddie no doubt had made many—and, yes, some were to protect her child.

But her mistakes were not as big.

And yet, he was her father.

She sucked in her cheeks, held her breath, then slowly let it out.

"Dad?" she finally said. "Can you stay for the day? I'm not good at walking, which you probably noticed. But you can drive my car. We can have lunch somewhere. And maybe see some places where you and Mom used to go? Would you like that?"

"I would."

She reached across the table and covered his hand with hers. "So would I." He was a good dad. And a good grandfather. And she couldn't let her self-pity override those facts. Even if the story he'd just told her was another big fat lie.

With her father behind the wheel, they drove up to the cliffs and the Gay Head Lighthouse; they browsed through the shops, which, she explained, were owned by the Wampanoags, and pointed out that most of the crafts and jewelry they sold were designed, carved, and woven by them. She didn't add that Joe had told her those things. Then they went to Lobsterville Beach, and Maddie pointed out where her grandmother's other properties were, and where she had tumbled.

He laughed. "Well, you did say you fell down a hill. But you failed to mention it was made out of sand."

When it was lunchtime, they went back to the cliffs, because her father once liked the clam chowder at the restaurant there. After they finished eating, Maddie had an idea.

"Grandma Nancy had a climate-controlled storage unit by the airport," she said. "She kept Mom's paintings there." She waited for him to comment.

"I'd love to see them."

"Good. And the key's right there on my key ring." She pointed to the jangle he'd set on the table.

In spite of GPS, they got turned around and wound up back in Menemsha. They laughed at themselves, two PhD college professors, who couldn't find their way around an island.

"Or probably out of a paper bag," Maddie said, and they laughed again. It felt good to laugh with him; maybe laughter would help her forgive him.

Once at the storage facility, he was startled to see the pickup.

"Good Lord," he said. "I remember this—your grandmother drove it everywhere. I think it was old even then."

Maddie told him about the note Grandma left inside and that she'd stopped driving when she turned eighty.

He guffawed. "She was a realistic old bird."

Then they went to the cabinet, and Maddie showed him the paintings, one by one, sliding each one back into its slot after he'd studied it; sometimes he quietly nodded, other times he muttered, "Uh-huh" or "Mmm." Then she showed him the one of the old man with the bronze skin and the wampum arrowhead on the rawhide cord.

He stopped. He took it from her. And stared at it. "It's Isaac Thurston. Your great-grandfather."

She caught her breath. "What?"

"No doubt about it. It's Nancy's father."

"But . . . he died before you met Mom, didn't he?"

"Yes. I never met the man. But your mom had a photograph of him. Exactly like this. She must have used it for reference. Wow. It's amazing, isn't it?"

Warmth flooded into Maddie's face; it moved to her heart, her stomach, and down to her feet, even the broken one.

"Are you sure?" Her voice squeaked as it often did when she was nervous.

"I'm sure. Your mother kept the photo. I could always see him in her. Rafe looks like him, too." He smiled a quick, sad smile. "The picture your mother used is somewhere in our attic. I put it away with a few other things when . . . well, it was all part of what I'd planned to give to you one day. When you were a grown-up."

She couldn't tell whether he was lying again. She tried to convince herself it didn't matter, that the only important truth was that she now knew her heritage. On top of that, she had a portrait of her great-grandfather—her mother's grandfather—another man Maddie had never known.

Wasn't that enough?

As badly as she wanted to believe that, she couldn't pretend that not knowing her history all these years had no impact on her, that it hadn't been a huge loss. Then grief, anguish or just plain anger took over. And a wave of silent fury came thundering into her, the way an incoming high tide crashes onto a beach in a storm.

She no longer felt sorry for him.

Snatching the portrait from his hand, she said, "I'll keep this." Her words were sharp and biting. "I'll show it to Rafe. If you talk to him before I see him, do not say a word about any of this."

He put a hand on her shoulder and patted it, the way he'd done when she was young and told him a secret. Like when she'd found a tiny goldfinch lying by the brook behind the house; she dug a small grave and buried him, then placed wildflowers on top to mark the spot. Or the time she told him Jimmy Hastings had kissed her on the playground and she was so scared she ran back into school and told her teacher she needed to use the girls' room, where she promptly threw up. A pat on her shoulder was her father's way of saying that everything would be all right. And it always was.

But this wasn't about a dead goldfinch. Or a childhood kiss.

And this time, it felt condescending.

She jerked her shoulder from his hand, her indignation spilling out.

"How could you do it, Dad? If Rafe looks so much like his great-great-grandfather, how could you look at him—look at *his face*—and not tell us that we're Wampanoag?"

"Half Wampanoag, for you. Only one quarter for him."

His answer fueled her ire.

Locking the cabinet and yanking out her keys, she clung to the portrait while navigating her crutches toward the door. "Go. Back. To. Green. Hills," she shouted, panting between each word. "And close the door on your way out. It will lock behind you."

She didn't wait for him to answer.

Her left foot stuttered as she moved it from the gas pedal to the brake, back to the gas. Amazingly, Maddie arrived at the cottage without incident. She had no idea how she'd done it, but she was grateful that traffic had been light.

How or if her father made it to the ferry was his problem. He was a grown, educated man; chances were, he'd call a cab or an Uber, or walk over to the airport and catch one there. She also hoped he'd have the good sense not to take anything from the storage unit. He'd left his bag at the cottage, but Rafe and her could bring it back with them. Or she'd ship it, if Rafe didn't show up. And if she decided to live on her own. Maybe it was time for that, too.

No matter what her choices would be, Maddie would no longer do things her father's way.

Before going to bed she stood the portrait of her great-grandfather on the mantel, between her mother's painting of the sunset and Maddie's pottery bowl. Then she opened all the windows to let the night air in. She no longer worried that a big bad wolf could crawl inside and do whatever to her.

Chapter 18

Rafe called in the morning to say he couldn't make it until Friday, maybe Saturday. Damn.

"I'm sorry, Mom. I couldn't get anyone to take my place. Will you be okay till then?"

"Sure, honey," she said, masking her disappointment. "I'll be fine." She never wanted him to hear her sounding needy. So, yes, she was guilty of trying to protect her child, too. Squaring her shoulders, she raised her chin, determined to act chipper. "Maybe by then the doctor will let me go home."

He hesitated. She knew Rafe was sensitive to her emotions; maybe it was common for an only child with a single mom. Or maybe he was more like her than she imagined.

"Okay," he said after another beat. "I'll let you know what time I'll get there."

"Great!" she said too exuberantly. "And before we leave here, I'll have lots to show you." If she'd said she'd have lots to *tell* him, he would have asked for a hint. That can of worms was far too big to open over the phone.

After hanging up, Maddie called Evelyn.

"Hello, dear," the woman said. She did not sound as upbeat as Maddie expected. "I'm not having a good day. I know Brandon spilled the beans about my condition. I asked him not to, but he enjoys dancing around my wishes. He says it's for my own good—that there's no shame in people knowing. Anyway, I'm afraid I'm not well enough today to drive you to your appointment. Can someone else bring you?"

If Brandon hadn't told Maddie about his mother's situation, she might have thought Evelyn was making an excuse—which she would have taken personally.

"Oh, Evelyn, I completely understand. And I'm sorry about your health issues. But you do well most of the time, don't you?"

"I do. Sometimes I even forget about it for a while. But not today."

"Well, please take care of yourself and don't worry about me. If I can't get someone else, I can call a cab. My dad was here yesterday, and he had no problem getting one."

Evelyn fell silent, then asked, "Your father came to the island?"

"Yes."

"Is he still here?"

"No." There was no need to elaborate.

"He came a long way for just a day."

"We had a nice time," she lied. "My son wanted to come with him, but he had to work; he'll be here later in the week."

"Oh. What does he do for summer work?"

Was she really interested?

"Environmental things. Mostly related to water. And he'll be a senior at Amherst this fall; he's studying business, too." Right now, however, she did not want to explain her family to Evelyn. So Maddie changed the subject. "I'm sorry I won't get to see you today, but I hope you'll feel better soon."

"I will. I always do!" Her spirits either brighter or she was pretending they were.

Good grief, Maddie thought, *another protector.*

"In the meantime," Evelyn added, "call Joe for a ride. He's usually free on Tuesdays."

"Thanks. I'll figure something out. But please let me know if I can do anything for you. Obviously, I'm not great at running errands right now. But I feel fine and can find a way to get anywhere if you need anything. Okay?"

"Thank you, Maddie. That's very kind."

Maddie rang off before the conversation went further. As for her doctor's appointment, she knew that Lisa would be working, that Brandon and Jeremy were gone, and that Joe . . . well, she hadn't spoken with him since Saturday. And once again, she hated to feel needy.

So instead of calling Joe, Maddie went to her Uber app, which she didn't need often but was glad Rafe had installed it. She scheduled the driver to come early enough so she'd make it to the hospital in time for lunch.

Walking into the hospital wearing Evelyn's gift of the white skirt and pale blue top, Maddie was happy she'd also tucked the denim jacket in her cross-body bag—the hospital was up the hill from the harbor, and she'd learned that, despite the summer-sunny sky, a chilly breeze often rippled off the water.

Engaging her crutches with growing confidence, she walked into the waiting room. It was an unlikely adventure for her, to be on her own in a strange place and going to see a doctor she'd seen only once.

Her first stop was the café. It was noisy and busy with appetizing aromas. Maddie was used to eating in the dining hall at the college, where everyone and everything was familiar, including the food. This was different. Her intuition told her this would be fun.

She opted for baked cod, corn on the cob, salad greens, and a cup of tea; instead of dessert, she chose clam chowder. FRESH CLAMS TODAY, a sign read.

At this rate, she wouldn't need dinner.

A kitchen helper offered to carry her food to a table. Maddie wondered if everyone on the island was innately kind. Maybe it was from the salt air.

Once settled, she began with the chowder. She stopped from turning to the people at the table behind her to ask if they'd tried it and tell them she thought it was good. But to them, it was probably commonplace, the way shepherd's pie was in the Green Hills dining hall.

While eating, she eavesdropped on the voices around her, on snippets of whispers and laughter. Then she realized someone was standing at her table.

She looked up. And blinked.

"Hi, Maddie." It was Francine, the dark-haired girl with the soulful eyes who lived on Chappaquiddick and had come to the cottage with her kids and Rex looking for Nancy. She was holding a tray with a sandwich and a soda.

"Francine!" Maddie said. "I never thought I'd see someone I know here. Join me? Please?"

The young woman thanked her, smiled, and sat.

"Do you have an appointment today, too?" Maddie asked.

"No," she said with a sly grin. "I went to Vineyard Haven to pick up a few things for the Inn. I like to sneak off Chappy when my husband, Jonas, can watch the kids. I don't get much time on my own. Anyway, I'm hungry. Between Bella and Reggie, I've been to the hospital lots of times. And I like the café food, so today I thought, why not?"

"Why not, indeed."

Looking around, Francine asked, "You're alone, too?"

"I am. My follow-up appointment is at one o'clock; I can't drive with this silly cast on, so I took a cab. I didn't want to bother anyone."

What followed was a nice conversation, the back-and-forth banter of two people getting to know each other over lunch. Francine revealed that she'd come to the island when Bella was a baby, which was when she was given one of Nancy's baskets. Then she told her about the Vineyard Inn, and how she wound up part of its mismatched family, which included Rex as one of their loveable patriarchs.

Maddie enjoyed the stories—they almost made her feel as if she, too, belonged. She responded with a brief synopsis of her life, leaving out the part about being half Wampanoag so she wouldn't be tempted to explain the rest. She'd save that for a later date, after her anger with her father had cooled. So she told Francine about Rafe and that she was a college professor and pleasantly divorced; she told about her summers on the island long ago, and how she remembered she'd loved it. Though she figured she was about two decades older than Francine, Maddie learned they had something important in common: their mothers had died before either one of them had been ready. Not that she supposed most people ever were.

By the time they finished their meals, Maddie was almost late for her appointment.

"I'm so sorry," she said, "but I have to go. It's been great seeing you." She grabbed her crutches and tried to stand gracefully, which didn't work very well.

Francine quickly stood and helped her with the crutches.

"One day soon you must come to Chappy and see the Inn. And our little island."

"Sounds tempting."

Then Francine gave her a crooked smile. "In the meantime, since I have nowhere to be right now, I'll walk with you. And I'll tell you a good reason you might want to get to know my gang."

They left the café and went into the corridor that led to the physicians' offices.

"Feel free to start sharing," Maddie said, intrigued.

"Okay, I'll be blunt. I heard you had lunch at the Lord James."

She didn't know what she'd expected, but it wasn't that. "I did. With my attorney."

"Well . . ." Francine dragged out her words. "I don't know how long you plan to stay, or if you're interested . . . but seeing as how you're available . . ." She stopped. She paused. "What I'm trying to say is that Rex likes you. I tried to get him to ask you out, but he's pretty shy."

They went through the lobby toward the doctor's office.

"Really?" Maddie finally asked.

"Yes, really. So maybe it's not a coincidence that I ran into you today. If you say yes, I'll tell him. If you say no, I won't say a word. Like we never had this conversation."

Maddie let out what sounded like a cross between a laugh and a chuckle. She'd allowed herself to get so wrapped up in her work and her family and applying for tenure, that she'd justified not dating. Which, of course, was easier than trying to find a nice man over forty. One without a secret wife and three kids in the wings. And yet Rex seemed different. Older than her, but not too much. Besides, his spirit seemed younger, more lighthearted than hers. Which she found attractive.

Then she heard someone say, "Yes. I'm interested." She was surprised that the "someone" was her.

"Great!" Francine cried as they reached the office. "But go easy on him, please. He's really a gem."

Maddie smiled again and thanked her. Then she marched into the reception area, standing taller and feeling so very happy.

What on earth had she been thinking?

The doctor said she was healing well and reassured her she would not be in a cast or on crutches for the rest of her life, at least, not due to this. Frankly, however, Maddie half listened because she was preoccupied thinking about Rex. After making another follow-up appointment for two weeks from then, knowing she'd wind up cancelling it because she'd be back in Green Hills by then and would see her own doctor, she Ubered her way back to the cottage, and busied herself by brown-bagging dozens more issues of her grandmother's outdated magazines—*Yankee*, *Good Housekeeping*, *Farmer's Almanac*—for recycling. All the while, she worried about what would happen if she liked Rex. Or more specifically, what if she fell for him? Would she change her mind and keep the cottage? She could sell the two other properties and live quite well off the proceeds for the rest of her life and put Rafe through grad school, too. She could withdraw from the tenure race and let Manchino have it because he was young and probably deserved a break.

But . . . what if Rex didn't like her as much as she liked him? How could she stay there? It would be humiliating.

Besides, she knew nothing about him. He could be a ladies' man or a con man or simply a creep. Francine said he was a gem . . . but she was young and married and maybe naive.

If he called, Maddie could always say no. In mere days she'd have her grandmother's things sorted and dispensed or disposed of. She'd list the properties with CiCi, because it would be easier than trying to vet someone else.

Yes, there was no way Maddie could go out with Rex. She had too much at stake to make a decision based on a man. This was her life, not a romance novel. She hoped he would not be disappointed.

She sped up her chores. When she was done, she returned to Grandma's bedroom and tackled the clothing. She already knew she'd trash most of it.

She was right. The worn-out shoes and all the clothes— including what was in the dresser—went into trash bags. The lone exception was the skirt that was decked out with the colorful beads, which she decided to give to the tribe.

With the clothing completed, she deserved a rest. She couldn't remember ever napping so much. She blamed it on the pain meds. Then she lay down on the bed, slept, woke up, slept again. She repeated that for a couple of hours, her brain barging in on her forty winks with reminders about what remained on her to-do list.

Finally, she gave up and assessed the tasks, congratulating herself for having made a good dent in her grandmother's personal things. As for the rest, all the furniture and all the old dishes and glassware, pots and pans, and cooking and eating utensils in the kitchen could probably be trashed, unless someone wanted any or—God bless them—all of it. Maybe CiCi could take care of getting it hauled out of there. For the size of her commission, it seemed like the least she could do.

Before calling CiCi, Maddie decided to have Joe stop by and offer his input on whether the things she'd designated for the tribe would be appreciated. She'd want him to distribute them however he wished.

Which would take care of the personal items and the furniture. Except for the contents of the linen closet, which was packed with ragged sheets and towels. There also was the hobbit house—she'd ask Rafe to drag out the seaman's chest so she could sort her childhood riches. At least the closet in her mother's bedroom was empty. Sad as that made Maddie feel.

With too much on her mind to relax, she knew that if both of her feet were in good working order, she would absolutely go for a run. But with that not being remotely possible, maybe a snack would suffice.

Besides, it was almost seven o'clock and, surprisingly, she was hungry.

Once in the kitchen, she took a spoon from a drawer, rinsed it in hot water, then sat at the table, picking her way through the plastic container of potato salad leftover from Lisa's get-together. Which didn't stop her brain cells from churning like the eddy of fish she'd seen when canoeing with Joe.

She thought about how invasive it was to weed out a lifetime of someone else's stuff . . . and that, one day, she'd have to do that with her father's belongings. Of course, thinking of him caused her anger to resurface.

Men could be so weird!

Not surprisingly, she supposed, that thought brought her back to Rex.

And to her disappointment that Rafe still wasn't there.

Then she thought about her damn foot. And the damn cast. And how it was a damn stupid way to have to spend the rest of the summer.

Closing her eyes, Maddie realized that maybe her boring, predictable life wasn't so bad after all. There was some comfort in knowing what to expect nearly every minute. Every day. Which was why she knew that, realistically, she'd be home soon. She would patch things up with her father, of course she would. Rafe would be off to Amherst. The fall semester would begin. All would be forgiven . . . and everything would be safely predictable again. Except that she'd be rich.

She took another bite of salad.

And then her phone rang.

Chapter 19

"Maddie? Hi. It's Rex. The bald guy."

She laughed. "Hmm," she said, "let's see. I know a lot of bald guys. Could you be more specific?"

"The one from the restaurant in Edgartown."

"Okay. That narrows it down."

"Ha!" he replied. "You're a funny lady."

Funny? Maddie would not have used that word to describe herself. While she enjoyed people who had great senses of humor, and she loved to laugh, she never thought she inspired others to laugh, too.

"I'm not sure my son would always agree," she said.

"Then he's missing out."

She chewed on her lower lip, glad Rex wasn't there to watch her do it. "I'll be sure to tell him." Pushing the fork around in the salad, she moved the potatoes and the chopped egg and the bits of green onion from one side to the other.

"So," he continued, "would you like to have lunch with me?"

A different Madelyn Clarke must have entered the cottage—different from the one who'd been rooting through her grandmother's possessions, then been frustrated, restless, annoyed. And, most importantly, preparing to leave the island.

"Yes," the new Madelyn Clarke replied. "I'd like very much to have lunch with you." She paused, as if waiting to come to her senses and take back what she'd just said.

"Great. How about Thursday?"

She hesitated. Was it too late to change her mind? But did she really want to go back to her old self? "Thursday's fine," she said. "I'm sure I can get a taxi to Edgartown . . ."

"No way! We won't be dining at the Lord James. I need a few hours off; my sous chef can cover lunch for me. I'll have to be back by four to start dinner, though. He hates it when I take advantage of his good nature."

She laughed, relieved that he expected lunch and nothing more. There was, after all, no such thing as love at first sight. Especially when both parties were well over forty.

"So, I'll pick you up around noon?" he was saying.

"That's fine. Yes. Great," she jabbered. She didn't ask where they'd go. Chances were, she did not know the place. "I'll look forward to it." She supposed that was the right thing to say.

"Good. Me, too. See you then."

They hung up. Maddie blinked.

She had a date.

The day after tomorrow.

She moved around the cottage, opening the windows, trying to stave off a rush of heat that suddenly billowed inside her.

The next thing she thought was, *Yikes. A date.*

What'll I wear?

Her jeans were off the menu as they now were shorts on the right leg. And she didn't want to wear the same white skirt she'd worn when she and Brandon had gone to Rex's restaurant. The denim one or the faded black one she'd arrived in were far too casual. Her navy sundress was tired and worn out, like her. But she didn't dare attempt driving again. Maybe in the morning she could call a cab and go clothes shopping in town. Or maybe Evelyn would feel up to going with her.

No! she scolded the new Madelyn Clarke. First, she'd rather not have Evelyn involved; second, she didn't want to think of this date as requiring a new outfit. Millionaire or not, it might make her feel that this was more than a casual lunch.

And third, she really needed to stop thinking of herself as tired and worn out.

Then, one of her famous intuitions kicked in. Rex might like to see her in Grandma Nancy's skirt, the one that Maddie had put in the tribal pile, the one with the colorful beads in the diamond-shaped pattern just above the hemline. It would be perfect. Before getting too excited, she hobbled into the bedroom, dug it out, and tried it on just as the sunset applause rose from the beach as if cheering her on. But the applause did no good—the waist was too tight.

Discouraged, she stepped out of the skirt . . . which was when she discovered a fist-sized bump in the backside of the waistband. Examining it closely, she found a burlap pouch attached to a fabric loop. She unknotted it from the loop and eased the drawstring open. Something inside was wrapped in tissue. Slowly, she pulled it out and unwrapped the tissue. And in her palm lay three strands of necklaces, all made of wampum.

She was pretty sure she knew where they'd come from.

Holding them gently, she rushed to find the box of photos she planned to save. It didn't take long to find the one of her grandparents on their wedding day. She'd been right: along with the skirt, Grandma Nancy wore the same strands of wampum around her neck.

Maddie cried. She was overcome. Overwhelmed. Over-everythinged.

When she finally stopped blubbering, she put on the beads, then stepped into the skirt again. Without the pouch at the waistband, it fit. The hemline fell halfway between her knee and her foot, which helped camouflage her cast. With her white knit top, the outfit would be fine. The only jewelry she'd need were the wedding necklaces.

Then she checked her image in the full-length mirror.

And gasped.

She looked as if she'd stepped out of her grandmother's photo collection. She looked, well, pretty, she supposed. But, mostly, she looked very much Wampanoag.

Staring at her reflection, whirling in another pool of emotion, she barely heard a faint knock on the front door.

"CiCi," Maddie said after she struggled to make it to the front door.

The woman didn't speak. She stared at Maddie the way Maddie had been staring at herself.

"Wow," the real estate agent finally said. "That skirt, those beads . . . you look like a Wampanoag."

Maddie let out a nervous bubble of a laugh. "Do I?" She promptly forgot that, like with Evelyn, she hadn't wanted CiCi to get too close. She opened the screen door and invited her in. "I kind of thought so, too."

"Well. The skirt and the wampum help."

"Agreed. But you probably didn't stop by to catch me trying on my grandmother's old clothes."

Shaking her head, CiCi said, "No. But I was in the neighborhood."

Maddie was tempted to ask her to swear to that on her grandmother's Praying Indians' Bible.

As if reading her mind, CiCi started to toy with her long, dangling earrings—shiny, bright coral discs that evening that almost, not quite, matched her flaming orange sheath that was splattered with a design of pink hibiscus blossoms. Maddie guessed it was a holdover from the nineties.

"I have a client who wanted to see the sunset on the beach," Maddie's flowered visitor said. "We came in separate cars—he and his wife had late dinner reservations at the Outermost Inn, so they went on their way, and I went on mine. But when I looked up the hill, I saw your lights on and . . . well, I decided to check up on you. I noticed your cast when you were at lunch with Attorney Morgan. And I presumed that the crutches standing in the corner belonged to you."

Two days and several hours had passed since then. Maddie thought there was a better chance that CiCi had stopped by the Chilmark Town Hall yesterday or today and pumped Lisa for details about Maddie's leg.

She sat on a kitchen chair again and asked her to take a seat. CiCi chose the sofa. Maddie declined to offer tea; instead she launched into details about her embarrassing spill. When she was done, CiCi whistled.

"I've never known anyone who broke a foot on a sand dune. Maybe you're lucky it wasn't worse."

Maddie looked at the cast that barely peeked from below the beaded hemline. "The doctor told me not to be impatient. Easier said than done." She was proud that at least she also remembered that from her appointment, in spite of her head being stuck in a cloud of romantic potential with Rex.

"Years ago," CiCi continued, "my second husband broke his foot windsurfing at South Beach. He hit the water too hard thanks to an offshore wind. It didn't help that it was his first time out, or that he always acted like he knew how to do everything. He never took a single lesson or listened to anyone who knew better." She squinted. "Damn fool."

Fiddling with the wampum necklaces, Maddie said, "I guess I'm in the same category. It was pretty dumb of me to think I could climb sand dunes while wearing sandals."

CiCi smiled. It was a soft smile, a nice smile. "You get a pass because you didn't grow up here. Pete, however, did."

Maddie smoothed a few wrinkles from the skirt. "Would you like a cup of tea?"

"No, thanks. But can I fix one for you before I go? Or do anything for you?"

As CiCi stood up, Maddie spotted the woman's orange patent heels. They weren't exactly stilettoes, but Maddie doubted that the agent had worn them on the beach while watching the sunset. Maybe that wasn't why she was in Menemsha. Maybe there never was a client and his wife with late dinner reservations at the Outermost Inn. Maybe she'd manufactured the excuse in order to check up on Maddie, to see if she'd made her decision. Or maybe she'd really stopped by to see how Maddie was.

Worst of all, Maddie wondered why it was taking her so long to trust people and why she was so lousy at it.

"Thanks, but no tea," Maddie said.

"Do you have food?"

"I do. And my son will be here Friday."

"You're sure you can wait till then? You must not be able to drive. And as good as lobster rolls are from the market or the Galley, a person can only eat so many before getting tired of them."

Maddie smiled. "Do you know Jeff Fuller?"

CiCi's eyebrows went up. "Jeff? Sure. Nice guy. Nice family. He's one of your neighbors."

"Do you know if his father, or maybe his grandfather, owned an ice cream shack here forty or so years ago?"

She sat back down and studied Maddie. "You were here that long ago?"

So Maddie told her the story of Grandma Nancy's deal to buy her a double-dip cone if she helped shuck corn for dinner. She mentioned her pink shorts and the T-shirt with the glitter heart that Grandma made for her, and the fact that Maddie was allowed to go barefoot. Back home in Green Hills, she'd thrown a tantrum on the first day of kindergarten because her father insisted she wear lace-up shoes.

Encouraging her to continue, CiCi ignored Maddie's wishes and got up and made two mugs of tea.

The more Maddie talked, the longer the story became. She told the agent how her mother had died that same year, and how she barely remembered Grandma Nancy at her mother's funeral, not knowing it would be the last time she saw her. She told her how her dad raised her alone, how Maddie went to college, married the wrong guy but had her wonderful son, Rafe, so it had been worth it. She skipped the part about getting her PhD and having tenure hanging in the balance because she didn't want to think about that right then. She did admit, however, that she hadn't known she was Wampanoag.

"My whole life," she added, "I wasn't told until now."

Then she stopped talking. The sunset was long gone, the sky was dark with sleep.

She looked into her empty mug. "Oh, CiCi, I'm so sorry! I never intended to bore you with my life story. And certainly not to keep you so long." She hoped the woman wouldn't broadcast the details about her life before sunrise.

"I enjoyed it. It's not often that someone who is—or might become—a client talks to me like we're old friends. Usually they turn off their lights and lock their windows and doors when they see me coming."

Maddie didn't confess that she might have done the same if she'd seen her walk up the path.

"I'm sure it's no consolation," CiCi continued, "but I never knew who my father was. My mother was a hippie in the sixties. I'm not sure she knew who he was, either. Anyway, here on the island, I wasn't the only single-parent kid back then, so that helped. I used to think—I used to hope—I was Wampanoag. I love everything about the tribe. And they've always been so nice to me; I liked to think they knew I was one of them. A few years ago, I got up the courage to have a DNA test. It turns out I'm mostly Scandinavian, with some Irish thrown in. Not a Native American in sight. I was very disappointed." She pressed her lips together, as if trying not to cry.

Maddie was ashamed that she'd underestimated the woman. Like many people, CiCi had had a difficult life. But beneath her questionable style, the woman's skin wasn't as thick as she seemed to want others to think.

"I'm so sorry," Maddie said.

CiCi shrugged. "To tell the truth, I'd been hoping for a genetic match, too. Like, maybe I'd find my birth father. No such luck there, either. So I decided it was time to forgive my parents and my ancestors for whatever or whoever they are or were. I've had a good life, ya know? And I've tried to be nice to everyone." She stood up again, then picked up her oversize, shiny silver purse, and said, "I'll leave now so you can get some sleep. Please call me if you need any help." She offered a quiet smile, and added, "Don't get up. I'll let myself out."

And so she did.

After CiCi left, Maddie stayed at the table awhile, her thoughts returning to the eddy of small fish that Joe said was a sign that the fish were growing up. Maybe his words—and CiCi's—were signaling that it was Maddie's time to grow up,

too. Which needed to start with forgiveness. And with reaching outside her safe cocoon and being grateful for the people
in her life who'd done so much for her.

Hoisting herself from the chair, she moved into her
mother's bedroom. The first thing she did was open the door
to the closet; she tried unsuccessfully to picture what had been
there. She felt sad for Grandma Nancy, who had lost her only
child first to Green Hills, then to life. Maddie couldn't imagine her life without Rafe.

Shutting the door, she changed into her nightgown, leaned
the crutches against the nightstand, and slid into what had been
her mother's bed, knowing that if CiCi—of all people—had
said she'd had a good life, Maddie certainly had, too.

She turned off the light on the nightstand. But when she
closed her eyes, Maddie would have sworn someone had been
watching her. Again.

*It was dark now. Inside the cottage and out. But it had been good
to sit outside the kitchen, below an open window, and listen to the
conversation between Maddie and CiCi. People say such interesting
things when they think no one else is listening.*

*It was too bad about my lost thermos, however. Iced coffee would
have made sitting and listening more enjoyable.*

Chapter 20

Wednesday morning, Maddie knew she had to make a few calls before starting to sort the kitchen things and before obsessing about lunch the next day with Rex. *Lunch*, she reminded herself. That was all.

Taking her grandmother's seersucker robe out of the trash pile, she pulled it on over her nightgown. The fabric was frayed at the collar and the cuffs and carried a musty scent mixed with an essence of salt air. Maddie wondered if all of Grandma's clothes—and maybe Grandma, too—had the same fragrance.

She tucked her phone into the pocket of the robe, then hauled herself to the kitchen, made coffee, and decided to eat half of the remaining blueberry muffin. After getting her breakfast to the table without spilling or dumping it, she took the same chair that she'd sat in last night when talking with CiCi. Then she closed her eyes and sent good vibes of gratitude to the universe that her foot was one day closer to being healed.

After breakfast, she checked her phone for the news (there wasn't much), the weather (sunny, warm), and the stock market (because she should start educating herself for when her

inheritance came through). Then it was ten o'clock, a reason-
able time to tend to her "must-dos."

She was beginning to feel like a robot.

So she went to her contact list, scrolled to Evelyn's name,
and called her.

"Good morning, Maddie!" the woman said when she answered on the first ring. Her cheerful voice could have been
genuine or fake, depending on what she wanted Maddie to
believe.

"Good morning. You sound perky. Feeling better?"

"I am. Thank you. As much as I hate my down days, I try
to roll with them because usually the next day is better."

"That's good advice. Even when people aren't in your situation."

"To be honest, sometimes I'm downright miserable to be
around. Ask my son. No. Please don't." She laughed. "But
today is a good day. How are *you*? How did your appointment go?"

"He says my foot is healing well. And that I need to be patient."

"How does it actually feel?"

"It no longer hurts. Well, hardly at all. But I'm afraid it
still has a way to go."

"Then your intuition is telling you something, dear. Your
ancestors would tell you to listen to it."

Of course she meant the ancestors on Maddie's mother's
side. Then Maddie wondered why Evelyn had mentioned intuition . . . and if she was hinting at something . . . else. But it
was an awkward topic for Maddie. One her father had never
understood. So Maddie just said, "Thank you, Evelyn. That's
more good advice."

"Now that I'm seventy, Brandon calls it wisdom. Which
makes me sound old. He thinks that's funny. So," she said, her

exasperation with her son having sounded both loving and annoyed, "how's the cleaning out going? I can't imagine all the
things Nancy collected over the years."

"I think a better word than 'collected' might simply be
'saved.' Newspapers, magazines, Wampanoag recipes. They
must have meant something to her. But . . . let's just say when
I get back to Green Hills I shall purge my own boxes of stuff.
I want to save my son from having to do this someday.
Thankfully, most of my detritus is on the computer, so he can
dump the whole thing in a bin." She hoped she sounded upbeat and not critical of Grandma.

"Speaking of Rafe," she continued, "he won't be here
until Friday or Saturday. I need a few things from Cronig's to
hold me over until then, but if you're not up for driving, I'll
call Lisa. Maybe she can get them on her way home from
work."

Evelyn sighed. "I'm sorry, dear. As much as I'd love to
help—and to see you—my book group is meeting here at
noon today. We were going to Mary Beth Braga's, but I
don't want to drive to Edgartown. Not after the day I had
yesterday."

"So, you really aren't as perky as you're trying to sound."

"You're getting to know me well, Madelyn."

"Well, then, there is something I really would like your
help with. But we can do it by phone. Maybe this evening?
Or tomorrow?"

"What is it?"

She swallowed. "I don't know how to start planning a
small memorial service for my grandmother. What to do.
Who to invite. I'm hoping that Brandon gets the death certificate this week, so we can have the service while my son's
here." She didn't realize until then that having Rafe there for
moral support would be wonderful. "I know you're busy
planning the wedding, but . . ."

"I appreciate you asking, dear. And though I'd be honored to help you, I have a better suggestion."

Maddie waited.

"Ask someone else," Evelyn continued. "Someone who knows much more about how you should do this, about the way your grandmother would want it." She paused again, giving Maddie time to digest what she'd said.

"Joe?" Maddie asked.

"Exactly. Joe, after all, was her half brother. And he knows how to follow Wampanoag traditions. I think Nancy would have liked that."

Maddie lowered her voice. "You're right," she whispered. "I'm embarrassed that I didn't think of him first."

"This is all new to you, dear." Then Evelyn said that when she spoke with Brandon in the evening, she'd ask him to rattle whomever he needed to rattle to get the certificate. And she asked Maddie to keep her posted if Joe needed her help, because she'd love to be given a chore or two, to help make the memorial service special.

Then they said goodbye. And Maddie called Joe.

"I'll be honored to help," Joe said, and added that he could stop by the cottage the next afternoon so they could get started.

Tomorrow? Maddie wasn't sure how to respond.

"How about after four?" she asked quickly. "I have a lunch thing earlier." A lunch thing? Well, that sounded childish.

"Let's make it four thirty," he said, and thanked her for thinking of him.

He was helpful. And kind.

They rang off.

Then Maddie called Lisa but got voice mail. So she left a message, asking if Lisa could pick her up something for dinner; a fish sandwich from the Galley would be fine. Then she added, "And I'd love a vanilla frappe, too."

After all, like Joe, Lisa was helpful. And kind.

With those calls out of the way, Maddie stared out the window at the sky and dunes, her thoughts reverting to Evelyn's comment about her intuition, that her ancestors would tell her to listen to it.

Little did Evelyn know, Maddie's intuition had been gnawing at her since she'd sensed that her grandmother's fatal fall might not have been accidental. And though everyone was, indeed, helpful and kind, she still couldn't stop wondering if they were merely hiding something from her. Like what about her feeling that she was being watched?

If her ancestors would tell her to listen, they might also suggest that she act on her suspicion. So she decided to call Brandon. To be honest with him. To ask him, point-blank, if she might be right. She hoped he would laugh and say she couldn't be more wrong, that everyone there was just as they seemed, and everyone had cared about Nancy.

Brandon, however, was in Boston and didn't pick up.

She did not leave a message.

With a disheartened sigh, she knew she had one more call to make. But in order to do that, she'd feel better if she were dressed. And acting like a professional.

"Professor Jarvis, please," Maddie said once she was fully dressed and back at the kitchen table, a glass of iced tea in front of her. She also had a spiral-bound notebook, open to a blank page, and she was holding a pen—all out of habit.

"This is Madelyn Clarke," she added.

The receptionist in the faculty department must be new; she obviously did not recognize Maddie's voice or her name.

While waiting to be connected, Maddie doodled in the notebook. Flowers had always been a favorite doodle; she loved swirling loops into petals, creating a round blossom, then putting a dime-sized dot in the center and adding a stem and two leaves, only two, never three or four. It was the same doodle she'd done throughout her school years, as both student and teacher. But now, as she glanced at the finished picture, she froze. Her eyes drifted from her notebook up to the mantel and the pottery bowl. It was the same flower. For her whole life, Maddie had unknowingly mimicked the flower Evelyn had taught her how to draw.

"Madelyn? Hello?"

Startled, she dropped the pen.

"Professor Jarvis," she said. "Yes, sorry. I'm here." She cleared her throat and quickly unscrambled her brain. "I wanted to thank you for letting me know about Dr. Elliott. That's exciting for him."

"And it should be for you, too, as it narrows the field." An older man, even older than her dad, he guffawed. Maddie wondered if all old men guffawed. Perhaps it was part of aging.

"Yes, well, I'm sorry it's taken so long to get back to you, but I had a minor incident . . . I broke my foot and it's topsy-turvied my schedule." She had no idea what a broken foot would have to do with her not calling him sooner. She also had no idea why she'd said "topsy-turvied." Maybe it made her feel more like a creative academic. The same way she felt more professional after trading her grandmother's seersucker bathrobe for her tan skirt and one of her new tops.

"Also, I'm not in Green Hills," she said. "I'm on Martha's Vineyard visiting family." She loved that she'd thought to add the part about the island and family. As if it took her credibility up a notch.

Then she hated that she was trying to impress him.

"Will you return in time for the fall semester?" he asked.

"Yes, of course. I should be out of the cast and off crutches by then. Or, soon after."

"Good," he said. "Good."

She thanked him again and said she'd let him get back to work. Then she mentioned she was working on a new article that she hoped would be published in *Journalism Review.*

"Good," he repeated. "Good."

He did not need to know that she'd barely finished the outline.

"Thank you for calling," he said. "We'll see you soon." The "we," of course, meant the English department.

It wasn't until the call ended that Maddie realized he hadn't asked how she'd broken her foot or how she was feeling. Professor Don Jarvis was all business. He was a gifted instructor and a decent department chair; what he lacked in warm fuzzies, he made up for in the classroom with his vivid lectures and keen way of listening to his students' ideas. His classes filled quickly.

Being around him made Maddie feel successful, too. She'd always liked that. Now, she was no longer sure.

For the rest of the day, she couldn't get motivated.

Owen called, but she didn't answer. She was not in the mood for him.

Lisa phoned and said not to worry, she'd pick up dinner for her.

Maddie thought about calling her father and telling him about her conversation with Don Jarvis. But she wasn't ready to talk to him yet. And he might not be ready to talk to her.

She thought about calling the Vineyard Inn and telling Francine she was going to have lunch with Rex tomorrow. But she didn't do that, either.

She wondered if she was depressed, if her worlds were on a fast-moving collision course and she wasn't sure which way to turn.

After wallowing for another hour, she changed back into her nightgown and went back to bed. If she couldn't run, she might as well take another nap.

With the noon sun warming the cottage, she fell asleep quickly. And dreamed of her grandmother again. But this time, Grandma Nancy was lying on the ground, the wampum necklace dangling from her throat, her head split open on the corner of the granite slab.

Lisa woke Maddie up by shouting through the window that dinner was there. She brought the vanilla frappe, but instead of the fish sandwich, she offered a lobster roll.

"Mickey brought home half a dozen. He got them at a fundraiser for one of the old salt guys who died last week. We had extra, so it's our treat. And it comes with Cape Cod chips, which are the best."

Maddie smiled through her cobwebs as she eased back into life. She asked Lisa if she could sit for a minute and chat.

After arranging the roll and chips on a plate for Maddie, Lisa sat across from her. "So, how're you doing?" She didn't mention the shabby seersucker robe Maddie had donned again.

"I'm fine. I think the foot's getting better every day." There was no point in sharing needless information. "And thanks so much for this," she said, biting into her dinner.

"Happy to help. So, now that you've seen the doctor, have you made any . . . plans?"

"I'm trying to. My son should be here this weekend. I'd like to have a memorial service for my grandmother while he's here."

Lisa nodded but did not interrupt.

"Evelyn suggested I invite people from the tribe; I'm meeting with Joe about that tomorrow." She crunched a chip. Then she was ready to say what was really on her mind.

"I hate to ask you to remember this," she said, "but I'm haunted by how my grandmother died. Have you wondered any more about whether it was an accident?"

Lisa looked at her with one of those deer-in-the-headlights, just-seen-a-ghost stares. "Um . . . actually . . . I've been trying not to think about it. It was so upsetting. . . ."

Oddly, Lisa seemed more upset now than when she'd first told Maddie what happened.

"I'm sorry," Maddie responded, "but it's taking forever for Brandon to get the death certificate. I keep wondering if it's because the medical examiner, or whoever does that, is suspicious about what happened. Like maybe he's doing extensive testing or something."

Lisa was no longer looking at Maddie but at her hands. She started weaving her fingers in and out.

"Oh, Maddie, it really was just like they said, that she hit her head and bled out. Pay no attention to my stupid rambling. I was trying to make sense of her dying, hoping there was someone I could blame. But I honestly can't imagine why anyone would harm her. She was a nice old lady." Then she stood up. "I'm sorry, but I just remembered I left the kids alone with Mickey. Which isn't a great idea when he's been working all day. Sometimes he falls asleep by mistake. You know?"

Maddie studied her a couple of seconds, then nodded. "Well, please thank him again for the lobster, and thank you for getting the frappe. If you bring me my purse, I'll reimburse you. . . ."

By that time Lisa was at the front door. "No," she said. "I told you. Our treat!" She smiled a smile that looked terribly phony. Then she waved, the screen door closing behind her.

And Maddie was left with an uneasy feeling that Lisa either was still too upset about not having found Nancy sooner . . . or she, like others, was holding something back.

Chapter 21

At some point either late at night or early in the morning, Brandon sent a text: *Saw that you called. Will def be on-island this wknd. Talk then.* That was it.

Maddie had slept late—which seemed unbelievable with all that was happening—so when she got up, there was no time to reply. She needed to get ready for her date that wasn't really a date. Not that she could be sure what a date actually was. The last one she'd had—a year or more ago—was with a guy named Norm Connors, who was so quiet she'd felt compelled to keep a conversation going. Thankfully, they went out for dinner, when chewing reduced the chance to politely speak; then they attended a play where the actors did all the talking. But the driving from place to place, the sitting while waiting for menus and again before the theater lights dimmed, were unnerving. By the time she got home, she was catatonic.

She was fairly sure Rex would be a more animated companion. As an added bonus, he most likely did not have a wife and kids because, on an island, dating another woman would certainly be noticed.

She checked the clock; she needed to forget her dating

mishaps and get a move on, because putting the plastic bag over her cast, showering, then removing the darn thing while not allowing water to seep in, was time-consuming.

Managing to shower, dry off, and dress in her grandmother's skirt and wampum necklaces, she had enough time left to dry and fix her hair.

He knocked on the door exactly at noon. *Eight bells*, Maddie thought with a smile.

"Great skirt" was the first thing he said when she opened the door.

"Thanks. It's bizarre how a silly cast on one's leg can limit a wardrobe."

He smiled. He looked nice. He was in what must be a no-iron, short-sleeved pale blue shirt that was tucked into knee-length denim shorts; he wore a woven belt that looked handmade. Maddie wondered if the belt was Wampanoag. Or . . . was Rex? She decided that, though it would be nice, it didn't matter. Then she hobbled to the table for her purse, and he escorted her out the back door.

"The *back* door?" she asked.

"Trust me," he said.

Right or wrong, she did.

He led her up the hill through the backyard; he said there was no need to walk down the hill on all that shifting sand. She walked beside him, curious. As they reached the larger, now unlocked, empty shed, he guided her around the back to an almost hidden dirt-packed path. Maddie took one careful step at a time as they cut through a grove of scrub pines. After about twenty or thirty feet, the trees parted and a small, open area appeared. A silver pickup sat there.

"I don't believe it," Maddie said. "For the past week I've been hobbling down the hill, terrified I'd fall, when all along, there was a parking space on level ground right here."

"Not exactly," Rex replied. "I actually hauled in a heavy equipment roller late last night. It was dark, so it was tough, but . . . voilà. An accessible parking lot."

She didn't believe him for a second. "How thoughtful of you."

"I was afraid the noise would wake you up." He guided her to the truck.

"So," she said, as he helped her into the cab, "in addition to being a chef, owning a restaurant, and constructing parking lots in the middle of the night, you're also a comedian."

"Yeah. I learned everything I know from Bill Murray. He has a house here, you know. He comes into the restaurant from time to time."

"Seriously?"

"Yup. Except the part about me learning anything from him. I'm not sure he knows my name. Oh, and the part about me chopping down trees, hauling out stumps, and hard-packing the dirt last night? That's not true, either. The rest is, though."

Maddie laughed.

Closing the passenger door, Rex rounded the truck and jumped in on the other side. And Maddie knew she'd been right: Rex Winsted was definitely not Norm Connors.

"Almost there," he said.

Maddie knew they'd been heading north, probably toward West Tisbury. She had no idea what, if any, restaurants were there.

"I've got all day," she said, then frowned. "Actually, I have to be home by four thirty."

"And I have to be back in Edgartown before then. But we have plenty of time."

He turned down a narrow, secondary road. Gray stone

walls bordered the sides; hefty trunks of tall trees—towering, stately oaks, perhaps? Curvy, knotty chestnuts?—shaded the green meadows beyond. Clusters of flowers sprung up here and there—lavender-thistle-topped stalks were sprinkled along the roadside, delicate pink blossoms poked their heads from between the rocks, deep red trumpets sprouted between the tree trunks.

Maddie was often shy on a first date, which she decided this really was. But it felt different with Rex. Their conversation was comfortable, not forced. Maybe her guard was down because she felt no pressure; after all, she'd be leaving the island soon. There was no need to obsess over whether he was relationship material.

Finally, he slowed the truck and pulled into a paved lot, big enough only for two or three vehicles. Surprisingly, no one else was there.

"Wait here," he said, as he turned off the ignition and got out.

She heard rattling sounds from the bed of the pickup. Then he was at the passenger door. A large backpack was slung over one shoulder.

"Your Majesty," he said. With a sweeping gesture, he revealed a wheelchair parked next to him. "We shall now exit you from the motorized vehicle and into a manual one that I'll have to push."

Maddie laughed again. How could she not?

After he helped her get seated, the chair began to wheel, and she was delightfully free from the crutches. They headed toward what looked like another packed-dirt path through more trees. And then an opening appeared; straight ahead was the blue sea. Even better, there was a wood-plank boardwalk. Rex deftly steered the wheelchair onto it, and less than a minute later, they were at the beach.

Setting down the backpack, he pulled out a blanket and spread it on the sand. Then he helped Maddie out of the wheelchair and onto a folding beach chair that he'd strapped to his back. Returning to his pack, he pulled out refrigerator containers, plates and paper cups, utensils and bottles of iced tea. While he staged the production, neither of them spoke.

Then he brushed his hands together, sat on the blanket, looked at her, and grinned.

"Welcome to my portable beach restaurant. Today is opening day . . . I'm thinking of franchising it. Are you interested?"

"How can I resist? You've thought of everything. But I'm sorry, I already have a job." Which led to a discussion about her career.

They talked and talked while Rex arranged small pink crab cakes; seared scallop sliders; green salad with feta cheese, cranberries, and an array of herbs; roasted fingerling potatoes; and a mix of grape tomatoes, mozzarella, and basil. He served her the plate, a napkin, and utensils. Then he poured a cup of the iced tea and secured it in the sand next to her chair.

"This looks fabulous, Rex. But I'm not used to eating so much all at once." She almost giggled, then remembered she no longer was a teenager.

He waved off her comment. "Eat what you can."

"You've gone to so much trouble. . . ."

"Just another day at the office."

Once they started eating, their banter resumed. Again, it was comfortable, easy.

He asked more about her career, then about Rafe, then about her father. He asked her what Green Hills was like, and if she'd liked growing up where the only body of water was a river and an occasional freezing cold lake.

She laughed and asked him to please stop quizzing her

about her life because it wasn't terribly exciting. She said she wanted to know more about him.

"Oh," he said, "you might regret that."

A small twinge sparked in her heart; she recognized it as her guard moving into position now, ready to lock up her emotions the way her foot was locked into the stupid cast.

"Try me," she said.

"Well . . . ," he started slowly, either for effect or because he wasn't sure where to begin. "I was born and raised on Chappaquiddick, like almost a dozen generations before me. I have a sister named Taylor. I was a rambunctious kid." One side of his mouth lifted in a half smile. "The island offers adventurous boys lots of things to explore. I loved to race around Chappy, chasing innocent birds and four-legged critters, and I liked riding my bike all the way to Aquinnah. My father had a plot of land there where he built the cabin."

"Was he a Wampanoag?" Maddie asked. *There,* she thought, pleased that she'd asked.

"Nope. He won the land in the annual fishing derby in Edgartown."

A small piece of her was disappointed. "It sounds like you grew up as an outdoors kid."

"I did. Until I learned how to drive. That's when, from time to time, I spent a few nights at the Graybar Hotel. In Edgartown."

She frowned. "Did you work there?" She expected he'd say he worked in the kitchen, and that his passion for cooking had started there.

"Not really." The half smile returned. "The Graybar Hotel is a reverential name for a jail."

Maddie was startled. Was he serious?

"I got myself into a few scrapes back then," he continued. "Nothing serious. I think my father was trying to teach me a lesson. He knew all the cops, so he had them arrest me for things like chasing squirrels with a twenty-two pistol or speeding down Chappy's main road in January, when no one was around."

It was kind of funny, but Maddie wasn't sure if she should laugh. Instead, she said, "I'm surprised there's a jail here."

"They need a place to put miscreants like me. And ours is a classic. It was built in 1870, when Ulysses S. Grant was president. It still has some of the original, iron-bar doors with the giant lock and key. Which is why the name 'Graybar Hotel' is fitting."

She took another taste of the incredible crab cake. "Basically, then, you're an ex-con."

He nodded. "You haven't heard the half of it. My business partner can tell you an even juicier story that happened to me up in Boston. Not many people on the island know about that. For some reason, it didn't scare her off from fronting the money so I could buy the Lord James. You'd like her. Her name's Annie Sutton. She used to write best-selling mystery novels, until she got hooked into Hollywood, where she lives now and works as a screenwriter. She owns part of the Vineyard Inn, where Francine works. Anyway, we keep hoping that someday she'll move back."

Maddie couldn't tell if he had more than a business relationship with Annie Sutton, whoever she was. But because it was none of her business, she digressed to the ex-con part of his story. "I don't picture you as someone to be afraid of."

"You haven't seen my battle scars," he said in a sweet, endearing way.

Then she got him to move on to happy things, like how the restaurant was doing ("Terrific"), where he lived ("In an apartment above the shop"), and if there was anything about the island that he disliked ("*No*").

They ate; they talked about food, music, and films. They shared silence, too, as they lazed under the sun and watched the gentle waves. It was a perfect afternoon. Until Maddie's phone rang in the side pocket of the wheelchair, which was still up on the boardwalk.

"Your phone?" Rex asked.

She nodded and said she'd call whoever it was back, but he'd already hopped up and retrieved it for her. But by the time he handed it off, the call had gone to voice mail. It had been Rafe.

Quickly, Maddie called back.

"Hey, Mom," he said, "guess what? I just got on the ferry. I'm almost to Martha's Vineyard."

"Today?" she asked. "Now? But it's only Thursday."

"I got someone to take my place. I still have a couple of weeks left till I have to be in Amherst. So I figured why not surprise you? And stay there a few days? Anyway, the ferry docks in Vineyard Haven at three fifteen. If you can't pick me up, can I walk from here?"

More than a little ruffled, Maddie said she'd arrange a ride.

"Thanks, Mom. And by the way . . ."

She said he could tell her the rest later. She rang off and looked at Rex.

"How long does it take to get to the ferry terminal? I'm having such a good time and I hate to interrupt it . . . but my son's on the ferry, and I'd love to be there when it comes in."

Rex glanced at his watch, then swiftly started packing the leftover food. "He must be on the two thirty. If we shake a leg—oops, no offense—we can make it. Is he coming into Vineyard Haven or OB?"

"He said Vineyard Haven." She wasn't sure, but thought that OB stood for Oak Bluffs. Or Oaks Bluff. Something like that.

"It's closer, then. And after we get him, I'll run you both up to Menemsha."

Maddie frowned. "But you need to be in Edgartown at four."

He shook his head. "I'll make a call. Your family is more important than pan-seared halibut with lemon pepper sauce. That's the special for tonight." He winked.

And Maddie laughed. Again.

The drive took forever. On the way, Maddie called Joe and canceled their meeting. She perched on the edge of the seat; she frantically tried to sort out everything she wanted to tell Rafe. She almost forgot that Rex was next to her. They arrived at the Steamship Authority, just as she finished preparing her agenda.

But the boat wasn't there yet.

When Maddie had arrived over a week ago, she hadn't paid attention to the size of the crowd—unsure of where or how to get around on the big boat, she'd stayed in her car on the freight deck during the crossing. While waiting to disembark, she'd merely set her GPS for Grandma Nancy's address, then followed the car in front of her as they clunk-clunked down the ramp onto the pavement.

But as Rex found what he said was a miraculous parking space and she exited his pickup, the crowd made her feel terribly claustrophobic. But with her crutches firmly in place, she told Rex she'd be fine without the wheelchair and that she'd like to do this alone if he didn't mind waiting. He agreed and gestured toward an area where people with dogs on leashes and others wheeling suitcases were crammed together, either waiting to board or there to meet someone. Praying she'd stay upright, she thanked him, limped across the pavement and joined the masses.

Leaning on her left leg, her right one bent at the knee and dangling in the air the way CiCi's earrings dangled, Maddie waited. And waited. When she'd been standing all of four or five minutes, a man shouted, "Here she comes!"

Heads turned, voices hushed, and eyes, Maddie's included, riveted their gaze to the not-too-distant jetty where the big white ferry turned into the harbor, inching along so slowly it was barely leaving a wake.

Like others around her, Maddie couldn't help but smile.

Several minutes later, the boat bumped against the pier. Dockworkers in neon-yellow vests performed their mechanical routines—aligning, cranking, and hooking up all things that needed aligning, cranking, and hooking.

The herd then shifted to the left; a boat worker unlatched a heavy chain and signaled the vehicles to start departing. It was a rhythm Maddie figured was repeated many times every day, every month, of every year. But she also knew she shouldn't think about that now; her mind should be on Rafe, her 25 percent Indigenous son.

The crowd swayed again, this time drawing Maddie's attention to the side of the boat where another mass of people, dogs, and rolling suitcases were descending down an enormous angled ramp. Like many around her, she bobbed her head this way and that, hunting for Rafe.

And there he was!

In cargo shorts and an Amherst T-shirt, his step was as jaunty as his smile was big, as he was scoping the area, too, searching for her, his mom, the person who loved him the very most.

Making sure not to knock anyone with her crutches, she lifted one and waved it toward the tall, so-handsome boy approaching.

He reached the bottom of the ramp and saw her. Waving back, he laughed and turned his head as if telling the person behind him that he'd just seen his mom.

Her love for him began to swell . . . until she noticed that the person behind Rafe looked an awful lot like her ass of an ex-husband.

Chapter 22

Maddie's first instinct was to rush over to the pickup and tell Rex to leave without them, that she'd get a taxi. But she was hardly able to sprint on crutches, let alone across the lot where people were dodging the stream of vehicles parading off the freight deck.

Then, as her gaze gravitated back to the person who now ambled next to Rafe, her body stiffened, as if she'd become one of the life-size sculptures in the garden at Field Gallery on State Road.

"No," she whispered. "No, no, no."

"Mom!" Rafe called, weaving his way toward her, and rewarding her with a nice, big hug. "We made it! And I tried to warn you, but . . ." He offered a wry smile.

She looked over his shoulder.

Crap. It really was him.

She drilled her eyes into his. "I thought I made it clear that you aren't needed here."

Owen shrugged. And chuckled.

She wanted to lift her crutch again and jab him in the gut. Or lower. Instead, she turned to Rafe. "Honey," she said, carefully choosing her words, "would you please wait by the terminal? I need to speak with your father."

He winced, then stepped away, having received the message that his mom wasn't pleased.

"I get it," Owen said. "I'm not welcome. But our son thought it would be fun. You know, like a family vacation." His robin's-egg-blue eyes bored into her.

Maddie cursed herself for the years she'd wasted—before and after the divorce—pretending that she and Owen got along. She'd done it for Rafe's sake because she was a mother, and she supposed that's what mothers did. And fathers, too, she now knew. She also now knew that families often screwed things up despite their best intentions.

"It won't be fun," she said to Owen now. "For starters, I have too much to do, including having to negotiate every physical step I take. And I don't want to have to deal with playing nice in front of Rafe. Besides, there's no room for you at the cottage, and I doubt you'll find anywhere on the island to stay; rooms here have been booked for a year or more." She had no idea if that was true. "Please, Owen. Get back on the ferry."

He smirked. "I can't. We came in my car, which I left in Falmouth. If I go now, Rafe will have to drive your car back to Green Hills, so you'll have to leave this place sooner than you might have planned because he has responsibilities and a life back home. From what I hear, so do you."

Rafe also must have told him about the tenure possibility.

People walking past them—some strolling, having just arrived, others hurrying to catch the boat—were giving them lots of elbow room, keeping a safe distance from the negativity they must be exuding. Maddie was embarrassed; she despised public displays of anything. Not to mention that Rex was in his truck, hopefully unable to read their lips.

"It's hard to believe our son will start his senior year at Amherst," Owen said, straightening the collar of his Armani linen shirt, one of his favorite summer go-tos; he once told her that though the Armani was costly, the price would be higher if it had run-of-the-mill breast pockets.

"It seems important to Rafe to spend quality time with both his parents," he kept yammering. "Who knows where he'll land after graduation?"

She knew that Owen was annoyed with Rafe for not yet having picked a grad school. She wondered if her ex feared that his plan to bring their son into his business might now be threatened thanks to her inheritance. Unless he got his hands on it.

"Excuse me." A woman in a neon vest suddenly stood next to them. "You'll have to move. You're too close to the vehicle queue, and we need to load the three forty-five."

Adjusting the crutches, Maddie said to Owen, "Go get Rafe. I'm in a silver pickup in the lot." She clumsily turned away but held her chin up high as she made her way back to Rex, hoping that the drama wouldn't ruin her friendship with the nicest man she'd met in years.

Maddie didn't think it would be amusing to introduce Rex to Rafe and Owen. But when Owen didn't seem to know what to say beyond muttering, "Nice to meet you," followed by looking at his shoes—Gucci loafers, naturally—she found it hilarious. What was even better was when they agreed there was only room in the truck's cab for three of them.

"You'll have to ride in back," she said to Owen. "With the suitcases and the wheelchair." She wished that—like with the old farmer who'd driven her from Evelyn's house—sheep were back there, too. One might have drooled on the Armani and the Guccis.

Perhaps embarrassed for his father, Rafe said he'd climb into the back, too, so Maddie would have more room, what with her cast.

Once everyone was settled, Rex gave Maddie a side glance and a half smile, then backed out of the parking space and drove off the lot.

"My son's excited to be here," she said. "But I think his father smells my pending inheritance. His wife's a big spender, and he has twin daughters who already are expensive."

Rex nodded. "He has a lucrative career?" So the restaurateur and chef knew designer attire when he saw it, though Maddie supposed there hadn't been a lot of that at the Gray-bar Hotel.

"He's in finance," she said flatly.

"Well, then," he said, "chances are he won't need to steal any of my tools back there."

Maddie tried unsuccessfully to suppress a laugh.

Then Rex reached over and put his hand on hers. "Guys like that don't scare me."

She turned her hand over and lightly squeezed his. "Thanks. Because he scares me sometimes. But please don't tell him." With Rex sitting next to her, she felt better. Her father had always remained neutral about Owen, so, for once, Maddie had someone on her side. Physically, maybe as well as literally. It was also nice that neither she nor Rex needed further conversation on the subject.

When they reached the secret turn-off that led to the pine grove behind Grandma's cottage, he looked at her and said, "You have my number. Call me if you need the cavalry. I can drum up a battalion of musclemen in a heartbeat."

She said that though that sounded sexist, she would definitely call. Then she thanked him for an unforgettable afternoon and, hesitating only for a second, she kissed him on the cheek. He gave her a sweet look that let her know he had liked it.

"And by the way," he added, "take the wheelchair. It might come in handy for a while."

He parked the truck and walked around the back. In the side-view mirror, Maddie saw Rafe take out the wheelchair and set it on the ground. Then he and Owen jumped over the side of the truck, Rafe much more adeptly than his father.

Rex stood still, watching the male routine, not needing to fluff his plumage. Once Rafe had handed Owen the crutches and helped Maddie into the wheelchair and Maddie directed them toward the path that abutted the yard, Rex walked toward them. He was toting the insulated bag that had held their picnic lunch.

"Wait," he said, "take this. There are lots of leftovers and, even better, two hefty servings of tiramisu that we didn't get to eat."

Maddie wanted to kiss him again, this time on the mouth.

Owen stared at the ground.

Rafe reached out and took the bag. "Thanks, Rex. That's awesome." He slung it over his shoulder, said thanks again and goodbye to the big, bald stranger, and wheeled his mom in the direction that she told him.

And Owen tagged along behind them like a cocker spaniel.

"What's with the skirt?" Owen asked. "Not exactly your style, is it?"

Maddie set down her crutches and sat at the table. She really, really wanted to tell him to shut up. "It was given to

me. It's easier to wear a skirt while I'm wearing the cast."
Amazingly, her voice was calm.

"Rafe, honey," she said, "why don't you put your things
in the back bedroom? The front room has boxes on the bed
and piles on the floor. I've been getting organized in order to
get rid of things."

"This place is cool," Rafe said, looking around. "Why are
you getting rid of stuff? Was this where your relative lived?"

Owen glared at her.

Still, Maddie didn't want to tell Rafe all she had to tell him
while Owen was breathing the same air.

"Honey, please," she said to her son, "give us a few minutes, okay?"

He nodded and went down the hall.

And Owen paced.

Over the years since the divorce, the number of times that
mother and father had been in the same room—without their
son or her father to maintain civility—were few.

"I honestly don't want you here," Maddie told her ex
now. She kept her voice low, though she supposed Rafe
could hear through the thin walls. "Please, Owen. Leave."
How many times would she have to say it?

"Not until you tell me what's going on. If you do, I'll go.
And not before. In spite of lame threats like men with shot-
guns. Or bald guys who seem to think that they're in charge."

She sighed and closed her eyes. She was tired, so tired. It
had been such a wonderful day, up until Owen had walked
toward her.

"Rafe," she said, raising her voice, "you can come out
now. We need to talk." This wasn't how she'd planned it.
But sooner or later, Owen would find out about her grandmother. Right now, if it would get him to leave, it would be

worth it. She would not, however, tell all of it as long as he was there.

"Great," Rafe said as he rounded the corner and flopped onto the sofa. "'Cuz I could hear every word, even when you were whispering."

Maddie would have laughed if her mind wasn't knotted up, trying to decide what and what not to say.

"Owen," she said, "please sit. Your pacing is irritating. I'll tell you both what I know. After that, only Rafe is allowed to ask questions."

Her ex-husband huffed, then strutted to the chair that matched the faded blue sofa and plunked. He paid no attention to the handwoven blanket that slid to the floor between him and the wall.

Rafe sat up straight, propped his elbows on his knees, and leaned forward, eager to listen.

Maddie squared her shoulders, determined to keep eye contact with her son and not his father.

"When I was ten, my father thought my grandmother had died," she began. "But she hadn't." There was no need to mention it had been a lie; she didn't want Rafe to be angry with her father, too. "My grandmother had drifted away from us; she'd been devastated when my mother had been killed."

"She was hit by a car," Rafe said, as if reminding himself.

Maddie nodded and kept her attention on him. She had no idea what Owen was doing.

Next, she talked about the letter from her grandmother's attorney, leaving out that her father had sent the first one back. She said that, in her will, her grandmother left her what few things she had: "Boxes of memories and this cottage." She would save the information about the other properties until after Owen left. She glanced around the room. "As you can see, there's not much to the place. The last time I was here was the summer I was five. Mother died shortly after that."

Suddenly, a flashback of a policeman at the door leaped into Maddie's mind. For some bizarre reason, the door wasn't back home in Green Hills but right there at the cottage. And the blue lights of his cruiser were blinking through squatty, scrub oaks and not through the tall pine trees in Green Hills.

She shook her head, trying to push away the image that made no sense, as her mother had been killed on a dark road back home in the Berkshires, not on the Vineyard.

"My grandmother was a basket maker whose work had built a decent following," she continued, struggling to regain her demeanor. "Her husband was a fisherman who died at sea when my mother was a girl. I don't know much about him, but I found a few pictures that I set aside for us, so we'll have something from that side of our family."

A loud yawn came from the chair by the window. Maddie ignored it.

"Grandma Nancy—that's what I called her—wrote that she wanted to be cremated. She asked if I'd scatter her ashes on the beach at sunset. She can't be cremated until her death certificate arrives, so it's good that I'm still here, though I hadn't planned to be. Anyway, it's also why I wanted you to come. So you can learn a few things about your roots."

She smiled at her son. "That's about it. Any questions?"

"Why didn't you know she was still alive?"

She shook her head again. "I'll never know. Maybe she was traumatized when my mother died, and it was too painful for her to be with me." There was no reason not to say that.

"Was she sick? Your grandmother?"

"She was eighty-nine, and as far as I know, she was still in good health, which I was happy to hear. So, no, she wasn't sick. She fell. The front door has three granite slabs that are steps. She tripped over one, landed, and hit her head on the corner of another one. One of the neighbors found her. But she already was gone." Her heart felt as if someone had squeezed it. The image of the policeman flashed again. She gripped the edges of the table for support.

"No surprise she fell," Owen barked. "Those so-called steps were put there by an amateur. Totally unsafe."

Maddie summoned all her strength not to erupt. She resumed focusing on Rafe. "I'm sorry I didn't tell you when I first found out. And I'm sorry you never got to meet her." Then she turned to Owen. "Would you please get me a tissue? They're in the bathroom. Down the hall."

With a look that now was smug as well as bored, Owen pushed himself up from the chair and meandered from the room. She stopped herself from asking why he'd insisted on being there when it was obvious he was not really interested.

Rafe stood up, went to her, and put his arm around her. "I'm so sorry, Mom. And I'm really sorry you didn't have her all the years you could have."

Maddie nodded her thanks. "She would have adored you." She didn't know if that were true, but she wanted to give Rafe some happy thoughts about Grandma Nancy. There was no harm in that.

Owen returned with the tissue box and handed it to Maddie. Then he spoke to Rafe.

"By the looks of this shack, son, I think we can agree it's a good thing I've worked hard for you to have everything you wanted while you were growing up."

Maddie had to look away. She wondered if Owen would have become whatever he thought he was if they'd stayed together, if he hadn't gone on to marry the material girl of one of the smallest towns in the state.

"Because I respect your mother's wishes, I won't ask her questions," he continued prattling. "But please find out what she intends to do with this place. It's worth a small fortune not because it's nice"—he chuckled again, surveying the room—"but because of the location. It's not waterfront, but it does have a small water view. And second best is still pretty good here in the land of dough-re-mi."

Rafe stared at his father as if he didn't know him. Then he looked back at Maddie.

"Mom? Isn't it too early to decide what to do? Like, wouldn't it be more respectful to at least wait until after you scatter her ashes?"

Maddie smiled. "Yes, honey, it is. And it's what I intend to do."

He nodded and said, "Good."

Owen folded his arms across his chest.

"But for now," she said, "I'm exhausted. And my foot is throbbing again. How about if the two of you walk down to the beach? Have some alone time, while I take a nap? And, Owen, when I wake up, please be gone. Rafe can use my car to drive you to the boat. When he wants to leave the island, he can take my car then, too, with or without me. I can make my own way home when I am ready." There was no need to add that before going back to Green Hills, she'd have to reconcile with her father.

She turned to Rafe again. "Honey, my car keys are in my purse. The key to the cottage is on the same ring. Please lock the front door on your way out."

It wasn't until they'd left and Maddie had changed into her nightgown and stretched out on her grandmother's bed that she had a disturbing thought. When Owen had come to the cottage the first time, and again when Rex had brought them there, he'd entered through the back door. How had he deduced that the granite slabs at the front door were unsafe?

Then she remembered that the first time he'd been there he'd said he tried the front door, but it had been locked.

She closed her eyes and wondered when she'd stop wondering if everyone she met could have caused Grandma Nancy's death. And yet, her intuition still hinted that something was not as it seemed. Like her vision of the policeman at the cottage door.

Chapter 23

In spite of the squeaky springs, Maddie didn't wake up until long after dark. She checked her phone: nine forty-five. She stayed in bed, listening. Then she heard what sounded like paper rustling. Unless it was the mouse, someone else was in the cottage. Hopefully, it was a friend, not foe.

Then she thought, *Rafe!* Of course it would be him.

Pushing back the covers, she swung her legs to one side until her feet touched the floor. Then she pushed herself up to a sitting position and grabbed the crutches. But as she pulled them toward her, one slipped from her hand and bounced onto the floor.

She let out a groan just as her son appeared in the doorway, silhouetted by the hall light.

"Mom? Do you need help?"

"Believe it or not, that's the first time I've dropped one of these."

He picked it up and, without waiting to be asked, he moved closer and hoisted her up. His well-muscled arms were a sad reminder that her little boy's thin limbs had now been lost to manhood, no doubt accelerated by years of rowing crew and cleaning the banks of the Hoosic River.

Holding her upright with one arm, he handed her the crutches. "Here," he said with a grin. "Don't drop 'em."

She was grateful that Owen's genes played a minimal role in his personality.

Knowing Rafe would help her if she couldn't get up on her own, she sat in the cushy living room chair by the window. Once he was settled on the sofa, she asked if he was hungry; he said he and his dad had dinner at the Homeport, the sit-down restaurant by the water.

"I wanted to ask you to join us, but Dad said it wasn't a good idea. I'm sorry he upset you, Mom. I never should have let him come with me."

"It's not your fault. I expect he'll harass me until your great-grandmother's estate is settled." It was the first time she'd admitted to him that things between his parents were not amicable.

"If it helps, he called a cab right after we ate. He said I didn't need to drive him, that the last ferry was leaving at nine thirty and he wanted to be on it."

Though she would have loved to say, "Thank God," she simply asked if he'd like to split a tiramisu with her.

Never one to say no to desserts, Rafe got up, opened the refrigerator and removed the tiramisu. He cut the slice in half, found two plates, and served her. He told her he'd emptied Rex's cooler before she woke up, and that he'd snuck into the front bedroom and taken a couple of boxes out of there and brought them into the living room. He said he looked through them, and that one had lots of pictures and newspaper clippings.

"I found lots of Indian stuff," he commented. "Is there a tribe on the island?"

And Maddie knew it was time to tell him the rest.

"One of the reasons I was kind of nasty to your dad is because I need to talk with you about something. Just you and me. Not even with your grandfather."

He took a forkful of the creamy dessert. "Sounds serious."

"It's not a bad thing, honey. But, yes, it's serious." She paused, also took a bite of tiramisu, then looked out the front window at the diamond stars shimmering in the night sky.

And she told him.

She told him that her inheritance wasn't only the cottage but also the two other parcels of land that were worth a lot of money. She told him about her mother, her grandmother, and what little she had learned about her grandfather. She told him they'd all been Wampanoags, and that she'd only found out last week. She told him it meant that she was half Native American. And that he, too, had Wampanoag blood, 25 percent.

She waited for his reaction. His eyes were fixed on hers, his hand still gripping his fork.

"So that's it," she said. "It's the whole story as I know it to date."

He set down the fork and put the plate next to him. "That's incredible."

She nodded. "It is. All these years, I thought I was half Iberian. A descendant of a Portuguese fisherman."

"Kind of a shock, huh?"

"That's one word for it."

"But why didn't anyone tell you? Didn't Grandpa know?"

So she told him that, too. "I don't think anyone was trying to be malicious. When your grandparents got married they moved to Green Hills, where he was already teaching. Apparently my mother had planned to explain it all to me when she thought I'd be able to understand better, but then the accident happened. Grandpa also said that once I was told, she was going to share her culture with the people in Green Hills."

"Wow," he said again. He leaned forward as he'd done earlier, eager to absorb every morsel. "So where do we go from here? Is there like a next step or something we should do to let the tribe know that we're here?"

Maddie grinned. Her son was wonderful.

"You have the kindness of a Native American," she said. "And I've been wondering if your affinity to care about the environment and all its 'critters,' as you like to call both humans and animals, also comes from your twenty-five percent." Then she had a thought. "Rafe, if you want to find out more about the tribe, about their background, their traditions, or anything, I know the perfect man for you to meet."

"The guy you were with today?"

She hadn't expected that. "No," she said. "No, that's Rex. He has a cabin not far from here, and he owns a fabulous restaurant in Edgartown, but . . ."

She realized that, like Owen, she was about to start prattling. She had no idea how to shape Rafe's opinion of Rex. Or why it mattered.

"Anyway," she cut off her rambling thoughts, "not him. But your grandmother had a brother, a half brother, actually. His name is Joe Thurston. He lives on tribal land, and I think he'll be more than glad to spend time with you. I don't know how long you can stay, but I think he'll make you a priority."

Rafe smiled. "Cool. And like I said, I don't have to be back to school for two more weeks."

Though the hour was late, Maddie called Joe.

Then she and Rafe stayed up until long past midnight, going through her grandmother's mementos. Before going to bed, Maddie turned Isaac's portrait to the wall so Joe wouldn't catch a glimpse.

Later, she slept peacefully.

And at nine o'clock Friday morning, Joe knocked on the front door. At least it wasn't five thirty. And Maddie was already up and dressed.

Joe and Rafe shook hands. Then Joe leaned closer and gave Rafe a hug.

"Nancy would be so amped," Joe said, as if he were Rafe's age. Then he asked how Rafe felt about kayaks and if he wanted to paddle around the ponds.

Rafe nodded enthusiastically. "Every summer I work with a crew that helps keep our river clean."

Joe said, "You're one of us, all right." His eyes twinkled the way the stars had done the night before. Maddie wondered if her grandmother's spirit was at work.

Making her way into the kitchen, she left Joe and Rafe to talk while she limped around on one crutch, repacking leftovers from her picnic with Rex and putting them into the cooler. Surely the kayakers would like sustenance while they were out to sea. It was marvelous that already they didn't sound like strangers to each other. On a spiritual level, perhaps they weren't.

Finally, she gave Rafe the cooler with the crab cakes, lobster sliders, mozzarella salad, and two bottles of iced tea that Rex hadn't opened.

"Make sure you wear the life vest," she instructed.

"I know, Mom," he said with an eye roll that sadly reminded her of Owen. Then he looked back to Joe. "When I'm at the river, we use both kayaks and canoes. So I know my way around water. Fresh water, anyway."

Maddie grinned, unashamed of having slipped into her Mom role. "Okay," she said, "you're set to leave. Do you have sunblock?"

His eyes rolled again.

Joe said, "I keep it in the kayaks. For my fair-skinned guests."

With that, the males jaunted off on their journey into Rafe's heritage. Her son seemed to be walking on a cloud.

Cloud nine, in fact. She pressed her fingers to her mouth, holding back joyful mom tears.

Buoyed by Rafe's happiness, Maddie returned to the mess they'd made the night before while rifling through her grandmother's papers. She reorganized it into the three piles in less than an hour. Not long after that, Brandon called.

"You've probably had breakfast," he said when she picked up the phone.

"Are you kidding? I haven't had time. My son's finally here—well, he's not with me right now. He's off on an adventure with his uncle Joe. His twice-removed great-great-half-uncle, I think?"

He chuckled. "Things are happening fast for you. How's the foot?"

"Better. Sometimes I even forget I'm lugging a concrete abutment around." Today, that was true. "How's your mother?"

"She's well enough to be helping out at the artisan fair today."

"Good for her. She wasn't having a great time the other day."

"Yeah," he said solemnly. "That happens sometimes." Then he perked up again. "So how about breakfast? Or call it brunch? Jeremy had to stay in the city, so I'm on my own. I was hoping you'd want to ride up to the cliffs. The restaurant up there has great omelets. Or you can get my favorite—two fish cakes with poached eggs, salsa, and melted cheese. And it comes with a view that can't be beat."

"Sounds fabulous." She didn't have the heart to say she'd been there with her father. Or that it seemed like this whole trip was designed around good food.

"Can you be ready by ten thirty?"

She said she was ready anytime.

In what felt like no time at all, she and Brandon were on the deck at the restaurant, sitting by the railing atop the Gay Head Cliffs, gazing out over the water toward Cuttyhunk. Brandon explained that "Cutty," as it was often called, was the most western island of the Elizabeth Islands, and that only a handful of people lived there year-round. The rest of the Elizabeths were privately owned by one family and were mostly populated by birds and flowers. As with every day that she'd been there, Maddie was enchanted.

Once the food arrived—Maddie chose blue-corn pancakes, because they sounded like one of the tribal recipes in her grandmother's collection—she brought up the business of Grandma Nancy's ashes.

"I can't believe we're still waiting for the death certificate," Brandon said. "My mother says because it's summer, people are on vacation. I guess it makes sense. But I mostly deal in real estate, so some of this is new to me. The death certificate comes from the medical examiner who works out of the regional office in Sandwich. George somebody, according to my mother. Apparently he either hasn't determined the cause of death . . . or he hasn't had the time to work on her case yet. My guess is it's the latter."

At least she now knew something. She hated to ask the next question but really wanted to know.

"Brandon? How long can they keep a body before it has to be cremated?" At least by saying "a body" and not "Grandma Nancy's body," she hoped she hadn't sounded insensitive.

He shuffled his fork around the plate. "With cremations, they have to wait until they've signed off on the paperwork. If it takes weeks, they have ways to keep the body preserved. Because, unlike with burials, once the cremation happens, there's no going back to double-check."

And then came the big question lingering in Maddie's mind. "Do you think the delay is because he suspects foul play?" There. She'd said it.

Brandon looked surprised, then slowly said, "Not that I know of." It was obvious he hadn't considered the possibility. "Why?"

She tried to brush it off. "I don't know. I guess I'm just still trying to make sense of all that's happened. And why it's taking so damned long."

He seemed appeased. "I'm afraid it's a reflection of our times. Aside from short-staffing almost everywhere, these days some autopsies—unattended deaths require one—aren't even handled in person, so to speak. The ME can use photographs, consult the person's medical records, and follow other clues to come up with the cause. And the fact that Nancy was almost ninety will most likely be added to the mix."

"So he might never see her . . . body?"

"Maybe not."

"How bizarre."

"I thought so, too, when I first heard it. But I've been told that with today's technology, it's become a solid method for learning cause of death."

"And probably saves money."

"For the state, yup. But I think if they do suspect foul play, they do a full-blown, old-fashioned autopsy."

"No matter how they do it, I hope they get it right. And soon." She was glad she'd at least addressed the possibility.

They ate in silence.

Then Brandon asked, "Maddie? Do you honestly think someone killed your grandmother?"

The words "killed your grandmother" jolted her. According to Lisa, no one on the island would have wanted to kill the "nice old lady." Would CiCi have killed her to profit from the commission she'd get selling the property? Or what about Lisa? Could she have somehow hoped to cash in on Grandma Nancy's death? But she'd known about Maddie all along, so she wouldn't have expected the property would go to her.

Unless . . . unless Lisa and CiCi were in cahoots. Maybe they were a team . . . with Lisa's job to convince Maddie to hire CiCi for a percent of the agent's commission. Judging by the value, even a small percent would be significant to a lobster-man and an administrator at the town hall. And it would surely buy their son, Charlie, a set of braces.

And Maddie couldn't discount Owen. Had he seen the first letter her father sent back? It would be like him to have steamed it open . . . and would account for why he seemed to know more than she thought he could by eavesdropping on Rafe's side of her phone conversation with him.

She ate a bit more, thought a bit more. Then she decided that her ex didn't have the guts to kill anyone. He often acted like a bully, but in reality, he was consumed with trying to convince people that he was the star of the show, any show. Murder would not achieve that.

"Maddie?" Brandon waved a hand in front of her face.

"Oh. Sorry. I know I'm overthinking this. But I feel like I'm not getting the whole story about much of anything, so I'm grasping at straws."

He laughed.

She finished her pancakes while trying not to think.

But suddenly . . .

She gulped.

She wondered about Joe. Had his comment that some people had donated their land in Aquinnah back to the tribe been preplanned? Could that soft-spoken, gentle man who'd built her hobbit house have killed Grandma Nancy? The same man who right now was with . . . *Rafe?*

It felt as if a thousand fireworks exploded in her mind. She leaped out of her chair. She teeter-tottered (as Evelyn had warned her could happen) on her cast. She grabbed for the wooden railing, then lost her balance, flipped over the rail, and began to tumble down the Gay Head Cliffs.

It happened so fast, Brandon couldn't catch her.

Chapter 24

Buzzing, humming, and beeping buzzed and hummed and beeped in Maddie's head.

"Her eyes are blinking!" A man's voice was familiar, but she couldn't place it. It was drowned out by the buzzing and the rest. Then, between blinks, she saw a blurry image bend down close to her where she was . . . lying down?

Where was she?

What was going on?

"Get the nurse!" the voice shouted. "Hurry!"

She wanted to open her eyes and keep them open, but it was exhausting. So she closed them again.

"Mom? Wake up!"

Her eyes opened that time. She tried to smile at her son.

"Hi, honey," she said. "What happened? Where am I?"

He sat on the edge of the bed, his sturdy shoulders slumping just a little.

Which was when she realized she was in a bed and had tubes snaking out of her.

"You're in the hospital, Mom."

Then two nurses rushed in.

"What happened?" she muttered again.

The nurses calmly moved Rafe out of the way and went to either side of the bed. One nurse had a smiley mouth painted on her mask; she checked a monitor and tap-tapped the screen of the tablet she was holding. The other nurse aimed a beam of light into Maddie's eyes.

"You had a fall," the nurse with the painted-on smile said. "At the cliffs up in Aquinnah. Do you remember?"

No, Maddie did not.

"That's okay," the nurse said kindly. "Can you tell me the last thing you do remember?"

The other nurse flicked off the beam of light and entered something into her tablet.

Maddie closed her eyes again, trying to remember . . . anything. Then . . . slowly . . . a vision formed.

"Brandon," she said. "I was with Brandon. My attorney. We were having brunch. Blue-corn . . ." Her words trailed off. She was so tired. Then a thought jarred her back to life. "Is he okay? Please, tell me!"

"Brandon's fine. You lost your footing, fell over the fence onto the cliffs, and rolled partway down. A clump of shrubbery stopped you. You sustained a head injury. Brandon rescued you. He didn't wait for the medics; he climbed over the fence and carried you to his car. I'm told he drove like a bat out of hell to the EMTs in Chilmark, which saved time. Your doctor—Brenda Wilson—will be in to see you soon." She squeezed Maddie's hand. "Welcome back."

Maddie blinked again, in disbelief.

The nurses left.

"Mom," Rafe said as he went back to her bedside and stooped to kiss her cheek. "I was so scared." Tears welled in his eyes.

"Oh, honey," she said, "I'm sorry. But see? I'm fine now. At least, I think I'm fine." She forced the widest grin that she could force. "I don't think anything hurts."

Rafe sat down again. "So the guy who saved you was your attorney. Geez, Mom, first I meet this guy named Rex. Now there's Brandon. What the heck have you been doing on this island?" He tried hard to laugh again.

"Brandon is going to settle the estate," she managed to remember. "Am I really okay? I'm sorry if I scared you."

"You really are okay. Or you will be. When I got here, Brandon and his mother were still here. She said you almost got airlifted to Boston, but your CT scans came back better than they expected. While you were asleep the ortho doctor gave you a new cast. But you avoided surgery."

Again, she thought.

"When did they put the new cast on?" she asked.

"Not until the guy sawed off the first one," Rafe said.

"How thoughtful of him. Now, can you please tell me what time it is?"

"Almost one o'clock. In the afternoon. Sunday afternoon."

"I've been asleep two whole days?"

Rafe bit his lip the way she often did. "You've been in a coma, Mom. They called it 'medically asleep.' Sedated."

Wow. If she'd ever wondered how it felt to lose two days from her life, she now knew: it felt like nothing. As if she'd passed over a skewed international date line—twice—where the calendar insisted time was fluid. Oddly, she did not recall having a single dream.

"How long will I be in the hospital?"

"It's up to Dr. Wilson. She's been the lead on your medical team." His face was pale, as if he hadn't slept.

"Okay. I expect you haven't slept."

"They've been letting me use a recliner," he said. "I haven't slept much, but they're really nice here, Mom. They brought me a sandwich and a muffin during the night."

"Good. But right now I want you to get out of here. Have

a decent meal at the café down the hall. Then go to the cottage and go to bed. I don't want to see you until later. Or, better yet, tomorrow. If they spring me out of here, I'm sure Brandon or Evelyn can give me a ride home." The word "home" had unconsciously slipped out too late to change it to "cottage."

Maddie had no idea how someone could be medically "asleep" for forty-eight hours and then wake up tired. And as grateful as she was to see Rafe, she was happier to see him leave. Because she needed to try to stay awake long enough to piece together what had happened after her last bite of the pancakes. In order to do that, she had to go back to the beginning, starting with why she'd been at the cliffs with Brandon in the first place. Especially since Rafe was on the island—at least she remembered he was there.

But why hadn't he been at brunch with them?

Then two words she'd been searching for surfaced in her mind: *Joe. Thurston.*

Slowly, methodically, her mind backtracked to when she was sitting on the deck at the restaurant, her mind sifting through possible suspects of who might have killed her grandmother: Lisa, CiCi, even Owen, though she might have ruled him out. Then there was Joe. And the parcels of land that once belonged to his people. And hers.

Maybe he hadn't succeeded in convincing Nancy to give them back to the tribe, so he'd done away with her.

Then Maddie had remembered that Rafe was with Joe, paddling around the ponds that were cared for by the Wampanoags.

She'd jumped up from her chair. And the rest had happened.

The sensation of her body tipping sideways over the split railing, rolling, rolling, one thud after another, came thundering back. Especially the part when she landed with a bump into a bunch of spiny shrubs.

That was it. She couldn't recall anything else until she'd woken up to the sounds of machines—and her son's voice.

As entrapped by sinuous tubes as she now was, she struggled to check the bedside stand for her phone. She needed to call Brandon. Maybe he'd come back—without his mother— so they could finish their conversation. But the bedside stand was crowded with boxes and sealed packets of medical paraphernalia; her phone wasn't there.

Right then, a tall, thin woman with short red hair and big eyeglasses entered the room. She had on a white coat and was carrying another of those tablets that must have replaced old-fashioned patient charts. Three young men, also in white coats, trailed after her. They, too, carried tablets. None of them had smiles on their masks.

The redhead's brown eyes glanced at her tablet, then fixed on Maddie. "I heard you're awake."

Maddie nodded. She would have thought that her state of alertness was obvious without confirmation from a ten-inch screen.

"I'm Dr. Wilson, and these are . . ."

As she continued, she turned toward the young men, so Maddie didn't hear their introductions. Hopefully, it didn't matter.

The doctor then explained Maddie's injuries in more depth than the nurse had, which didn't matter, either, as most of it was medical lingo regarding test results and procedures. Except when she said "mild concussion." Maddie recognized that term, also from when Rafe had fallen on the ice at the frog pond a hundred years ago. But while she appreciated what the doctors and nurses had done for her, she only wanted to know when she'd be released. And where her phone was.

"So," the doctor said, "everything appears to be okay with this injury. But with the additional trauma to your foot, Dr. Blais replaced your cast, so you'll have to follow the same protocol as before. In other words, you'll be starting over with that—elevating it for a couple of days, and so on. If you don't have enough medication, Dr. Blais will prescribe more."

When she said "Dr. Blais," it took a few seconds for Maddie to recognize the name of the orthopedic doctor who had cemented her foot and half her leg the first time, and who'd given her kudos for a good job of healing when she'd seen him the other day. She wanted to peer under the covers to determine if this cast was as enormous as the previous one.

"Dr. Blais is off today, but his office will notify you about your next appointment, which should be in a week or so. In the meantime, we'll keep you here another night. Your vitals are fine, so it's just precautionary. For a while, you might experience occasional confusion. Typically, it's nothing to be alarmed about, but if it's too frequent or too intense, give us a call."

Maddie kept listening, though she'd rather be sleeping.

"When you do leave the hospital," the doctor added, "it will be best if you're not left alone for a few days. Head injuries can have a mind of their own. That's about it. Any questions?"

Maddie couldn't tell if the doctor knew she'd just made a joke about head injuries having a mind of their own. So instead of laughing, she tried to think of a question. Nothing surfaced. "No questions. But thank you. This is a great hospital."

"It is. But next time—if there is one—it would be better if you plan to visit us some other time than summer."

Ah. A joke.

That time, Maddie smiled.

Then the woman nodded and led her ducklings from the room.

Once they were out of sight, she sat up and lifted the sheet. *Argh*, she thought. The cast did look bigger, more cumbersome. *Great*. Then she remembered she should have asked if someone could look for her phone. But she supposed that wouldn't qualify as a medical question. So she tousled the sheets, trying to figure out where the call button was. Finally she found it on the wrong side of the bed. It had fallen out of reach.

Determined to stay awake until a nurse passed her door again, Maddie waited with vigilance. A few minutes later one obliged. And Maddie called out, "HELP."

Brandon arrived twenty minutes later. Maddie had been in and out of sleep when he came into her room.

"You're tired," he said as he moved a chair next to the bed.

At first, she wasn't sure why he was there, or, for that matter, why she was. Then the word "concussion" filtered to the forefront of her mind. As did the doctor's mention of "confusion." She sighed.

"I was so glad to hear your voice," he said, "and to know you're back among the living. But you sounded a little crazed, so I got here as fast as possible, what with summer traffic, which was touch and go all the way down State Road. No surprise."

All the time he was talking, Maddie was thinking . . . *I called him?*

Moment by moment, her memory cells regrouped. She'd borrowed a nurse's phone because no one knew where hers was. The nurse looked up the Morgans' number. That's all she remembered. Her was in a fog, like the kind that had been on the beach the morning she'd met CiCi. Back when Maddie was still able to run but had been walking thanks to the high tide.

She rubbed her eyes, grateful that at least part of her memory seemed intact. "My phone. Do you know where it is?"

He lifted her purse. "I didn't want to leave this here Friday. Do you want it now? I expect your phone's in it?"

"You really are my savior. Thanks." She took her purse and quickly found it. "And it's still charged."

"Do you want to keep your purse here?"

"No. Just the phone for now." She handed him the purse. "I'll be out of here tomorrow."

He nodded. "That's all you wanted? It's why you sounded so crazed?"

She lowered her eyes, then raised them to meet his. "If there was another reason, I've forgotten it."

"Hmm," he answered with a frown. "If it's any help, you insisted that I come alone. Which I took to mean I shouldn't bring my mother."

"Ah," she said, the fog starting to lift. "Right. It's about Joe Thurston." She waited several seconds to allow the letters in her brain to fall into words as if being prompted by Vanna White of *Wheel of Fortune* (her father watched that, of course) or teasing her while she played *Wordle*. When the words finally formed, she asked, "Brandon? Do you think Joe killed my grandmother?"

Brandon let out a sharp laugh. "Joe? You're kidding, right?"

"Well . . . no."

"Why him? He's probably the kindest, most decent guy I've known on the Vineyard."

So Maddie explained how Joe had told her about some people giving property back to the tribe; she asked Brandon if he thought Joe might be hoping she'd do that with Nancy's.

Brandon frowned. "Sorry, Maddie, but I don't believe it. I know you want answers about Nancy's death, but let's not jump the gun, okay?"

"So we have to wait for the death certificate."

"Yes." Then he fidgeted with the edge of the sheet. "The truth is, sometimes they can't tell for certain. And, if so, we'll have to accept that."

She closed her eyes, wondering why it mattered so much to her to try to solve a mystery that might not even be a mystery, about a woman who hadn't reached out to Maddie in forty years. Maybe she'd only left Maddie her estate in memory of her daughter.

"I guess you're right," she said. "But when we were having brunch, I thought about the people I've met here. I guess because my grandmother's land is worth so much, I've been feeling compelled to try to figure out if one of them might have wanted her dead."

"The land is only worth 'so much' if someone sells it," he said.

"Or returns it to the people it once belonged to."

Her comment was punctuated by the steady beeping of a monitor.

"Brandon?" she asked. "You really don't think Joe did it?"

He took her hand, careful to steer clear of the IV port.

"Maddie, you won't remember this, but when we got to the hospital—I rode with you in the ambulance—I called my mother. Earlier you'd said Rafe was with Joe; I asked my mother to call Joe and have him get your son to the hospital. She said Joe was awfully upset, but he didn't tell Rafe what had happened, or that you were in the hospital. Which, to me, was a super kind thing to do. But that's Joe. All he said was that something had come up, and he needed to head back to dry land. When they docked the kayaks, he asked Rafe to go with him—he said he wanted to show him something.

When I saw Joe here in the waiting room, he told me he hadn't wanted your son to be worried all the way to the hospital, that he figured there'd be plenty of time for the poor kid to be upset, that there was no sense alarming him ahead of time. And while Joe was telling me all that, he was crying. He's a good man, Maddie. Not a killer. And, by the way, with Nancy gone, you and Rafe are Joe's closest relations. Don't for a second think he takes that lightly."

Then Brandon let go of her fingers. "So try not to worry, okay? My mother said George should be back in a couple of days, and I'll be all over his case for the death certificate."

She felt as if she'd shattered Michelangelo's *David*. How could she have suspected Joe? He was her family. And from what he'd told her about Grandma Nancy, it seemed that they'd been close.

It was time to stop tormenting herself into thinking that her grandmother's death had been anything but an accident. Time to stop trying to make more of things than what they obviously were.

Then another image of the policeman at the door flashed into her mixed-up mind.

This has to stop.
Maddie's back in the hospital.
Which, on so many levels, is totally messed-up.

Chapter 25

Rafe returned at four o'clock.

"I thought I told you to get something to eat, then go to the cottage and sleep," Maddie said, proud that her brain cells were alert. Even better, *she* was alert; she'd been napping since Brandon left.

"The café's closed on weekends," Rafe said. "So I walked over the bridge to a place called the Black Dog and ate there."

"That's near the ferry, isn't it? Isn't it a long walk from here?"

"Yes, to both questions. But it was nice. And it took longer coming back because the drawbridge went up."

She sighed. "How was the food?"

"Great. Fish and chips. I'm stuffed."

"Good. Now, as you can see, I'm fine. So go back to the cottage and sleep. No excuses. Do you know how to get there?"

Rafe laughed. "GPS, Mom. On my phone." He waved his iPhone at her.

"Very funny." Then she scowled. "Wait. Your car's in Falmouth. Is mine here? If not, you'll have to get a cab—"

Rafe stopped her. "Joe left me his truck."

She blinked. Joe. The kindest, most decent man Brandon knew on the island.

"Can you drive a truck?"

"It's only a pickup, Mom. I'll manage."

He asked if she needed anything before he left.

"I'm all set, thanks. And this time, please, don't come back until tomorrow. Brandon brought my phone, so I'll let you know when they're going to let me out of here." The thought of being "let out" made Maddie think of the Graybar Hotel. She wondered if she should have asked Brandon to tell Rex where she was. Then she decided Rex did not need to hear about her latest misadventure. Once she left the Vineyard, chances were she'd never see him again.

Then Rafe kissed his mother on her cheek, moved into the corridor, and was gone again.

She closed her eyes, drifting back to sleep, just as her intuition began to peck at her again, trying to break out of the Graybar in her mind.

The toughest part about sleeping on the hospital bed was having her foot elevated the "correct" way. But the night nurses took turns stopping by to check on her and, when she was awake, they stayed a few minutes to visit. Lucky for Maddie, it was a quiet Saturday night; one nurse said Saturdays typically were, as lots of renters left earlier in the day and the ones who took their places didn't need medical attention. Yet.

Dr. Wilson arrived at ten o'clock Sunday morning and reiterated that she'd discharge Maddie as long as she wouldn't be alone. "And I mean *not at all* for a full week, when both Dr. Blais and I will see you again."

Maddie assured the doctor that she wouldn't be alone. She had a feeling Rafe wouldn't budge without her at his side.

Her theory proved right: half an hour after she called to be picked up, he arrived. She hoped Evelyn was busy with wedding plans and wouldn't feel slighted.

Even better than having her favorite person on the planet as her custodian for a week was that when the hospital's paperwork was signed and Maddie was wheeled outside, Rafe had not only brought her comfortable old Volvo but also the wheelchair Rex had offered, which was in the back seat.

"Otherwise, those damn crutches might permanently maim you," Rafe commented, as if the crutches were responsible for her losing her balance and careening down the cliffs. She saw no point in explaining that there was much more to the story.

Seeing the wheelchair, however, made her hope that Rex would call. Then she could casually mention her latest mishap. And hope he wouldn't think she was a catastrophe-in-waiting.

With Maddie in the passenger seat and Rafe behind the wheel, once they were on the road, he asked, "Don't you want to know how I got into your car?"

"No. I gave you my keys when your father was here."

"You did, but I dropped them back into your purse when I got back. I also couldn't get back into the cottage last night."

"So, how did you manage to do both?"

"Well, seeing as how Brandon had your phone, I figured he might have your purse, too. I didn't have his number, but I had Joe's—he gave it to me in case we need anything. So I called Joe and Joe called Brandon, who fished around and found your keys in the outside pocket. I hope that was okay. So your purse is in the back seat of your car now, keeping the wheelchair company."

"I guess it takes a village to manage me," she said. "Thank you for doing everything. And mostly for being here."

He smiled. "It's a nice little island, isn't it?"

"That it is. And speaking of Joe," she made sure she sounded upbeat, dismissing her previous suspicion, "how was your day with him yesterday?" She blanched. "I mean Friday."

He glanced at her. "It was incredible, Mom."

She nodded, waiting for him to continue.

Then he replayed his kayak trip from the moment he strapped on the life vest: paddling from Menemsha Pond to Quitsa; seeing the varieties of birds that showed off their distinctive songs; watching the eelgrass beds and their ecosystem ballet. It was as if, in no time at all, Rafe had both met and embraced his Wampanoag roots.

She wondered how Owen would take the news. Hopefully, he wouldn't try to minimize it.

They stopped at Cronig's in Vineyard Haven; Rafe pushed her in the wheelchair up and down the aisles while, at her direction, he plucked things from the shelves. Though she'd never liked having attention, she admitted that right now, it was fun.

After they cashed out, Rafe loaded the bags of food that Maddie hoped would last a week. After that . . . well, she wasn't going to think about that now.

They drove up State Road, past the postcard view of Lake Tashmoo, then the rustic farms and rolling hills into West Tisbury. Maddie told him to turn right onto North Road. It was the route Rex had taken in the opposite direction when they'd picked up Rafe at the boat two days ago. No, she thought. Four days. She kept forgetting that she'd passed the date line of deep sleep.

Like so many Vineyard roads, North was two lanes, one in each direction, edged only by a white line that indicated caution because beyond it was no shoulder, just trees. Lots and lots of tall, thin- and thick-trunked trees that allowed the summer sunlight to keep winking like a mirrored globe high above a dance floor like the one at Maddie's high school prom whose theme was a retro-disco extravaganza. She had no trouble remembering that but not that four days had passed since Rafe arrived. *Sheeesh.*

Before they reached the turn to the access road that rimmed the backyard of the cottage and the parking spot Rex claimed he'd built for her, a siren blared behind them. Rafe pulled as far right as possible and stopped; they craned their necks as an ambulance hurried past, its lights flashing the way Maddie supposed they'd flashed for her. She squared her jaw to keep the blue police lights of her imagination out of her thoughts again.

"He's probably headed to the beach," she said.

"Maybe Jaws is back," Rafe added.

His mother looked to him. "Poor taste, my son. If there's an ambulance, chances are someone's hurting."

"Scolding noted and approved."

With the ambulance well past them, he steered the car onto the access road. But as they reached the parking area, Maddie saw red lights blinking through the trees, the way the sun's rays had danced along North Road. This, however, was alarming. Because, unlike the blue ones of her visions, these lights were real.

Rafe stopped the car, bounded to the back door, and yanked out the wheelchair. Then he helped Maddie out and set the crutches on her lap and they hurried toward the footpath. Which was when she heard heart-stopping sounds from down the hill: voices shouting, water gushing, footsteps clomping—all set against a crescendo of crackling and popping.

Then the thicket of trees parted at her grandmother's backyard, and Maddie saw what the commotion was about.

The cottage was on fire.

★　★　★

In a lightning-fast instant, Maddie grabbed the crutches from her lap, hauled herself up off the wheelchair, and got a little dizzy. She inhaled a long breath—and tasted smoke. Throwing the crutch on her right side onto the ground, she grabbed Rafe's arm.

"Help me!" she cried. "I need to get down there!"

Rafe steadied her. "Without the wheelchair?"

"Too confining!"

Propping her right side against his left, she held on to his arm; they made it to the sheds and toward the orange flames and the smoke that threatened to suffocate anyone who approached. Then a figure emerged from the heavy haze and ran up the hill toward them.

"Stop!" It was Lisa.

They stopped.

Tears formed in Maddie's eyes. Her gaze jerked back to the cottage.

"What happened?" she cried.

"It started a while ago. They don't know why yet. But about two dozen people are working to shut it down before the wind picks up."

At which time, Maddie figured, the flames could spread in a direct line to Lisa's house, the pier, and beyond.

"They don't want us any closer," Lisa added. "I've been yelled at twice to get out of the way." She wrapped her arms around her denim dress, hugging herself.

"Are your kids okay?" Maddie asked, her gaze locked on the blaze. "Is anyone hurt?"

"No one's hurt. Tri-Town ambulance is here just in case. The Tisbury one just got here as a backup. My kids are at camp. I was at work, but the word spread fast. I don't want the kids here until it's out. If I don't pick them up later, a counselor will bring them to her house." Her words were racing, racing, the way Maddie's heart was beating.

Lisa rubbed her hands. "I'm going back. I don't care if I get yelled at." She ran down the hill, keeping a wide berth around the cottage. Then she went around the corner and vanished into the smog of smoke.

Maddie leaned on her crutches. "I'm glad my grandmother isn't here to see this." She thought about the things inside: the family photographs she'd wanted to save; the testaments to so many Wampanoag traditions she'd reserved for the cultural center; the portrait of her great-grandfather. Even the things she'd allocated to be recycled. Together, the collection represented the belongings of nearly ninety years of life. And now it was going up in flames. Cremated, like her grandmother would be.

"Mom?" Rafe asked. "Sit. Please." He grasped the handles of the wheelchair, moving it closer to her.

She sat. Rafe stood. And they watched. Unable to do anything. But wait.

Then Rafe said, "I'm going around to the front. Maybe I can help."

Another mom might think that keeping her child safe was more important, might say something like, "We don't live here, Rafe. We don't know these people. Let them handle it." But now that they both knew the island was part of them, it seemed only right for him to want to help. And for her not to stop him. Besides, he was smart. And old enough to make his own decisions.

"Promise me you won't move?" he asked.

Maddie nodded. "I'll stay right here." Not that she had anywhere to go. Or any way to get there. She didn't add that she also wanted to witness the demise of the cottage—and the end of what might have been a new beginning for Maddie. If she had wanted it.

Having received no negative reaction, Rafe, like Lisa, ran toward the cottage. And Maddie stayed seated, gripping the armrests of the wheelchair, staring at the fire, tears glazing her cheeks as she thought about her mother.

She watched a while longer, until the flames either were diminishing or tricking Maddie into thinking that they were. Then another figure—large and hulking—hiked through the haze and up the hill toward her. And Maddie knew right away that it was Rex.

Chapter 26

"So you're using the wheelchair?" were Rex's first words.

"So you're putting out a fire?" she replied. "And aren't you a long way from Edgartown?"

He had on tall black boots and a thick fireproof jacket; soot was smeared across his nice face. He carried a firefighter's helmet. "Didn't anyone teach you not to answer a question with a question?"

"Should I ask the same of you?" It was not a time for humor, and yet . . .

She sat there, and he stood there, the cottage now smoldering in the background.

Then he looked at her, his face serious. "Are you okay?"

"Okay enough." She held his gaze a moment until he gestured toward the cottage. "I'm so sorry about . . . this, Maddie. But it's under control now. The worst should be out soon."

Good news, perhaps.

"It won't spread?"

"Nope. It shouldn't."

"And no one's been hurt?"

"No. It wasn't as bad as it might have looked from up here."

So it wasn't going to harm Lisa or her family or anyone else. Except Maddie. And Rafe. And possibly her father, whose memories of the place must run more deeply than hers.

"Will it be . . ." She knew the right words but didn't want to ask them. "Will it be a total loss?"

"I honestly don't know. But I'm no expert. Just a volunteer."

"Did you come all the way up-island for this?"

He shook his head. "Nope. Not that I wouldn't have. I was at my cabin. I don't rent it anymore, but Francine and Jonas like to use it for a few days in the spring and fall. So I wanted to spruce it up before summer's over. Anyway, my phone alerts me when there's an emergency anywhere on the island. If I can get there, I go."

She studied him a moment, unsure if he was being truthful or trying to impress her. She couldn't tell.

"Is everything inside ruined?" she asked. The smoke had, indeed, begun to dissipate, the flames now sparked only in spotty places. The roof over the kitchen, however, appeared to be heavily damaged.

"It's too soon to know that, too. Sorry."

She nodded, then felt a tear, maybe two, leak out again.

"Until it's livable again, you're welcome to use my place."

She blinked. "What?"

He turned and pointed toward the harbor. "My cabin's not far from the other side of the water. I could drive your car over there for you, and you can easily take the bike ferry back and forth whenever you want to check up on what's happening here . . . or maybe just stay over there while you're figuring out what to do next." He spoke in a take-charge tone layered with empathy. "This time of year, you'll be hard-pressed to get even a single room anywhere else. My place isn't big, but it's big enough. If you plan to stay."

It was a generous offer. She might have been able to stay at Evelyn's, but somehow Rex's cabin sounded closer, maybe cozier. Besides, she'd have nowhere else to go except back to Green Hills. And she wasn't up for the ferry trip followed by a four-hour drive.

"That's so kind of you, Rex. Not to mention that right now I'm exhausted. And in pain. And there are groceries in the car, some of which need refrigeration." The shelf life of groceries, refrigerated or not, hardly seemed problematic compared with the fire, but at least it was something she could fix.

"How about if I run both you and the food over to the cabin now? It's not the Ritz, but it has a bathroom and two bedrooms and a kitchen with fairly new appliances. There should be room in the refrigerator. And you can lie down and rest." It didn't sound as if he wanted her to leave the island.

"Thanks, Rex. My car is up the hill . . . well, you know where it is. Will you tell Rafe where I'll be?"

"Absolutely. I have to make a quick call, but I'll be right back." With that, he trotted back down the hill.

Maddie took a long look at the cottage and what might have been her future. Then she said goodbye to her mother. All over again.

"I'm glad my father wasn't here to see the cottage burn," she said on the ride to the cabin. "It would have been hard on him. He never got over losing my mom. Not that he ever talked about it."

"Some guys aren't great at showing that last part. Or, actually, at showing any of those things."

"Some women aren't great at it, either."

"Present company included?"

She shrugged. "Probably. Though I think—I hope—I've been a better mother than I was a wife."

"That might have had to do with the husband you had."

She laughed again. "And to think you're not a rocket scientist, too."

Rex grinned. "I take it that the ex has left the island?"

"He has." She could have said more, but didn't want to waste her time or breath talking about Owen. Then she said, "I can't believe this has happened. My grandmother's . . . my mother's home . . ."

Rex reached over and held her hand.

Several minutes later he steered the Volvo onto the bumpy road that he said led to his cabin. Maddie commented that Joe hadn't been kidding when he'd noted that crossing on the bike ferry was a quicker route to Lobsterville Beach.

"My grandmother's properties are around here somewhere," she added.

"I know. Keeping them all these years was a good investment for her."

"Do you know how my grandparents got them? Like if my grandfather won the derby, too?" She wanted—needed—to talk about something happier.

Rex laughed. "I don't have a clue." Then he took a left turn onto what only looked like the footpath behind the cottage, where so many trees were shading the ground, sunlight could hardly sneak through. It might have been a driveway, though it didn't have a mailbox posted at the entrance or a brightly painted wooden arrow nailed to a tree with block letters that read: WINSTED.

And then, there were no more trees. A wide expanse of bright afternoon sky and green grass greeted them; a small cabin sat atop a small slope, not as high as Grandma Nancy's cottage sat up from the road, but enough so anyone inside could look out the picture window and see a car approach. Maybe off to the west, they could see the ocean when the leaves were off the trees. Rocking chairs beckoned up on the porch; a small garden ran along the front and displayed a number of bright green-leafed bushes with plump hydrangea blossoms in shades of blue. Blue like the summer sky; blue like Menemsha Creek and Vineyard Sound.

She glanced at Rex.

"Like I said, it's not the Ritz."

"It's wonderful, Rex. Did your father build it himself?"

"Pretty much. But I helped. Manual labor was often my comeuppance for doing something stupid. I can't remember the specifics as to why I was commissioned here; I did so many stupid things back then." He smiled and shook his head, as if calling up unpleasant memories. Then he gestured toward the passenger door. "Stay put. I'll come around and help you out. Sorry, but I never thought we'd need a ramp."

Thankfully, though, he'd remembered to bring her crutches. Between them and his arm, Maddie made it up the four stairs and into the living room, which was when she knew that she desperately needed to lie down.

"Make yourself at home," he said, his eyes scanning the place as if checking for a bachelor's mess. Whenever Rafe wasn't at college, he tended to create what her father called explosions in his room: workout clothes scattered on the floor, socks tangled in the comforter, sports gear wherever it landed. Rex, however, was an adult. A quick sweep of her eyes indicated that he also was a neatnik.

"I'll get the food," he added, then went back outside to retrieve her groceries. He returned in a flash, set down the grocery bags, and handed over her purse. "In case you need anything in here."

He moved into the kitchen; Maddie watched as he adeptly organized the Cronig's collection.

"Looks like everything but the ice cream survived," he said. "Don't worry, though—you can get better at the Galley. It's a quick trip on the bike ferry. Later I'll show you how to get there from here. Right now, you look like you could definitely use a nap."

Maddie nodded. She was too tired to tell him she already knew about—had, in fact, been on—the tiny ferry on the day that she'd broken her foot.

"And you can tell me anytime why you were back in the hospital," he added. "If you want."

She leaned on her crutches and stared at him.

He motioned toward her hand. "Wristband," he said. "I've seen more than a few of those."

She looked down at the bracelet strip. "Oh. Well, I had a little tumble over the railing at the restaurant on the cliffs. Nothing much."

He set down a small bag of apples. "Huh. I heard that rumor, but it was hard to believe. Like falling down a sand dune and breaking a foot. I don't think anyone's done that one, either."

Though she had no excuse for her broken foot, she could have told him that her tumble down the cliffs was because she thought Rafe's life was in danger. But because Maddie disliked being dramatic, she simply said, "I guess I'm just a trailblazer."

He laughed. "Let's hope not." He closed the refrigerator door and put both hands on his hips. "And you sure you're okay?"

"I am. I was in a coma for a couple of days, thanks to a small head injury. While I was sleeping, they gave me a new cast. But I'm fine now. Honest." She smiled as if that would prove it.

"Okay, then. Go. Rest. Take the guest room in the back.

It's not used very often, so it's probably cleaner. And maybe quieter, if anything could possibly get quieter around here."

She started to navigate toward the bedroom when he said, "And the bathroom's between the two bedrooms—you probably figured that out. Do you need any help getting"—he paused—"into bed?" His voice went tentative; perhaps he was embarrassed.

Sheeesh, she thought. *Men*. "I'll be fine, thanks."

"Okay, but if you need anything, shoot me a text or call. I hope you kept my number in your phone."

"I did," she said a little shyly, as if she was embarrassed, which she was. She headed to the guest room, sat on the bed, and parked her crutches next to it. And Rex was right behind her, standing in the doorway.

"If you think you're going to sleep, I'd like to go back to the cottage and see how it's going."

"Trust me. I'll sleep. You are free to go."

"Right. Well, I won't be long. With any luck, I'll come back with more good news."

"I'll count on that."

He smiled a soft smile. "Get some rest. I'll be back soon."

After he was gone, Maddie remembered she was not supposed to be alone. But she fell asleep so fast, it didn't really matter.

She dreamed about her grandmother. Again.

"You know the rules," Grandma whispered, "A double-dip cone if you help me shuck corn for dinner."

This time, though, Maddie had trouble running down the hill toward Mr. Fuller's ice cream shack; it was hard to negotiate the sandy path with a cast on one leg and crutches under both her arms. To top it off, she wasn't a child but a full-grown woman.

When she finally opened her eyes, she sensed that hours had passed. Bands of late-summer sunlight slanted through the windows; a light breeze fluttered the sheers.

She listened for movement elsewhere in the cabin but only heard birds trilling outside. Then she got up and limped into the bathroom on her crutches. Next, she checked the living room, then the kitchen, then the other bedroom. And both the front porch and smaller one outside the back door. She was alone; it didn't look as if anyone had been there while she'd slept. If they had, there were no signs—there wasn't a towel on the floor or a spoon in the sink. Which ruled out her non-neatnik son.

Groping around, she found the makings for tea; she filled the kettle and set it on the stove. Then she opened the refrigerator door and stared inside: their stop at Cronig's had produced some inviting offerings, but she'd learned that trying to cook while standing on crutches wasn't fun. It would be safer if she could find crackers and a can of soup. Not exactly an August meal, but at least she could dump chicken noodle into a pan without making too much of a mess. In spite of being a gourmet chef, maybe Rex kept a few cans of Progresso on hand for emergencies.

She opened one cabinet: glassware and mugs. The next one had plates and bowls. But Maddie struck gold with door number three: canned fruit, canned vegetables, canned soup. *Hooray.* Elated, she chose chicken and wild rice. And then she realized she needed a can opener. And a microwave container for nuking or a pan for simmering.

Sometimes nothing was easy.

Setting the can on the counter, she opened the next cabinet door; amazingly, there sat what looked like a perfect heat-it-and-eat-from-it bowl. She set it on the counter next to the can.

Then she turned to three vertical drawers under the counter—maybe one was a junk drawer where a can opener might live. But the top one held silverware; the drawer below that, large cooking utensils. Not ready to quit, Maddie took a step back, then, leaning her crutches against the counter, she cautiously bent down, aware she could tip sideways and fall at any second. She could break open the cast. Or worse, whack her head again. And this time, no one was there to rescue her. Still, she decided to risk it.

The bottom drawer was heavier than the others. She reached up and held on to the edge of the counter, mindful of keeping her balance. Then she grasped the handle and gave it a good jerk. With reluctance, the drawer popped open. At a quick glance, however, she didn't see a can opener. Instead, there was a bag of white candles, a box of wooden matches, several placemats, and a pile of matching cloth napkins. But no can opener.

So she retreated to the living room, plunked down on a chair, and closed her eyes.

Chapter 27

It sounded like a thousand trains were roaring through her head, their whistles blowing, blowing, blowing as if hundreds of people were standing in the middle of the tracks ahead of it and the engineer was warning them to get out of the way. *Now.*

Then Maddie's eyes blinked and blinked until they fully opened.

Had she been in a coma again—or had she just fallen asleep? Maybe she'd dreamed everything that had happened. Was the cottage on fire—or wasn't it?

The whistles kept blaring. She blinked again. She was sitting in a comfy chair but could not remember where she was. Her eyes darted around the room to the fireplace, the big picture window, the braided rug that must have been at least half a century old. Nothing was familiar.

She squeezed her eyelids shut and covered her ears from the piercing sounds.

Then *Rex's cabin* buzzed into her mind. She wasn't sure if she was happier she'd remembered, or disappointed that she knew why she was there. The fire had been real. Her grandmother's cottage might still be burning. And the whistling sounded like it was coming from a teakettle.

She remembered that Grandma Nancy had a whistling teakettle when Maddie was a little girl. Grandma had said the whistle was because old ladies needed to be reminded that they'd started to make tea before they got busy doing something else and forgot about it. Maddie had found that fascinating.

Then she remembered she'd been boiling water for tea.

She would have jumped up if she could have. Instead, she had to wriggle her body sideways to get enough leverage from the armrest to stand up. Then she slogged her way into the kitchen, one wobble at a time, all the while thinking: *This is why I shouldn't be left alone.* But Rex hadn't known that because she hadn't told him.

Amazingly, about half an inch of water remained at the bottom of the kettle.

Leaning against the sink, she added water to it and tried again.

She stood and waited until the kettle whistled, that time only twice.

After fixing her tea and using just one crutch so she could carry the mug in her other hand, she slowly made her way into the living room and sat where she'd been sitting. It wasn't long before the front door opened and Rex came inside.

"You're awake," Rex said. "How are you doing?"

"Fine," she lied. "I had a nice nap."

"Great. Because I have good news." He crossed the room to where she was sitting; he squatted in front of her and took her hands in his.

"They saved the cottage," he said. "It's going to need renovations to the kitchen, and the side walls and the back will have to be replaced, but it's not as bad as it could have been. I really thought it was a goner."

Maddie didn't think she'd ever heard someone say "goner." She closed her eyes. "Oh. That's wonderful."

"You might not know," he added, "but there was a huge, fast fire in Menemsha a while back. It destroyed the coast guard boathouse and the pier. It would have been a lot worse if it reached the other buildings and the houses up on the hill. But when there's an emergency, islanders react fast. The coast guard fire tested every bit of that. And it was a miracle no one was seriously hurt."

He didn't know it also was a miracle that she was sitting, sipping tea, instead of having caused his cabin to also catch fire.

"And you won't have to worry about rebuilding," he continued. "Several islanders have volunteered to help out come fall—once the summer folks are gone."

Come fall, Maddie thought. When she'd no doubt be back in Green Hills, back in the classroom, awaiting final news of tenure. When she would have resumed her routine life with her father as if the past couple of weeks hadn't happened. She would stuff down the hard feelings she still harbored against him. She'd find a way to dismiss the past. Life would be more livable that way.

The only trouble was, she didn't want to leave the Vineyard now. Not until she learned how the fire had started. And not until she could properly dispense of her grandmother's ashes.

As if reading her thoughts, Rex said, "With so much damage in the kitchen, the old wiring might have caused it. But the officials will figure that out. Nancy never installed a detector, or it would have left a less costly mess. At least it didn't happen in the middle of the night. A couple of neighbors called it in as soon as they saw smoke."

Maddie wondered if it would take as long for the officials—whoever they were—to determine the cause of the fire,
as it was taking the medical examiner to cough up a death certificate. She tried not to wonder if anyone would have set it.

"Have you eaten anything?" he asked.

"No." Then she remembered she'd left the can of chicken
and rice on the counter. "I thought about making soup, but I
couldn't find a can opener. What about Rafe? Is he still at the
cottage?"

Rex nodded. "The active fire's out, so they're letting him
help outside with the equipment. They won't let him inside.
But he's been great."

"How long will he be there?" Maddie asked.

"He'll call when he's ready to leave. I would have left
your car for him, but I was over here when the alert sounded.
I ran down to the dock and used one of Joe's canoes to row
across the harbor. It was quicker than driving. How about if I
throw some food together?" He moved into the kitchen area
and opened the refrigerator door.

Food again.

Shuffling things on the refrigerator shelves, Rex then set
several items on the counter. "Rafe also wants to ask the fire
chief to let him get a few things. He said your grandmother
had lots of Wampanoag memorabilia that you and he were
going through."

Maddie didn't want to think about the things up on the
mantel: the sunset painting, the pottery bowl with the daisy
painted on the front, the quahog shell. And the portrait of
Isaac Thurston.

Then again, Maddie didn't want to think about a lot of
things right then.

It was five o'clock when Rafe finally showed up. Rex had
gone outside to gather wild blueberries for cobbler; Maddie

was resting—again—but she woke up when her son whispered, "Hi, Mom."

"Hi, honey," she said. "Please. Come sit beside me."

"One of the firefighters brought me," he said as he stepped into the room. He was carrying a blanket. "They still wouldn't let me in, but Joe was there—he's a firefighter, too. I asked him to get the three metal boxes—they're in the living room. And he found this. The blanket's kind of smoky, but . . ."

She recognized it. It was the lap blanket Grandma Nancy wore in her wedding photo, the one that Maddie's great-great-grandmother, Gladys Nightingale, Spotted Fawn, had woven by hand. The blanket Grandma kept on the living room chair. And that Owen knocked onto the floor.

Rafe unwrapped the blanket. Inside was the portrait of Isaac Thurston. Joe must have been too preoccupied to realize it.

Maddie cried. "It's your great-great-grandfather, honey." She studied the careful brushstrokes, the way her mother had depicted his dark eyes in a way that showed deep character. She sighed. "What about the other things that were on the mantel? Are they okay?"

He sat down. "I don't know. Why don't you call Joe?"

She asked if he'd do it for her.

Pulling out his phone, he stood up, scrolled to Joe's number, touched it, and started to pace—one of his few Owen tricks, which, come to think of it, her father did as well.

"Joe?" Rafe asked. "Yeah, sorry to bother you."

Maddie listened to the silence, followed by her son asking about the items that had been on the mantel.

He waited for a response, then said, "Uh-huh. No, that's fine. I was just checking. Thanks." He hung up and looked at his mother.

"They burned," she said.

He shook his head. "Don't know. They aren't there."

She frowned. "Seriously?"

"Yup. Joe said he knew exactly what I meant. But he didn't see them. Not on the mantel. Or anywhere else. Sorry, Mom."

"It's okay, honey," she said as she reached out and touched his hand. "They were only things." She hoped he couldn't tell that her throat was constricting. She set the painting down beside her on the bed, happy that at least this had been retrieved. "Now let's get you some food. Rex turned what we bought into a feast."

Rafe helped her off the bed and followed her into the kitchen. She heated up the leftovers; in less than half an hour, he had devoured them. Which was when Rex reappeared.

"Hey, man," Rafe said to him. "Great place you have here."

"Thanks. Did your mother tell you that my father won the land in the fishing derby in the fifties?"

He plunked her keys down on the counter and helped himself to a beer. Maddie was back in the chair by then, watching the interaction.

Rafe said that was really cool, which launched a conversation about the derby and how it had changed and grown over the years, and how chances were the organizers could no longer afford to donate a chunk of land, what with the increased value of real estate.

Then Rex explained that his father had preserved the land and its habitat long before many people on the mainland recognized that it was important to live together as one with the earth. Then Rafe asked if he was Wampanoag, but he said no, which then led to a discussion about growing up an islander where lots of their friends and neighbors were Indigenous, so the rest of them adopted many of their ways, not because it was expected but because they made sense. And they were cool.

"No kidding," Rafe exclaimed. "Joe believes that the trees and the plants—like wildlife—are living, breathing things and deserve respect. I've always felt that way. It's been hard for me to understand that not everybody does. It came natural to me. Now I know why."

As Maddie listened to the banter, she cautioned herself not to feel guilty that Rafe hadn't known about his heritage. Though it hadn't been her fault, at some point in time, when she'd looked in the mirror, she should have noticed that her face was different from the faces of her friends in Green Hills; she should have been smart enough to make the connection to her time spent on the island.

But Maddie hadn't noticed. And though she still was angry with her father, she knew she ought to call and at least let him know what was going on. So as the man talk continued, she slipped out of the living room.

It took several rings before her father answered. Maybe he was watching reruns of *Jeopardy!*

"How are you doing?" he asked. "And please tell me the truth." Wherever he was, there was a lot of background noise—sounds of people talking and things clattering.

"Where are you?" Maddie asked, sitting back on the bed, toying with the corner of the frame of her grandfather's portrait. "It's awfully noisy."

"Sorry, I'm in a restaurant. I'll go outside."

While she waited, she reminded herself that he only knew about her broken foot. Unless Rafe had updated him. She decided not to ask.

He returned in a couple of minutes. "Quiet now?" he asked.

"Yes. And to answer your question, physically, I'm okay. I'm healing fine. Mentally, I'm still trying to process everything."

Her father hesitated. "I've thought about it every minute of the day. And here's what I think. I want you home, Maddie. You've already met the attorney; whatever you'll need to do next can surely be done by email or phone. Please," he said. "I want you to be safe."

She frowned. Why would he think she wasn't safe? "But, Dad . . ."

"I think that getting back to your friends, to your work, to your routine, will be better for you, Maddie. You don't know the people there. They might mean well, and it's a lovely place, but you belong in Green Hills. It's your home. And I don't want anything else to happen to you. Or to Rafe."

So he knew that Rafe was there. "Dad," she said. "What's going on? What else are you keeping from me?"

He didn't answer right away. She pictured his blue eyes, the color of hers, the only visible link they had to each other. And yet, Maddie knew that her scholarly instincts, her need for circumspection about so many things, and her sensitive, yet pragmatic heart, came from him. Some people might say those common traits were from having been cooped up too long in a small, academic town. But Maddie now knew that as much as she had Stephen Clarke's British/Scottish bloodline, she was also Wampanoag.

On the other end of the line, she heard a loud whooshing sound.

"Now it sounds like you're in a wind tunnel," she said loudly.

"This is not a conversation for a phone call," he replied. "We'll talk about it later when you're home."

"Seriously?" she said. "Are you trying to scare me into leaving the island?"

"No, Madelyn. It's just that there are things about your grandmother you simply do not know." He said he hoped to see her soon. And then he hung up.

Chapter 28

"No, Mom," Rafe said as he was polishing off a dish of blueberries that Rex had picked and topped with fresh cream he'd just whipped. "If you want to go back to Green Hills, I can't stop you. But I want to stay here."

Maddie blinked once, twice, three times. "But, Rafe . . ."

He shook his head. "I've learned more about myself in the past few days than I've known my whole life. And I'm not talking about my heritage; I'm talking about . . . me."

She thought he must be kidding. "But you've survived living in Green Hills for twenty-one years."

"Almost twenty-two," he corrected her. "And you don't really know if or how well that's worked for me. I didn't even know. But let's face it, I've been on the other side of the planet compared to here. You and Grandpa have sheltered me, maybe too much. My father has made sure I look the part that he and his wife want me to look—prep-schooled, Ivy League business major, heir apparent to his financial world. I've lived in his huge house on Wednesday nights and alternate weekends. I never told you how much I hate that place. I feel sorry for my half sisters, who won't grow up knowing anything else. I love living with you and Grandpa. But I'm no longer a kid, and this is where I want to be."

She was stunned. Her son had never challenged her before. More important, she had no idea how to rebut his feelings. Or if she should try.

Rex briskly wiped his hands on a dish towel and said, "I'll go walk on the beach before the sun sets and leave you two to talk." Then he departed, leaving Maddie still at a loss for words.

"But, honey," was all she could think of to say. "We don't know the extent of damage to the cottage yet. You won't have anywhere to live. It wouldn't be right to take advantage of Rex's generosity—"

"Joe said I could bunk in with him," Rafe interrupted. "He's family, too, you know."

Stumped. Stymied. Flabbergasted. She wished her father were there. He had such a level head. After all, he was the reason she'd gone back to college. He was the reason she was in line for a secure future. Then she wondered if, given half a chance, she, too, would have chosen the island.

Then she recalled his words: "There are things about your grandmother you simply do not know."

She shook her head. It was getting hard to think; maybe that was thanks to her concussion. "We have no idea what it's like to live here all the time. Right now it's summer. There's kayaking and concerts and art shows and great food. There's cheering on the beach every night at sunset. Fun is all around us. But I doubt if that's what it's like in winter, when most people are gone and places are closed." She had no idea if that was true.

"I don't care about that, Mom. And sure, the kayaking's great. But I don't need the rest. I've had my fill of fun in Green Hills. And in Amherst, too." He took a final bite of the few blueberries left in his bowl.

Her foot started to throb again. She wanted a pain pill.

She sighed. "What about school? You're so close to fin-
ishing."

"Maybe they'll let me finish remotely. They did everything online when all the students were stuck in the dorms
when Covid started." He seemed relaxed, as if he'd just announced that he liked strawberry ice cream better than choco-
late.

She tried to come up with a decent argument. But she
could tell that he'd already thought this through.

"And if I was here," he added, his voice not at all combat-
ive, "I could oversee rebuilding the cottage. Your grandmother left you the place, Mom. Wouldn't it be nice for us to
keep it? I could find some kind of job that would pay the taxes
and utilities. And whatever else the place might need. I hope
you'll at least think about it. Because my mind's made up."
He set down his spoon and turned his chair to face her, waiting for an answer.

Rafe needed to know the rest. And so did Maddie. She
wasn't going to leave him on the island, on his own, until
she did.

So she said she needed time to think about what he'd pro-
posed. She suggested that he head toward the beach and look
for Rex.

With reluctance, he agreed.

Once he was out of earshot, she called the only person she
knew she could trust—and who might know something she
needed to know.

"Maddie!" Brandon said when he answered. The connection sounded hollow, as if he was in his car. "Are you out of
the hospital? Are you okay?" Apparently, he hadn't heard the
rest.

So she told him about the fire.

The line went silent.

Then: "You're kidding."

"I wish."

"Was it arson?" It was curious he asked that before assuming it was caused by a frayed wire or something else not sinister.

Suddenly Maddie wondered if her earlier concerns that things weren't as they seemed had been correct. "They don't know how it started yet."

He paused again. "I can turn around. I can get there in time to catch the last boat."

Ugh. He wasn't on the island. Again.

"You're on your way back to Boston?"

"Yup. I have to be in court tomorrow."

Disappointment skittered through her. "Don't turn around, Brandon. You have to work. I'm fine. Rafe is with me. We're going to stay in Rex's cabin tonight. After that . . . I don't know." She decided not to tell him they might go back to Green Hills in the morning. Maybe she'd overreacted when he'd mentioned arson so fast.

"I wanted you to know about the fire, that's all. I'll keep you posted." She needed to shift the topic. "How's your mom?" Making this about Evelyn helped Maddie breathe more easily.

"She claims she's fine." The drone of highway traffic humming filled the dead air space. "Maddie?" he said. "Can you do me a favor?"

"Anything."

"Give me a couple of minutes, then call her."

"You're worried about her."

"No. I'm worried about you. There's something you don't know."

She hadn't expected that. All along, she'd been second-guessing herself, blaming herself for not trusting others, for letting her intuition get the better of her. But Brandon, like her father, had just confirmed her angst.

"What is it?" she asked.

"I don't know the details. But my mother does. She said it wasn't our concern, and she swore me to secrecy. But I hate the way this is ripping you up. It isn't fair."

Her pulse started to hammer at the base of her throat. "Am I in danger? Is my son?"

"Just, please. Call my mother. But first, give me ten minutes to shame her into telling you the truth."

They rang off, which left Maddie to wait. And to try not to think about what she was about to learn. Or that Brandon hadn't answered her question about her and Rafe being in danger. Maybe her best choice would be to go to Green Hills tomorrow. She'd insist that Rafe come with her; she'd lie to him if she had to. She'd leave her car there; they could get his on the Cape. Once she told him whatever it was that Evelyn would say, maybe Rafe would hate her less for tearing him away.

She checked the Steamship Authority schedule but found that walk-ons didn't need reservations. She noted the departure times.

Once Rafe agreed to go with her, she'd call the cultural center and donate her old Volvo. She'd call Joe and ask him to disperse anything left in the cottage that wasn't ruined. At least for now, she'd keep the metal containers with photos and the other things Rafe had salvaged. She'd give the portrait of her great-grandfather to him. He would like that. She hoped Joe didn't know about the painting, as Isaac Thurston had been his father as well as Nancy's.

As for scattering the ashes, Maddie decided that her grandmother's spirit would most likely still rest in peace without a dramatic send-off in Menemsha Bight.

★ ★ ★

Ten minutes later, she picked her phone up again, held her breath, and made the call.

Evelyn answered on the first ring. "Hello, Maddie."

"Brandon told me to call you." Her tone was flat, but she couldn't help it.

"Yes. And I'm glad. Secrets are fine unless—or until—they hurt innocent people."

"Like me."

"Yes."

Taking a short breath, Maddie wondered if she was going to hyperventilate. "Okay. Tell me."

"It's about your father," Evelyn said. "And your grandmother."

She sat up straight, her spine stiffened.

"My *father*? What about him?"

"And your grandmother," Evelyn repeated. "It started when your mother was killed."

Maddie pressed a hand to her temple. She didn't think her confusion was from the coma. "I don't understand. First of all, it was forty years ago. My mother was killed by a hit-and-run driver who was never found. It happened in Green Hills. My grandmother only was there once—for my mother's funeral. My father wouldn't let her park a camper in our driveway. She was angry. She went home. End of story."

Evelyn paused, then said, "Not exactly."

"Well, for God's sake, tell me."

"You're right that your mother was killed in a hit-and-run accident. But it didn't happen in Green Hills. It happened here on the Vineyard."

Maddie frowned. "*What?*"

"At the end of your last summer here, a few days before you and your mother were going back to Green Hills, your grandmother took you to the Ag Fair. Do you remember?"

"No. Well, yes. Maybe." A faint memory arose of music and sawdust and a joyful crowd, along with aromas of sizzling burgers and farm animals. And there was a building where quilts and vegetables and all kinds of crafts were on display. Grandma had entered something that won a blue ribbon. *A basket*, Maddie suddenly remembered.

"Your mother hadn't been feeling well," Evelyn continued, "so she didn't go with you. When you got home, she wasn't there. By then it was dark, and the full moon was up. She left a note saying she was feeling better and had gone clamming at Red Beach, and that she'd make chowder later. She always made chowder to bring home to your dad."

Maddie froze. *Feeling better. Gone clamming at Red Beach. Low tide and a full moon. Will make chowder later.* The note had been in one of her grandmother's steel boxes. She wanted to hang up. She wanted to rush out to the porch and rip through the containers, hoping that—thinking it was another piece of Grandma Nancy's trash—she hadn't tossed it out.

"The accident happened when your mother was on her way back," Evelyn said next. "She canoed across the harbor— Red Beach is on the other side, technically, it's in Aquinnah. She and I went clamming lots of times when we were growing up, but never at night—things can change too quickly by the water. Anyway, by the time Hannah reached the Menemsha side, dark clouds had rolled in and covered the moon. The coast guard verified that. When she started walking up the road, she was hit. The driver kept going—without the moonlight, it was pitch dark. The police speculated that the driver might not have even known he'd hit her because the impact wasn't hard. Apparently, the way she landed on the street was what killed her." She paused, then added, "The quahog shells flew all over the road." Then she cried. "I'm sorry, dear, I shouldn't have added that."

The quahog shells. The one next to the pottery bowl on

Grandma's mantel. The one that was scuffed and had a big crack along one side and wasn't very pretty. Maddie closed her eyes. Her grandmother must have gone to where the accident had happened. She must have taken one of the shells.

"Evelyn?" Maddie asked, her voice a soft whimper now. "Why wasn't I told?"

"You were so young, dear," the woman whispered. "And it was such a . . . nightmare."

And then Maddie remembered. The blue flashing lights. The policeman at the door of the cottage. He had come there to tell Grandma.

"Your grandmother blamed herself. She said if she hadn't insisted on taking you to the fair, the accident wouldn't have happened. If Hannah had wanted to go clamming, Nancy—and you—would have gone with her. And you would have gone long before the sun went down."

Chapter 29

In a very strange way, things were starting to make sense. The split between her father and grandmother. The fact that Maddie hadn't been told that she was Wampanoag. The reality that her father had tried to do all he could to shield his little girl from the horrible tragedy.

Her grandmother blamed herself for what had happened. Her father probably blamed her, too.

After a bit more conversation, Maddie asked if Evelyn had any more surprises.

"I think this is enough for now, don't you?" the woman replied.

Yes, Maddie had heard all she needed to hear, all she could digest.

After they hung up, she hobbled back to Rex's guest room and crawled between the covers, not caring that tomorrow she'd be a wrinkled mess. If she had a pain pill, it might help her sleep. But the pills were in her purse, which was in the living room. Too far to have to walk again.

Turning onto her side, too sad now to cry, Maddie wished she'd never received Brandon's letter, wished she'd never

known what happened to her mother, wished her grandmother had simply bequeathed everything to the tribe.

More than anything, Maddie finally understood why her
father hadn't wanted to come back to the island. Why he'd
protected her. And now, she wanted to go home to Green
Hills, to hug her father and not let him go.

But as Rex knocked on the guest room door, she was reminded that life often just sucked, and she could either shove
the awful things into those deep recesses of her mind or buck
up and get on with it.

This time, she chose to buck up and resolve. "Come in."

The door opened.

"Rafe went back to the cottage to try to get your things.
Apparently, the bedrooms aren't damaged, so your clothes
and whatever is in his backpack should be okay. And your
laptop."

She briefly closed her eyes. "Great. Thanks."

"Still no hint as to what caused the fire."

"It's okay," she said quietly, pulling herself to a sitting position, arranging the pillow behind her.

He pulled up the chair and sat.

"Maddie," he said, "I'm so sorry about everything. This
has gotten way out of hand."

"What has?"

Was he going to say that she should leave, that he didn't
want her to get the wrong impression of how much time he
wanted to spend with her?

He rubbed his bald head as if killing time.

"Right from the start," he finally said, "I didn't like it . . .
I knew it was a mistake . . ." He averted his eyes.

Maddie recognized his hesitation as coming from someone
unaccustomed to lying. She often saw it in her students, when
they tried to conjure a reason why their papers were late, or
why they hadn't read the assignment.

Then Rex stood up and went to the bureau. He opened one of the bottom drawers. He took out what looked like an artist's canvas and handed it to her.

She froze. Again. Yes, it was a painting. Of a beach. A sunset. And two silhouettes—a woman and a child—walking along the shoreline. It was the painting from the mantel in the cottage. Or one that looked an awful lot like it.

Maddie started to tremble. She tried to reassure herself that her mother often painted the sunsets, some replicas of others. Her father once said she sold them at island fairs. Studying the painting now, every shade of orange, every gentle wave, every ripple of soft sand, Maddie ran her finger across the artist's signature: *Hannah Clieg*. Then she turned the canvas over. There was an inscription: "My mother, Nancy, and my daughter, Maddie. Menemsha Beach. 1983." She hadn't looked at the back of the painting over the mantel until now.

Her stomach flip-flopped. She looked back at Rex, who still stood at the dresser.

He leaned down, and removed something else from the drawer. Something small. And round.

She set down the painting as he handed her the object. But before she took it from him, she knew it was the pottery bowl. The one with a daisy painted by what looked like a child's small hand. Inside the bowl, the quahog shell quietly rested.

Which was when Maddie knew the rest of the story.

She should have figured it out earlier. She was a college professor; she was supposed to be smart, wasn't she?

Gnawing on her lower lip, Maddie asked, "Where is she, Rex? Where's my grandmother?"

Putting the pieces together had been simple. Evelyn said their talk had been "enough *for now*." Joe said, "I know Nancy's death seems strange. But life—and death—often are, aren't they?" Lisa told her in a robotic way about finding her grandmother's body. And now, the painting, the bowl, and the quahog shell had been hidden in the bureau drawer. Right there, in Rex's guest room.

He stayed motionless for what felt like a long time. Then he sat down again.

"Jesus," he finally said. He wrung his hands, then scooped one over the arc of his skull. "Please believe me. I told her not to do it." He bent his head and studied the floor.

Maddie's body went limp, as if the stress of the past days had been expelled from her like air from a balloon. "Just tell me the truth, Rex. She's still alive, isn't she?"

He raised his head, and met her eyes. "Yes."

She closed her eyes. Tears began to flow. She'd been right. It was why the bowl and the quahog shell and her mother's painting had been hidden in the cabin. Maddie might be the only one who knew what those things meant to Grandma Nancy . . . or would mean to her. So Grandma removed them from the cottage and made sure they were safe—before she set the fire.

"Where . . ." Her voice quavered as she repeated, "Where is she, Rex?"

He huffed. And sighed. "That's the worst part. I don't know where she is. She was staying here until the fire. As far as I know, she was still here when I called her from the cottage to tell her I was bringing you over."

Maddie remembered when he'd left to tell Rafe they were leaving, he also said he needed to make a quick call.

"So you've known all along. And you've been an accomplice."

He didn't respond.

"Who else knows? Brandon?"

"Brandon? God, no. He wouldn't have allowed it. He's a lawyer. It would have made him complicit."

"At least this explains why he hasn't been able to get the death certificate," she said. "It would be hard to get one if the person isn't dead."

"Evelyn said she'd take care of it, that she'd contact George, the ME. They're on a town committee together. The one about the beach erosion. Anyway, she told Brandon not to worry, that she'd get the certificate. Brandon's a busy guy, going back and forth to Boston, juggling clients in both places. She convinced him it was a small thing she could do to help and that his father would have wanted her to do. George, of course, knows nothing about it. He would never have gone along with it, either."

Rex was talking too fast, as if he had to pour out his culpability all at once.

"So, Evelyn knows," she said. She was surprised she wasn't angry, that she hadn't raised her voice.

"Yes. But we—none of us—know how the fire started. It could have been a fluke. Your grandmother is too attached to that place to want to destroy it. Not to mention that it's so close to other structures. Nancy was home when the fire engulfed the coast guard boathouse and the pier. She remembered the fear that it would spread up the hill and burn every shop, every restaurant, every house and cottage in its path. But as for faking her death . . ." He paused again. And huffed. "Evelyn knew Nancy wanted to see you before she turned ninety. To try to make things right before she died for real. So Evelyn came up with the plan of how to fake it. She'd always felt bad for Nancy. And for your father. And you. On account of what happened to your mother."

Maddie cringed. *Do not talk about my mother*, she wanted to snarl. Then, in her mind's eye, she saw the blue lights flashing again, the image of the cop at the cottage door. She quickly flicked it away.

"Lisa, my neighbor? Does she know?"

"Yes. Evelyn offered her money, but Lisa declined. She said she'd be happy to do something nice for your grandmother. Nancy's a quirky lady, but Lisa thinks she's wonderful. She checks on her every day."

Turning her head, Maddie looked out the window. "CiCi, the real estate agent?"

"CiCi? Nah. She wouldn't have been able to keep her mouth shut."

She looked back at him. "What about Francine? I don't really know her, but . . ."

He shook his head. "No. Francine doesn't know. She'll be shocked. And totally pissed. At me. She looks up to me like I'm her father." He tried to smile, but the corners of his mouth quickly drooped.

They sat, breathing but not speaking.

Maddie ached from her head to her heart to her foot. There was one more person she needed to know the truth about, not for her sake, but for Rafe's.

"Joe?" she asked quietly. "Was he hoping I'll give the land back to the tribe?"

"Try to understand, Maddie. You're Nancy's only heir. If she'd given the land to them herself, you wouldn't have had the chance to make the choice. But, yes, both she and Joe were hoping you would. She claims she has no idea how her grandfather came to have it, though she thinks he might have made a deal with the government a long time ago. She did, however, want to know 'ahead of time' what you'd do. She knows the properties are worth a lot. But more than that, she wants you to be happy. And your father, too."

"And Joe knows all this."

Rex stood up. "He does. But he didn't like being part of it, either. Once you see your grandmother again, I think you'll understand. It's always been easier to agree with her than contradict her."

"Who says I'm going to see her? We're leaving in the morning. Rafe and I. On the earliest possible ferry."

"Please. Don't leave the Vineyard until I've found her. Then you can decide whether to see her."

"And I should do that because . . . ?" Maddie did not like feeling duped. Cheated. Made to feel as if her feelings hadn't mattered.

"Because Nancy won't be around forever. I think she used the land as an excuse. I think she just really wants to see you before she dies. She figured if you thought she already was, that you'd come to the island to settle her estate. So, she'd get to see you. She's pretty spry for her age, but not enough to jump into her old rattletrap pickup and drive up to Green Hills. And she's too proud to have anyone take her. Joe already offered."

Maddie sat there without moving, trying not to cry again. "Why didn't she just wait at the cottage and see me when I got here? Talk to me? Hug me? Why all the theatrics?"

"She didn't know if your father would be with you. I also think she wanted to know if you'd reclaim your heritage or just sign a few papers and be on the next boat home."

"I never knew about my heritage."

"She didn't know that. Now she does. Because we told her."

It made no sense. Or maybe it did.

"Please, Maddie, don't hold this against her. The bottom line is, she loves you and she wants to see you. Promise me you won't leave until I've found her."

It still was hard to tell if Rex was on her side.

"I have a question about you, Rex. How did you get hooked into this? Did you feel sorry for her, too?"

"That's another story," he said. "Maybe she'll share it with you, if you let her. But first, we have to find her. I'll go get Joe. She can't be too far; she hates even going down-island when she has to."

He left the bedroom, then left the cabin, too. She heard him start his truck and drive out of the driveway. And Maddie still didn't know how she was supposed to feel. Or what in God's name she should do.

Chapter 30

She needed to call her father.

Hauling her exhausted body from the bed and then out to the living room, she grabbed her purse and fished inside it for her phone. Then she brought the things into the guest room, climbed under the covers, and sat with her back against the headboard. And she made a commitment to let those pesky bygones just be bygones.

"Dad," she said when he answered. "Are you okay?"

He paused. "Yes. Are you?"

"Dad, I hate to ask, but can you come back to the island? I really need to see you, and I can't go home yet."

"Neither can I," he replied. "Not until this is settled."

She was puzzled, to say the least. "What do you mean?"

"Where are you now?" he asked.

"On the Vineyard."

"But where? Exactly?"

"At a friend's cabin in Aquinnah. There was a fire at the cottage. . . ."

"Are you at Rex's place?"

She paused. "How do you know about Rex?"

"I'll tell you when I see you. Do you know the address?"

"No. It's in Aquinnah."

"Never mind. I'll find out from Evelyn. And I'll be there in a few minutes."

"*What?*"

"I'll be there in a few minutes."

He disconnected.

And, once again, Maddie became a statue, dazed.

Rafe and his grandfather arrived at the cabin at the same time. Stephen explained that he'd never left the island, that he couldn't leave with her there. Rafe was carrying her cross-body bag and her laptop; he wheeled her suitcase into the bedroom.

"You were at Evelyn's?" Maddie asked her father.

He nodded and sat next to the bed. "I was. At first I considered staying in the storage unit at the airport—I remembered that the code to get into the unit was your mother's birthday. But I wasn't sure I'd be able to sleep well enough on the seat in the pickup. In fact, that's where I was, at the restaurant in the airport when you phoned—I'd hitched a ride there. Hitchhiking used to be popular on the Vineyard. And I wanted to see Hannah's paintings again."

Her heart pinged a little. "How did you end up at Evelyn's?"

"I had to go somewhere. And she has a very nice guest room. But you already know that."

She never dreamed that her proper, stoic father could be so exasperating.

"Did she tell you what's been going on?"

"She only suggested that I wait for you to call. That you'd know when it was time to leave, and that chances were, you'd call. Or you'd have Rafe call."

"Well, it isn't time yet. But before I explain, I need you to brace yourself. You, too, Rafe."

Her son looked bewildered; he sat on the edge of the bed while his grandfather took the only chair in the room.

"So . . . ?" Rafe asked.

She smiled. "Okay. I'll start with the best part. My grandmother is still alive."

As evidence of the curiosities of genetics, Rafe and her father suddenly wore the same expression: their mouths fell slightly open, a small vertical line appeared between their brows, and their foreheads scrunched in a way that made them look as if they wanted to say, "Huh?"

"You're joking," Rafe said.

"Madelyn," her father interrupted, in his best professorial tone, "we need more information."

She laughed. *Laughed?* She had no idea where the humor came from, other than she finally realized that the whole situation was, and had been, absurd.

"So, Evelyn didn't tell you."

"No. She only said you'd be fine. Eventually."

Maddie laughed again. "Well . . . once I found out that my grandmother didn't die when I was ten"—she was careful to try and say that without accusation—"I never questioned that she'd recently passed. Why would I? At almost ninety, it wasn't surprising. Well, it turns out that because her ninetieth birthday was approaching, and she feared she'd die soon, she wanted to see me. She no longer drives, so she and Evelyn devised a plan to get me to come here. Which, of course, worked. Grandma Nancy had lost both her daughter and her granddaughter; the least I could do was show up and fulfill her last wishes to scatter her ashes in the 'bight' at sunset."

Rafe looked at his grandfather. "The bight is where the water from Vineyard Sound follows the curve from Lobsterville Beach to Menemsha Basin. Most of the land there belongs to the Wampanoags." He must have learned that from Joe.

Maddie nodded and continued. "Obviously, my grandmother had a few more helpers to pull this off, but apparently, none of them did it maliciously." *Or for profit*, she could add but didn't want to put that idea into their heads.

"As for the fire," she continued, "I don't know if she set the fire or if it was a coincidence. Rex doesn't know yet, either. All he said is that she's quirky. I guess we can ask her the rest . . . if I decide to meet her."

"*If?*" Rafe asked. "You're not seriously going to go home without meeting her, are you?"

She opened her pill bottle, shook one out, and gulped it down without water.

"I don't like feeling that she played me," she said. "But I do understand that she wanted to see me again." She leaned toward her father. "Dad? You're the one who might have a bigger reason for us to leave. I know what happened to my mom—and Rafe, I'll fill you in later—but I won't meet Nancy if it's going to upset you. I came here alone because I naively thought I could meet with the attorney, settle the estate, and slip back to Green Hills without having to drag you into it. I had no idea it would get so complicated. Not to mention that I'd land in the hospital. Twice."

Her father studied her a moment, then fixed his eyes on the quilt. "Yes. I heard about your second incident. In fact, I snuck into the hospital and saw you in the middle of the night. Evelyn insists that you're okay now?" It was sweet that he said that as if it were a question, as if he wanted to be sure it was true.

"I'm fine, Dad."

"Good. And, yes, your grandmother and I have a 'history.' We actually got along well until your mother died. I think Nancy was as tormented as I was, maybe more. I know she felt guilty. We both did. I felt like my life had been ripped apart—well, it had. Your mother and I had wanted to have more children. 'Three more!' she said just before she kissed me goodbye and the two of you left for the island that last summer." He stopped speaking then. The only sounds in the air were from the crickets as they moved closer to the cabin, getting ready for autumn.

"Oh, Dad." Maddie turned onto her side and reached for his hands. "I'm so sorry."

He sighed. "You would have had a big family by now."

She brushed a tear from his cheek. "I have all the family I need."

Rafe said nothing.

Then Stephen cleared his throat and resumed his explanation.

"Your grandmother and I acted like we were in a game of tug-of-war for you. Which was immensely juvenile. But I didn't want you to be caught in the middle. And, yes, it bothered me that you didn't know your Wampanoag heritage. But sometimes the longer someone waits to right a wrong, the easier it becomes to procrastinate. At some point, I convinced myself it was too late, and that, in reality, no harm had been done. I'm so sorry, Madelyn."

Maddie understood. She'd put off asking Owen for a divorce; she'd tried to keep the "happy family" ruse alive for Rafe. But even at three years old, their son had sensed the growing hostility. Once, after he'd heard a late-night argument, he asked her if Daddy was mean. Though Owen was not right for her, he wasn't an evil man—and he was Rafe's father. She knew it wouldn't be right to deprive them of each other. And that divorce would be the best way to protect their son from his parents' toxicity.

"I don't know what to do," she said now, feeling her own tug-of-war growing inside her. She wanted to say that in one way, she was afraid to meet her grandmother, afraid she'd want to stay. And never see Green Hills again. But she couldn't, wouldn't say it.

Rafe twitched in the chair, crossing and uncrossing his legs, biting a fingernail, which he rarely did. Maddie figured he'd opt for her to meet Grandma. He likely wanted to meet her, too. She was, after all, his great-grandmother. A full-blooded Native American. Who had passed so much of her spirit on to him.

"Where is she?" Rafe asked.

Maddie shrugged. "I don't know. Rex is out looking for her. He made me promise to wait here until he finds her. But he won't bring her here unless I agree."

The room was quiet, the sky was drifting into twilight— the "gloaming" her father called it, a word from old Scottish dialects referring to the light that lingered after sunset. And Maddie thought, *I am half Wampanoag and half British and Scottish. What a marvelous feeling it is to know I am a blend of ethnic groups who were once enemies, that I am a symbol not only of diversity but also of global peace and forgiveness.*

It almost seemed unbelievable.

Chapter 31

"We can't find her," Rex said. He and Joe had come into the guest room and were squeezed between Rafe and the closet. Maddie hadn't been in such close proximity to so many men since she'd mistakenly wandered into the wrong locker room at the college.

"What do you mean, you 'can't find her'?" her father asked.

"She didn't go to Joe's, and she's not at the tribal center."

"I haven't seen her since yesterday," Joe said. "We even checked Winnie Lathrop's. She's got a big house in Aquinnah that people could get lost in, and she's a friend of Nancy's. We looked in a few other houses on tribal land where we knew she'd be welcome to take shelter. But she's not there, either."

"She can't be far," Rafe interjected. "This is an *island*."

"It's a big island, son," Joe told him.

Maddie grew impatient. "Did you go to the cottage?"

"I was just there, Mom. Remember? The only other person there was the policeman who was guarding the front door. He wouldn't let me in, but he got our stuff. There's now red tape across the kitchen doorway where the back door used to be, and a 'No Trespassing' sign is posted there."

Maddie suspected that a sign would hardly stop her grand-mother, especially since it was her house.

"We didn't try Evelyn's," Rex said to Joe.

"She isn't there," Stephen said.

The men didn't ask how he knew that.

The room was starting to close in on her.

"Out of here, all of you. Please," Maddie said. "Rex, you and Joe should go to Evelyn's. And anywhere else you can think of in Chilmark. Rafe and I will check Lisa's. And find out if she knows where Nancy might hide in Menemsha." She turned to her father. "Dad? Do you mind staying here? Grandma was living here. Maybe she'll come back."

He hesitated, then nodded. Perhaps he'd decided to let bygones be bygones, too.

"It's after eleven," Rex said. "Shouldn't we have a little something to eat and get a good night's sleep? Then pick this up in the morning?"

Maddie glared at him. "No. We don't need more food. For all we know, my grandmother has hopped the last boat to the mainland. The longer we wait, the trail will get colder." She knew she sounded like one of the old black-and-white movies that her father liked streaming when he was not watching game shows.

Rafe spoke up first. "I'm hungry again, Mom. I like Rex's idea better."

Her father and Joe muttered and nodded.

Then her father said, "I'll tell you what, Maddie. In the morning, I'll stay here in case Nancy comes back. In the meantime, you can get some rest and keep your foot elevated, like you're supposed to do. I don't want you to have to go back to the hospital."

Maddie didn't often contradict his wishes. Before she had the chance to, Rex stepped up again.

"And Joe and I will go to Evelyn's in the morning. And

we'll comb all of Chilmark. You and Rafe can go to Lisa's and wherever else you want. Maybe if we're less tired, we can outsmart your grandmother."

If he was trying to make a joke, it wasn't funny.

"If it's any help," Joe said, "Nancy's only been off-island once since your mother's funeral. And that was for cataract surgery, which she only agreed to have because she could barely see. I brought her. She was cantankerous the whole time. And I doubt she hopped a boat now, because she'd have no idea where to go."

Maddie finally agreed. "I hate being outvoted. But okay. Please make these starving men a snack, Rex. And I'll go to sleep."

Rex retreated to the kitchen and pots and pans started to clatter. Twenty minutes later, he announced that eggs Benedict and asparagus with freshly made hollandaise sauce were ready. If the man hadn't participated in this ridiculousness, she definitely might start to like him too much.

Maddie, however, could not settle down. Maybe it was her concussed brain. Or she still was in shock. She got up and meandered into the living room, listening, for another hour or so, to more useless chatter. Then Rex directed her father to take the main bedroom; he offered Joe the sofa while he tossed blankets and pillows on the living room floor for Rafe and for him.

With the men all relatively tucked in, she retreated to bed for what she hoped would be the last time that day. However, two hours later, she was still awake, trying to imagine what it would be like to see Grandma Nancy again. What if Maddie wasn't how her grandmother had imagined? What if she was too bookish, too quiet, or not pretty enough? Would Grandma be sorry she'd gone to all this trouble only to be disappointed?

The longer Maddie brooded, the more upset she became.

What was most confusing was the fire. Even if it was due to frayed wiring, it sure picked a bizarre time to spark.

Then Maddie remembered feeling as if someone had been watching her. Had it been Grandma? When Maddie was in the hospital, could her grandmother have thought Maddie had left the island? That she hadn't wanted to stay because the cottage was too old and rundown?

And where on earth was the woman? Other than being smoke-filled, the bedrooms apparently hadn't been damaged. Was she actually there, hiding in a closet or under one of the beds? Had she set the fire because she thought Maddie had left and she had nothing left to live for?

It seemed preposterous, but so did the whole situation.

Then an odd shudder started to rumble inside her, like when lava began to shift before a volcano erupted. She pulled the covers more closely around her and closed her eyes tightly. And in that instant, her fuzzy brain kicked into its long-awaited gear. And Maddie knew exactly where Grandma Nancy was.

She wasn't going to wait until morning to find out if she was right.

Slowly, quietly, Maddie peeled back the quilt and swung her legs off the bed, still wearing the same clothes she'd been wearing for days, not counting the hours she'd been in a hospital johnny. She didn't care about the wrinkles. She slipped her sandal on her left foot; then, helped by the crutches, she heaved herself upright. But as she stood by the bedroom door, she knew she could not pull this stunt off by herself, not in her compromised condition.

She considered going back to bed.

But the thought of waiting until after sunrise gave her agita. And she knew there was at least one person who'd be on her side.

★ ★ ★

As the moonlight glowed softly through the windows, Rafe stirred under his makeshift bed. Then he rolled onto his side, looked up at his mother, and rubbed his eyes. She put her finger to her mouth to stop him from speaking.

He closed his eyes again, but only for a second. Then he got up off the floor. She was glad that he, too, was still fully dressed; it would save time and lower the risk that they'd be caught. She headed for the back door, because it was closer and might not disturb the others.

It was, however, hard to tiptoe when one was using crutches.

Then Rex lifted his head. Luckily, Maddie was out of his view. But Rafe was not.

"You okay?" Rex whispered to Rafe in a sleepy baritone.

Rafe paused long enough for Maddie's heart to beat a little louder.

"Yeah," he finally said. "I just need to use the bathroom."

Maddie stopped from exhaling a bucket of gratitude.

Rex pointed toward the bathroom door, closed his eyes, and went back to sleep.

With her hand on the doorknob, Maddie suddenly remembered they'd need the car keys. Resting the crutches under her arms, she mimed two-hands-on-a-steering-wheel, then gestured as if she were starting an ignition, while raising her casted leg as if she were stepping on the gas.

Despite the cobwebs of sleep, her boy was smart. As he moved stealthily toward her, he patted the front pocket of his jeans: the keys must still be there from when he'd gone to the cottage for their suitcases. Yes, he was a smart boy. She made a mental note to thank Owen for the money he'd spent at both Deerfield and Amherst.

Then Maddie turned the doorknob; there was a small *click*.

Without further hesitation, they made it out to the back porch and down the steps without any floodlights going on or alarms to stop them.

And without Maddie falling on her face.

They walked around the side of the cabin, then quietly opened the doors to the old Volvo. They did not latch them shut. Then, because the driveway was pitched up a slight hill to the cabin, Rafe put the gearshift into neutral and they coasted out toward the road. Once out of sight and hopefully sound, he started the engine, and they escaped.

"Well," Maddie said once she no longer feared they'd be exposed, "we never would have made it without nature's night-lights." She gave a nod to the softly glimmering sky.

Rafe gave her a side-glance. "Care to tell me where we're going?"

"Back to Menemsha. To the cottage."

"Let's hope I remember how to get there from here."

"You'll be fine. You just did it a few hours ago. If you forget, I'll remember." There was no reason to mention she'd been on this road only four times recently—twice when she'd gone to the cliffs with her father, then Brandon; once when Rex brought her to the cabin; the other time in the back of an ambulance, when they'd gone straight to the hospital without a side trip to Menemsha, so that didn't count. The bottom line was, Maddie didn't really know where they were, either.

"Meanwhile," Rafe said, "feel free to tell me why we snuck out at"—he checked his phone—"two thirty in the morning."

"Is it that late?"

He snickered. "Mom. Why are we going there? I was already there. Joe was there. For crying out loud, your grandmother's not there."

"Humor me, honey, okay? I won't sleep until we do this."

"Right," he said.

As State Road appeared, she directed him to go left. The rest of the hilly, windy route—lit only by the moon and stars and very few streetlamps—came back to Maddie so easily she might have been guided by her mother's spirit. Or her grandmother's, if she'd been dead.

They parked in the back where Rex had showed her. It was kind of secluded, so they wouldn't disturb the neighbors or the policeman on guard at the front door. As they got out of the car, they quietly closed the doors; Maddie said a quick prayer that no dogs were around to let out a howling alert. For one thing, it would scare her half to death and she might drop her crutches and try to race back to the car, forgetting about the cast. And she would fall. Again.

But Rafe was right behind her to stop her from all that.

By another miracle, they made it without incident to the path that led through the cluster of scrub oaks. But the trees were thick; they blotted out the light from the sky. Maddie hesitated; she thought of her mother on the dark road not far from where they were now. Then she cleared her throat and her mind and stepped gingerly. Which was when her very smart son held up his phone with the flashlight app turned on.

They maneuvered between the trees and down the path; she was glad she'd taken the pain pill earlier. They moved cautiously, stopping only when either of them stepped on a twig and it snapped like in those goofy old movies. Each time it happened, they waited and listened, but there were no sounds, no visible lights snapping on. The island was quiet at night: she remembered that from years ago.

Once they crossed the boundary into the backyard, Maddie allowed herself to stop and breathe again.

"Okay," she whispered. "There's a strip of tape across the back door, right?"

"Right."

"I took my manicure scissors out of my purse; they're in my pocket. We'll use them to clip the tape."

"Um. Okay. But what about the cop? Will we get in trouble if he catches us?"

"Doubtful. He's around front, right?"

"Yup. Sitting on a chair."

"Good. Even so, if my grandmother really was dead, the cottage would be mine, so we won't really be trespassing." She smiled. She wondered if she, the spinster college professor, had become a younger version of Miss Marple. "Come on," she said, keeping her voice low, "let's go before I chicken out."

They went down the hill, one tentative footstep at a time, until they reached the back door, or, as Rafe had said, where the back door used to be. Maddie took out the clippers; it took three tries for the red strip to split, fall to the sides, and allow them easy access.

"Phone," she whispered, and held out her hand.

Rafe handed it over, beam side down.

She refused to think about the germs that might be on the case and clenched it between her teeth.

With the light directed at her feet, Maddie moved one crutch then the other over the doorjamb and onto the kitchen floor. So far, so good. Until she breathed in an ugly odor of ashes. Closing her eyes, she struggled to call up her resolve. Then she thought about the wildflowers her mother had loved to pick when they were there, fragrant summer blossoms of Clerodendrum and echinacea and summer sweet. Like the wildflowers in Evelyn's meadow.

The odor dwindled.

Maddie opened her eyes again, and, with a slight pivot back to Rafe, gestured for him to take the phone out of her mouth. But as he removed it and held the flashlight up so they could see into the room, something big was in the way. Rex.

★   ★   ★

Maddie screamed. She nearly dropped the crutches; Rafe quickly grabbed them.

"What took you so long?" Rex asked. "Did you come by way of Edgartown?"

"How . . . ?" Maddie asked, trying to catch her breath. "How did you know we'd be here?"

Rex smiled. "I have psychic gifts."

She might have believed him until Rafe said, "I think he followed us, Mom. A couple of times I saw headlights in the mirror." He looked at Rex. "That was you, right?"

"You didn't really think I'd sleep through the two of you sneaking out of my house, did you?"

"Why are you still up-island, anyway?" Maddie snipped. "Don't you have a restaurant to run?"

"I've learned that when you have a good staff, you don't have to hover over them."

"But . . . how did you get in? I had to cut the red tape. . . ." She was stalling, trying to dream up her next move while she spoke.

"I know the cop at the front door."

She couldn't think of anything else to say.

"So," Rex continued, "do you mind telling me what you plan to do here?"

Then an idea gelled; if she were honest, maybe it would work. "As a matter of fact, I do not mind telling you. But first, I need you to wait here. Both of you. If you hear a crash, come get me. Otherwise, please respect my privacy for a few minutes." She wanted Rafe to accompany her, but not Rex. Maybe he'd be less offended if she left them together, standing where the back door used to be. She snatched the phone/flashlight back from Rafe.

Rex shook his head, not as in saying no, but as expressing that she bewildered him.

"Are you sure, Mom?" Rafe asked, but she chose not to reply. By then the flashlight was between her teeth again, and she was halfway to the small hallway that led to the bedrooms.

When she reached the back bedroom that had been her mother's, Maddie stopped and recharged. Then she went inside, one crutch after another. She made it to the closet where her mother's belongings once had been; she stood her crutches against the wall and went inside. And slowly, ever so slowly, she scrunched down and opened the tiny door that led into her hobbit house.

Chapter 32

"Grandma?" Maddie whispered.

A lump of bedding was on top of the narrow cot. It looked too small to be hiding Grandma Nancy, at least as Maddie remembered her. Besides, the bedding wasn't moving.

"Grandma? It's me. Maddie. I came home to see if you're okay."

She waited another moment.

"Grandma?" She was reluctant to touch the pile, in case her grandmother really was under it, and this time she was really dead.

And then the blankets stirred. For a second, Maddie considered that a large critter might lunge out—a skunk perhaps, or a raccoon. Bigger than whatever had been in the cottage on the day that she'd arrived.

"Maddie?" a small voice growled from the cot. It came from a person, not a four-legged thing.

"Grandma?"

A few seconds later, when nothing else happened, Maddie wondered if she thought she'd heard something she hadn't. Maybe her intuition had once again taken control of her senses.

Then the covers stirred. An arm appeared: it was blue-veined, its flesh almost as wrinkled as Maddie's skirt.

A head wriggled out next: it was mostly covered by a mass of long white hair that needed a good brushing. It didn't look as thick as Grandma's black hair once was.

Then the bedding started to move rapidly. Maddie took a quick step back and somehow didn't wobble. Her thoughts were spinning. How would she recognize someone she hadn't seen in forty years—and not since she was five? But then, a pair of eyes—the semi-sweet chocolate-colored eyes that looked crafted from the smooth, shiny confection—peered out from under the blanket and over at Maddie. It was Grandma Nancy. Without a doubt.

"I've ruined everything," the old woman cried.

Maddie, too, started to weep. She sat down on the cot; Grandma reached up and folded her arms around her. Maddie welcomed the tender, familiar pat-pat of her grandmother's hands.

"Grandma," she said again. "It's okay. You're okay. I'm here."

"Will you ever forgive me?"

"It wasn't your fault, Grandma. Mommy's accident wasn't your fault. My dad knows that, too."

They stayed like that for a few minutes, shedding tears and murmuring, then holding each other in silence, until Maddie heard Rex's voice.

"How's a guy supposed to fit through this stupid door if you need help?" He'd contorted his lumberjack body into what clearly was an awkward position in order to see past the hobbit door.

Maddie laughed.

"I made sure Joe built the doorway so it was big enough for girls but not for the likes of you, Rex Winsted," Grandma said, her voice now clear and definite.

Rex groaned.

"We'll be out in a second," Maddie told him.

But as she tried to get up off the cot, the whole damn thing collapsed.

The nurses in the emergency department now knew Maddie by name. She wasn't sure whether that was something to be proud of. They sat on the same bed in the same room because Grandma Nancy refused to let Maddie out of her sight. Which was fine, as Grandma was smaller now. *And a bit more stubborn*, the thought of which caused Maddie to laugh again.

When the orderly wheeled the bed to radiology for an X-ray of Maddie's foot, Grandma went, too: they took some pictures of her right elbow after she owned up to landing on it when she fell on the floor.

Maddie's foot showed no further damage, though she was berated for not having followed the doctor's instructions, and was told she most likely would take longer to heal. Grandma had sprained her elbow; she'd have to wear a sling for a couple of weeks and was told to put ice on her injury, rest, and take an anti-inflammatory, for which she insisted that chewing willow bark would do the trick while not encouraging Big Pharma toward more profit-making madness.

Rex and Rafe and Joe and Maddie's father had congregated in the waiting room; by the time the women were examined, tested, patched up, and discharged, Evelyn was there, too. As was Brandon, who'd canceled his court appearance in Boston due to a "family emergency."

As the pair of wheelchairs was rolled out to the big room, the audience of six stood up to greet the wounded women. After they answered the initial "How are you?" questions, Maddie addressed Brandon.

"Is it true you knew nothing about this little scheme?"

He glared at his mother, then looked back to Maddie.

"Not until I asked my mother if she thought someone might have killed Nancy."

"I laughed," Evelyn confessed. "I said, 'Brandon, my darling son, I can't believe you haven't already figured out that this is a hoax.' He's been furious with me ever since. He said I could have put his license to practice law at risk because he lied to a client."

Brandon interrupted. "To which she had the nerve to say if that happened it would not be so bad, because then Jeremy and I could move to the island and take care of her."

"I was joking," Evelyn added.

Then Maddie's father stepped forward. "Nancy, it's nice to see you again."

The woman didn't seem to recognize him.

"It's Stephen, Nancy," Evelyn said, "Hannah's husband."

Nancy offered an unsettled smile. He leaned down, placed his hands on her shoulders, and gently hugged her. Then he stood up and squared his jaw.

"While the two of you were being tended to," he said, addressing her, "we concocted a revised plan. We decided it will be best for you and Maddie to stay at Rex's cabin for now. Joe said he'd be pleased to have Rafe bunk with him; I'll be at Evelyn's for a short time. It will give me a chance to pick her brain about when she and Hannah were girls." He drew in a breath, but managed to avoid getting misty-eyed. Which must have taken a great deal of effort. "You and Maddie will be able to get to know each other again. And we won't be far away." If he had any hard feelings about their decades-long estrangement, or the reason for it, he didn't show them. Stephen Clarke, after all, was a consummate gentleman. "As for Rex," he added, "well, he'll be in Edgartown, where he supposedly lives."

A few chuckles rose from the group.

"Thank you, Stephen," Nancy said. "It sounds good.

And . . . it's nice to see you again, too." Perhaps Grandma guessed that they'd both been at fault for not having put Maddie's needs ahead of their own anger and sorrow.

But if anyone was waiting for Grandma to apologize for her rather large ruse, it didn't happen. More than likely, she didn't feel an apology was needed. She had done what she'd needed to do, and had not needed anyone's approval. And who would dare say she was wrong? Her family was together again, just as she'd intended.

Then Rex announced he had to go to Edgartown because a large party was booked at the restaurant for that night, but he'd be back up-island the next day and stay next door in a vacant cabin. He added that he'd ordered lobster Cobb salads from MV Salads and an assortment of treats from Sweet Bites.

More food! Maddie thought with a laugh.

Joe said he'd pick up the goodies on the way back to the cabin; he and Rafe would then help Nancy and Maddie get situated, as if the women couldn't manage on their own.

"I have a question," Nancy said, and Maddie sensed the rest of them bracing themselves. "By any chance, is the tall boy who's standing, half hidden, next to Stephen, my great-grandson?"

The air in the room relaxed, if air could do that sort of thing.

And Rafe cautiously stepped forward. "Only if, by any chance, you're my great-grandmother."

"Come closer," she said. "Let me have a good look. You look like your great-great-grandfather Isaac Thurston, except for those blue eyes, of course. Isaac's Wampanoag name was Walks with Thunder. If you stay here long enough, maybe you can earn the right to have that name, too."

Rafe moved closer and smiled shyly. Maddie knew he was ecstatic.

Then Nancy said to Maddie, "As for you, you took the

portrait of my father out of my storage unit at the airport, didn't you? You put it on my mantel."

Maddie grinned. "I did. He was very handsome, wasn't he?"

Nancy gazed at Rafe again. "That he was. And so is this young man."

"By God," Joe said. "I thought Rafe looked familiar." Isaac, after all, was his father, too.

Then everyone laughed again, and a young woman wearing a name tag came over and politely asked if they would mind moving their nice reunion outside the emergency department, where they wouldn't disturb the other patients.

Brandon and Evelyn went home, ostensibly to get the guest room ready for Maddie's father. Maddie expected that the real reason was so Nancy could spend time alone with her relations.

When Nancy, Maddie, Rafe, Joe, and Stephen reconvened at the cabin, they found a loaf of fresh bread waiting for them on the kitchen counter. It was wrapped in an embroidered tea towel and set inside a handmade basket. A note next to the basket read, *So glad you've all had a happy ending.* It was signed with several *X*'s and *O*'s.

Maddie and Nancy left the meal preparation to the men; the ladies went into the living room and sat down. Maddie asked her if the basket on the counter was her work. "Of course," she replied. "Which reminds me, did you find the rest of them in my storage unit?"

"We saw lots of them, but I didn't look in all the boxes," Maddie said. "I was eager to unlock the cabinet."

"And . . . the other things?"

Maddie frowned. "Well, there's the truck. Orson, I believe it's named?"

Grandma laughed. "There are more than baskets in the back of him. Your mother's things are there, too."

It would be easier for Maddie to ask what she meant if her tongue hadn't gone partially numb. "Such as?"

"The tribal clothes she wore at our ceremonies. Photos of her with her friends. Her high school yearbook. Memories, I suppose."

The things her mother had kept in the closet in her bedroom in the cottage. The things that Maddie had presumed Grandma threw out.

"Thank you for saving them, Grandma," she said, as a tear trickled down one cheek.

"Actually, she's the one who saved them for you. The last time I spoke with her, we decided I'd bring them when Joe and I went to Green Hills for Christmas. Did you know we'd planned to go? We were going to tell you then that you are Wampanoag. All four of us, including your father."

Maddie had no idea—none—about what to say. It answered so much. And left her feeling . . . full. She couldn't wait to look through her mother's things; somehow she'd have to find the patience to wait until the current commotion simmered down.

After they had their fill of food, Maddie asked Rafe to get the painting of the Menemsha sunset, the pottery bowl, and the quahog shell from the dresser. He brought them into the living room.

"When did you sneak these out of the cottage?" Maddie asked her grandmother.

Eking out a Cheshire grin, Nancy said, "After Evelyn called to say you were in a coma, I had Rex get them out in case someone decided to steal them."

"Steal them?" She didn't say the notion was preposterous because the items were worth more to Nancy and Maddie than to anyone else. And because they'd clearly been there for years and no one had grabbed them yet.

"All right," Nancy groused. "I was afraid you'd figure out

what they were and you'd take them back to Green Hills."
Her voice dropped. "I didn't want to lose them. I've looked at
them every day for forty years. The quahog shell . . ."

Maddie smiled. "I know where it came from, Grandma.
I'm glad you saved it." She didn't really know if she was glad,
but her comment seemed to please her grandmother.

Then Maddie struggled to get up from the chair; she tot-
tered to the corner of the sofa where Grandma Nancy sat, and,
careful not to touch the damaged elbow, she leaned down and
gave her a hug.

Then, with cool composure, Nancy said, "By the way, in
case anyone asks, I'm the one who started the fire."

Maddie grabbed the back of the sofa to stop herself from
falling over. She wished she'd misheard Grandma, but her intuition told her that she hadn't.

Joe and Stephen left their cleaning-up duties in the
kitchen, came into the living room, and stood next to Rafe,
who was standing like a statue, still holding the painting and
the shell and the pottery bowl with the daisy on the front.

Maddie plopped back down on the chair.

"Seriously?" Rafe asked. "You tried to burn down your
house?"

Nancy eyed everyone in the room. "It wasn't intentional.
When Evelyn first told me that Maddie was coming and that
she was going to meet with Brandon, I had to get out of the
cabin and over to Rex's fast. We'd already planned that. I
threw some clothes in a bag—which, by the way, is still under
the bed in the front bedroom here, where I've been sleeping—but I forgot my eyeglasses, so I couldn't see to read.
Since my cataract surgery, I only need them for close-up, but
I figured I wouldn't have much else to do except read, what
with being holed up here at the cabin. Anyway, with Maddie
on the verge of showing up, and me not remembering where

my glasses were, I didn't want to bother Lisa to go in and get them. So I made do without them, which wasn't easy."

Then she redirected her explanation to Maddie.

"When Evelyn said you were back in the hospital, I asked Rex to get these treasures off the mantel, but I forgot to have him look for my glasses. Yesterday, I snuck over just after dawn, when anyone who might have heard I was dead would still be sleeping, except for a couple of fishermen, but they're real good at minding their own beeswax. Anyway, I used Joe's old canoe to cross the creek.

"I forgot it would still be dark inside the cottage. Instead of turning on the light, I took the matches from a kitchen drawer and lit the candle that I keep on the stove. That's when I saw that my eyeglasses were right next to the candle. I slipped them into my pocket—my distance vision's great now—and then I looked around and was happy to see you'd been hoeing out; Lord knows my place has needed it. Anyway, I set the candle up on the windowsill so I could see better. That's when I saw your mother's portrait of my father, Isaac, up on the mantel. I guess Rex didn't figure that I'd want that, too; I don't think he knew who it was, and I hadn't asked him to take it. So I rescued it and wrapped it in my grandmother's lap blanket, which had fallen off the chair by the window and was on the floor. I probably only saw it because by then I'd put on my glasses and bent down for a good look."

Maddie remembered when Owen had plopped onto the chair and knocked the blanket off it.

Her grandmother paused and closed her eyes again, as if she'd grown dizzy and was trying to regain her balance. When she reopened them again, she sounded tired.

"And then I heard something crackling," she continued. "I yanked off my eyeglasses, looked back to the kitchen, and saw that the candle flame had caught the corner of the old

gingham curtain and had set it to burning. I remember thinking I should have burned those ugly curtains years ago. But
the fire was spreading faster than I could think. I dropped the
painting; it fell between the chair and the wall, I think, and I
ran back to the kitchen. I grabbed a dish towel so I could pick
up the candle and dump it in the sink, but it was too late. The
curtains were blazing. So I used the dish towel to try and put
out the fire, but then the dish towel was on fire, too. I
dropped the towel on the floor; on the way down, it set fire to
the other towel I always hang over the handle on the oven
door, and . . ." She lowered her head. "I tried to put the damn
fire out. But I hadn't noticed that the windows were open.
And that there was a breeze. Of course there was. There's always a breeze so close to the harbor. I don't know how much
time passed, but I heard someone yell 'Fire!' and I knew whoever it was must have meant at my place. So I ran to the safest
place I could think of, where no one would look for me . . ."

"My hobbit house," Maddie said.

She nodded.

"It didn't take long before I heard sirens. And voices. Lots
of people must have showed up to put it out. I was so afraid
they'd find me and be mad at me . . . but, worst of all, I never
got to save my father's portrait."

Maddie held her hand and tried to soothe her. Then she
looked at Rafe and nodded toward the guest room.

It took only seconds for Rafe to leave the group, then return, the portrait of Isaac Thurston under his arm.

"Here it is, Grandma," Rafe said, and no one corrected him
by saying that, technically, Nancy was his great-grandmother.
"Joe found it. It isn't damaged; it's as good as new."

And Grandma Nancy cried.

Once her crying eased, Rafe said that the fire hadn't been
her fault.

Joe told her not to worry, that it obviously was not intentional.

Stephen tried to reassure her that the damage to the cottage was contained to the kitchen and only part of the living room and that it could be fixed, good as new.

Maddie wasn't going to tell her grandmother that she could have died if someone hadn't seen the smoke as early as they had. Nancy no doubt already knew that.

They talked in low, comforting voices. Soon, however, it was obvious that Nancy was weary from her ordeal, and Maddie ached all over, and they decided it was naptime.

Maddie's father left for Evelyn's, and Joe and Rafe cleaned up the kitchen. Then they hugged both of the women, and left for Joe's house. Maddie knew that Rafe would love being on tribal land.

Then Nancy followed Maddie into the guest room. She said that, even with one arm, she wanted to tuck her granddaughter in; Maddie didn't say she could do it alone. Then once Maddie was under the covers, Grandma Nancy leaned down and softly whispered, "*Cowàmmaunsh.*"

Maddie was startled. "That's the word! I remember it. Does it mean 'good night'?"

Her grandmother smiled. "No, Madelyn. It is how a Wampanoag says, 'I love you.'" She kissed her fingertips and placed them on Maddie's forehead. Then she whispered *cowàmmaunsh* again and tiptoed from the room.

Epilogue

Maddie decided they should have a surprise celebration of her grandmother's life while the woman was still alive to witness it. In the morning, as Grandma Nancy still slept, Maddie went out to the porch, sat down, and called Evelyn.

"What a marvelous idea," Evelyn said. "Of course I'll help you plan it. A real celebration will be much more fun than a memorial service."

"You're sure you won't be too busy planning the wedding?"

A sigh of discontent fluttered down the line. "My son is still angry with me for encouraging your grandmother's 'little stunt,' as he calls it. He implied that he and Jeremy might get married in Boston, after all."

"Maybe if he sees how happy we all are, he'll change his mind."

"Good idea. You are smart. Your mother was smart, too. And she was desperate to see the rest of the world. So when your father came along, and she fell in love . . ."

"I know," Maddie said. "And I understand."

"But what you don't know is that the last summer you

were here with her, she told me she was going to tell you everything that Christmas. She had it all planned—she had asked Nancy and Joe to spend the holiday in Green Hills; she said she wanted to help you become comfortable with both sides of your heritage."

So Evelyn confirmed that Maddie would have learned about her Wampanoag blood that Christmas. She wondered if her life would have taken a different course; if she still would have married Owen. But if she hadn't, she would not have her precious son.

"I guess life turns out the way nature wants," Maddie said.

To which Evelyn replied, "I believe most Wampanoags would agree."

After she and Evelyn talked, Maddie sat for a while, peacefully rocking, gazing at the wooded land that Joe had said was sacred to the tribe: "Like the earth and its creatures," he'd said, "plants and trees are living beings, too."

She looked at her phone: it was ten fifteen. The offices at the college would be open by now. Without hesitating, she called the direct line for Don Jarvis. She'd made her decision the night before; she knew it was the right one.

"Don?" she asked when he picked up. "Is this a good time to talk?"

She asked him to withdraw her name from the list of tenure candidates. "I'm going to stay on Martha's Vineyard and take care of my grandmother." She didn't add that, after her cast was off, she also planned to run on the beach at low tide every day.

He didn't say he had no idea she had a grandmother there, or anywhere, for that matter.

"But with classes starting in a few weeks," Maddie continued, "I won't put you in a tough position. I can teach the semester remotely if you want. We did it during Covid, and it worked fine. If you haven't found my replacement by spring semester, I'll do it again. After that, we'll see. Okay?"

Don said he was disappointed.

She tried to end on a happy note by saying that with only one candidate left, he'd now save time filling the tenure post. And that Manchino would be delighted.

"Maybe we'll hold off a while," Don said. "Until we're sure he's the right fit. In the meantime, another candidate might come along. Or perhaps you'll have a change of heart."

So he wanted to leave the option open for her. It wasn't the right time to tell him that her mind was made up, or that she wasn't going to write the article she'd sort of outlined. She hoped to turn over her research to one of her students who could bring it to fruition, because Maddie believed the message of journalistic integrity was important. She also didn't tell Professor Jarvis that now that she knew her Indigenous roots, maybe she'd revisit her interest in archaeology. Joe had said the Wampanoags had been on the Vineyard for more than ten thousand years: she'd love to work with the tribe to study their—her—cultural history and maybe help them find ways to enhance their education efforts.

But Don Jarvis didn't need to know any of that. She hoped he'd come to know that, though she appreciated her years at Green Hills, Maddie was resolved. Happy and resolved. In a place where she belonged.

Five days later, Rex arrived at the cabin just before sunset. Maddie had told her grandmother that he was going to take them for a drive. While waiting for her to finish getting ready, Maddie stood by the front door and looked into Rex's eyes.

"Will you ever tell me how you got mixed up in this? I don't want to ask my grandmother. She might still be a spitfire, but I don't want to bring up something that might upset her."

He rubbed the back of his neck. "It's a long story, Maddie. Like I told you, I've known Nancy almost my whole life."

"A lot of people have. But I doubt that most of them would have gone along with this."

He smiled. "Touché. But I don't suppose a lot of people would have had a father who, for many years, loved a woman who wasn't his wife. A man who once asked his son to look after the woman if he died before she did. Which is all I'm going to say."

Maddie started to form the word "*What?*"

But Rex simply smiled again.

And Maddie knew she did not need to know more. Rex Winsted had looked after her grandmother, that was clear enough. He was, after all, one of the good guys. And they all were good people. Imagine that. Her intuition, she supposed, was like many things in life: sometimes it worked well, sometimes it didn't. From now on, she vowed to pay attention to it but not let it hold her back from allowing good people to love her.

Then Grandma came out of the bedroom.

"I don't need to go for a drive," she grumbled.

"You'll like this one, Nancy," Rex said as he guided Nancy to the door. "It's a perfect evening to check out the sunset at Menemsha."

"I've seen that damn sunset nearly every day for almost ninety years."

"And what year did you grow tired of looking at it?" Rex asked as the three of them walked outside toward his pickup.

Nancy snarled. "You always were a bratty kid, Rex Winsted."

He laughed and helped her, and then Maddie, into his truck. They fit comfortably; no one needed to ride in the back.

As they approached Basin Road, he reminded Nancy that

322   Jean Stone

they wouldn't stop at the cottage because the restoration couldn't start until the insurance claim was settled.

Then, as they had planned, Maddie said, "Rex, I'm sorry, but I rushed to leave the cabin. When we get to the restrooms, would you mind stopping?"

"No problem," he replied.

"Maybe I should go, too," her grandmother said.

Rex shot Maddie a glance.

Then Nancy added, "Oh, never mind. I'm fine. And it's too hard to fuss with that now that I only have one arm that works."

If Maddie suggested she'd help her, it would spoil the rest of the plan. Besides, in her pocket was a small, tissue-wrapped package that she needed to deliver.

Rex pulled into the parking area, and Maddie got out and made her way to the whitewashed building that typically had a long line on a summer day. But with dusk imminent, most people were at the beach. Except Lisa. Who was waiting inside.

"Got it?" Maddie asked as she hobbled in.

"Got it," Lisa replied. She opened a bag that Rex had dropped off at her house the day before. "And it doesn't smell like smoke."

Maddie wouldn't have cared if it did.

Quickly removing her denim skirt, she stepped into the beige one with the hand-beaded diamond pattern around the hemline. Then she bent her head, and Lisa slipped the three strands of purple-and-white wampum around her neck. Maddie glanced in the mirror, liking the way the necklaces looked against her white top. The way they'd looked for her picnic with Rex.

"Did you bring the other thing?" Lisa asked.

Maddie tucked the small package into Lisa's hand. She'd retrieved it from one of the metal boxes the night before.

"You know what to do with it, right?"

"Absolutely," Lisa said. "I'll see you on the beach. Give me a head start, okay? I want to see the look on Nancy's face when she realizes the crowd is there for her." Then she snuck out the side door and darted out of sight.

Maddie took another look at her reflection and was reminded how much the outfit suited her. In so many ways.

"You're wearing my skirt," Grandma Nancy said when Maddie returned to the pickup and Rex drove toward the water.

"I didn't think you'd mind."

Nancy grinned but didn't ask if Maddie had changed in the ladies' room—perhaps she thought she hadn't noticed it when they'd still been at the cabin. She was, after all, almost ninety. And deserved to forget a thing or two.

In a minute, Rex parked again; they got out and stepped onto the pavement. Which was when the crowd came into view.

"Oh," Nancy sighed, "there are too damn many people here. We should go back."

"Not a chance," Rex said. He looped his strong arm around her good one, and the big man—accompanied by an old woman with one arm in a sling and her granddaughter with one leg in a cast and walking with crutches—approached the crowd.

As they drew closer, Nancy slowed.

"Oh, look," she said. "Is that Lisa and Mickey? And their kids?"

"Huh," Rex said. "What a coincidence."

"Are they with what's her name? That real estate girl?"

"CiCi," Maddie said, "CiCi Cochran."

"Come on," Rex said, gently tugging her arm. "Let's see

who else is here, even though they, too, have probably seen the sunset nearly every damn day of their lives."

And then the others stood up from their beach towels and chairs, while more slipped from their hiding places between clusters of tall beach grass. Most of them had known Nancy for years: Vineyard artisans who, like Nancy, sold their wares at the island fairs; neighbors—even Jeff Fuller, who it turned out was, indeed, the grandson of the long-ago ice cream man; and a bevy of islanders who Evelyn said had learned a thing or two from Nancy—from basket making to herbal remedies, from foraging wild berries to preparing recipes from the crops they grew.

Best of all, a large contingent of Wampanoags was there; some wore colorful, cultural attire, a culmination of traditions from the thousands of years the tribe had been on Martha's Vineyard.

As the group moved closer, a few tribal members started drumming, and everyone cheered:

"Nancy! Nancy!"

Grandma Nancy bit her lower lip, the way Maddie did when she was speechless. The way Rafe did sometimes, too. Maddie made a mental note to tell her that later.

"Why are they all here?" Nancy asked. "Why are they calling my name?"

Maddie tucked one crutch under her arm, reached over to her grandmother, and smoothed her long hair, the way her grandmother used to smooth hers.

"It's a celebration for you, Grandma," she said. "For your life. These are some of the people who love you and wanted to be here for you."

"Are you sure it's not my funeral? I did not really want one."

Maddie and Rex laughed.

Then the mass of people stopped and parted, revealing a wonderful banquet of food and beverages laid out on long tables. Evelyn, Brandon, and Jeremy emerged, cheering with the rest as they walked toward them, down the aisle that the crowd had formed. Behind them were Joe and Stephen. Joe stepped forward and took Rex's place as Nancy's escort, then led her to her tall, handsome great-grandson, who carried a small wreath of wildflowers.

When she spotted Rafe, Grandma bit her lip again. He wore a denim shirt and a rawhide necklace that had a wampum pendant carved into the shape of an arrowhead. It was the necklace that once belonged to his great-grandfather Isaac Thurston, Nancy's father. It had been in the small package that Maddie had given to Lisa.

Then Rafe stood before Nancy, his mouth forming a tender smile, his eyes filled with tears. He set the crown of wildflowers on his great-grandmother's head, and Maddie glowed with pride—and joy. She knew she'd felt more love and more fun in the past couple of weeks than she'd felt in . . . well, she could not remember when. Including that morning when she'd been in Rex's kitchen and had reached in a cabinet for paper towels and noticed a shiny, stainless steel thermos. She'd paused for only a second . . . and smiled.

Lifting her gaze to the big sky now, Maddie watched as it turned red and orange, the fiery sun then dipping behind the horizon where the heavens met the water. Applause and cheers erupted, and flickering sparklers and yellow glow sticks streaked ribbons of festive lights as "*Nancy! Nancy!*" echoed down the beach and over the dunes.

Then Rex took Maddie's hand in his, and the night felt safe and warm. And all the love around them became beautifully infectious.

She doesn't need to know.

Maddie Clarke is someone special. . . . I hope she'll stick around. And be in my life. As long as Nancy never tells her I'd spied on her through the windows of the cottage, invaded her privacy, and reported to Nancy everything I learned. Including when I heard her tell someone on the phone that she had a doctor's appointment . . . and I came up with a lame plan for Francine—who did not know what was happening—to be my front man. Front person. Whatever. To "coincidentally" run into Maddie at the hospital and ask if she'd consider having lunch with me. Francine actually did it. And Nancy had approved.

Of course, if Maddie found out, it would be the end of whatever we might have together. But I won't tell her. Just as I'll never tell her that her grandmother was my father's lover for many years, from the time he'd won the up-island land, to the day he made me promise to look after her. And the next day he'd died.

When their affair started, Nancy's husband had already drowned. She was still young and had a little girl to raise. She once told me she wouldn't have survived without my father's financial help. Or without him, period.

As for my mother, she drove my father crazy, accusing him of dragging her to a remote island in the middle of the sea. Even so, he did not have the courage to tell her he wanted a divorce; after all, she'd given up her career with the symphony and her life in New York City when he'd asked her to.

"Young love," he'd told me, "is sometimes stupid."

And so, my parents stayed married. But my father loved Nancy the whole time.

So if Nancy can keep her promise not to tell her granddaughter any of this, either, maybe Maddie will learn that life can begin again, when we least expect it. It's something I learned the day that the Lord James Restaurant became mine.

Be sure to look for the next Up-Island novel by Jean Stone

in which Maddie opens a little bookshop on the harbor . . .

On sale Spring 2025.

Visit our website at
KensingtonBooks.com
to sign up for our newsletters, read
more from your favorite authors, see
books by series, view reading group
guides, and more!

Become a Part of Our
Between the Chapters Book Club
Community and Join the Conversation

Betweenthechapters.net

Submit your book review for a chance to win exclusive
Between the Chapters swag you can't get anywhere else!
https://www.kensingtonbooks.com/pages/review/